Children of the Day

Louise Lenahan Wallace

To Miriam and Dean Gibeson—
Thank you with all my heart.
From the littlest of your "Children of the Day,"
With love

For ye are our glory and joy …
Ye are all the children of light,
And the children of the day.

~I Thessalonians 2:19, 5:3

CHAPTER ONE

Union County, Ohio
April 1870

Anxiously tweaking the apple-green bedroom curtain aside, Larissa Michaels checked the progress of the ever-strengthening dawn light. Impatient as she was to be out of doors viewing the sunrise on this early spring morning, several annoying and time-consuming occurrences worked to delay her exit from the room.

As she tugged at her skirt to fasten it, a button popped off, necessitating a thready reunion with the waistband it had deserted. Next, she buttoned her left shoe all the way up, only to discover at the end that she had one more loop than button. With considerable exasperation, she backtracked down the button path, unhooking each one with the expectation that the next would wink up at her as a pair. She finally found it, the next to last. Sighing, she began wielding the buttonhook with dangerous speed. Fortunately for the buttons' continued co-existence with her shoe, they and the loops came out even this time. She stood and twitched her skirt down over her correctly buttoned shoes. A last hasty glance in the mirror assured her that at least her hair, in its customary heavy bun, was cooperating and hadn't suddenly taken on Medusa's snake-like qualities.

Hurrying from her bedroom off the kitchen, she almost collided with her daughter. Now sixteen, Rose had inherited Larissa's violet blue eyes, and her short stature, which didn't thrill Larissa, but didn't seem to bother Rose at all. She'd been wearing her hair up since her birthday last Christmas Day, and it had recently begun to take on the rich chestnut hue of Larissa's own. Rose was now also wearing long skirts. These indications of maturity still caught Larissa off guard if she unexpectedly came upon the young woman who was her daughter.

A little over three years ago, Rose had become deathly ill with the measles. The high fever accompanying the episode had left her profoundly deaf. With the slight amount of hearing remaining, she could now understand what someone said only if they leaned very close to her ear and spoke slowly and distinctly.

Remembrance of those first soul-shriveling days for Rose—and all of them—in the adjustment to her newly silent world, and the realization of the bleak future it foretold, still had power to make Larissa shudder. But the tears and prayers and fears that had rippled through that darkest of times, as a tossed stone spreads ripples to the farthest edges of a pond, had caught the sunlight of a thousand prisms of brightness. Even as Samuel's priests and diviners of old, Larissa could murmur, "... *it is not his hand that smote us; it was a chance that happened to us.*"

A lifetime's weavings of chance had fashioned a blessing for Rose that they had not even known existed: the opportunity to learn sign language. Still able to use her own voice, in learning to read the hand signs and lips, facial expressions, and body movements of others, Rose had regained the miracle of communication—and her rightful place in society.

"You all right, Ma?" she asked, stooping to pick up Merry, not quite a year old, who was tugging at her skirt. "You look a little frazzled."

Larissa managed a small laugh and bent close to Rose's ear. "'Frazzled' is putting it politely." As Merry stretched out eager arms, Larissa took her from Rose and kissed the top of her strawberry blond head. "I suspect this is not going to be one of my better years today."

Rose's eyes sparked with laughter and she moved her chin slightly in a pointing gesture. Larissa followed her gaze to Merry. The little girl, diminutive fingers staunchly erect, was holding up her right hand, determinedly rapping it against the side of her mouth. Since Larissa's arms were full of daughter, Rose gently tucked the not-yet-cooperative thumb into the tiny palm and signed, "Eat breakfast?" Merry responded with an enthusiastic, if wildly erratic, circle of her palm against her chest. "Please?" Rose clapped the small hands together in jubilation and dipped her fist. "Yes!"

The back door burst open. Larissa's husband Ethan called to them even before he entered, interrupting their delighted praising of Merry's accomplishment. Hurrying to the doorway, they found him standing beside Charity, his sixteen-year-old daughter from his first marriage, who had inherited his tall stature and her birth mother's honey-gold hair. Hans Druid, the mute but hearing young man who had taught them sign language, hovered just behind them. All three were grinning from ear to ear.

"Come on outside," Ethan urged. His eyes, the blue of a jay's wing, entreated Larissa.

She wavered. "I can't," she finally protested weakly. "You and Hans have finished the chores and we've not even started making breakfast."

"Just for a second, I promise."

"Come on, Ma," Charity chimed in. "We want to show you something."

Unable to resist their joint pleading, as they had known perfectly well she wouldn't, Larissa gave in. "All right, but no complaints and falling on the floor in a starving faint because breakfast is late."

Still holding Merry on her hip, she stepped out ahead of Ethan, who was crowded closely behind by a gleeful Charity and a puzzled Rose.

Hans, his expressive brown eyes full of the mirth his voice could not produce, had wisely retreated to the side to let the procession pass.

Larissa walked to the edge of the porch, and then she felt it. The morning breeze still held a hint of coolness but lacked the bone-chilling cold of the past days. The early-morning sky was the vivid blue of a newborn kitten's just-opened eyes. She stared at Ethan and a sudden welling of joy erased all the frustration of the minutes in her bedroom. "It's time to plant," she whispered. The grin behind his short brown beard widened, confirming her certainty.

She knew many women considered gardening sheer drudgery, a boring chore to be hurried through on their endless work list. But growing flowers and tending her vegetable garden had always satisfied a creative, colorful outlet that Larissa yearned for in her otherwise orderly, ongoing world. Each morning for the past three weeks, she had stepped onto the porch, scanned the sky, felt the chill breeze tickle her hands and face, and turned back to the house in acute disappointment.

Each morning, seeing her crestfallen expression, the family had forborne to tease her. Charity and Rose had made some lighthearted remarks the first day of this process, but Ethan, seeing Larissa's very real disappointment, had taken them aside and, with quiet firmness, impressed upon them that it would be to their future benefit not to poke fun at her again. This morning, with her various bedroom mishaps, he had beaten her to the weather forecasting expedition.

He reached to take Merry from her and she almost tripped over the hem of her skirt in her haste to descend the back steps of the white-painted farmhouse. Impatiently yanking the offending material away from her ankles, she reached the path to the drive without smacking forward on her nose, and headed toward the fenced garden area. She had been waiting for this moment heralding the new planting season ever since the final vegetable harvest last fall.

"Appears we should have kept it a secret." Ethan's rueful voice trailed her. "At least until after breakfast. We'll never get her back in the house now." He'd followed the family rule to sign while speaking, so that Rose was included in the conversation, similar to not whispering to one person in a group of hearing individuals. Laughing, the girls rushed forward, grabbed Larissa by the arms, and began tugging her back toward the kitchen door.

Digging in her heels, pretending to struggle all the way, Larissa allowed herself to be dragged back inside. "All right, you win. I'll behave myself and fix breakfast for my poor, starving family."

They let go of her, and she immediately dashed for the door. She'd miscalculated, however, because Ethan, still holding Merry, with Hans behind him, stood firmly in front of it, barring the way. With a squeak of dismay, she skidded to a halt and threw out her hands in surrender. "I give up," she said sulkily and stuck her lower lip out in a pout that would have made a four-year-old proud. Rose and Charity marched her to the stove. Rose retrieved the green-checked apron hanging from the hook beside the top oven and fitted it over her mother's head. Charity deftly tied the sash.

"My goodness," Larissa muttered, "delay feeding you and you go absolutely wild. It's a good thing Mac isn't here to side with you against me, too." As soon as the teasing words were out, she fervently wished she'd never uttered them. Charity ducked her head, but not quickly enough to hide her suddenly flaming cheeks. She became very busy unfolding Merry's bib as Ethan settled the baby in her high chair. Mac, Larissa's son, was in Philadelphia. He would complete his fourth year of courses at the Pennsylvania University Medical School this spring.

Charity had loved him for as long as she could remember. Unfortunately for her, he had no idea and was happily seeing Amity Terrill, a young woman he had met in Philadelphia, who was the daughter of the head of the medical school's teaching department. Aware of the situation, the family, in day-to-day conversation, didn't deliberately avoid talking about Mac, but they tried not to pour salt upon Charity's hurt. A very long second of silence followed Larissa's little speech.

"That's right." Ethan's grumpy reply splashed into the pool of quiet as he handed Merry her spoon. Since his hands were occupied, Hans signed the words for Rose's benefit. "I'm hungrier than a snapping turtle with a stuck jaw."

"And with the same one track mind, I see," Larissa retorted quickly — and gratefully. "Do you think hotcakes and maple syrup would sweeten your ornery disposition?"

To Charity's credit, she joined in as Larissa's tormentors looked at one another for a long moment before shouting "Yes" in perfect harmony.

"Then let me get to it," Larissa said severely, "if you know what's good for you." Ethan, suddenly noticing the reduced supply of firewood beside the stove, backed meekly out to the porch, where he was joined by Hans. Charity and Rose industriously turned to grinding coffee beans and setting the table, and the awkward moment slipped past.

Once more reining in her impatience to be outdoors, Larissa tended to the hundred and one details of preparing breakfast, certain that somehow the list had expanded to one hundred and three. Mostly owing to the girls' efficiency, the meal was cooked, served, and eaten, and Larissa dutifully consigned the dishes to the soapy wash pan in the dry sink. With the biggest smile she could muster, she saw the girls and Hans safely on their way into town in the buckboard. Hans, who had long dreamed of becoming a doctor, was working as an assistant to Doc Rawley who, after nearly forty years as the town's physician, was still going strong. Because of his inability to use his voice, Hans could never become a certified medical practitioner. But as Doc put it when he took him on, "Poking around patients with me, I figure he'll come lots closer than he would otherwise." Hans would drop Rose and Charity off at school, where they would complete their formal education in June, before he went on to the office.

Charity was already making plans to assist in the classroom next fall, in preparation for her long held goal of becoming a teacher. Thanks to planning, ingenuity, and patience on the part of Charlotte Sullivan, who had been teaching in Fairvale almost as long as Doc had been practicing medicine, Rose had been able to go on with her schooling in spite of her severe hearing loss. The ability to continue her education, and her blossoming talent for sketching the scenes of daily life about the farm, were two constants that deafness had not taken from her.

Larissa resolutely returned to the waiting breakfast dishes. Ethan watched her glance stray out the window in front of the sink. Abruptly, he remembered the overwhelming number of barn chores requiring his immediate attention, kissed her lingeringly, and headed outside.

Fully aware that he was fully aware of what she was about to do, Larissa promptly abandoned the syrup-sticky plates. Settling Merry's knitted cloak around the child's shoulders, she tied the sunbonnet that matched hers under the small chin and jammed her own onto her head. She fought and lost the notion to speed things up by not fastening the strings, but only because her finicky conscience nagged that she had to set a good example for Merry. After yanking the bow into submission, she snatched her cape from its peg. Without even a backward glance toward the heaped-up dishpan, she lifted Merry into her arms.

Descending the steps, she felt a tug of joyful anticipation. Talking to Merry, describing their destination as they headed toward the fenced garden area, Larissa knew she could never put her gratification into words simple enough for the child to understand. She had no way to explain that, besides the deeply satisfying physical act of participating in the creative, colorful production of food and beauty for her family, in touching the earth, she felt a kinship with God through this most basic of elements.

She recognized another cause for her pleasure. Since her marriage to Ethan, however, it was one that she preferred not to put into spoken words, and one which she tried not to dwell on, even in the recesses of her heart. It brought up memories of her first husband, Zane, dead these past seven years. On the heels of the outbreak of the Civil War in 1861, he had joined up with the North. Early in the war, Nebraska Territory's regular army troops were pulled east to fight in the larger conflict. Zane and other Ohio Union cavalry soldiers had been sent to Nebraska Territory to protect the Overland Trail and its accompanying stage stops from increasing Indian harassment. In the spring of 1863, Zane died in an Indian attack against one of these stage stations. He was buried at Fort Laramie.

Zane had always been deeply attuned to the earth and the ways of nature. Not that he'd spoken much about it. He'd never been one to easily express his deepest emotions. But she had known his feelings. Oh, yes, she had known. Always before a source of deep satisfaction to her personally, in the first years after Zane's death, she had come to cherish her own moments of working with the earth because, in some strange way, it had seemed to allow him to continue to be a part of the farm, too. Then had come her marriage to Ethan.

The half-formed reflection faded as she stepped inside the garden enclosure. Contemplating the plot of ground, she wondered when Ethan would plow and fertilize the area, as he had promised. There was really nothing for her to do here at the moment. She had, weeks past, decided where each planting was to go. She set Merry on her feet and, still bent down, pulled a weed. It came easily from the moist earth, a few grains of dirt clinging to the root as though reluctant to be parted.

Symbolic of my feelings for Zane? The question popped into her head. In the rich fullness of her daily living with Ethan, she didn't often dwell on the past. But her heart knew exactly why Zane was so much in her thoughts now. Tomorrow was the anniversary of the morning he had held her tightly against his heart and then ridden away to war, the anniversary of the last time she had ever seen him. Eleven spaces later, the small, neat square on the calendar would relentlessly designate the day he had died two years later.

A sharp tugging by her knees brought her full attention back to Merry. Even in her musing, a part of her mind had been aware of the little girl clinging to her skirt for balance as she tried to reach something in the soil where Larissa had pulled up the weed. Obligingly, she bent down beside her daughter and caught sight of the brown worm that had squirmed out of the hole. "It's an earthworm." Larissa wiggled her right index finger against her other palm in a creeping motion. "It's very good for the soil and will help us grow huge peas for you to eat."

Merry, green eyes wide, studied the worm rapidly burrowing into the earth, but obviously couldn't make the connection between this slithery creature and the food she was so fond of. Straightening, Larissa scooped the baby into her arms. "Yes. Worms, and peas the size of marbles. Peas the very color of your eyes!" Exuberantly she twirled, Merry giggling delightedly.

"Worms and peas?" Behind them, Ethan's puzzled voice joined their laughter.

Larissa continued twirling until they faced him. "We were just trying to decide what to have for supper, weren't we?" Merry clapped her hands.

"I hope she's clapping because she's happy to see me and not because she's looking forward to such a tasty meal," Ethan said dubiously. After making an appropriately outraged face, which caused more giggles from his small audience, he unlatched and swung the gate wide. As he reached for Merry, Larissa saw the digging plow sitting behind him.

When Hans first came to the farm and was overwhelmed with the abundance of equipment needed to put a meal on the table, he had assigned the various implements nicknames that helped him remember their primary function. He had quickly dubbed the digging plow "Socrates Spade" when Ethan had first explained this plow turned the earth much as a spade did.

"Ethan? I didn't expect you to start plowing so soon. At breakfast, you had a full list of other things to do."

He grinned broadly at the anticipation in her voice. "If we want to eat something besides worms and peas tonight, I'd better get to plowing here." Merry wiggled her index finger against her palm and he swung her in his arms into the air. "Yes. Worms for supper. I can hardly wait!" Their laughter joined hers as, in the safety of his grasp, she swooped back down.

Once more in her peaceful kitchen, with Merry down for her morning nap, Larissa tended to the pesky pan of dishes and a dozen other necessary chores. Hands busy, her thoughts turned again to the question she had asked herself but had not answered as she stood in the garden plot. Of her feelings for Zane during their marriage, she had not the slightest doubt. Theirs had been a true joining of mind and heart and self. She had lived with the expectation that nothing in her life could ever change the happiness and contentment of knowing she and Zane would grow old together on some always far-distant day.

She remembered the April morning, just eleven years ago, when she had met Ethan Michaels for the first time. How young she had been then, how safe and sheltered in her home and family and her love for Zane, and his for her.

Ethan had come into their lives via his daughter Charity's unfortunate—and messy—encounter with a mud puddle, and Larissa had learned that even the most inviolable marriages could be shattered. Two years before meeting Zane and Larissa, the unexpected death of his wife Nettie had ripped Ethan's marriage from him, as surely, as heedlessly, as one rips a page from a book or a plant from the earth, and left him torn and bleeding. Larissa had taken his sorrow to her own heart, never knowing, never dreaming, that in four short years, with Zane's death, she would be walking Ethan's path.

Memory of that time of blinding, all-encompassing grief still made her heart shiver. During the nightmare months following Zane's death, the only constants in her life had been Mac and Rose, for whom her mother instincts remembered, through her dull despair, that she must be strong. Mac and Rose ... and Ethan, who had promised Zane upon his departure for war that he would take care of the family Zane was leaving behind. Unaware as she was of it at the time, Ethan's steady comfort, his quiet, having-been-there-understanding, had enabled her to get up in the morning, put one foot in front of the other, and walk through all the days following Zane's death.

She and Ethan had been married for three years now, and her heartbeat still quickened upon hearing his voice calling to her when he returned after any length of time away. She had been deeply blessed twice in marriage to men who, in spite of their similarities of honesty and steadfastness, were unique unto their own selves.

She knew his first wife sometimes came to Ethan's thoughts, even as Zane did to hers. They didn't make an issue of it, but either of them pretending otherwise would have been ludicrous. She would never forget the last Saturday in April seven years ago when, as she washed the noon dishes, she had a sudden urge to go to the cornfield to see if any plants were showing yet. When she'd run over her list of chores earlier in the day, that expedition certainly hadn't been among the chosen ones. But Zane had always been ecstatic at sight of the first spiky leaves emerging from the rich soil. Since the war wasn't over yet, and he was still guarding the Overland Stage Road in Nebraska Territory and couldn't go check for himself, she'd do it for him.

Amused at herself for coming up with such a feeble excuse to get out of the house on a fine spring day, she'd wandered out to the cornfield. On the way she'd shaped in her mind how, in her next letter to Zane, she would describe this defection in her housewifely duties. Reaching the field, seeing a definite green stripe along the rows, she had stopped in surprise. Ethan had mentioned the evening before that there was no sign of life out there yet, and he'd grumbled that he sure hoped the crows hadn't snitched every last seed kernel.

Looking out over the newly green-spiked earth, she had had a sudden sensation of Zane's presence. She knew he couldn't be there since he was still a thousand miles away at Fort Laramie. A few times since he'd been gone, she had felt his nearness and it had given her immeasurable comfort. This time it seemed as though, if she turned around, she would actually find him standing there. She'd turned and, of course, he wasn't, but the feel of his presence was so vivid, it seemed as if she could reach her hand and touch his face. His face … the joy and sorrow and love in his brown eyes … she'd blinked and the image vanished.

Three days later, word had come that he had died the afternoon she'd stood in the cornfield and felt his presence.

Just as working in the soil put her in mind of Zane, she knew that, for Ethan, sunsets could bring memories of Nettie. On an October evening after Zane's death, when she was on her way back from shutting the chickens in their coop, she'd come upon Ethan, eyes lifted to the vividly painted sky. He was standing so motionless, gazing so fixedly at the panorama that she knew he had no clue she was anywhere near.

She'd hesitated, not wanting to distract him, but knowing she couldn't stand there spying on him, either. She took a couple of careful steps backward, but he shifted stance at the same time and his attention flicked her way. The expression in his eyes was still so far away, she wasn't certain he even saw her. But she recognized only too clearly the grief and the ache of longing stamped on his features before he blinked and truly focused on her.

"I'm sorry, Ethan," she said softly. "I didn't mean to disturb you." She took another step back, although it occurred to her that fleeing to the chicken coop wasn't exactly practical. A swift mental picture formed of her apologizing to the hens for disturbing their rest.

"Larissa." His voice sounded slightly rusty, as if he hadn't used it for a long time, but the sorrow had eased from his features. Now it lingered only in his eyes. "You needn't go." He'd reached out his hand to her, then had dropped it back to his side. Only much later had she understood that he was reaching out to her as one wounded human being to another. At the time, she had taken it simply as a natural gesture of friendship.

Reassured, she'd moved slowly toward him. "You were such a distance away. I truly didn't mean to disturb you."

He'd sighed. "It was time to come home anyway." He gestured toward the dying but still magnificent sunset. She'd followed his gaze. "Nettie loved sunsets," he said quietly.

His words had startled her, because he very seldom said anything about his wife or the time they'd spent together. Larissa knew she'd died after being bitten by a rattlesnake when Charity was four, but she'd never asked for, and he'd never provided, any further details.

He drew in a deep breath. "Tonight is the anniversary of her death. Six years ago. A lifetime ago." The words came out a bare murmur and he once more fell silent.

In that moment Larissa, for the first time since Zane's death, became attuned to someone else's hurt besides hers or her children's. Great as her own ache was, she felt it nudge aside and make room in her heart for his pain. It felt strange, but it also felt right. She'd kept her eyes steadfastly on the lingering colors. "Maybe's she's saying hello to you tonight." They were standing a few feet apart, looking toward the west, but she didn't miss the start that went through him. She turned questioningly, but, even as she did so, he recovered himself.

"That's exactly what Charity said when we were looking at a sunset shortly after Nettie died. It's entirely possible." He'd smiled a little crookedly. "She always did like bright colors."

That night had marked the beginning of Larissa's journey out of pain, had enabled her to take the first step, however small, toward life without Zane—

A sudden crescendo of jabbering from the bedroom cut across her thoughts and told her in no uncertain terms that Merry was done napping.

"I'm coming." Even as she hurried into the bedroom to lift the baby out of her crib, she answered her own earlier musing. *Zane was, and always will be, a part of my past. But Ethan is, and always will be, a part of my present and my future.*

CHAPTER TWO

Ethan, carrying Larissa's newly repaired Seth Thomas clock, emerged from the dusky interior of Enos Gibson's combination jewelry store and watchmaker's shop into the bright May sunshine. Carefully lowering the blanket-wrapped bundle into a crate in the back of the buckboard, he made certain the box wouldn't shift position on the three-mile trip back to the farm. As he straightened, someone called his name. He looked up to find Alvin Thompson, Fairvale's current postmaster, hailing him from across the street. He raised his hand in acknowledgment, waited for a team and wagon to lumber past, then crossed to the opposite boardwalk. They shook hands. "Good to see you, Al. What's up?"

"I'm glad I caught you today, Ethan. Saw you in town yesterday but you'd already left by the time the mail came in." Thompson ducked back into the post office, which was tucked between the candle maker's shop and the cooper's store. "Letter came in for your family," he said over his shoulder as he disappeared behind the wrought iron grillwork and reappeared a moment later, bearing a white envelope. His brown eyes twinkled. "It has a Philadelphia postmark. Thought you might like to have it sooner than later."

Ethan took the envelope and glanced at the handwriting, confirming that it belonged to Larissa's son Mac. "Thanks. Larissa will be mighty glad to get this."

"Now that he's a full-fledged doctor, with a year of experience under his belt at that fancy hospital, you reckon he'll be coming home pretty soon to help Doc Rawley out?"

Ethan couldn't keep his grin down. "That's the plan. I don't know who's more excited, Larissa or Doc. Every time I walk into the kitchen, she's making sure she has all the ingredients for another one of Mac's favorite dishes. Every time I talk to Doc, he tells me how he's rearranging the office floor plan to accommodate a new desk or chair 'so Mac'll have his own space when he gets here.' And we're not even sure yet when it'll be."

Al tugged at the upturned end of his mustache. He'd only been Fairvale's postmaster for three years, but his snowy eyebrows and soft beard, plus the frontal pillow Nature had so kindly provided, had made him a natural for the part of Saint Nick at every community Christmas service for the past decade. His kindly eyes sparked with laughter at Ethan's spot-on mimicry of testy Doc's attempt to appear casual. "Sounds like Mac better get a hustle on and show up before those two wear themselves out."

The door behind Ethan opened and Sylvie Mayhew, the town's hypochondriac, entered. Before she could say anything, Ethan raised the envelope in a farewell salute. "I know Larissa will appreciate not having to wait longer for this. Thanks for tracking me down." Passing Sylvie, he responded to her greeting with a smile and a touch of his hat brim, and kept walking. Before Ethan shut the door with firm finality behind him, Al's polite but resigned greeting and her response drifted to him.

"—and this pain in my big toe, land sakes!"

Shaking his head, Ethan chuckled as he climbed into the buckboard and gathered up the lines. *I know there are lots of advantages to being a farmer, and I do believe Sylvie just reminded me of one. At least out in the field, the oxen don't talk your ears off.*

On his way out of town, he saw Shawn Gallaway, the minister of the church he and Larissa attended, descending the stairs from John Shearer's third floor *Tribune* office. Ethan could never pass the building without reliving the odors of ink and newsprint surrounding them the day John had told him that Zane was dead. He maneuvered the team to the side of the street as Shawn, good friend as well as spiritual advisor, raised a hand in greeting. "Ethan, how's the family? When's Mac coming home?" His black hair now showed white wings along his temples, but his voice had never quite lost the rich accent of the Welch village of his childhood. He approached the buckboard and the men shook hands.

"Everyone's just fine. And as for hearing from Mac—" Ethan waved the letter.

"That's great. I'll be sure to tell Martha. I think my wife's been almost as anxious as Larissa to hear he's set a definite date for coming back. When will it be?"

"Now, you don't really expect me to read it and get the news before Larissa does?" The glimmer in Ethan's eyes belied his indignant defense. "She gets such a kick out of opening his letters. Problem is, she waits and waits for one, then takes forever to actually get to reading it. She always studies his handwriting on the envelope first to assure herself he's well and happy. It looks the same to me every time, but she says it's just one of those things a mother can tell."

"I expect she's prolonging the suspense, more than anything else," Shawn offered. "I've seen Martha do the same thing when she gets a letter from New York City."

The two men exchanged a baffled look, and Shawn stepped back. "I sure don't want to be the cause of even more delay over opening this one. Martha was mentioning making a visit out your way. I'm betting she'll make a point of it now that you've heard from him."

"Larissa'll be expecting her. You know you're both more than welcome any time." Ethan lifted the lines. As the buckboard rattled across the little bridge over Mill Creek at the edge of town, he reflected on his and Larissa's good fortune in having not only a compassionate spiritual advisor, but also a deep blessing in Shawn's and Martha's friendship. For a certainty, both attributes had been proved more times than he or Larissa could count.

Pulling into the farm driveway, he halted the team beside the kitchen path. Retrieving the swaddled clock and making sure the letter was still in his shirt pocket, he stepped quietly across the porch and eased the back door open, looking for Larissa. He had quickly learned to walk softly—or face the consequences—when Merry might be sleeping, because the most innocuous noises could rouse her where she napped in the bedroom off the kitchen. Even after the briefest of catnaps, she was bright eyed and ready to go, which tended to annihilate Larissa's hopefully laid plans to accomplish various tasks during that time.

He found her in the sitting room, dusting the fireplace mantel. In his quest for quiet on behalf of Merry, he'd proved so successful that Larissa hadn't heard him, either. Watching her pick up a heavy silver candlestick and run her cloth over it, he decided retreat was preferable to scaring her half to death while she had such a hefty weapon in hand. He eased back out to the kitchen, opened the door, and shut it more firmly than before. She heard him this time, and met him in the doorway between the kitchen and sitting room, with no candlestick in sight.

Her face lit as she saw the blanketed shape cradled in his arms. "The clock's fixed?"

"Right as rain, Enos told me. He said to tell you hello. So did Al Thompson and Shawn—and Sylvie Mayhew's big toe, in a manner of speaking."

She raised her eyes heavenward at mention of the last contributor. "In that case, I'm surprised you made it home before tomorrow."

He chuckled. "I expect cobwebs are sprouting all over Al and his grillwork by now." Laying the bundle on the kitchen worktable, he unwrapped the blanket. Lifting the clock carefully, he returned it to its rightful place on the sitting room mantel. Larissa set it to the correct time and gently touched the pendulum into motion.

At the soft ticking, she clasped her hands and let out a happy breath. "There. All's right with the world, again."

"More than right." He pulled the letter from his pocket and held it out to her.

"From Mac?" She scanned the envelope. "His handwriting is still firm and legible," she said with satisfaction.

Ethan's lips twitched at this confirmation of his prophecy to Shawn. "How about finding out what he has to say?"

After drawing a pin from her hair and deftly using it to slit the envelope, she pulled out the sheets of paper, counting them, as always, before she began reading. She'd followed this little ceremony from the first letter she'd received from her son. Long before Shawn had suggested it that afternoon, Ethan had suspected it was a tactic to extend the anticipation of discovering what Mac had to say. "Four pages, both sides," she confirmed.

They settled on the bottom stair step, which had, somehow, become the place they most often read Mac's letters. She leaned against Ethan who, his back resting against the spindles, slipped his arms around her waist as she began reading.

"Dear Family,

"I didn't expect to be writing to you again before I knew exactly when I'd be coming home. I assure you that I am well, but two things have just occurred that I need to let you know.

"First, the University Hospital Board has approached me again. Unlike last year's joking session, before they got around to suggesting I stay another year and take their new, advanced classes, this time they veered the other direction and were completely serious. I realized only later that their gravity came from the fact that, for the first time, they were regarding me not as a student but as an actual member of the medical profession. It's probably just as well I didn't realize it until well after the meeting was over. They are 'extremely pleased with the way I have conducted myself throughout all aspects of the four-year medical experience.' Their words, Ma, not mine, I promise. The upshot is they have requested that I stay one more year to work in the hospital, this time with full medical credentials."

Larissa's voice had become softer with each sentence and trailed off altogether on the last words. Ethan felt her go rigid, then slump against him. "Lizzie?"

"I'm all right."

The words were so soft he barely heard her. "Do you want me to read the rest?"

The back of her head moved from side to side against his chest. "No. I'll do it." Her voice held an underlying note of determined strength that he recognized only too well from other times that circumstances had added another rock to the basket of stones she had been forced to carry through life. She smoothed out the wrinkles where her fingers had inadvertently clutched the paper, took a breath, and continued.

"I know you were planning on my coming home, and I know Doc was, too. He's usually so restrained in conveying his emotions, but in his letters he's actually been expressing genuine excitement and making plans for me to join him as his associate. I'm writing to him, too, of course. I know I gave my word that after completing my studies I'd come back and practice with him. That's been our understanding all along. I feel like I'm betraying his confidence, and your expectations of my future, by staying. But it's the opportunity of a lifetime and would incalculably benefit my future practice of medicine.

"I haven't given them an answer, yet, but will have to do so very soon."

She stopped reading, and once again slowly shook her head, a silent protest for the things she would not say, because she already knew what her answer to him would be. "He said two things," she murmured. "Whatever the second one is, it can't be more earthshaking than that he's been asked to practice 'with full medical credentials' in one of the most prestigious hospitals in the country." Ethan's arms tightened about her in silent reassurance that he understood her disappointment—and her decision. With a small but definite upward tilt to her chin, she picked up where she had left off in the letter.

"The other news I wish I could tell you in person is that I am going to ask Amity Terrill to marry me." Larissa's voice failed her completely. Mutely, she pushed the letter at Ethan.

When he found the place where she had stopped, his voice wasn't any too steady, either, as he continued with Mac's announcement. "Nothing short of a year-long engagement is socially acceptable in Philadelphia. The hospital position is for a year. Accepting the offer means that I will be able to stay in Philadelphia with Amity to fulfill the hospital commitment and the engagement requirements at the same time."

Ethan lowered the letter and said thoughtfully, "A year's engagement is certainly wise, even though they've known each other for several years now. I wonder what her father thinks. Combining the engagement and the hospital opportunity could produce a sticky situation if he asks her before he officially accepts the position." He raised the letter. "Might as well see what other firecrackers he has in mind to set off.

"After my interview with the Board, I felt I had to meet with Amity's father immediately, to discuss my wish to marry her. All during the last four years, as head of the teaching department and one of my instructors, Dr. Terrill has been completely professional, yet cordial and understanding in our encounters, particularly when difficult situations have arisen. This morning, he coolly informed me that, should I work in the hospital for a year, this announcement of my intention to marry his daughter would afford no leniency whatsoever on the Board's expectations of my performance. I told him I understood and that I expected it to be no other way. He pointed out that I'd be distracted from my hospital work. I assured him that, for Amity and me, nothing would change in our manner of seeing each other, only the awareness that our feelings are validated. He quizzed me with that same snowball in his voice for ever so long. I tried to answer him sensibly, and all the while my heart was thumping so hard, I just knew he could hear it. To be honest, I don't recall a single word I said. Finally, in that same iceberg tone, laying out strict terms to be followed, he gave his consent to the engagement. I plan to ask Amity this Saturday evening.

"It's late and I must write Doc tonight. Thank you for the understanding you have always shown me.

"Your loving son,

"Mac.

"P.S. Jeff Kinsley has also been asked to stay on and has accepted."

"Easy for Jeff to accept," Larissa said crisply. Jeff and Mac had shared a room at the school's dorm for most of the four years. "His family lives in Pennsylvania and they can see him whenever they want to get together."

Ethan saw her tart comment for the delaying tactic it was and pointed out as gently as he could, "This letter was a week on its way. That means he must have asked Amity last Saturday."

Larissa pressed her knuckles against her mouth. "I should be happy. We decided when we met her in Philadelphia that she seems a nice young woman. But we really hardly know her."

He rested his chin on the top of her head. "We'll have to tell Charity."

"God, help us all," Larissa murmured. "Please," she added with a shiver.

Ethan stood and reached his hand to pull her to her feet. They held each other for a long moment, drawing comfort from the other's understanding that, whatever might happen, they were in it together.

Ethan went back outside to tend the team. Hearing sounds that indicated beyond doubt that Merry was awake and desiring to be freed from her crib-cage, Larissa opened the bedroom door to squeals of delight from her daughter. Merry, facing the door, had pulled herself up and, clutching the bars, was vigorously bouncing up and down. At sight of her mother, her face crinkled into a dazzling smile. Larissa imagined herself being that energetic after napping for only an hour, and smiled ruefully at such an extravagant flight of fancy. Lifting Merry over the bars, she buried her nose in the damp, sleep-tangled curls and cradled her baby against her heart. Merry snuggled against her in one of those moments Larissa wished could go on forever. "Did you have a good sleep?" she murmured. "Apparently, it rained while you were snoozing."

After Merry was once more socially presentable, Larissa slid her into her high chair. When she handed her the wooden clown that Mac had sent for Christmas, Merry squealed in glee and began enthusiastically attempting to maneuver the jointed arms and legs. Hearing the sound of a rig on the drive, Larissa looked out the window over the sink just as Doc Rawley's grouchy piebald mare Bella halted with a jerk that shook the buggy she was drawing and Doc who was riding in it. Larissa's lips twitched. Bella and Doc were both getting on in years, but neither one had lost the contrariness that had marked their relationship for as long as Larissa could remember. The only problem was when they butted heads, as now, Doc invariably lost the argument.

She watched as Ethan, coming up from the pasture, waved a greeting to Doc and gestured toward the house. She sped to the wash bench, checked in the mirror above it for sagging hairpins and unsightly splotches on her apron, and turned to the door with a smile of glad welcome as the men came in. When Mac was ten years old, Doc had taken him under his wing as his "apprentice." He'd given him the medical training the boy had yearned for from the time he was old enough to attend to injured birds, rabbits, barn cats, and all the parade of wildlife he came across that needed patching up. Doc's financial contributions had made possible Mac's four years of medical schooling in Philadelphia. Compensation, he'd told them gruffly, to cover his unwonted pride in his pupil, for the seven years Mac had worked for him without pay.

Doc had weathered more family crises with them than they could count. He'd been there following Zane's death, and during Rose's nearly fatal measles illness and her hearing loss. Through his intervention, in Philadelphia Rose had been linked with those who taught her sign language and thus returned her to her rightful place in society. He'd also been witness to a highly memorable fit of temper Charity had once produced, stemming from her emotional predicament over Mac's total lack of awareness of her love for him. Brusqueness, crankiness, and all, Abe Rawley was to them much more than the town doctor. He was family.

His hair and beard had grown snow white during the war years, but Doc was still not one to beat around the barn. He accepted Larissa's offer of coffee, admired Merry's clown as he passed by, sat down at the kitchen table, and pulled an envelope from an inside pocket of his perpetually rumpled black suit coat. "Got a letter from Mac yesterday. He said he'd already written to you, but I figured you'd be interested in hearing it anyhow."

Larissa jumped and the water she was pouring into the coffeepot sloshed over the side. Ignoring it, her eyes sought Ethan's. A muscle in his jaw twitched as he waited for her to speak. "We received a letter, too." She took a deep breath. "I'll wager our letter is much more newsy than yours." Clearly, her lighthearted teasing didn't fool Doc, whose hazel eyes shuttled to Ethan, then back to her. She grabbed a cloth and began sopping up the water she'd spilled. "Your letter first," she urged.

Doc hesitated, then drew his glasses from his coat pocket and perched them on his nose. He cleared his throat and began to read. The letter contained essentially the same information Mac had written to Ethan and Larissa, except for his direct apology to Doc for breaking his promise. It was clear his decision was a struggle and that he was not taking for granted Doc's acceptance of his defection, even though Doc would understand better than anyone else what the extra year's experience would mean to Mac's future practice of medicine.

As Larissa and Ethan had suspected, the letter made no mention of Amity Terrill. Mac had based his consideration of the opportunity solely on the impact it would have on his and Doc's relationship. Doc finished reading and sat in thoughtful silence for a few moments before tugging at his shaggy beard. "As he says, it's the opportunity of a lifetime. At the rate he's going, I'll have to go back to school to keep up with him." His gaze traveled to each of their faces as he added slowly and carefully, "When he comes back next year."

Larissa closed her eyes and stood totally still for several seconds before looking directly into Doc's eyes. "Thank you for understanding," she said softly.

He waved his hand in casual dismissal of her gratitude. "On second thought, I won't have to go back to school. I'll have my own private tutor right at hand." Recovering his normal testiness, he frowned at Larissa. "Now just what do you mean about your letter being 'more newsy' than mine? Seems like he would have newsed himself out with that morsel."

Larissa drew the letter from her apron pocket and threw him an excellent imitation of a mischievous smile. "It's probably a good thing you're sitting down." She skipped over the repetition of Doc's news. Her voice was remarkably steady as she got right down to the basics. When she finished, she lowered the letter so she could see Doc's reaction.

He, too, got right down to the basics. "She's city. In spite of being city for the last four years, he's coming back to be country. I'm presuming both of them are aware of this. We know beyond doubt that he's level-headed. When I met her in Philadelphia, I was quite frankly impressed with her maturity and her lack of pretension in coming from a family with money." As he spoke, Larissa had moved to sink into the chair beside Ethan. Now he studied their clasped hands and said quietly, "In my expert medical opinion, they're both lucky. They've found each other."

He refused Larissa's offer of a cup of coffee. "I have to get back to town and send a telegram. 'To my dawdling associate. Stop. All is understood. Stop. Unless I'm not invited to the wedding. Stop. If not, scrounge up your own patients. Stop. Except for Sylvie Mayhew who will be my wedding present to you. Stop.'" He clapped on his hat, backed out the door, and closed it with a decisive thump.

***

As was her custom, begun in the days when Zane was away at war and wrote from whichever Army location he currently inhabited, Larissa told Rose and Charity as soon as they arrived home that a letter had come from Mac. She blithely neglected to mention the letter Doc had received. Rose's eyes lit with anticipation and she gave her mother a big hug. Although Larissa responded automatically, her attention focused on Charity. The girl made no spoken response, but quickly bent to pick up Merry, who had scooted on hands and knees to them when they came in. Larissa saw clearly, however, that the glow of pleasure lighting Charity's face came from deep within. Already perching precariously enough in her chest because Mac's news, Larissa's heart wobbled ominously.

As was also her custom, Larissa waited until they were all seated at the supper table before she pulled the letter from her apron pocket. Hans looked disconcerted, as he always did when he thought he was intruding in "family matters." They had assured him from the beginning that, as a member of the family, they expected to include him. He'd accepted their reasoning with a graciousness that conveyed his deep-felt appreciation, but he'd never taken it for granted. Now, catching Ethan's quick nod and half wink, he quietly settled back. As Larissa began reading, she concentrated on giving Mac's news every drop of optimism she could as Charity, ever the dramatist, signed the translation for Rose with exuberant facial expressions and body language that brought the words to life.

Larissa knew Rose missed Mac deeply. Although he was older by five years, the brother-sister bond had been there from the beginning. Whether it was Mac's naturally nurturing nature or Rose's gentle disposition, Larissa had never been sure. When Zane died, Rose had turned even more to Mac, the only other person in the world on an equal footing with her in understanding what their father's death meant to her.

Now, as Larissa read, Rose sat raptly watching Charity, her supper plate forgotten in front of her. Charity, too, busily signing and communicating the nuances in Larissa's voice, listened with an attentiveness that only reinforced Larissa's fears. Risking a glance at Ethan, she saw he, too, was watching his daughter and the play of emotions flickering across her face at Mac's news. When Larissa reached the part about his having to give the hospital an answer very soon, everyone at the table except Merry already knew exactly what that answer would be. Charity flinched, but her hands didn't waver as she continued signing. Watching Rose's crestfallen expression, it flitted through Larissa's mind that Rose actually showed more disappointment than Charity did. Then Rose's head came up in a gesture Larissa recognized because she herself had made it a thousand times as she faced some hard fact that could not be changed. Just as you'd better face this one, she told herself sternly.

Her hesitation was so perceptible that Rose asked, "Is that the end of his letter, Ma?" Stoic as Rose was about accepting the many large disappointments that life had flung at her, Larissa heard the dismay in her daughter's voice.

Larissa's eyes met Ethan's directly, and she read in them, as surely as if he had spoken the words aloud, the silent message of support and encouragement he was sending her.

"Ma?" Apprehension, overshadowing dismay, crept into Rose's voice. Charity obviously sensed something wasn't right because she stared at the letter, the unasked question large in her eyes.

Larissa forced a shaky laugh. "Of course it's not the end of the letter. I'm just not sure your delicate young ears should hear this next part." Once again, Charity's hands moved. Understanding her mother's teasing, Rose immediately relaxed, but Larissa's already sinking heart fell with a thud down to her toes as Charity tensed even more. Having done the best she could to prepare her, however briefly, Larissa had no choice but to continue with, "'I am going to ask Amity Terrill to marry me.'" As she read the words, she saw Charity's hands drop and the light in her eyes die. As Hans repeated the news for a bewildered Rose, Larissa wished for the first time in her life that Mac had not written.

CHAPTER THREE

Later that night, Larissa stood on the porch and looked out over the darkened yard. The moon in its first quarter cast little light, but she didn't need it to know every detail of the scene before her: the barn, the apple orchard, Mill Creek rippling and chuckling as it hurried about its business. And, skilled as she was about filling in the details of the farm world, she knew she would never even come close to Zane's ability. He had known every stone and slope of ground and tree with knowledge that comes only from caring so deeply about the land that it seemed to be an extension of himself. *Just the way you cared about your children, Zane.*

Her throat so tight she could scarcely get the words out, she had finished reading aloud Mac's letter. Rose had absorbed the news about Amity Terrill with younger sister enthusiasm for her brother's marriage and for a sister-in-law on her own horizon. Her concern clearly centered around Mac's not coming home for another year. She'd accepted the change in plans with regret, but also with good grace for the larger picture of his incredible opportunity to enhance his medical skills. No, she was not worried about Rose. Her daughter's disappointment would right itself, Larissa was certain.

But what of Charity? Remembering the hurt in the girl's eyes, Larissa blinked rapidly to keep a sudden mist of tears at bay. She rarely cried anymore. After Zane's death, nothing had seemed important enough to shed tears over. Then had come Rose's hearing loss. *Why is hurt to our children always so much harder to bear than our own?* Especially when Charity was not even her blood child. *You may not have carried her under your heart for nine months, but you've certainly carried her in your heart for the past eleven years.* Ever since that long ago spring morning when Mac had brought her home, a mud-caked bit of humanity fearful of facing her father's wrath, she had tugged at Larissa's heartstrings.

Both Larissa and Ethan had known marriages that had fulfilled their wedding vows in the deepest sense of those spoken words, just as their marriage did now, every day of their lives together. The sharing of mental and spiritual as well as physical emotions was so much a part of them that they could not now simply sweep away those characteristics as one swept away unwanted wheat chaff after the threshing.

She knew Ethan wanted that type of fulfillment for his daughter every bit as much as Larissa wanted it for Mac and Rose—and for Charity. She recognized painfully how Charity's well-being and future encounters with life's inevitable deep blows would stem from acceptance or rejection of this present harsh reality. *Were Ethan and I wrong? Should we have crushed her hopes a long time ago, as one crushes a black-widow spider, instead of waiting for "the future" to do it? What have been the chances all along of Mac and Charity eventually marrying?* In her own dismay at Charity's heartache, the question came to her, not in a fruitless chasing of possibilities, but for an honest evaluation. *Make a list.* Unlike the interior voice that chastised her, this suggestion did not come from an unbending conscience, but from practical experience. Listing points, positive and negative, was a trick Zane had often used when faced with a thorny question. It was a tactic she could put to good use now.

She continued to gaze out upon the star-speckled farmland, but she was no longer seeing the shadows that spilled over the acreage. *It's evident that Mac cares deeply for Amity Terrill.* In all the time he had been gone, he had never made mention of any other young woman he had met in Philadelphia. Today's letter answered any doubts about why.

And why shouldn't he reach beyond the farm world? Fairvale was a small town. Mac had gone to school with, had known all his life, each of the young women who lived in the community. Philadelphia was a large city. He had been bound to meet and become friends with many people. Hadn't she been happy because that had been an added benefit to his venturing into the larger world? Hadn't she been thankful that he would expand his horizons by gaining knowledge of people as well as medicine? An opportunity he never would have had by staying in Fairvale.

All well and good thinking, but Charity is one of the young women he has known practically all his life. They had a history, a knowledge of each other that he would never achieve with someone he met as an adult. The chances of his hauling Amity Terrill out of a mud puddle were, after all, rather small. *He's coming back to Fairvale to go into practice with Doc Rawley. Will a city bred young woman be able to adjust to small town life?* Doc apparently thought so. But other than their trip to Philadelphia four years ago to validate Doc's verdict that Rose's profound hearing loss was unalterable, small town life was all Charity knew. There would be no such adjustment for her to make.

When all is said and done, in spite of his big city experiences and his clear attraction for Amity, does Mac really want to reach outside the element he has known all his life? Here, she faltered. Here, she had no answer to balance the list because Mac alone could fill in the blank. She had only a mother's intuition and a mother's prayers.

Larissa had experienced many emotions since Zane had been killed: agony, desolation, loneliness, and the ache that would be in her heart until she died. In those first bitter days, she had been forced to face life without his support and encouragement, a totally different experience from making judgments about the farm and children when she had known that, in spite of his being a thousand miles away, she was making decisions she was sure he would have agreed with. But that new time of coping after his death had had to come from her heart and strength alone. During that first dark isolation, another emotion had occurred, one she had never before encountered with Zane and one she had certainly never expected to experience: resentment. Never again would she and Zane make a joint determination. From that day forward, he was released from all answerability for whatever the future held for the farm and for the children. The entire burden had been thrust upon her. Horrified to acknowledge such anger at him, she had fiercely denied it. But denial hadn't made it go away. Only day-by-day living and the relentless, repeated assumption of those responsibilities had dulled it. Tonight, for the first time in so long that she had relegated its existence to the hazy past, that bitterness resurfaced.

Zane, what would you have said or done about this situation between your son and Charity? A situation that might never have arisen had you not died, so that he's looked on her as his "sister" these past years, not as the young woman she's becoming. In her frustration, she flung the question at him.

If you trust him enough to choose what's right, you must also trust him enough to do it.

The words seemed to come from deep within her. An answer that was so completely Zane's he might have been standing next to her as he murmured it with all the old, quiet assurance that had had the ability to comfort her spirit.

***

Wary as they had been about Charity's reaction to Mac's news, the girl's response was more unnerving than anger or weeping. Listening to Larissa voice his intentions, she'd gone pale, and her darkening eyes had betrayed the hurt she was not experienced enough to mask.

During the following days, she maintained her inner stillness. Ethan and Larissa each approached her, making openings to talk. She obligingly discussed every topic they broached, except the one that mattered. She was unwaveringly polite, saw to her chores and tasks about the house, and joined in the nightly discussions at the supper table. But the exuberance and high spirits with which she had always faced all the small details of living had retreated into a dark cavern. As the days passed, Ethan and Larissa found no way to retrieve them.

They turned, as in so many other times of crisis, to Shawn and Martha Gallaway. The death of Martha's first husband Ross, in the First Battle of Bull Run at the start of the Civil War, had left her to raise four small children alone, as best she might, on their family farm. With heartbreaking similarity, Zane's death out in Nebraska Territory two years later left Larissa to raise her own two young children. The unendurable situation which after all must be endured formed a bond of understanding between the two women that no one else in their community could share, because no one else had experienced such a devastating wartime loss. Much later, having walked the bitter path, Martha had rounded yet another curve—and found Shawn. When faced with the agonizing choice of sacrificing either their love or Shawn's commitment to the church, they had turned to Larissa and Ethan. Battling their own emotions and doubts before their marriage, Ethan and Larissa knew well the frustration arising from the necessity of choosing. When they faced the reality of Rose's deafness, Martha and Shawn had given them strength when they had none of their own. So now they sought spiritual guidance and were warmed from the glow of friendship so freely given. Shawn and Martha could not provide ironclad answers to their fears for Charity's future, but, by sharing the tangled emotions, they were able to ease some of the burden of uncertainty.

***

April's plowing had become May's eternal hope for good crops, followed by the heat of summer's "corn growin' time." September's russet mantle brought Larissa a letter from Wyoming Territory. Anne Clayton's husband Ben had served with Zane in Nebraska Territory during the war. The men became friends, and Ben had fought in the same Indian attack that had cost Zane his life. After Ben had returned home to Marietta, Anne had written to Larissa, conveying her sympathy for Zane's death and offering a gift that Larissa had come to treasure: friendship. The two women had never met, but the bond they had forged through their letters was so deep and strong that it startled Larissa to remember they had never had a face to face conversation.

This letter assured Larissa that the family was well, but that the Clark's Valley community certainly was jumping with many things happening in a short time. The excitement over last year's linking of the continental railway in Utah was simmering down, but folks—that is to say, the men—were still going on about the ruling the past December that granted women in Wyoming Territory the right to vote. Ben wasn't so enthusiastic, but Anne thought it was a good decision. Now that women had a say in how things were run, maybe the Territory could attend to the business of getting settled. She'd never tell Ben so, "but, quite frankly, men don't always make good choices." The past war was a perfect example. "If women had been in charge, they would have settled it straight off, gone home, and had supper cooked by sunset."

The most important news, however, was that the neighborhood schoolhouse was within a "hoot and a whistle" of becoming a reality instead of a far off day possibility. Everyone had been contributing funds a little at a time to buy the lumber and other materials. After seemingly unending discussion, because of the lay of Willow Creek bordering the neighborhood properties, the participating families had actually chosen a spot only a couple of miles from Ben and Anne's Arrow A ranch, and "*that* was a cause for jubilation." Once it was up and running, she intended for her children to be on the doorstep first thing, hair combed and faces scrubbed. She could scarcely take it in that her dream of a formal education for them was finally going to come true. She admitted she was worried about her young ones fitting into their correct grades after all their home schooling. Ben kept telling her she was fretting for nothing, but still … the men would begin working on the building next year as soon as the ground thawed and spring roundup was out of the way.

The weather not always cooperating as it should, the board had decided, once the school was open, to hold classes as long as possible before the winter's storms could set in and freeze their efforts. This would also help the older boys make up the time they'd miss when they went on the annual trek with the herds to the summer grazing grounds. None of that, of course, would affect their oldest son Jason who, at seventeen, wouldn't attend. But twelve-year-old Luke, determined to make the summer trip, talked about nothing else but going with the herd. At least eight-year-old Matt and five-year-old Catty had no room to argue. Eve, of course, being only two, would have to wait a few more years. They were still searching for a teacher. They'd had a couple of nibbles so far, but "all the applicants decided, after all, that they were unwilling to come out to such a falling-off-the-end-of-the-world place as this."

Sharing the news at supper, Larissa and the girls had a good laugh at Hans' and Ethan's consternation over women voting. At the mention of the school project, Charity's eyes lit up. She'd completed her formal education last spring. When school had started earlier in the month, she'd begun assisting Miss Sullivan in the classroom. Her teaching goal thus strongly reinforced, she questioned Larissa eagerly about that part of Anne's letter.

Rose, whose long-cherished expectations of teaching would never be realized, leaned over to pick up the slice of peach that had slithered out of Merry's hand and landed on the floor. In light of Rose's battle to accept that her dream had been crushed, they tried not to wave Charity's success in front of her. But neither could they deny Charity her well-deserved recognition. With Rose's face shielded as she bent down, only Larissa saw her daughter's desolation.

CHAPTER FOUR

October's hunter's moon brought a letter that changed the course of their lives forever.

Larissa was scrubbing the mirror above the wash bench in the kitchen. She had been standing in front of it, holding Merry, and making funny faces at their images. Merry, in her delight, had patted the mirror, sprinkling it liberally with miniature fingerprints. As she polished, Larissa thought of Mac and Rose and how many times she had removed their baby smears from various surfaces. She remembered her vexation at the extra work they had caused. *What I would give for even one of those smudges now.*

She heard the buckboard rattling along the drive. *Surely Hans and the girls aren't home already.* Hans stopped by the kitchen path to let Rose and Charity off before turning the team toward the barn. In contrast to their old way of bursting through the back door, they entered sedately and hung their coats on the pegs beside the door. After giving Larissa her usual hug, Rose went at once to Merry, who was sitting on the floor, playing with a box of wooden sewing spools. Charity hugged Larissa with more spirit than usual before following Rose. It blinked in Larissa's mind that Charity's cheeks were pinker and her blue eyes were brighter than the brisk air outside warranted. The thought vanished as Merry, knocking over the tower of spools Rose had obligingly set up, chortled with glee and, tapping her fingertips together, begged her to stack them "more."

Only after they were seated around the supper table did Larissa learn the cause of Charity's sprightliness and Rose's subdued behavior. Charity glanced around the table before pulling an envelope from her apron pocket. "I received a letter from Mrs. Clayton today." She said it as casually as if she'd announced she was going out to feed the chickens. Since Charity's hands were otherwise occupied, Hans unobtrusively began interpreting for Rose, who, from her downcast expression, already knew what Charity was revealing.

"From Anne?" Larissa's heart gave an odd twitch. Ethan, at the other end of the table, looked as blank as she felt.

Clearly nervous, but striving to hide it, Charity unfolded the paper. "I wrote to Mrs. Clayton about the teaching position at their school." After tossing this keg of lighted gunpowder into the middle of the table, she continued. "I asked if they would consider me and told her about my schooling and how I'm assisting Miss Sullivan this year."

"What did she say?" Larissa didn't even recognize her own voice. *Surely Anne wouldn't ignore Ethan's and my parental authority.*

"She said I'll need my teaching certificate and a letter of reference from Miss Sullivan," Charity announced cheerily.

"What else does she say?"

Larissa cast Ethan a grateful glance, both for the response and for his carefully measured voice. She wasn't at all certain she could have even produced any words to frame the question.

"She needs to know I have your permission before they'll even consider taking me." Charity's reluctance in admitting this small snag was in approximate proportion to the relief that flooded Larissa as she realized yet again how close she and Anne were of mind and heart. *And we've never even met.*

The following morning, Larissa dashed off a letter to Anne. She had Ethan take it in to the post office when he picked up Rose and Charity from school, although she well knew it would not actually go out in the mail for several more days. An image that had frequently come to mind during the times she had waited so impatiently for the arrival of Zane's letters returned to her as she found herself once again waiting, with no means to speed up the process. A gleaming silver bird, grasping her envelope as the dove had once grasped Noah's olive leaf, soared across the cloudless blue sky and deposited her letter at Anne's feet. Not only that, it returned with Anne's response the very next day. *There are more things in heaven and earth than are dreamt of ...* She shook her head ruefully. Her inclination to let her imagination run wild in private was one thing. *If I ever mentioned any of my fantasies in civilized society, they'd probably lock me up and throw away the key.*

Anne's response came later in the month. "I well understand your concerns about Charity taking the teaching position here. I would have the same fears were it Catty or Eve considering an action that would take her so far from home at such a young age. She's your daughter, so I have every confidence that she would do an excellent job, but if you don't wish her to consider it, I won't continue to forward information that will encourage her." Her reassurance that she would never deliberately come between them and their daughter was music to Larissa's heart.

When she read the letter to Ethan, the relief in his eyes reflected her own. Yet over the next days, she could not bring herself to flaunt Anne's letter in front of Charity. The still-green memory kept intruding of another young woman asserting to her fiercely opposed parents that marrying Zane at such a young age would not ruin her life, but would fulfill it. Even as they gave her their consent, Larissa had seen the fear for her they could not hide. How swiftly the years had gone, and now she was looking, with the fear that had been in her parents' eyes, at her own beloved daughter. *Dear God, you know I don't want to press the issue, but I know what I would have done if they had not finally agreed. I would have followed my heart in spite of their objections. Can I expect Charity to do any less if we don't give our approval? Should I show her Anne's letter as proof of our side of the argument?*

She was straightening the quilt in Merry's crib when the hardest truth of all hit her. Anne had merely mentioned the teaching position as interesting news. It was Charity who had picked up on it and run with it. *But I'm making Anne the scapegoat to try to keep Charity from going.* She sank onto the edge of her bed and stared without seeing at her wedding ring. *I've made Anne responsible for the solution. How could I do that to her?*

At noon, when Ethan answered the dinner bell summoning him from Mill Pond, her thoughts were still as roiled as the waters he was clearing of debris from the last storm. As he began to comprehend the truth of her insight, his face, too, darkened. "We've always prided ourselves on facing facts," he said gloomily. "Looks like we've thrown the horseshoe mighty far from the stake this time. It puts me in mind of when Charity was learning to crawl. Nettie had made a little stuffed lamb that Charity was really attached to. When we'd put it on the floor in front of her, she'd giggle and reach out for it. But when she tried to crawl toward it, she'd go backward. She couldn't figure out why, the harder she tried to reach it, the farther away from her it got. She'd end up squawking so loud, she sounded exactly like she was cussing a blue streak. Seems like that's what we're doing here. We're trying so hard to get her to go forward with her life, we're sending her in the very direction we don't want her to go."

"We can't simply toss aside the fact that she's upset over Mac coming home with Amity." Larissa put all the fairness she could muster into her voice. "Even if we don't agree with her solution, she sees this as the perfect answer to not having to face him."

"If she runs away from this problem, what will she do next time she's faced with something unpleasant? We've worked hard to teach her better than that."

Larissa had no answer.

Over the next days, the verbal and emotional conflict between anxiety-ridden parents and determined daughter continued. Throughout this parent-child tug-of-war, Rose hovered in the background and forlornly watched the turmoil, and wondered how she would endure it if Charity won the battle and went to that far-off place. *Pa went there and he didn't come back.*

CHAPTER FIVE

On a blustery November evening, Mac Edwards, totally unaware of the tumult he was causing at home, walked briskly up the steps of the building he shared with other unmarried doctors who worked at the University of Pennsylvania Hospital. Finally possessing the coveted M.D. after their names, he and Jeff Kinsley had moved from the student dormitory to rooms in the doctors' residence hall. He paused at his mail slot. The days were long past when each member of the family wrote him once a week, both cheering and dispiriting him by their letters that brought them close, yet made them seem so very far away. He was no longer that homesick young man, but he looked forward to a weekly letter from at least one of them. One glance at the envelope waiting for him tonight confirmed that it was Charity's offering.

For no reason he could determine, he thought of his "hideaway" under the cedar trees across the hospital grounds. He hadn't been there for a long time, and had almost forgotten about the sense of reassurance it had given him during his first anxiety-ridden months as a student. The wish to go there swung through his mind, startling him. With a bemused shake of his head, he took the stairs two at a time to the third floor.

Mac passed Jeff's closed door as he headed for his own room. Tossing his coat and hat onto the bed, he absentmindedly pushed back the auburn hair that was forever falling into his eyes, and opened the letter. He unfolded it and a white square fell from the closely written pages. Curious, he turned it over. His heart gave a strange twist as he saw two young women seated on a wicker bench with a toddler perched between them. Could it really be coming up on four years since he had tugged Rose's braid and Charity's curls at the Pennsylvania station? They had been boarding the train with Ethan and Larissa to return to Fairvale at the end of the trip that had enabled Rose to learn sign language. Now they sat demurely, their hair pinned up, flowing skirts touching the floor. That could only be Merry with them, small hands clutching a large ball, her eyes wide and her mouth open a little as she gazed in wonder at something out of camera range.

Before he could read the letter, Jeff knocked on the open door and stuck his head around the frame. "Are you coming down to supper? I hear they're serving—" He broke off as he saw the picture in Mac's hand. Bending for a better view, he gave a low whistle of disbelief. "They can't be those two giggling girls who visited a couple of years ago?"

"They're my kid sisters, all right."

Jeff's brick-dust red eyebrows shot up. "They may be your sisters, but they're sure not kids anymore."

Startled, Mac studied them more closely. Rose's big eyes and heart-shaped face. He'd never noticed before how much she looked like Ma. Charity's blonde hair appeared darker in the picture, but in spite of her decorous pose, her eyes sparkled with mischievous humor. Again he felt that unaccountable twitch in his heart. "I guess they have changed some since they were here," he conceded.

Jeff grinned. "The rest of us fellows with sisters should be so lucky!"

Long after he was in bed, Mac, arms crossed behind his head, lay wide awake. Charity's letter kept circling through his mind. She'd related how Ethan had taken the three girls to the new photographer's store in town to have their picture taken to surprise Ma for Christmas. She didn't mention how she just happened to come into possession of the print she had sent him.

She had told of the possibility of going out to Wyoming Territory to teach, and how Ma and Pa weren't exactly thrilled with the idea. "But I'm almost eighteen years old. Surely, they don't expect me to live at home forever!" He smiled in the dark. By his count, her "almost eighteen years old" wouldn't happen for six more months. *I bet Ma and Ethan have their hands full trying to win this battle.* But he could see their point. It wasn't as if she planned to go to the next county. She had her sights set on moving half the country away from home. They must be feeling that potential loss keenly. For himself, he'd always pictured her being at the farm. Rambunctious as she was sometimes, he couldn't imagine home without her.

Again his heart twisted oddly. *What's the matter with me?* He couldn't wait to show the picture to Amity and tell her of Charity's latest stunt. *She'll get a good laugh out of it, too. Amity.* It felt so right and good to be with her. It made him feel the same as he used to when he saw Pa and Ma happy together in their day-to-day lives. He'd taken it for granted, then, had accepted the warmth and security of their love for him and each other as a simple fact. When he'd ridden out with Doc Rawley to visit patients, and even more so here at the hospital, he'd realized how rarely such a companionship existed. *How very fortunate I am to have found it with Amity.*

CHAPTER SIX

Another Christmas and New Year's Day had hurtled past. Already February's dreariness had slid into late March's enticing promise that springtime would soon beckon to them with the white and pink of apple and peach blossoms, the fragrant purple stars of lilacs, and new farm life in the pastures. Larissa was changing the heavy winter robin's-egg-blue woolen kitchen drapes for lighter, daffodil-yellow curtains. She dutifully climbed up and down on the stool, arranging the fabric into its proper pleats and gathers. Her heart, however, was outside with the almost-springtime day. The feeling of urgency she experienced every fall and spring, of wanting to go somewhere, do something—she knew not what—had poked at her for the past two days. She glanced over at Merry. The little girl, almost two now, was sitting on the floor, playing happily with the spoon and spatula Larissa had given her and the pans and lids she had filched out of the cupboard all on her own. She was, clearly, oblivious to her mother's fidgety feelings.

Catching herself daydreaming for the third time in half an hour, Larissa shook her head impatiently. The afternoon was flying by. Rose and Charity were due home from school shortly. This past year, Charity had continued working as a teaching assistant to Miss Sullivan, who was now instructing the grandchildren of some of her first pupils. Rose had completed the highest grade available in the Fairvale school system, but she, too, continued to go each day.

Miss Sullivan, still capable of striking terror into the hearts of even the biggest and oldest boys with one glance of her piercing black eyes, had sent to her old seminary for materials at a higher level to further Charity's burgeoning ambition to teach. While she was at it she had casually requested some extra textbooks and was now also leading Rose, who loved mathematics, through the intricacies of geometry and classical literature. Larissa smiled, recalling the payment Miss Sullivan had early-on exacted for those extra sessions. Upon the family's return from Philadelphia four years ago, Miss Sullivan had watched Rose and Charity, fresh from Hans' sign language tutoring, put their newly acquired skill to use. Thoroughly intrigued by their ability to communicate with their hands, she had promptly brokered sign language lessons in exchange for tutoring. The teacher had proved to be an adept pupil, and the hands-flying mathematical discussions she and Rose now carried on left Larissa in the dust. In her nightly prayers, Larissa doubly blessed Miss Sullivan. Because of her generosity, although she would have tartly denied it was any such thing, Rose was not only continuing the education in which she delighted, she was participating in social situations outside her family circle.

Unless there was an emergency, Hans, who was still riding out regularly as Doc Rawley's medical assistant in training, would be back with the girls in time for supper. Ethan, too, would be returning from his errand to the grist mill, and here she was, standing with her work undone. *Guess I won't be flying with the wild geese back from far-off lands this year. It's probably just as well.*

She was on the porch, shaking out the crocheted patchwork rug that normally lived on the kitchen floor in front of the dry sink when she heard the buggy coming around the curve of the drive. The chestnut coats and flaxen manes of Lyra and Lynx, the matched pair of Morgan horses Ethan had been training to drive in harness, gleamed in the sun as he halted them beside the kitchen path. Years before, when Zane and Larissa realized they would need more than simple dirt farming if the place were to succeed financially, they had begun raising Morgans for sale. Over the years, their carefully established bloodline had grown to attract attention in far counties of the state. The war and Zane's death had derailed the project, but now Larissa and Ethan were finally in a position to begin putting it back on track. Lynx and Lyra, named from the constellations, as all their horses were, with their proud carriage, strongly muscled quarters, and expressive eyes, showed extraordinary promise in contributing to this success.

Larissa raised her arm in greeting, then realized that the hand Ethan was waving held something white. Her breath caught in pleasure and she hurried to the porch steps as he climbed from the buggy. Going to the horses' heads, he stroked their muzzles and murmured softly in reward for a lesson well done. His blue eyes were twinkling and the mouth behind the soft brown beard curved in a teasing smile as he turned to her. Behind her, Merry's lively discussion with the spoon and spatula carried clearly to Larissa, who, with a glance back at the open kitchen door, resolutely resisted the impulse to dash down the steps to Ethan.

The first few months after their daughter's birth, when she had obligingly stayed neatly where they put her, Larissa and Ethan hadn't given a thought to how, in a split second, little ones could zip away. After Merry became a mobile and swift child, it came rapidly back to them. After one particularly giggle-filled chase on Merry's part—and a winded one on Ethan's—Larissa had caught him examining Merry's feet. He'd sheepishly confessed he was checking her heels to see whether a pair of wings had been stitched on before she was born.

Prudently waiting at the top of the steps, still clutching the shaken-out rug, she waited for Ethan to reach her. "Don't tell me you were so sure there'd be news from Mac that you've been standing here waiting all this time." He didn't pause for her reply but handed her the letter and took the rug.

"Do you think he's writing to tell us he's coming home?"

Ethan's lips twitched at her familiar request for him to help her second-guess the contents. Now, as each time previous, he offered his suggestion. "Why don't you open it and find out?" And, just as she had each time at his practical masculine response, she withdrew a pin from her hair and slit the flap. As she drew out the paper, Merry's scampering feet and squeal announced her presence in the kitchen doorway. With a crow of delight, she launched herself at her father. Dropping the rug, he caught her and swung her up into his arms.

As she had with each envelope, Larissa unfolded the pages and hastily counted them. "Only two, but both sides. It must not be something earthshaking this time."

Even as he chuckled at her conclusion, he had to admit that the few times Mac's letters had contained sobering information—the two times he wasn't coming home as planned; his announcement that he intended to ask Amity Terrill to marry him; his announcement that she'd accepted—they had been more lengthy. He watched the joy that leaped into Larissa's eyes and knew she'd been right again.

By the time Hans and the girls rattled up in the buckboard, Larissa had got herself under a semblance of control. This time, however, she didn't wait until suppertime to make her announcement. As soon as they came in, she waved the letter. "Mac's coming home, for sure this time."

At supper that evening, as they had earlier agreed, Ethan handed the conversational oars over to Larissa while he sat back and observed the family's reactions. Hans, watching Larissa keep the leaky boat of family harmony afloat, apparently decided it was prudent to stay on shore, and didn't contribute to the discussion. Ethan's eyes rested on Charity, and his parental heart squeezed with dismay. She was clearly struggling, not very successfully, to appear nonchalant by contributing cheerful remarks.

Rose's face harbored the same serenity as when, having labored over a sketch, she saw in the completed version what she had intended to express. "He doesn't say exactly when in June he'll be back."

That observation caused Larissa to scan the letter once more. "You're absolutely right. I was so excited, I didn't even notice that small detail. We'll have to see if we can pin him down a little more closely." Her faintly scolding tone didn't fool anyone.

***

Upstairs in her room that night—the room which had originally been Mac's and in which her possessions had gradually taken up residence after he left for medical school—Charity sat at her desk. Theoretically, she was correcting arithmetic papers from yesterday's homework. In reality, her mind was repeating, over and over, the words of Mac's letter, hoping that if she did so enough times, her heart would hear the truth.

… coming home in June for a month … Amity will stay in Philadelphia to make her final arrangements to come to Fairvale … working with Doc getting settled into the practice … look for a place in town for us to live, the boarding house, perhaps, at first … going back to Philadelphia … to Amity … the wedding….

At that point in her fourth repetition, a rap on her door startled her so she jerked and ripped the paper she had unconsciously been gripping. She stared wildly from the sorely damaged evidence of her distraction to the door. She knew it was Rose. Long ago, they had devised a knock whereby Rose could identify herself if Charity's door was shut, as it was now. With a flash of gratitude that it wasn't Ma or Pa, and still clutching the hapless homework, she hurried to let Rose in.

"I just—" Rose broke off her explanation at sight of Charity's woebegone face, then caught sight of the ragged edges of the papers clutched in her hands.

"Charity!" Since Rose could no longer correctly hear the volume of her own voice, the dismay in her exclamation came out more forcefully than she intended. Charity pulled her into the room and slapped the door shut against Ma and Pa hearing.

"Charity?" This time her name came out little more than a whisper as Rose stared from the pieces of paper to Charity's face.

Charity suddenly threw the pieces into the air, where they floated, still separate, to the floor.

Rose bent, picked them up, and attempted to fit them together. "I came to see how you're doing. I guess this answers my question. I'm so sorry," she added softly.

Charity blinked rapidly and slumped down on the edge of the bed, patting the space beside her for Rose to join her.

"I wish I had words to help you, Kinsee." Rose sank down beside her.

Long before their parents had even thought of marrying, Charity and Rose had decided that they wanted to be more than friends—they wanted to be sisters. Since they possessed neither a magic wand nor three wishes to help them achieve this objective, they'd decided to take matters into their own hands. After much earnest juggling of words, they agreed they would become *heart sisters*. Determined to make it a forever-pact, they had discussed ways to seal the pledge. They knew that boys became *blood brothers* under similar circumstances, but both girls hastily vetoed such a gory method as too obvious to their parents' eagle eyes. They chose and rejected several options, until eight-year-old Rose finally came up with a solution. "Your Pa was reading to us about 'kith and kin' and I asked him what it meant. He said 'kith' means 'friends' and 'kin' means 'relatives.' We're already kith and when we figure out how to do it, we'll be kin. We've made up lots of hand signs since we learned the finger alphabet from that book at school. Why don't we make up a sign for 'heart sisters' that no one else in the whole world can figure out what we mean?"

In spite of growing up on a horse farm, Charity's mind had already shifted from walk to gallop, without benefit of trot or canter. "We could hold our hands together over our hearts, like this." She clasped her laced fingers together over her heart. "In our hearts, we're kin, see?"

Rose had gravely repeated the gesture. "Kin, see," she'd agreed solemnly.

Through the ups and downs of childhood and adolescent temperaments and squabbles, the pact had stuck. Even after Rose became deaf and they learned the true *heart* and *sister* hand signs, they had kept *Kinsee* as something that, out of all the world, only they knew.

The young women sitting on the bed were years removed from that hot summer day and the two little girls making a solemn promise as they sprawled in the fragrant hay filling the barn loft. Now, because Rose could no longer hear the word spoken, Charity clasped her laced fingers over her heart, and they exchanged a shaky smile.

Rose drew a deep breath. "What are you going to do?" She dreaded the answer, for she already suspected what it would be.

Charity stood and, unnecessarily, checked the door to make certain it was shut. Turning back to Rose, she gripped her hands together nervously. Ever the talker, never at a loss for words, she now seemed unable to form a coherent answer.

Rose, always the quiet one, wrenched it from her own heart. "You're going to go out to Wyoming Territory, aren't you?"

Charity pressed her lips tightly together and nodded. "I can't stay here." She whispered the words as she signed them. "I've tried to make myself think I could, but I just can't. Do you think I'm a coward?"

"No!" Rose's forceful response, in sign and spoken word, burst from her. "You could never be a coward. I think it's tremendously brave of you to even think of going clear out there, so far from home."

Charity's knees gave way and only the edge of the bed behind her saved her from becoming a graceless heap on the floor. She flopped beside Rose. "I know Pa and Ma don't want me to go."

Rose looked straight into Charity's eyes. "Do *you* want to go? Would you go even if Mac weren't a reason?" There, she'd said it. After all the weeks of everyone tiptoeing around the truth, she'd brought Mac directly into it.

Charity's mouth opened, then closed again as a look of surprise swept across her features. "Yes." Even though Rose couldn't hear her, she repeated it, more emphatically. "Yes. I hadn't really asked myself if I was choosing to go or needing to go. I just knew I wanted to be gone." She stood, her fingers fluttering with a lightness Rose had not seen for a woefully long time. "I really do want to do this. It will be such an adventure. Remember how we always talked about someday going out and seeing the world, instead of just staying on the farm, with our entire social life centering around boring Fairvale? And this way I'll be teaching, too."

Her voice and her hands froze in horror as she realized what she had said. For Rose, in addition to the loss of her teaching ambitions, there would be no going out and seeing the world. She would remain at home, on the farm, three miles distant from the social life of boring Fairvale. Pain flicked in Rose's features and was as quickly gone.

"I'm sorry, Kinsee. I didn't mean—"

Rose's chin came up in a gesture her mother would have recognized. "It's all right, truly. I know what you meant." She tugged Charity back down beside her. "You'll just have to have enough adventures for both of us."

Charity bit her lip. "It won't be nearly the same without you there."

"You have to promise that you'll write about absolutely everything that happens, in school and out."

"I will. Just the same as if we were talking about it like we are right now." Charity's eyes widened. "We're talking about it like I'm really going to go," she said wonderingly.

Rose swallowed hard and laughed. "We have you there already, but there's still the small detail of convincing Ma and Pa."

Charity sighed. "I know. But knowing you're with me on this, that you understand what it means to me to go, I'm so relieved. I just couldn't do it without your support. That'll help me so much when I face Ma and Pa." Charity threw her arms around Rose and spoke into her ear. "Thank you for being my sister."

CHAPTER SEVEN

Over the next weeks, Charity's resolve to speak to her parents didn't waver, but, as a precaution, she practiced with Rose what she would say, while Rose vigorously and ruthlessly threw in their certain objections. "You'll have to promise to tell me everything they say, so we'll know how close we've come," she implored.

Charity stared at her. "But you'll be there, too."

Rose shook her head. "This is between you and them. I can't interfere—"

"But I was expecting you to be there with me. I know you can't say anything, but please just be there. I need all the moral support I can get for this."

"Charity—"

"Please, Rose!"

Even without hearing her tone of voice, the desperation in Charity's expression was too much for Rose to resist. "All right."

Charity hugged her tightly. "Thank you. I guess it doesn't sound very grown up to be so glad to hear you say yes," she said ruefully.

Rose gave a choked laugh. "You'll have to be doing so many grown up things from now on, I guess this one last occasion won't hurt."

***

On a Saturday in the middle of April, Larissa, with money in hand from her sale of the week's surplus eggs and butter, strolled among the goods displayed in Fairvale's mercantile. The farm had had good crops the past two years, and they had sold one of their Morgan horses, so they were not scrimping at the moment. But always there was the knowledge that Nature could turn on them at any time during the process of bringing crops to successful fruition. It had happened before and must be expected to do so again, so they continued to spend carefully against the eventuality.

The income from the butter and egg money was so specifically her own it even bypassed the formality of first placing it in the farm's coffers. With the satisfying knowledge that she could fritter away her windfall on anything her heart wished, she now perused the possibilities. Wandering among the displays of glassware, bolts of silk material, and other luxuries, she pointedly avoided the foodstuffs, brooms, washtubs and other practical items. One Saturday a month, she came to town alone. When she'd left Ethan and the girls that morning, they had been planning to stack the firewood he and Hans had cut and split. There had also been mention of cleaning the henhouse when they were finished with the wood. Larissa hadn't waited around to hear more.

She stopped before a tray of jewelry and carefully inspected the pieces. *A ring?* She had one. Ethan had placed it on her finger four years ago at their wedding. The necklaces were pretty, but she hadn't worn one since she took off the quarter eagle gold pendant and chain Zane had made and given her before they were married. Nothing she'd seen since had really suited her fancy. *A brooch?* She had the one that had been a wedding gift to her grandmother, worn and loved until she passed it down to her daughter, Larissa's mother. The daintily-etched, slender golden bar gleaming at her mother's throat was a childhood memory that had not dimmed with the years. Now it was Larissa's, to someday pass down to one of her daughters. *No brooch, either. S*he paused beside a paisley shawl. On Mac's first Christmas in Philadelphia, he had sent her a cherry red shawl, made of the softest yarn she had ever seen or felt. So a shawl, even a paisley patchwork of gold and brown and rust, didn't stir her to want to own another.

She had the butter and egg money, she had the chance to buy something lavish for herself, and she saw nothing around her to spend the money on. *I already possess everything I desire.* She smiled to herself because she knew exactly what she would purchase with the money, had known before she even started her treasure hunt. Mac and Amity's wedding would, of course, be in Philadelphia, at the home of the bride. Upon receiving Mac's letter in which he announced that Amity had accepted his proposal of marriage, Larissa had told Ethan that, expensive or not, the whole family would attend the wedding. She had vowed that she would eat bean soup for a year, if that was what it would take to save enough money to purchase train tickets for all of them. Ethan had not argued. He had smiled and begun quietly forgoing little luxuries such as the more expensive pipe tobacco he enjoyed and Mark Twain's newest book, *Innocents Abroad*, which he had been looking forward to reading.

"Good morning, Mrs. Michaels."

Startled out of her reverie, Larissa turned to find Charlotte Sullivan's direct gaze upon her. "Why, good morning," she managed without squeaking.

Having dispensed with the pleasantries, Fairvale's school teacher got right to the point. "I saw you drive by earlier, alone. Did none of the family come with you?"

Larissa shook her head. "Today's my day in town, to shop as I please, without anyone else along."

Miss Sullivan didn't voice outright disapproval of such an extraordinary indulgence, but she didn't applaud it, either. Her black eyes fixed on Larissa so intently that Larissa felt as guilty as if she'd been caught red handed firing off a spitball.

"I've been waiting for an opportunity to speak to you privately, Mrs. Michaels, as soon as possible."

Larissa sighed inwardly. *That can only mean more trouble of some kind is brewing.*

"The bench in the courthouse square will be a suitable place to sit. I will complete my purchases first, since I am here, and meet you there in ten minutes."

That's our Miss Sullivan, needing to talk about something important. Larissa was unable to squelch the wry thought. *She never wastes time on idle chatting, then after getting me concerned, postpones it so she can complete her planned activities in an orderly manner.* "That will be fine. I've finished my shopping." *You don't need to qualify your acceptance.* The scolding thought promptly snipped at her. *After all, you're not six years old, even if you feel like it at the moment.*

Precisely ten minutes later, Miss Sullivan approached Larissa, who was standing beside the bench. The childish rebellion of standing while she waited, instead of sitting as the teacher had directed, fell flat as the older woman, back straight as a poker even on the curving seat, moved her skirts aside and gestured for Larissa to join her. With another inward sigh, Larissa sat.

"I wish to discuss a situation that has come up concerning Charity."

Larissa actually felt hasty relief. If Charity was the subject, at least it was not an entirely new disaster to add to their problems of the moment.

"I do not come to you with the intention of interfering in matters between you and your daughter. Nor do I come to be carrying idle tales. Because Charity has been under my supervision as my teaching assistant this school year, I have had several discussions with her concerning her future plans. During the twelve years since she became my pupil, I have had many opportunities to observe that she has an adventuresome spirit. I gather that she is now making plans to go to Wyoming Territory to teach in a new school there." Her black eyes fixed on Larissa with an unblinking gaze. "Is this true? Are you and Mr. Michaels aware of this? As responsible parents, do you consent to this scheme?"

Larissa did the only thing she could against the faint outrage evident in the rapid-fire questions. Holding Miss Sullivan's eyes with an unblinking gaze of her own, she said firmly, "We do know about it. The possibility has been building for quite some time. As responsible parents, no, we have not consented to this plan."

"Will you consent?"

The last thing we want to do is consent, Larissa wanted to screech. *Just how irresponsible do you think we are?* By great force of effort, she managed to answer calmly. "We are still discussing the matter. It's not a simple question and answer of shall we let her go or not. She's young, and it's a very long way for her to go." Larissa stopped as her throat closed around the words.

"Mrs. Michaels, again I assure you that I do not wish to interfere in a private family matter. However, as her mentor, it is my responsibility to help her with questions and concerns about her future teaching role. Therefore, I am authorized to discuss this situation with her." She added smoothly, "And with you, to achieve the best possible resolution. She has asked me to write a letter of recommendation to the Clark's Valley School Board. I believe she would make an excellent teacher and am willing to write a letter detailing my observations. However, I do not wish to proceed without your knowledge and without your parental authorization to do so. "

Larissa gripped her hands in her lap to keep them from trembling. "Has she talked to you about why she wants to go out there?"

"She said that she wants to experience life beyond Fairvale," Miss Sullivan said crisply. "She knows the daily, quiet routine of farm and village life as it is carried on here. When she was in Philadelphia, she saw all the glamour of city life. Now she wants to explore a part of the country that is just beginning to shape its life. She explained how, in that way, she'll gain a better understanding of people. She'll learn what motivates them to act as they do in striving for goals and achieving or failing to reach them—all the small details that make up a human being's personality and emotions. She feels that in this way she can better understand her pupils and the people they hope to become. It is a credible aspiration for a young person."

"Did she give you any other reasons?"

"She did not say specifically, but I sense that she is questioning her heart." Miss Sullivan's lips tightened at this rare wading into the waters of another person's emotions.

"Do you feel the 'experiencing life beyond Fairvale' quest outweighs the possibility that she might be running from her heart?" Larissa asked the question as casually as she could, then held her breath as she waited for the answer.

Completely out of character, Miss Sullivan hesitated for the space of two heartbeats. Drawing herself up—no mean feat since her spine was already rigid as a poker—she said flatly, "Before I started teaching school, I, too, had the opportunity to travel. To England, to be precise. The details do not matter. What matters is that I did not take the opportunity. I will tell you to satisfy the curiosity I see in your eyes, that no, I did not refuse because of a … romantic attachment." For the first time in her memory, Larissa saw the woman's cheeks turn pink. She was so amazed at this proof of emotion from unbending Miss Sullivan that she missed the next words.

"… although I am aware that such is often the case. Mine was not a situation out of *Wuthering Heights*, I assure you." She spoke sharply, as if Larissa showed signs of arguing the point with her. Again she paused before pushing resolutely on. "I did not go for only one reason. I was afraid. It was that simple. I did not have the courage to go out into the world and encounter all its pitfalls, or all its wonders. I chose to stay here, safe in Fairvale, secure in my teaching. It is a decision I have deeply regretted. Because of it, I determined that I would never again pass up an opportunity to gain knowledge, even about inconsequential things such as why giraffes in Africa, with the weight of their long necks, don't topple forward when they run." For the first time in their conversation, she shared a grim smile. "A student asked me that, and I had to tell her that I didn't know, that I would seek the answer. I never found it. I am still seeking."

If possible, Miss Sullivan's gaze was even more fixed than before. "What I am telling you is that I didn't seize my chance. I let fear dictate my decision. Charity is afraid, but she really wants to do this, and it may very well be the only way she can answer those questions of her heart which you implied. Besides which, I believe she would do an excellent job of teaching if given the opportunity." She stopped abruptly and rose from the bench. "Please let me know if you wish me to write the letter. Good day, Mrs. Michaels." And she was gone before Larissa could gather her wits enough to respond.

Alone in their room that night, Larissa described the strange experience to Ethan. He raised an eyebrow quizzically. "What we've always seen as rambunctious behavior, Miss Sullivan sees as adventuresome spirits. That's certainly 'a rose by any other name' if I ever heard one, considering some of the high jinks Charity's pulled. It's interesting that Miss Sullivan, of all people, brought up *Wuthering Heights*. Did she make any mention of suspecting Mac as Heathcliffe's parallel to Charity's Cathy?"

Larissa shook her head. "She implied that if Charity wants to do this for the adventure of finding knowledge, her heart will take care of itself."

"Things do have a way of working out, in spite our vigorous attempts to bend the results to our way of thinking. It just astonishes me that prim and grim Miss Sullivan would unbend enough to speak about such private emotions. She said she didn't have the courage to act when she was young," he mused. "Revealing what she did today, I'd say she has courage in abundance."

"Which brings us to the question of granting our permission for her to write the letter to the school board. I think we should." Larissa's eyes met the question in his. "There's no arguing that Charity's going to be a teacher. She'd need a letter of recommendation if she were going to Wyoming Territory or Columbus—or Siberia. Besides, we can make reading it before Miss Sullivan sends it part of the deal. It will be highly interesting to see what Miss Sullivan has to say about the 'adventuresome spirits' that are a very real part of the package she's recommending."

CHAPTER EIGHT

Larissa and Ethan knew the showdown with Charity was coming and braced themselves for it, but before it materialized, yet another problem reared its unhappy head. After Hans had weathered the first awkward days of adjustment, and had been assured that they regarded him as a member of the household, he had settled into his new farm and family life. Although he didn't place himself in the center of attention, they'd been confident that he was content in his new role, for he increasingly offered quiet participation. As he became more comfortable with them, he revealed a dry wit. He'd made more than one suppertime debate memorable when he summed up all their noisy opinions with one quiet comment that hit right at the heart of the discussion.

The last several days, however, Hans had been acting oddly. He no longer joined in mealtime conversations, and he seemed to sit on the fringe of the family circle when they gathered in the sitting room or kitchen after the dishes and other evening chores were completed. He was never sullen or rude, but the spark of liveliness they had grown to appreciate seemed dampened. Many nights he and Ethan had poured over the Farmer's Almanac for weather predictions and ended up discussing the suggestions and advice also found there. But he no longer asked a multitude of questions, some of which frankly stumped Ethan and caused him to see the illogic of ways of doing things he had taken for granted and never thought to change. Hans' quickness of mind seemed to have retreated along with his usual exuberance. Ethan tried to bring the reason to light during times they were alone milking or currying the horses, but Hans withdrew even more into himself, never taking advantage of the openings Ethan offered.

Discussing it, Larissa and Ethan wondered if he were interested in some young woman he had not worked up the daring to approach in the village. Or, infinitely worse, he had approached her and been sent away. He was, after all, twenty-one, plenty old enough to be thinking in terms of marrying and settling down in a home of his own. They had, as yet, seen no such interest brewing. His inability to speak would make a relationship somewhat more difficult to initiate, but, since he retained his hearing, not impossible. He had once spoken to Ethan about Ellen Damon, a young woman near his own age, who had asked him to teach her sign language. During the subsequent course of lessons, she asking the words, he responding in sign, the two had found an easy friendship which they had retained over the past few years. But to all appearances, that was what they remained: friends with no romantic intentions hovering in the wings.

It was a busy time on the farm, and the hard work and accompanying weariness at the end of the day didn't leave a lot of opportunity for other thought or action. So Ethan and Larissa wondered but came up with no way to draw him out.

On a sunny noonday, Larissa set a basin of hot water on the bench beside the back porch door for Ethan's dinnertime washing up. Hearing the sound of a rig rounding the corner of the drive, she glanced up. In just a moment, Bella appeared, with Doc in the buggy clearly attempting to slow her down as they approached the kitchen path. Larissa, lips twitching, watched fascinated as Bella refused to obey his instructions. Just when it seemed certain that she would overshoot the walkway, she stopped, so abruptly that the momentum thrust Doc forward. Fortunately, the dashboard intervened to spare him an up-close inspection of Bella's tail. Bella snorted. Doc snorted back. He clambered down from the buggy, indignation fairly sparking in his hazel eyes. Yanking his rumpled coat into position, he grabbed his bag and turned.

Larissa barely had time to change her wide grin to a less explosive smile. "Doc, it's good to see you. Have you had another letter from Mac?" As Doc approached, Larissa realized that his ill humor came from more than just Bella's antics. "Is something wrong?" Even as she asked, she felt all-too-familiar tightness squeeze her heart.

Doc waved the hand that wasn't holding his medical bag. "Everyone's in one piece, as far as I know."

His lopsided response illogically reassured her, although he continued to look grim. *But, truth to tell, Doc looks grim more often than not.* "Come in," she said hastily. "I just rang the dinner bell for Ethan. He should be coming up from the oat field in a minute. If you'd like to wash up before he gets here, I have plenty more hot water. And towels," she added, removing the one slung over her shoulder and holding it out to him.

"I didn't come to eat you out of house and home again," he protested gruffly.

"You certainly wouldn't want to make Ethan uncomfortable eating his own dinner while you looked on, starving," she argued just as gruffly.

He opened his mouth, shut it, shook his head, and reached to take the towel from her.

"Doc!" They both turned at Ethan's hail to find him striding toward them. Dirty and sweaty as he was, his grin was all warm welcome.

Larissa disappeared into the kitchen. Doc held out the towel apologetically, but Ethan waved it back. "Go ahead. If I don't get shed of these muddy boots first, Larissa will never let me in the house."

"That's right," she said sternly as she reappeared with a fresh towel and soap. Doc sighed, gave up, and thrust his bushy chin into the basin.

Seated at the table a short while later, with Merry in her chair industriously straining the last bite of her mashed peas through her fingers, Doc set down his coffee cup. "A great meal as always, Larissa," he pronounced as she fetched a damp cloth to scrub the bright green remnants from her protesting daughter's face and hands. His eyes softened as he watched the little girl, set free from the high chair, immediately toddle off to reclaim her abandoned stuffed squirrel. He hesitated another moment, the softness vanishing as he spoke decisively. "Hans is off keeping Grandma McCormick company."

"Is Grandma ill?" Larissa's concern was well grounded. Birdie McCormick, at ninety-two Fairvale's oldest citizen, possessed a lively wit, a hearty laugh and a fierce independence. Her beautifully pieced quilts still took prizes at the Union County Fair each year. Her death would leave a very large hole in the community.

"She's fine. We stopped on our rounds to check on her. When we were ready to leave, she asked if Hans could stay just a while longer to chat. I suspect she asked him because he's the only one who hasn't heard every one of her stories a bushel basket of times. When I left, she was regaling him with the story about how Fairvale, not Milford Center, came to be named Union County's 'Seat of Justice' back in 1820. Since she lived in Milford Center when it happened, she was taking pains to assure that he 'heard the true story.' It gave me a good chance to talk to the two of you alone," he finished abruptly.

At the gravity in Doc's tone, Larissa put down the plates she had been gathering and sank back into her chair. "What is it?"

He saw Ethan and Larissa brace as if they knew, inevitably, the news would be bad. It seemed to him like he never brought any other kind. "I particularly wanted to talk to you without Hans around." Larissa and Ethan exchanged a quick glance, but he suspected they weren't surprised by the topic. "Hans has been acting odd lately. At least around me. He's quieter than normal and hasn't been flummoxing me with his usual slew of 'what's' and 'why's.' Have you noticed anything like this?"

Asked pointblank, Ethan and Larissa could not evade an answer. Again they shared a silent-message look, and she bit her lip. "He *has* been acting different. We've noticed it, but if something's bothering him, he won't talk about it. We've both tried, but he just withdraws into himself. If you're noticing it, too—"

"He won't talk to you? He clammed up with me, but I finally pried it out of him. Told him he couldn't let personal problems interfere with his work. That's when he opened up." Doc eyed them speculatively. "You really have no idea what's bothering him?" In unison they shook their heads, a typical reaction of like-mindedness that usually exasperated him. This time, deeply intent on his subject, he let it buzz past, much as he would a departing mosquito. "Think back. When did he start acting this way?"

"Why, a few weeks ago." Larissa's bewilderment was plain.

"And what happened a few weeks ago?" Doc prodded.

"The most exciting thing was getting a letter from Mac, but there was nothing negative in it. He just talked about coming home."

"What's Mac going to do when he comes home?"

"Go into practice with you, of course." She didn't say, "As if you don't already know that," but her tone clearly indicated it.

"And what's Hans going to do when Mac comes home?"

"Why, he's—" She stopped so abruptly it was as if her words had fallen off the edge of a cliff. Her eyes widened and once more met Ethan's, and Doc saw their shock and horror mingle in about equal parts. "Oh, no," she breathed.

"Oh, yes," Doc said dryly. "He's been working with me for four years. Took to it like a duck to water. Now, all of a sudden, that work is about to be yanked out from under his feet."

Shame, as he had never seen it before, suffused Larissa's features. "Dear God," she whispered. "We were so wrapped up in Mac coming home, we didn't stop to think what it meant for Hans."

"You can be sure he's been thinking about it. He's been worried sick about where he'll go, what he'll do."

The guilt stamped on Ethan's face mirrored Larissa's. "He's just become so much a part of the family, we didn't even consider the consequences to him, certainly never that he might think he'd have to leave."

"Take a look at it from his viewpoint," Doc suggested flatly. "He had his life ripped apart with that carriage wreck when he was six. His folks died and he lost his ability to speak. He went to that school for the deaf and learned sign language. When he finished his courses there, he was booted out. He made a life for himself at the Philadelphia hospital. He was yanked from there and transplanted here, which meant he had to piece his life together yet again. He's done well, all things considered, and you've certainly given him a home life he wouldn't have gotten anywhere else. I'm not belittling that in any way. But here he is, once more, without a clue what his future will be."

Ethan, beet red, started to speak, but stopped. No words were adequate.

"We never in this world dreamed that he'd think he'd have to leave here," Larissa said weakly. "He's so much a part of the family now I can't even imagine it."

"Well, he's imagined it," Doc said grimly. "But I'll take my share of the blame. I'm the one who suggested he come here. I encouraged him. I dangled the carrot of learning medicine in front of him."

"But you did it for Rose, too," Larissa said softly. "It gave both of them a chance they wouldn't have had otherwise. His medical learning and her opportunity to continue learning sign language. Surely it couldn't have been a wrong encouragement."

Behind his snowy beard, Doc's lips compressed. He had never easily accepted praise or acknowledgment of a kind deed. Now he said stiffly, "What's done is done. All the wishing or regrets in the world won't change it."

Ethan clenched his jaw. "We can't change the past, but we can attempt to make the future better. Has Hans said anything about his plans? Does he even *have* any plans?"

"He's thinking that he'll go back to Philadelphia, to the hospital if they'll take him back. At least there he had work and independence." He saw the flash of sorrow in Larissa's eyes.

"He's so much a part of our family. It would be a betrayal to send him back there."

"He can stay and help on the farm. God knows there's more than enough to do, so he needn't feel it's an obligation on either of our parts. If we give him wages, same as we would anyone else, he'd have work, independence, and a family."

Larissa brightened at Ethan's practical suggestion, then slowly shook her head. "He's done well, learning how to farm. But he wants to be involved with medicine, and we don't have the right to take that away from him if he has a chance to do it."

"Even at the cost of losing him from our family? That's what we'd be doing. It's not like Mac going off. Mac has and always will remain connected to us. He didn't go away because he felt there was no longer a place for him here." Ethan trailed to a stop at the distress in Larissa's eyes.

Doc had been watching their exchange and reading more in it than they would ever realize. He tugged at his beard. "I do have a suggestion." Seeing the hope that leaped into their eyes, he cleared his throat roughly. "I haven't spoken to Hans yet. I wanted to get your views first. I've been conferring with Gustav Ingemar over in Delaware County. His medical practice is growing by leaps and bounds, and he's been considering for a long time taking on an assistant, like I did with Mac and now Hans. He's just never gotten around to it. He'd like to have a go with Hans, see how it works out. Says he'll be getting a bargain since the boy's been working with me and already knows quite a few of the ropes. If Hans is willing, of course. His inability to speak might be a stumbling block for a while." Here Doc came as close to giving a sheepish grin as they'd ever seen him. "But Ingemar says if I could learn sign language at my age, he can, too." They stared at him, speechless. "Well," the gruffness was back. "What do you think?"

Ethan's wide smile and the look of joy on Larissa's face were more than enough answer.

***

Doc left, after warning them he wasn't going to say anything to Hans, that it would be up to them to get it all worked out. Because the planting couldn't wait for them to sit down and hash it out, Larissa walked with Ethan back to the oat field. Merry, holding their hands, swung happily between them, totally unaware of their disquiet. They paused at the edge of the field and Ethan summed it up. "So we should just apologize straight out for our lack of concern over his feelings and assure him it wasn't intentional. Then we can ask him about his plans, give him a chance to air his feelings. He's certainly entitled. After that, we'll lay out Doc's proposal."

She nodded. "I can't even begin to imagine what he's been going through. I pray he can forgive us."

"Misunderstandings and hurtful actions are all part of being a family," Ethan said ruefully.

"We've showed him that in large measure. I just hope we can convince him that love and caring are an even bigger part of it."

That afternoon, Ethan came in early from the field, so that he and Larissa would both be there when Hans arrived home. As it turned out, though, it was later than usual when he drove in. Ethan went out to help him unhitch, but said nothing about Doc's visit.

Larissa and the girls were finishing the supper preparations when the two returned from the barn. She flashed Ethan an anxious glance, but he only gave a slight shake of his head. Supper seemed interminable. There wasn't a great deal of talk, in contrast to their usual lively bantering. Hans was even more withdrawn than he had been. It didn't help the atmosphere any that Charity was clearly nervous about something, as well. She was so distracted that she even failed to sign for Rose the slogging conversation between Ethan and Larissa. Hans, head ducked, didn't translate either, so they made certain to sign as they talked. Rose was quiet, too, although Larissa was aware that her silence seemed more somber than nervous.

As they were preparing to leave the table, Ethan put his hand on Hans' arm. "Larissa and I would like to talk to you. May we come to the cabin?"

Even as he spoke, he heard Charity say to Larissa at the other end of the table, "I need to talk to you and Pa right away."

Larissa, fully aware of Ethan's request to Hans, shot him a panicked look as Charity persisted. "Please, Ma."

Her first wishful instinct was to dismiss the girl's plea as the over-dramatization with which they were only too familiar. Charity's demeanor told her, however, that this time, of all times, that wasn't the case. She looked down the table and saw Ethan's alarm that he had caught Hans' attention and that Larissa wasn't following through as they had planned. She knew then, with total certainty, how a woods creature must feel when it realizes that the door of the trap has swung shut behind it, leaving no escape. Here it was again, one of those moments of parenthood that every mother and father dreads: the need to make an instantaneous decision that would forever affect their child's life. *For you are my child, Charity, as surely as if you had been born to me.* Hans half-turned toward her. Ethan's hand still on his arm, they looked at her, waiting, even as Charity looked at her, waiting.

Ethan, not grasping his daughter's need, caught up in the import of his own necessity, said sharply, "Larissa."

She swiftly cupped her hand to Charity's cheek. "I have to go with Pa right now. But we will talk to you just as soon as we can. I promise." The shock, pain, and disbelief that swept across Charity's features would forever linger in Larissa's heart. Even as she watched, the girl's face emptied of all emotion. "Charity?"

She turned slowly away. "It doesn't matter." Her voice was as empty of life as her expression.

Hans and Ethan were standing by the back door, waiting for her. Charity was moving away through the doorway to the sitting room. With a wrench of her heart so hard that raw pain shot through her, Larissa watched the young woman go.

Because no one had translated for her, Rose missed the verbal thrust of this outburst. She had, however, learned to read body language as skillfully as she did hand signs. Grasping the bitter outcome of the exchange, Rose, looking back at her mother reproachfully, trailed after Charity.

Numbly turning to Ethan and Hans, Larissa wondered if, after so many years of loving Ethan's child as her own, she had lost her.

Ethan, with a mixture of confusion and resolve crossing his face, took her arm. "Whatever it is, we'll fix it. I swear."

His assurances seemed as fragile to her as the night breeze cool against her cheek, as insubstantial as the shadow cast by Hans, shoulders slumped and footsteps heavy on the path ahead of them, as trancelike as Ethan's hand grasping hers tightly, and his unawareness of the agony of the choice she had made.

As they entered the cabin, her thoughts continued to whir wildly. The joy she and Zane had shared here so many years ago. The times she had been here with Ethan, including the day of jagged lightning and drenching rain when she had learned of Zane's death and she and Ethan had come here to escape the storm's onslaught, only to be overtaken by a different kind of adversary. The December night she and Ethan sat at this table and worked out whether they should take Rose to Philadelphia to confirm her hearing loss and give her the opportunity to learn sign language. *Ethan built up the fire because it was so cold.* It slipped into her awareness that Hans had made a true home for himself in this small space that held the ghosts of so many life-changing choices. *And now, once again, this room will be witness to a choice that will change many lives.*

They settled around the table and Ethan laid out the facts to Hans. Carefully, honestly, without embellishment, he told the young man how it had been with them, and their regret that their preoccupation had caused him such pain. Larissa, still with a feeling of unreality, heard herself confirming Ethan's explanation and her regret. She thought she must have said something right, because Hans' shuttered expression slowly changed—to skepticism, to disbelief, to wariness, to comprehension. Haltingly, he revealed his idea of returning to Philadelphia. They offered him the choice of remaining on the farm and were gratified to see the relief that sparked in his eyes. Finally, they told him of Doc's suggestion that he work with Dr. Ingemar over in Delaware County. They saw the spark of relief in his eyes leap into blazing light and knew they had their answer.

Then, as he had never done before, he shared his innermost secrets. Gracefully, his hands sketched his initial uncertainties as he became accustomed to his new life and his new family. He told them of the deep satisfaction he had come to know in assisting Doc and becoming a part of the medical life he had hungered to enter. With slow gestures, he admitted his despair when he thought he would be displaced because of Mac's homecoming. And with bursting joy, he told them how much it would mean to him to work with Dr. Ingemar, to continue to be a part of the medical world that had become his life.

All the while, as Larissa read his words and lived those moments with him, she tried desperately not to think of Charity, who had not the faintest clue why she had been rebuffed in her hour of need by the people she loved and trusted.

As Larissa and Ethan finally made their way back to the house, she poured out her grief of rejecting Charity. He listened, astonished, as miserable as she that they had done this to their child, regardless of the twist of fate that had left them no choice. *There's always a choice.* Out of the past, Ethan heard his own voice admonishing Charity because she had made a poor decision. *Whatever you choose to do or not do, the outcome is your own responsibility and no one else's.* Blood thumping in his ears failed to drown out the certainty with which he had uttered that statement. *Talk about parental words coming home to roost.*

The kitchen, empty and still disheveled from supper, echoed with silence. There was no sign that Charity and Rose, having walked away after Larissa's failure to listen, had returned or ever planned to return. There was also no sign of Merry. Such desolation pushed at them from all sides that Larissa, in a moment of pure panic, wondered if Rose and Charity had fled the house, taking Merry with them.

At her catch of breath, Ethan's hand tightened on her shoulder. "I'm guessing they must all be up in Charity's room."

Larissa was already on her way to the sitting room doorway. Turning left to the foot of the stairs, she started to call to them, as always, to come down. But the words died in her throat. "I have to go up, not the other way around this time."

He took her hand. "*We* have to go up," he said firmly.

The upper hall was dim and ghostly quiet. Both girls' bedroom doors were closed. After a moment, though, they heard the faintest sound, as of a choked-off breath, coming from the right side of the hallway. Their handclasp tightening, Larissa rapped on Charity's door.

CHAPTER NINE

"Charity," she said softly, "may we come in?" There was a long moment of silence, then slow footsteps. Expecting Charity, they were taken aback when the door opened on Rose. Her face was flushed from weeping, her cheeks still damp with tears. Her expression mirrored the betrayal that had darkened Charity's eyes earlier as Larissa had turned from her to Hans. Searing pain, greater than her anguish at Zane's death, more scalding than her first, sharp knowledge that Rose would never hear again, scorched through Larissa. Those two times of agony had been beyond her power to prevent, but this time—this time. She felt Ethan behind her stiffen, heard his indrawn breath. Rose, who had neither felt him stiffen nor heard his sharp breath, stood, waiting.

"We need to explain what happened." Out of habit, Larissa had spoken as she signed. Rose made no gesture to open the door wider, merely looked at them with an expression from which all trust had fled. With a pattering rush of feet across the floor, Merry shoved past Rose and tugged open the door. Wailing, she threw herself against her mother's knees. By reflex, Larissa caught her up and cuddled her against her shoulder.

The little girl's movement had swung the door wider and revealed Charity sitting at her desk. She had turned at Merry's headlong flight and they could see that her face, too, was flushed from crying, but tears no longer dampened her cheeks. Hands clasped in front of her, still without speaking, Rose retreated to stand beside Charity, her stance making it abundantly clear where her loyalty lay.

For a moment that seemed to stretch across a gap far wider than the space of the room separating them, silence lay between parents and children. Then Charity stood. "Come in." They had expected mutiny or rebellious tears. She gave them neither, speaking lifelessly and watching them enter the room.

"We must talk to you. Will you listen?" At Ethan's appeal, Charity silently gestured to the bed and he and Larissa sat, Merry scrambling to reach his lap.

Her arms now empty, Larissa took up where he had left off signing. "We won't make any excuses for what we did, Charity, but we are more sorry than words could ever begin to tell you."

Still expressionless, still saying nothing, the girls looked at them.

"We know that for some time you have been wrestling with a dilemma." Larissa's fingers quivered and she stopped to steady them. "Then we became aware that Hans also had a problem. We couldn't get him to talk to us about it and we were getting more and more worried. Until today, we had no clue what was troubling him. Then Doc came by this afternoon and told us he'd found out what was wrong. Once we knew, we were so frantic to talk to Hans that we threw everything else out the window, including your need. But please never doubt we have been aware of your trouble, and we have been struggling for many weeks to find a way to help you."

Pain flicked in Charity's eyes at this assurance. In the continuing rigid silence, Merry switched back to nestle her head against Larissa's shoulder with a sleepy sigh.

"In the end, it came down to a choice." Ethan was very carefully controlling his voice and his hands. "We never in this world expected his problem and yours to meet with such atrocious timing. Lady Luck has engineered quite a few coincidences in the past. The old gal must be dancing on the roof with glee over this one." Neither girl smiled. He clenched his jaw then determinedly relaxed it. "But when it comes to assigning responsibility for taking Hans' problem over yours, I stand front and center." Beside him, Larissa stirred in protest, but he didn't pause. "Ma was aware that you couldn't be ignored for Hans. I was only aware that we had the opportunity to help him, and that we had to seize it. I'm sure you've figured out by now that Ma and I stand in agreement with each other in any discussions requiring, shall we say, parental guidance." Still neither girl lightened in any way. He plowed on. "I took the lead and, because of the agreement between us, I took away her chance to make her own choice."

Larissa, as he'd known she wouldn't, didn't contradict him, but she spoke with a firmness that left no doubt of her views on the subject. "I think what it all comes down to is why we make the choice we make in making our choices." Both girls blinked as Ethan signed the convoluted statement, their first show of positive animation since Ethan and Larissa had entered the room.

"Charity," Larissa said slowly, "I would never in this world want to deliberately cause you hurt. In all the years you've been in my life, long before your Pa and I married, in my relationship with you, I kept forgetting that you weren't my daughter. Remember when you and Rose snitched the batch of sugar cookies and ate every last one? Your Pa couldn't figure out why you were so sick that night. I knew, because I found the empty plate, but I didn't say anything. You were scared to tell your Pa. He'd already spanked you for helping Tal Enock hide the frog in Miss Sullivan's lunch pail, and you knew perfectly well this was a much worse offense."

Startled, Ethan, faithfully signing her words, darted his eyes toward her, but she kept her concentration on Charity, who gave one tight nod.

"You, Rose, and I discussed it thoroughly. You both solemnly promised never to steal anything again, and I promised not to tell your Pa. And I never did, until now. I thought about it later and realized I should have told him because I was taking responsibility for your actions when I didn't have the parental right to do so."

She eased Merry, now sleeping soundly, to a more comfortable position on her lap. "When I chose to go with Hans and Pa tonight, I didn't stop to think why. But now I know. I have come to love Hans dearly in the time he's been a part of our family circle. But before he came to us, he had a whole other life that we will never be a part of. I couldn't know for certain what his reaction would be if I brushed him aside. But you, you're my daughter. My heart trusted that you would understand."

Charity closed her eyes and sighed deeply. Then she straightened, and, with a poise and maturity new to her, said quietly, "My head understands, Ma. It's just going to take a while for my heart to catch up."

Beside her, Larissa felt Ethan's tenseness ease. She nodded, with no way to hide her gratitude that at least there was this much.

Rose looked questioningly at Charity, who gave her a taut smile. Before Larissa could get past more than a flash of wondering, Charity turned to them. "Ma, Pa, now I need to talk to you about the plans I've made to go out to Wyoming Territory and teach in the new school there."

Not asking for permission, but given as a simple statement of already carried out fact. In spite of Larissa and Ethan discussing it a hundred times from all sides to prepare themselves, Larissa found she wasn't prepared after all. Her arm had been resting lightly against Ethan in much needed moral support during this discussion. Now she felt his muscles tense. *He's not prepared any more than I am. Maybe there really is no way to be ready, despite all the attempts in the world.*

They listened to Charity, this new Charity who methodically laid out her facts, meeting each of their objections before they could even voice them. "I received a letter from the Clark's Valley School Board. Not from Mrs. Clayton," she said in quick reassurance in response to Larissa's sharply indrawn breath. "Mr. Ezra Clark, the board president, sent it. He wrote that, based upon their understanding of the situation, if Miss Sullivan will forward a recommendation, they are very much interested in considering me for the position. Miss Sullivan has agreed to write the letter. She says she talked to you and you've given her your permission to do so." Here, Charity's eyes flicked from Ethan to Larissa with a direct intensity, as if underscoring the point that this agreement signified their wholesale future blessing upon her plans. She paused fractionally. "But she says she won't send it without having you read it first."

Charity had no inkling that they were already fully aware of this condition because they had set it themselves. Ethan tipped his head once in grave acknowledgment of Miss Sullivan's consideration and support. "We truly appreciate that."

Having been honest about this hiccup in her plans, Charity hurried on. "I don't have my teaching certificate yet, but Miss Sullivan feels that I'm ready and she's offered to take me over to the school superintendant's office in Milford Center, where I can take the test. As soon as I have your permission," she added with the matter-of-fact assurance that they would not object to this activity, even if they vetoed everything else. "Mr. Clark explains they've arranged that if I can come out to Clark's Valley within the next month, they'll have the school ready, and if they know for certain that I'm coming, they'll send the money for my train ticket." She took a breath. "Within the next month gives me plenty of time to get ready. I can leave Fairvale on the train on the last Monday in May and reach Laramie, the nearest station to Clark's Valley, by Thursday. Members of the school committee will be there when I get in."

Larissa's mind spun forward. *But that's right at haying time. We're committed to being here.* Helping to bring in the June hay harvest, the largest one of the several summer cuttings, was a crucial neighborhood obligation. Ethan would join forces with Perry Sayers and his two sons, their neighbors to the south, and Jens Volker and his son, who farmed east of them. Using their combined strength and hands, the men would go to each of the farms in turn, sharing the hot, prickly labor of cutting the fodder, drying it in windrows, stacking, hauling, and finally pitching the hay into the barn or loft. The men weren't the only ones obligated. While they worked the fields, Larissa, both in her own kitchen and joining Ariana Sayers and Lena Volker in theirs, would prepare enormous meals for the proverbially hungry harvesters. Always dogging their heels was the threat of rain. If it came too soon, the cut but ungathered grasses on the ground would turn to a rotted black mass.

But commitment or no commitment, we certainly aren't about to allow her to travel all that way by herself, new maturity notwithstanding. Larissa's spinning mind halted so suddenly, it might have slammed into a hay stack. *She wants to leave on the last Monday in May. That's one week before Mac gets here.* With effort, she pulled her mind back to what Charity was saying.

"I know that you'll be haying then, and you won't be able to make the trip with me." Charity bit her lip before plunging on. "I plan to ask Miss Sullivan to go with me."

"Miss Sullivan? But she's—" Ethan shut his eyes as if to block out the picture. "I can't even begin to imagine asking her in the first place."

Larissa was already shaking her head. "No. It's far too much of an imposition. It would be a long, difficult trip, even under the best of circumstances and with a pleasant traveling companion. Do you remember how long it took to get to Philadelphia?"

Charity nodded calmly. "But why not Miss Sullivan? She's a *teacher*. She could look the school over and advise me about supplies I'd need." When this obviously didn't convince them, she added, "And she'll be able to tell if it's a good place with good people or whether I should run for the hills." Her voice softened. "I know you've been worried about that, even if you haven't said anything. I'm not a total birdbrain, you know." For the first time in days, she gave them a goofy grin, but quickly sobered. "I truly would feel more confident about it all if Miss Sullivan were along. I know I've said lots of mean things about her, but I trust her judgment."

Larissa's eyes met Ethan's in startled recognition that Miss Sullivan's promise to herself in the long gone past to expand her world had, by a most unexpected mingling, become their future. Her dismayed reaction also included the knowledge that, if they followed Charity's plan, they would thrust their daughter into a future with which they had no personal acquaintance. They would, literally, be sending her off into the unknown.

Ethan forcibly relaxed his clenched jaw. "We'll think about it. We can't possibly give you an answer right at this moment. Besides, Miss Sullivan might flat-out reject the whole idea."

Charity's expression told them clearly that she had absorbed the fact Ethan hadn't given an outright "No."

She continued demurely, each of her carefully planned details a shower of pebbles spraying against Larissa's heart. She had already listened to Hans tonight. Now, with that same sense of unreality she'd felt earlier, she was being offered the dreams of another young person who had all the world in front of her. She realized Charity had fallen silent and was watching them for a reaction. Her arms instinctively tightened around Merry, still cuddled sound asleep on her lap in spite of the light and noise in the room. With a swift, silent prayer for the right words, she voiced the one subject Charity had not brought up. "Mac will be home just a week after you leave. Surely you don't want to go before he gets here. He would think it awfully odd that you would deliberately choose to leave without seeing him."

Charity's eyes darkened for an instant, but she said steadily, "I don't want to be here when he gets home. I want to leave before he comes."

"You haven't seen him for over four years. Are you certain you want to leave without seeing him now? You're both four years older than when you were last together. You were a child then. Now you're a young woman. How can you be sure, if you leave before he returns, that your feelings are as you've been remembering all this time?" Ethan, who knew only too well about the illogical logic of persistent emotions through his own experience of waiting for Larissa to return his love, now waited for his daughter's answer.

Charity shook her head and her chin came up. "I'm certain. I'm not going just to get away from Mac. I know that's what you think. But I've gone over and over it in my own mind. I really want to do this. I want to go and teach." She said it calmly, but with such conviction that they had no argument for her.

"We cannot give you an instantaneous answer." Ethan spoke as quietly, but with less composure than Charity had.

Larissa cut across his barely suppressed frustration. "Pa and I will discuss the facts as you have presented them. We assure you we will consider all the details you've proposed, even about Miss Sullivan. When we have everything clear in our minds, we'll talk about it with you again."

They were fully aware that it wasn't the positive answer Charity had bargained for but, in this, their duty to do the very best they could for her rose above her youthful yearnings.

In bed that night, hands clasped, they discussed it detail by detail as she had presented it to them. "It took a lot of courage for her to approach us as calmly as she did," Larissa said softly.

"She was well prepared," Ethan admitted reluctantly. "Her points and solutions were sensible and well thought out. I must confess I was rather proud of the maturity of her argument."

"But what of Mac?" Finally, Larissa could give voice to her own distress. "That look in her eyes as she told us she doesn't want to be home when he gets here. Can we really insist she stay until he comes? If she were a child, yes. But she's not a child anymore."

"Maybe she'd take one look at him and wonder at her own imaginings for all these years."

"And maybe she wouldn't," Larissa said starkly. "In any case, I must admit that I know exactly how I would have responded when I was her age if my parents had put their foot down and ordered me to do the direct opposite of what my own heart dictated." *Fortunately, they didn't.* But she did not voice this knowledge to Ethan.

"'There's the rub,'" he said wryly. "The last thing we want to do is force her into a wrong decision."

They fell silent, knowing that they had come to the answer for all their circling questions.

Ethan finally spoke. "Our new Charity, and her new maturity, will take some getting used to. So will knowing her new maturity gives her the right to make her own decisions, including asking Miss Sullivan to accompany her. We must agree that she can go. There's no question of that. But we can't insist that she see Mac. She's earned the right to her feelings."

At last they slept, their hearts troubled at the first departure from their years of parental responsibility, but with the beginnings of reassurance that Charity's steps along the pathway of her future were guiding her in a positive direction.

The next morning, Larissa wrote to Anne, relating the most recent events on their end of the situation. She also asked for her frank opinion about Clark's Valley and its inhabitants, confident that Anne would provide the information that, were the situation reversed, she would want to know about Fairvale. She and Ethan drove into town to drop off the envelope at the post office and to talk to Miss Sullivan. Charity had been very quiet at breakfast, and they hadn't spoken to her of their decision, wanting to make certain first that all pieces of the arrangement were in place before telling her that she might go with their blessing.

Having safely negotiated the school yard gauntlet of students skipping rope, playing "Run Sheep Run" and hide and seek during the noon dinner hour, Ethan and Larissa entered the classroom. Charity was putting arithmetic problems on the blackboard. At their sudden appearance, her hand holding the chalk went to her throat, a gesture from earliest childhood whenever she was taken aback. Rose, head bent over a book, wasn't aware they had come in, but some sense made her look up and catch Charity's expression. Turning and discovering their presence, her eyes grew wide and she half stood before sinking back onto the seat. Miss Sullivan, grading papers at her desk, laid down her red pencil and rose to meet them. If she was surprised, she hid it well behind her imperturbable nod. She glanced at Charity. "Would you please go check on the children?"

At this not-very-subtle request, Charity motioned to Rose and they slipped past Ethan and Larissa out the door. Charity's hands were already moving, filling Rose in on her personal concept of the situation.

CHAPTER TEN

Larissa and Ethan emerged from the building nearly an hour later. Miss Sullivan, following them, grasped the school bell rope to summon her pupils from their lengthy noon recess. As they passed the two young women waiting at the bottom of the steps, Charity reached her hand to stop them, then drew it back, only her eyes asking the question. Larissa smiled, reassuringly, she hoped. "We'll talk at home." Miss Sullivan's ringing bell forestalled further discussion as the children surged past them. Rose, searching their faces anxiously, said nothing, and turned with Charity to trail behind the hurrying students.

Waiting until they disappeared inside, Larissa sighed and Ethan slipped his arm around her. "I think it went rather well," he said with hearty enthusiasm.

"I think so," she said tentatively. "It's just starting to become really real so fast."

His arm tightened about her for a moment, then eased. "We'd better get over to the parsonage and retrieve Merry, before Shawn and Martha think we've abandoned her."

Fortunately, no such dismal thoughts were in evidence when they reached the little house beside the white-painted church. Shawn and four-year-old Camden, hand in hand, were in the front yard, gazing up into the branches of a lofty buckeye tree. As they approached, the little boy announced in a loud whisper, "The mama bird is feeding her babies. We have to be very quiet," he warned solemnly. Shawn raised his eyebrows and his lips twitched at this proof that his words had been heard and heeded. Ethan and Larissa obediently craned their necks upward, and sure enough, the mother bird was poking a bit of worm into one outstretched beak while three others managed to gape and chirp at her at the same time. "God's beauty," the child explained earnestly to Ethan and Larissa.

After a speechless moment, Shawn scooped the little boy up into his arms and pressed his cheek against the curly black hair. "Yes, son," he murmured, "God's beauty, indeed."

Her own eyes misty, Larissa went on to the house, leaving the men to their talk under the leafy tree. Shawn had told her Martha was in the kitchen and to go on in, so she followed the sound of voices down the hallway. Calling out, she pushed open the swinging door. An unbaked pumpkin pie, ready to slide into the oven, sat on the worktable. Merry, dabs of flour on cheeks and nose, swathed from neck to ankles in a protective apron, knelt on a kitchen chair and leaned over the table as

Martha showed her the intricacies of shaping her own miniature pie crust in a small tin pan. Guiding the child's hands, she helped her to maneuver a spoonful of pumpkin filling onto the crust. When it landed on target without spilling any, they cheered. Merry, catching sight of her mother, crowed with excitement and begged her, "Come. See." Larissa, obliging, admired it extravagantly. It took a bit of persuading, but Merry finally agreed to let Martha put her pie in the oven, too.

Martha put the kettle on for tea as, against her protests, Larissa rolled up her sleeves. By the time the water boiled, they'd washed the mixing bowls and tidied the kitchen, and the two women sat for their first real conversation in several weeks.

While Merry busily patted, tugged, and nibbled at a scrap of leftover dough, Larissa told Martha all that had transpired and was about to happen. Martha listened gravely, her quiet understanding of her friend's mental ups and downs as soothing to Larissa's tangled emotions as a warm hug.

***

That evening, Larissa and Ethan had a long talk with Charity in the sitting room, making clear their side of the situation, so that she might better understand their actions. Larissa, standing behind her rocking chair, hands clasped tightly over its back, explained that she had written to Anne and promised to share her response as soon as it came. They showed her the copy of Miss Sullivan's letter of recommendation to the Clark's Valley School Board, and watched her eyes widen and her cheeks flame as she read the phrases that set forth her tyrannical teacher's opinion of her. "… excellent student for eleven years … exhibits a tendency to high spirits." She stole a glance at her parents and quickly ducked her head again as Ethan rolled his eyes heavenward. "… enable her to understand her pupils … trustworthy." She looked up and they glimpsed the shine of tears in her eyes. "'Honorable,'" she whispered in a tone of awe as the shine of tears became radiance.

Ethan, one elbow propped on the fireplace mantelpiece, cleared his throat. "We also discussed with Miss Sullivan the tiny detail about your needing someone to accompany you." Charity sat up alertly. "As she phrased it, she will consent to your request to be a traveling companion on this journey, and she will make a proper inspection of your new teaching position and living arrangements." He pursed his mouth to hide a smile. "We figured you'd be pleased to know that she showed just the faintest trace of excitement while she said it."

Charity's grin acknowledged that Miss Sullivan's faintest trace of excitement would be anyone else's shout of joy. She looked from him to

Larissa, anxiety overshadowing her earlier glow. "Does this mean I can go?"

"Yes. You have our permission to go."

"With just one more detail to set straight," Larissa added quickly.

Wariness edged into Charity's anxious expression, only to be elbowed aside by a haunting sadness. "Mac," she whispered. Before they could say anything, she lifted her chin. "If you want me to stay here until he comes home, I will." At their shocked expressions, she said in that same self-assured tone, "You've been so right about everything else, I wouldn't want to leave you with that kind of distance between us."

Larissa could scarcely speak for the tightness in her throat. "Are you sure?"

Charity's smile failed to erase the sadness in her eyes. "There's going to be distance enough if I go. I don't want to add to it."

Ethan, too, appeared to have a lump in his throat, for he had to try twice before he could speak. Even then, all he managed was her name. "Charity."

Larissa said softly, "That means more to us than you will ever know."

Charity watched them exchange another of those between-parents-only looks before they walked slowly to her. Ethan said gravely, "Our grown up daughter. Thank you. But we want you to know that we'd already decided to tell you that you can go without seeing him."

Her eyes widened. "But—"

"You have showed so much good judgment throughout all this discussion. Not just tonight, but all along. That kind of maturity deserves our trust that you are now adult enough to know your own heart and make your own decision about it." Larissa bit her lip fiercely. "'Our grown up daughter,'" she repeated softly as Charity came to their arms in a rush.

CHAPTER ELEVEN

On a humid Philadelphia May evening, Mac Edwards sat beside Amity Terrill in the wooden swing on her parents' back veranda. The lamps illuminating the area gave off a faint odor of gas and an occasional popping during which the jets briefly flared brighter. As he pushed the swing into languid motion with his foot, she smiled at him, tightening her fingers already intertwined with his across the short space that separated them. In a wicker chair near the railing her father, Dr. Oliver Terrill, perused the Philadelphia *Journal*. Her mother Matilda's hands and shuttle flew, shaping the doily she was tatting, her rocking chair drawn companionably close to her husband. The Terrills, living outside the city, were luckier than many of its inhabitants on this sweltering evening that portended a scorching summer. Finished dining a short time ago, they had sought the veranda in the hopes of finding a cooling breath of air.

When Dr. Terrill, with decades of medical experience, and Mac, now completing his first year as an official doctor, were by themselves, they frequently fell into discussions about cases, treatments, and other hospital subjects in which they shared a mutual interest. When in the company of his family, however, Oliver followed his long-standing rule of avoiding medical topics. Accordingly, the four had conversed about a number of subjects unrelated to hospital work. The happy exception to this restriction was Amity's sister Mercy, now married to Charles Huxford, a doctor practicing at Boston Hospital. The Terrills had found out only that day that Mercy would present them with their first grandchild before the end of the year. In Philadelphia social circles, pregnancy was normally a delicately conveyed topic, particularly in the presence of an unmarried young woman and her fiancé. In the privacy of their own home, however, the elder Terrills had no difficulty whatsoever voicing their joy. Not surprisingly, the doctor's daughter was so busy expressing her own delight that she didn't swoon, turn deathly white, blush rose red, or require medical assistance of any nature.

During dinner, Amity had mentioned the rumor that an archeologist by the name of Schliemann was digging around near the Aegean Sea in hopes of unearthing the long-sought city of Troy. Mac had told them how, in the evenings, his father used to read to the family from his mythology book. This brought on a discussion of ancient Greek and Roman legends.

Oliver had started on the topic of the moment. The "first major league baseball game ever," as it was being hailed, had been played earlier in the month between the Cleveland Forest Citys and the Fort Wayne

Kekiongas. The Indiana Kekiongas shut out the Ohio Forest Citys by a score of two to nothing. Fortunately, because Mrs. Terrill was from Indiana, Mac wasn't called upon to defend his Ohio loyalties at losing such a momentous match. However, he did point out with the utmost tact that it was the first such game only because the expected Boston-Washington opener was rained out.

Before Dr. Terrill could interject his opinion of this clarification, Mrs. Terrill put aside her tatting shuttle and thread and stood. "I think it's time for some lemonade. Will you come help me, Oliver?"

He hesitated, saw the twinkle in her eyes, and, with a glance at the two young people, resignedly disappeared after his wife into the house. In the weeks following the announcement of the engagement, Matilda had initiated these "chaperone breaks" during Mac's visits to their home. He wasn't totally certain of Dr. Terrill's opinion of the interludes, but Oliver never spoke of them during the odd times Amity and her mother chanced to be out of hearing. Not for the first time, Mac sent Matilda silent thanks for her motherly good sense and understanding. *Even if they do limit us to fifteen minutes.* Amity raised her face to his and responded to his kiss with a fervor that made the night spin. With his cheek against her soft cloud of black hair, all his bleakness at leaving her in Philadelphia while he went home, and the long weeks of separation this would entail, dissolved in the wonder of holding her in his arms.

Once he had set a definite departure date, they'd spoken little of the time they would be apart. Both accepted that it was necessary and that moaning would only steal from the time they had left. But now, alone with her for these swiftly diminishing minutes before her parents reappeared, he stood and drew her to her feet. She was tall and slender, and fit perfectly into his arms. After a moment, he stood her back, and, still holding her hands, studied her. Her eyes, questioning, were the color of the quiet places along Mill Creek back home, where the water didn't ripple past, but lay in still, blue-green pools.

"Is something wrong?"

At the concern in her voice, he smiled and shook his head. "At this moment, everything is very much all right. But I want to show you something." He tugged her over to the steps leading down to the lawn and gardens at the back of the house. The fragrance of honeysuckle and roses, blooming early in the intense heat, drifted to them on the sultry night air. At the bottom step, still holding her hands, he paused and looked up. "They're still there." Hearing his unconcealed satisfaction, she raised her eyes to the heavens. The gas lamps illumining the veranda didn't reach as brightly into this area, and the constellations winked as if diamonds had been tossed into the air and caught on a swath of black fur.

He drew her close to his side and pointed toward a semicircular cluster in the northeast. "Pa always said that with mythology's stars to guide us, we could never lose our way." His voice dropped, remembering. "I must have been all of four years old when he told me about the crown that Ariadne, the daughter of King Minos of Crete, wore when she married Dionysus. The *Corona Borealis*, he said it was called. He took me outside to show me where, right after Ariadne died, Dionysus hurtled it into the heavens between Hercules and Bootes. The jewels turned into stars and the crown became a constellation. The picture in Pa's mythology book showed how to follow the handle of the Big Dipper southeast to Arcturus." Unconsciously, he traced the sparkling path with his hand as he spoke. "Then west and slightly south to the *Corona* itself. Kind of like connecting dots." He chuckled ruefully. "I admit I still couldn't figure out what to look for in all that lumped-together brightness. But I'll never forget the night Pa and I were walking back from the barn and I looked up at all those glittery stars, as confused as ever, and there it was. Seemed like it just jumped out at me."

He felt his ears turning the approximate red of his hair in spite of the number of times he had practiced what he wanted to say next. "I want us to have our constellation. That way when we have to be apart, we can both look at the sky and know we aren't really separated."

"Oh, Mac," she whispered and buried her head against his shoulder.

Drawing a deep breath of relief at her uncomplicated understanding, he kissed her temple.

"With mythology's stars to guide us, we'll never lose our way back to each other." As she turned her face up to his, voices from the veranda signaled her parents' return. Raising her eyes one last moment to Ariadne's crown, she murmured, "Ours. Forever and ever."

Hand in hand, they retraced their steps onto the veranda, into the everyday world of talk and laughter and lemonade.

***

Days later, shortly after sunrise, with the heat already baking Philadelphia's streets, Mac and Jeff Kinsley, with four other doctors, lounged in the hospital's outpatient clinic. In a few minutes, the doors would swing open and the people from the city's poorer neighborhoods would begin streaming in for the treatment and medicines they could not otherwise afford. Cordell Watson, heavyset and perspiring, fanned the front of his white doctor's coat in the vain hope of circulating a little air beneath the heavy cloth. Turning to Mac, he remarked jovially, "Tomorrow you'll be on your way to the cool, quiet farmer life, while all of us will still be stuck here in this infernal heat."

Mac had been fiddling with his watch, tugging the fob to open it, then clicking it shut again. Of all his colleagues, only Jeff had any inkling of his emotional turmoil, how pulled in two directions he felt about leaving Philadelphia and going home, and he wasn't about to reveal it to anyone else now. He studied the watch fob as the other doctors, responding to Cordell's ribbing, threw in good natured jeers about his being paid in chickens, and how his medical services would doubtless include plowing a patient's rocky field. Rose and Charity had made the fob. They'd painstakingly embroidered his initials on it the Christmas his parents, along with Ethan and Doc Rawley, had presented him with the doctor's watch and chain, proof in hand of their full support of his fledgling medical career.

Without looking up, he drawled, "When I'm sittin' in the shade of the big oak tree down by the ol' swimmin' hole, I'll be sure to feel plumb sorry for all of you back here bakin' like Christmas turkeys in this fancy oven." The answering groans gave clear evidence that his little speech had conjured up a vivid picture of countryside coolness. He waited until the grumbling had tapered off before he added pitilessly, "And we farmer boys have ice houses, great big ones, that we can go and sit in any time of the day or night we want." Fortunately for the congenial work association of all concerned, the outside doors opened and the first wave of patients rolled forward, forestalling the colorful comments that would have been directed at him. As they stood to greet the surging crowd, Jeff glanced sharply at Mac, who grinned and shrugged his shoulders. Jeff gave him a short, vigorous thumbs up sign which he answered by curling his lip in a mock snarl.

By late morning, the clinic was stifling hot and swimming in enough humidity, Mac was sure, to boil an egg, a comparison he was certain would not have been lost on his earlier hecklers. The tide of patients had surged without ceasing and the odors of sweat-soaked bodies, unchanged diapers, and heavily perfumed oils were all-pervading. The clamor of voices raised in Italian, German, Polish, and half a dozen other languages blended and spun around the room.

Mac finished examining the arm of a man who, while on a construction crew digging a ditch for a new gas pipeline, had been hit by a bucket-sized rock that suddenly loosened and pitched down on him before he could jump aside. He concluded the arm was badly bruised but not broken. Between the man's Polish and halting English and Mac's growing grasp of the language, he'd understood enough to piece together a rough picture of the accident. He was also able to reassure him that his arm, with rest, would be all right. The man nodded and said carefully, "Thank-you-doctor," as he lifted his hat and backed away. Knowing how missing even a day of work could be financially disastrous for a laboring man, Mac was sincerely glad he could deliver good news, although he wasn't too confident that his instructions for rest would be heeded.

Next in line was a young woman, scarcely more than a girl. In spite of the heat, the infant she was carrying was wrapped, as was considered proper, in a gray woolen shawl. A boy of perhaps four and a younger girl, both with curly black hair, clung to their mother's skirts and peered at him dubiously. The woman spoke to the children in Italian. When they didn't move, she reached with her free hand to push the boy forward. Brown eyes wide, employing the same cautious curiosity he might have displayed if he were approaching an unknown, oddly shaped insect, he edged nearer to Mac. When his mother spoke sharply, the little boy held out his right hand. The index finger was badly bruised and swollen. Mac cupped the small fist in his, at the same time asking the child his name. At more vocal prodding from his mother, he responded almost inaudibly, "Enzo."

With a reassuring smile, Mac carefully turned the boy's hand. Among the swelling and bruising, a row of tiny tooth marks was perfectly imprinted along the upper edge of the finger. Lifting it gently, he confirmed the corresponding perfect row on the underside. His involuntary glance at the little girl, who looked to be about three years old, earned him an unblinking glare from her long-lashed dark eyes, as if daring him to blame her. He wasn't about to take the bait. He favored his fingers intact. Fortunately, the mother intervened with another rush of Italian, this time directed at her daughter. The child stared at Mac and, lower lip trembling, mumbled something he didn't catch.

"Bite," her mother offered. Holding her own index finger up to her mouth, she demonstrated with a snap of her teeth. "Take toy," she offered as further explanation, pointing to Enzo.

Stifling a laugh, Mac managed to keep his features properly solemn as he continued his examination. In spite of the swelling and bruising, the skin wasn't broken. He smiled at the mother. "*Buono*," he assured her with a nod and a smile. "He'll be fine." Holding up his injured finger, Enzo stared up at him, the pleading in those lustrous dark eyes as clear as if he'd said the words aloud. Mac reached for a can of salve and a strip of white bandaging. With the child following his every movement, he put a generous scoop of the salve over the bite marks and wrapped the cloth carefully and conspicuously around the finger. When he finished tying it, the little boy broke into a big grin and waved the badge of his combat wound at his mother.

She looked at Mac and her severe expression transformed into a warm smile. "*Grazie*."

"You're welcome." He smiled, reflecting that it didn't seem all that long ago how important it had been to him, too, to have proof for the world to see his bravery after suffering a grievous injury.

The mother, with the baby in her arms and one child on each side clutching her skirts, turned away. As the children retreated, Mac distinctly saw the boy stick his tongue out at his sister, who screwed her face up in protest and opened her mouth, revealing a perfect set of white, tiny, sharp teeth before mother and children disappeared from view.

Mac chuckled and turned to his next patient, but was interrupted by a voice at his elbow. "Dr. Edwards." A second year student was motioning him aside. Stepping a little farther away from Mac's table, the student murmured, "Dr. Kinsley asked me to find you. He requests that you come to examining room seven as soon as you can. I'm to watch your station while you're gone."

Mac nodded and spoke to Cordell Watson, who was at the table next to his. "Sure, Mac," he said easily, brushing aside the more formal "doctor" with which they were required to address each other while on duty and patients were present. "I'll keep an eye on him," he agreed cheerfully, as the student took Mac's place.

Wondering what Jeff had found, knowing that it must be something highly unusual or he wouldn't have been sent for, he made his way to the area where the more in-depth, private examinations were conducted in small curtained rooms. He knocked at the frame of number seven, moving aside the heavy canvas door when Jeff bade him to enter.

Jeff was standing near a young woman with three small children clustered around her chair. "Dr. Edwards, this is Mrs. O'Rourke and her children, Ronan, Maureen, and Daisey. This is Egan." He gestured to the baby in her lap, who leaned against her wanly, his tiny face fever flushed, his breathing labored. A sudden spate of coughing wracked him, and when it was over, he sagged against his mother again, his breath rasping.

Mac greeted them and looked questioningly at Jeff.

"Egan is eight months old and has been feeling under the weather for the past couple of days. His mother brought him in because he's having difficulty breathing, especially after he coughs. I'd like your opinion."

He spoke calmly, but Mac felt a sudden flash of uneasiness. Jeff wanting his opinion could only mean that he must have found something really serious. Keeping his expression pleasant, Mac bent down beside the mother so that she could continue to hold the baby in her lap. The other children stared at him solemnly. He checked the child's eyes and ears and, feeling his feet, estimated his temperature to be well over a hundred. He had to pause as another fit of coughing wracked the small body. He peered down the child's throat. At sight of the grayish-yellow membrane covering the swollen tonsils and palate, his earlier flick of concern lashed into full-blown dread.

It took all his years of practice at keeping his expression impassive to look at Jeff, whose features were also carefully controlled. He gave his friend an all but imperceptible nod. "I'll go talk to Dr. Terrill." Leaving Jeff to reassure the now understandably concerned young mother, he left the room at a normal pace. Once back in the press of the clinic activities, however, he broke into a swift walk. With effort, in order not to alarm anyone he passed, he forced himself not to run as he strode through the hospital corridors. Reaching the administration department, he asked the young man at the desk for Dr. Terrill.

"He's in a meeting," the clerk responded. "He'll be at least another hour if you'd like to come back. He gave strict orders not to be disturbed under *any* circumstances." He gave Mac a smug smile, clearly enjoying the power he wielded.

Mac bent over the desk. "I must see him now." Clipped as the words were, the clerk bristled at the implication that this man's white coat magically gave him enough supremacy to order other people around. The important doctors were sitting in the room just beyond his desk, and he had been charged with seeing that they were not disturbed. He opened his mouth to refuse, then took a closer look at the breadth of Mac's shoulders and the ice chips in his eyes. Very slowly, he reached for a piece of paper. With set lips, and failing to provide pen and ink, he pushed the paper over to Mac, who simply leaned in further and snatched a pencil from the holder on the desk. Shielding the paper from the clerk's efforts to see past his view-blocking arm, he wrote: Urgent I see you, sir. He signed, folded, and handed it to the clerk, who sniffed as he took it.

With Mac's glare firmly on him, the clerk made no attempt to slip it open. With a sense of unreality that at the same time felt only too terribly real, Mac watched him knock on a door marked Board Room and hand the note to someone inside. He then gave Mac a disdainful, see-what-happens-now smile.

In a matter of moments, Oliver Terrill emerged. Mac had been able to hurry the clerk along without alarming him. Dr. Terrill, on the other hand, had spent too many decades interpreting other people's expressions. Without asking questions, the older doctor led Mac to a room down the hallway, leaving the clerk staring after them. "We can talk in here." Once the door was securely shut, he turned to Mac. "What is it?"

Carefully, analytically, even as Doc Rawley had taught him long before he came to the university, Mac laid out the facts of Jeff's requesting his opinion, the fever, lethargy, strident coughing, and, finally, the grayish-yellow membrane covering the baby's throat.

A muscle twitched in Oliver's jaw, but he gave no other hint of his alarm. "And Dr. Kinsley's diagnosis?"

"Diphtheria, sir."

CHAPTER TWELVE

Diphtheria. It was called "the strangling angel of children" because the thick membrane, growing unchecked and with heartbreaking speed, would completely obstruct the throat and nasal passages, making it impossible for the small victim to breathe.

The next hours were a nightmare unlike any Mac had experienced during all his years of learning medicine. Dr. Terrill hurrying to examine baby Egan. Confirming the diagnosis of the younger doctors. Issuing sharp instructions. Isolating the little boy in the vain hope of preventing the disease from spreading. Examining his mother and siblings and finding Maureen's and Daisey's throats a dreaded tell-tale red. Reviewing the doctors' clinic notes to try to determine if any other patients that day had shown early-stage symptoms that could have been overlooked as a mere cold. Sending messengers to the other hospitals in the city to warn them and to learn if anyone else had been diagnosed. Receiving word that one hospital had two cases and another three. At this news, in spite of themselves, a sigh of fear went through every doctor in the clinic. The hospital turned to its emergency mode, even as everyone involved in the medical process knew that it was a futile effort. In the overcrowded, overheated, airless tenement buildings, the disease would spread as swiftly as a fire raging out of control.

The first victims started trickling in late that afternoon, but it soon became a flood. Mac lost all track of time as he bent over one small form after another, hearing the tortured breathing, the choked-off stillness that followed, and the cries of grief echoing in that too loud silence.

Sometime toward dawn, Mac, bleary-eyed and sodden with weariness, talked to a woman who had four children clustered around her. The oldest, a boy, looked to be about nine. Mac had confirmed that he did not yet show any symptoms of the disease, but two of his younger siblings had red throats and were coughing sporadically. As Mac straightened, a quiet but authoritative voice spoke behind him. "Dr. Edwards." Mac had become very familiar with that voice over the past five years. He turned to see Oliver Terrill tipping his head in a silent message to step away from the family he had been examining. He looked back at the terror in the woman's eyes. He opened his mouth to protest—to Dr. Terrill, of all people—who had the authority to dismiss him from the hospital for failure to obey. Dr. Terrill cut off his refusal by nodding toward a third year student who was shadowing him. "Dr. Quimby will relieve you." His tone left no room for either of the young men to argue. Mac put his hand on the woman's shoulder then stepped away with

Oliver, while Dr. Quimby bent over her and the children.

Oliver led Mac through the press of bodies and unceasing coughing. He stepped through a side door into the breaking dawn and the already overheated air. Mac breathed deeply for the first time in hours. It would be another stifling day, with more victims of the epidemic pouring into the hospital. Making certain they weren't being overheard or observed, Dr. Terrill faced Mac squarely.

Seeing the grief in the eyes of this older man who was unfailingly calm and capable, Mac's heart twisted so tightly that he could no longer feel it beating. "Amity? Is she—"

"Both she and Mrs. Terrill are still all right. It hasn't spread outside the city yet, as far as we know, but it can't be very long before it will. We have no way to prevent people coming into town and going out. We must be prepared. I've seen epidemics such as this. The entire city will be prostrate before it finishes its sweep."

As terror-inducing as the words were, Mac's heart untwisted enough for him to breathe again, knowing Amity was still safe. *But for how long?*

Oliver's words cut across his relief and his dread. "Your train leaves today, doesn't it?"

"At two o'clock this afternoon. But of course I won't go, now. I'll stay here and—"

"No! You must take that train out of here." There was fierceness in Oliver Terrill's expression that Mac had never seen in anyone's before.

Mac stared at him. "But the hospital—you'll need all the hands you can get to see us through this."

"Mac." In all the years he had known Dr. Terrill, the older man had addressed him as Dr. Edwards. Even when he and Amity had begun seeing each other on a serious basis, the formality had stuck. Only in the last few months, after the announcement of their engagement, and only in the privacy of his home, Dr. Terrill had called him MacCord. Never once, until now, had he called him Mac. Once again his heart contorted so hard that pain radiated through his body.

Oliver put his hand on Mac's shoulder, something else he had never done before, as if breaching the final barrier between medical instructor and son-in-law to be. "You will go home." It was nothing less than a direct command. "And you will take Amity with you."

Mac stared at Dr. Terrill, convinced that he had heard the words wrong.

Oliver's voice grated. "Mrs. Terrill and I have talked. We want Amity out of the city and away from this epidemic. We could send her to her sister Mercy in Boston, but we want her as far as possible from a big city. Your country atmosphere is the direct answer to our dilemma. With you providing for Amity's safety, we can concentrate on Mercy and the baby.

We've telegraphed her, but she's determined she's going to stay in the city with her husband. Short of chloroforming her, which she would probably not take kindly to, he hasn't figured out a way to make her budge, either."

Reeling under this onslaught of information, Mac's mind somehow snagged the important words. *You will take Amity with you.* "Does Amity know?"

"Her mother is advising her so right now. We are certain that she will object. In times past such as this, Mrs. Terrill has opened the house to friends who need care and have no one else to give it to them. I have never been able to dissuade her from this activity. But Amity is her mother's daughter and will insist upon helping. We simply cannot take the chance that she won't become ill, too. Therefore, we will send her with you."

With you providing for Amity's safety. Instead of the burst of elation the thought should have brought, dread touched Mac's spine with bony fingers. "But, sir." He literally had to force the words out. "Over the past twenty-four hours, I've been in constant contact with people exposed to it. I've examined a hundred patients who have it. If I've been infected, and I take Amity home, being with me will increase her risk of becoming ill."

Oliver was already shaking his head. "You're young and healthy. As a doctor, you've built up resistance to illness, much more than someone living in a tenement. We don't know why or how that works, but I've seen clear proof of it. Amity would be in much less danger going with you than she would be staying here." His eyes became iron. "Her mother and I trust that you will display the same sense of propriety at your home as you have in ours."

However else Mac's mind might be having difficulty assimilating their conversation, this pronouncement came through loud and clear. He straightened his shoulders and looked directly into the cold eyes fastened upon him. "You have my word, sir. I have no more wish than you to destroy what Amity and I have now or what we will have in the future."

Oliver stared mercilessly at him for another long moment, then his fierceness eased a bit and he nodded. "Are your belongings packed?"

Again, Mac had to shift focus. "Some, sir. Not all. I had intended to finish doing that last night." Last night—a thousand years removed from this moment of dawn just breaking over the crouching city.

"We will need you to work as long as possible. When it's time, I'll send someone to relieve you. The rest of your belongings will be packed and waiting at the depot with your ticket. Train service in and out of the city will undoubtedly be severely restricted, if not halted completely, as soon as it can be put into effect. That's why you and Amity must go today. Mrs. Terrill and I will take her to the station just before two o'clock, so that she can board without delay."

Not even to go back to my room one last time before leaving? Without saying goodbye to anyone, even Jeff? "I'll need to get word to my folks."

With this assurance that Mac agreed to the proposal, the faintest slackening of unyielding command touched Oliver's eyes. "Yes, they would probably appreciate knowing a little ahead of time. Having met them, I am certain that they will take in stride my rude actions in demanding that my daughter become their guest. But they would undoubtedly appreciate knowing it before she steps off the train, not after." The hint of lightness faded. "I will telegraph them immediately."

"Thank you, sir." There seemed nothing more to say.

Returning to the hospital and its wails and death was like stepping back into another world. Thoughts whirling, Mac edged past a dazed-looking young woman with three children clutching at her skirts and an elderly man staring around at the crowd with panic-stricken eyes. Intent on getting back to his station, only a small corner of his mind noted that the fellow, both hands clutching a black-shawl-wrapped form to his chest, was being buffeted unmercifully by the throng. As he brushed past in his white doctor's coat, now stained and wrinkled, the old man suddenly heaved a gusty, unmistakable sigh of relief, pushed his cocooned bundle at Mac, turned and melted into the crowd. Mac barely managed to grab the shawl and its contents before it pitched onto the floor. As the man's intention crashed over his dulled senses, Mac called out and started in that direction, but he was already gone.

He tried to push his way through the tightly packed mass, but, fearing that the baby would be hurt or smothered, halted his pursuit after only a few yards. His gaze fell to his squirming acquisition, which looked to be about six months old. Staring into the tiny face, he remembered another time that he had had an infant shoved at him. Many years before, Doc Rawley had thrust a newborn into his arms before wheeling to bend over the mother, who was in grave danger of bleeding to death. The weight of the baby had startled him so much, he had nearly dropped the little fella on his head before he managed to get a firm grip on him. At least this one wasn't slippery, although a tell-tale odor emanated from its nether region.

How can I tend to the needs of a single baby, when so many others are desperately depending on me for their very lives? His logical mind, dulled by fatigue, slowly teamed up with common sense. *Find someone to take it.* His quick survey of the misery-filled faces around him showed no one fitting that description. Clearly, they were so deeply involved in their own troubles, not one of them would have either the time or the desire to take on someone else's problem.

Even as logic and common sense beckoned, a deeper truth whispered to him, then stood quietly waiting. *I will follow that system of regimen according to my ability and judgment, and abstain from whatever is deleterious ....*

My ability and judgment. The oath he had sworn the day he became a certified physician, the solemn promise he had made to his future patients that he would do nothing to harm them, could not now be lightly set aside. Nor could the words of Someone Else, who spoke of leaving the ninety-nine sheep and going after the one.

Almost as swiftly as he had formed them, these thoughts melded into one simple truth. He could not desert this small one whose life at this moment had been entrusted to him.

For the space of a heartbeat, the child stared solemnly at him out of deep brown eyes before it screwed up its little face. It let loose with a yowl that would have done credit to a cat with its tail caught in a slammed-shut door. He jiggled it experimentally and was rewarded with a still louder squawk. Heads turned toward him with something very like curiosity, probably because it was a scream of outrage, not pain or fear. After a moment, however, everyone lost interest, re-submerging themselves in their own dire troubles.

Holding the baby close to his chest, he started edging through the tightly packed mass of frightened, distraught humanity. No one stepped forward to relieve him of his vociferous, fragrant burden. Knowing he would have to check the child to ensure that it was still healthy, he moved as quickly as possible through the crowd, searching for a clear-enough space that he could lay it down. He finally spotted an empty examining table. Grateful that it had somehow remained available, he eased his burden down onto it. Unsure whether his soft murmuring was getting though the noise, he began to loosen the inevitable black shawl. He still didn't know whether it was a boy or a girl. With the baby squalling in his ear, he hadn't been about to stop for the necessary inspection. It was wearing a long dress and crocheted bonnet which could make the call go either way, since boys not yet walking were dressed the same as girls.

Legs now freed from the tight wrapping, still howling to high heaven, the baby immediately began kicking its heels in thumping blows against Mac's stomach. One thing at a time, he told himself. Still murmuring soothingly, but now through gritted teeth—his ears were starting to ring—he began his careful examination to determine whether the child had diphtheria. Because he found no other symptoms of the dread disease, making a judgment call, Mac finally concluded that the red throat he discovered came from the vocal venting of wrath, not the strangling angel of death.

With vast relief, he set about performing his second examination. Holding the baby under one arm like a sack of flour—he really didn't need it rolling off the table and bouncing onto the floor at this point—he rummaged without much hope through the drawers of supplies used to fix the various aches and pains of the people who came to the clinic each day. He thought fleetingly of Enzo and his carnivorous little sister. Had they become ill? He hadn't seen them or heard anything about them, and could only pray they had been spared. Was it really only yesterday morning he had, with amusement, watched Enzo flourish his bandaged hand in the air as proof to one and all he had been gravely wounded? Weariness scuttled through him. With his free hand, he gripped the edge of the table and fought his way through it until his eyelids no longer insisted on closing.

A few minutes later, task finished, he wrapped the shawl loosely around the baby boy. The air was warm, but not nearly as stifling as it would be in a few hours. He hoped that, regardless of the heat, if the child was used to being swaddled, this would provide him a small sense of security. Whether it was exhaustion or the comfort of being cleaned up, about half way through the process, the howls of protest had evolved into sniffling hiccups. With the clean, if not precisely fresh-smelling baby cradled against his shoulder, he started once more on his quest for help, toward the one place that came to mind.

Emerging into the glaringly bright outdoors for the second time during that still-early morning, he finally caught sight of his goal. Singly and in loose groups, still unaffected family members were sitting on quilts and rugs beneath a large canvas shelter rigged on the farthest edge away from the cluster of hospital buildings. After the grieving din of the clinic room, the shouts of the children playing on the stubby, sun-browned grass nearby were as welcome as the sound of rain on parched earth. In a vast stillness, the men and women under the canopy watched his approach. Only as he neared them, he realized their utter silence, the agony mixed with pleading stamped on each face, came from their waiting for him to say whose loved one had died. He wondered how many times during the night such a messenger had come to them. The thought snapped off as a woman in the veiled white garments of a nun left the sheltering cover and determinedly cut off his approach.

"I'm Sister Bernadette. May I help you, Doctor?" Her voice, wrapped in an Irish lilt, was low, questioning, and firmly in control. He got the loud and clear message that if she didn't want him to come a step nearer to the waiting group, he would never take that step.

Gripping the baby a little more securely, he tipped his head courteously. "I'm pleased to meet you, Sister. I'm Doctor Edwards."

She glanced at the infant, now sleeping soundly against his neck. "He was left with me," he said in what he thought was probably the understatement of the year. "I have no idea who his family is or where they are. I was hoping someone here might recognize him."

Even as Sister Bernadette turned to the still-silent group and formed the question, they both knew that it had already been answered. No one stirred. No one came running with glad cries of welcome. In her lined face he glimpsed weariness that he suspected matched his own. "I've checked him, and he has a red throat." She looked at him sharply. "He has no other symptoms," he assured her hastily. "He's been crying hard enough to inflame his vocal cords." His second understatement of the year, he thought wryly. At this pronouncement, she studied him so grimly that he felt as if she were checking the back side of his brain for moral failure, but he kept his eyes steadily on hers.

She reached, finally, to take the limp baby from his shoulder, and his inward sigh of relief was so great that he feared she would hear it and change her mind.

"Poor little lamb," she said softly, rocking him in her arms. He didn't stir, but she looked up at Mac with a startled expression that also contained faint bewilderment. "What is that odor?" she asked cautiously.

"He needed tidying up," he said tactfully, fairly certain that she would not be amused at his solution. "I didn't have much to work with, but he's clean and dry, at least momentarily. I must get back to work. Thank you for taking him in," he added sincerely and tried not to break into a lope as he headed for the hospital. He had a strong premonition that very shortly Sister Bernadette would be saying more than "poor little lamb." It would be to his benefit to be a long distance away when she discovered he had cleaned the baby with the pungent smelling salve the doctors normally put over open wounds, and wrapped him in a long strip of the bandaging used for broken arms.

Re-entering the hospital, his lightness vanished as the noisy talk, and the odors, and the grief assailed him.

***

He was examining an elderly woman when he once more heard a voice behind him. "Dr. Edwards." He turned and recognized the medical student who had earlier been shadowing Dr. Terrill. "I'm to relieve you again. Dr. Terrill said you are to meet him at the east door."

Mac's glance went to the woman whose throat he had been checking. "He wants to see you immediately," the student insisted.

Mac paused long enough to take the woman's hand. "Dr. Quimby will take good care of you," he assured her with a smile. A look almost of resignation slipped over her wrinkled features as she nodded. He held her hand firmly in his for another moment. Then, with a jagged feeling of loss sawing at his heart, he straightened.

Having managed to thread his way through the clumps of people who were still waiting to be examined, he found Dr. Terrill standing beside a table holding a basin of water and a towel. "You need a chance to wash up before we go."

For the first time in many hours, Mac thought of his appearance. If he looked as tired and unkempt as Dr. Terrill did, he definitely needed to improve matters. Quickly, he washed his hands and face and ran a comb through his hair. Looking down at the rumpled white coat he was wearing, he closed his mind to what he was doing as he unbuttoned and removed it. Leaving it in a heap beside the basin of water and the towel, he followed Doctor Terrill out the door into the blinding midday sun.

CHAPTER THIRTEEN

Larissa stepped out into the last of the hot June evening, pulled the cabin door shut, and made certain the latch was secured. She stood a moment on the porch, pressing her hands to her aching back. Mac and Hans would share the cabin through harvest. Hans had volunteered to stay to help Ethan and the neighbors before going to Milford Center in neighboring Delaware County where he would assist Dr. Ingemar.

With some adjustment of furniture and a thorough non-Saturday cleaning, the place was ready for Mac's arrival tomorrow. *Tomorrow.* In spite of her exhaustion, her heart gave a bounce of joy. After being twice disappointed in expecting him to come home, only to find that he planned to stay longer in Philadelphia, she had scarcely let herself believe that now, after five years, he was really coming back, that he was actually on the train at that moment.

She began walking slowly along the path toward the house. The last few days had been exhausting, with the promise of more equally wearying days to come as Ethan, Hans, and the neighbor men worked to bring in the enormous June hay harvest from the three farms. Her own days, and those of Rose and Charity, of cooking and baking in the sweltering heat of Ariana Sayers' and Lena Volker's kitchens in order to provide mammoth dinner and supper meals for the famished harvesters left her limp with fatigue by nightfall. And they were not yet done. The plan was to finish at the Volkers' place tomorrow morning before Mac's train came in. Day after tomorrow, the men would come to Ethan's fields to bring to the loft the hay that had been windrowed and left to dry.

She knew she ought not to feel so relieved that there would be a break tomorrow afternoon. Each hour that the cut swathes lay on the ground brought closer the potential rainstorm that would turn any of the ungathered crop into a sodden black mass. She couldn't remember feeling this drained in other years, so why should she now? Martha and Shawn had summarily kidnapped Merry and would keep her at the parsonage until the harvest was in. That meant she didn't even have the excuse of tending the two-year-old bundle of energy her daughter had become. She was busy refusing to let the tendril of suggestion at the back of her brain—that she was older than she had been when she had participated in those earlier gatherings—take root as she arrived back at the kitchen path. The clatter of a rig on the drive at the far side of the house brought her sharply out of her musing. Who would be coming this late in the evening, when the family would have to be up and at it again long before dawn tomorrow?

As the buggy rounded the corner, she saw Shawn driving, with Martha seated close beside him, both their expressions anxious. *Something's happened to Merry.* The thought clawed at her throat with vicious fingers and she started toward them.

Martha must have read her terrified expression, for she called sharply, "Merry's fine! We brought you this."

Larissa's racing heart slowed a little as she glimpsed the yellow-brown envelope that Martha was waving. But as Shawn drew the team to a halt beside the path, Larissa's easing terror level shot up again. Ever since the news of Zane's death had come in a telegram, she was unable to view one without dread swamping her.

As Shawn helped her down, Martha repeated hastily, "Merry's fine. Gretta and Mara are watching her." Martha's daughters, fifteen and eleven now, took Merry under their wing whenever they were around her and seemed never to tire of looking after her. "We wanted to bring you this right away." Martha handed the envelope to Larissa, who was unable to stop the shaking of her fingers as she tore it open.

"I saw Miles Painter and he asked if we could bring this out to you. He knew you'd want to see it as soon as possible." Larissa scarcely heard Shawn's explanation as she unfolded the paper and read the message in one astonished gulp. Seeing her bewilderment, Shawn put his hand on her arm to steady her. "Are you all right, Larissa? Miles didn't tell us what was in it, just that it had been delayed reaching him because the telegraph wires were overloaded with backed up messages and it was important that you get it right away."

She dragged her eyes from the printing to Shawn's and Martha's worried faces. "Mac is bringing Amity home. She left on the train with him Friday afternoon." Their shocked expressions wavered in front of her and Shawn's grip on her arm tightened. "It's from Amity's father. There's an outbreak of diphtheria in the city and her parents are sending her here where she'll be safe from it."

"Diphtheria." Martha's face paled. Shawn slipped his free arm about her and she took a deep breath. "Of course they would. Our country air is the very best place to be."

Larissa pulled away from Shawn's supporting hand. "I have to tell Ethan. He and Hans are down by the pond, getting rid of all the chaff from today." She started off, then remembered and turned back. "Rose and Charity are in the house. They can fix coffee while you wait until Ethan and I come back."

Shawn shook his head. "A minister might think it his duty to stay and talk you through this. A friend will leave you to discuss it privately between yourselves."

Martha hugged Larissa tightly. "Whatever we can do to help," she said softly. "You know that."

Larissa nodded gratefully as Shawn turned the team and guided the buggy around the corner of the drive. Clutching the telegram, she sped toward the pond, calling out before she reached the bank where she knew they were swimming.

Ethan called back in answer as he and Hans appeared, fully dressed and looking considerably cooler than when they had trekked to the pond. "We're finished, Lizzie. Sure does feel—" He broke off at the still-stunned expression on her face and hurried to her. "Lizzie?" Catching sight of the envelope clutched in her hand, dread flashed in his eyes.

"It's all right," she gasped, a corner of her mind noting the irony that this time she was the one lending him comfort about a telegram.

Hans had stopped and was watching with apprehension as Larissa handed Ethan the paper. He read it as she had, in one gulp of amazement. "Amity's coming here. She's already on her way." His repetition of the words failed to make them more real, but at least it gave Hans a chance to grasp the situation.

Ethan drew Larissa tightly against him and pressed his cheek to her hair. Hans shuffled his feet and began to back quietly away. The movement caught Ethan's eye, and he put out a hand. "It's all right, Hans. You needn't leave. Come up to the house with us while we tell the girls, and we can all discuss it properly."

Larissa stiffened and her eyes went wide. "Charity."

At the single word, Ethan drew in his breath sharply. "Dear God," he murmured. "What will this do to her?"

The walk to the house seemed to take an eternity, yet it went by so fast that they still had no words to prepare Charity for this unforeseen turn of events. As she had promised, she had stayed to see Mac come home. And now it was as if she would be punished for her unselfish decision. As they entered the kitchen, Rose was sweeping the floor and Charity was lighting the coal oil lamp on the table. Rose, not hearing the door open behind her, didn't look up, but Charity did and her welcoming smile froze as she saw their agitation. She caught sight of the telegram in Ethan's hand, and her hand went to her throat, but she said nothing. He held out the paper and she reached, still without saying anything, to take it. Rose had turned around, her own expression stilled as she took in their distress. Charity read the words, and her face went white. Behind Ethan and Larissa, Hans responded to Rose's beginning panic by signing that Amity was coming home with Mac. Rose looked blank for a moment, then understanding swept her features.

Charity continued to stare at the paper as if so doing would change the words. Finally, Ethan cleared his throat. "Charity."

She gasped as if she had just remembered that she needed to breathe.

The hand holding the paper began to tremble. Larissa stepped toward her, but Charity shook her head. "No. Please leave me alone." She whirled and ran out of the room. Her footsteps rushed up the stairs and they heard, faintly, a door open and shut.

Rose, eyes enormous in her pale face, turned slowly and started up the stairs. They thought she was following Charity, but a moment later they heard the faint squeak of her own bedroom door opening and closing, leaving them standing in stunned silence. "We brought this on her," Larissa said dully. "If only we hadn't insisted she stay."

Ethan said nothing for there was nothing to say. They were responsible for this disaster. They had played with their daughter's heart, and she had lost. "We need to go to her," Larissa said. "We have to tell her something."

Ethan shook his head. "No. She asked us to leave her alone. The least we can do is listen to her for once."

"I have to fix the room upstairs for Amity. There's no other place for her to stay," she said wearily, desperately wishing she could just go to bed and pull the covers over her head. The room was the one that Larissa had shared with Zane all during their marriage until he went to war. Ethan and Larissa, each for different reasons, had chosen to add the downstairs bedroom rather than use the already available one. Larissa and the girls dutifully cleaned the upstairs room with the rest of the house every Saturday, but no one had slept in it since Larissa and Ethan's marriage. It had become a storage place for items they didn't currently need, but would use in the near future.

"Do you really need to?" Ethan peered anxiously at her drawn face. "I thought you did it up just last Saturday."

"It needs to be aired out and the extra boxes moved someplace else. I'll put some flowers in there tomorrow."

"Get Rose to help you." He added wryly, "I don't think this is a good time to ask Charity for help."

She mustered a half smile at his observation. "I'm not sure Rose wants to be the soul of helpfulness with this particular job, either. But putting it off isn't getting it done." She trudged up the stairs to her daughter's room. Since Rose could not hear someone knocking, they had hung a mirror on the back of her door. The jarring motion of the knock jiggled the mirror, producing prisms that caught her attention. They'd also installed mirrors on the other walls so that she could always see the room behind her. Thus, she was alerted when she had a visitor, and was still allowed the privacy of a shut door.

After a very long moment, Rose answered her knock. Larissa, having decided the direct approach was best, told her, "We need to fix the bedroom for Amity. Will you please come help me?" She thought for a moment that Rose was going to refuse, since she had signed it as a request. But after a moment she nodded and followed her mother down the hall to the unused bedroom. For an instant, as Larissa opened the door, she went back to the time she shared the room with Zane. The image flickered and faded even as she stepped over the threshold.

They changed the sheets, dusted, and set out a few things to make the room feel more homelike, putting a crocheted doily on the dresser, a fresh candle in the holder beside the bed, and Larissa's new washbowl and pitcher on the commode. She and Martha had run into each other in the mercantile on one of Larissa's Saturday shopping expeditions. She had paused to gaze at the set with its pattern of tiny roses and called Martha over to admire it, too. If she weren't putting all her butter and egg money toward train tickets to Philadelphia for the wedding, she would have succumbed, but somehow nobly resisted. When she returned to the store the following Saturday, half hoping it was still there, half afraid it would be, it was gone. Surprised at her sharp disappointment, she continued with her "what would I buy" game, but her heart wasn't in it.

She was even more surprised when, having been invited to the parsonage for dinner the Sunday before her birthday, Martha's daughters Gretta and Mara disappeared, only to return a little later carrying a large box wrapped in festive paper, with a huge red bow bobbing on the top. They set it front of Larissa. "Happy birthday, Mrs. Michaels," they chorused. Considering themselves mature young ladies, they didn't giggle at Larissa's startled look, but it was evident from their expressions that they were holding back their mirth with great difficulty, as were their brothers Garth, Noah, and Camden.

Larissa looked at Ethan, who was clearly as puzzled as she was, and at Martha and Shawn, who were both smiling warmly. Charity and Rose spoke in unison. "Open it, Ma." Martha made a go ahead gesture, so Larissa unwrapped it to find the washbowl and pitcher, complete with tiny, intertwining roses, that she had coveted.

Once home, she had carefully placed it on the wash stand in her bedroom, where a tickle of pleasure went through her each time she saw it. Now, readying the bedroom for Amity, Larissa looked at the perfectly serviceable bowl and pitcher that normally lived in the room. With a mixture of wanting to put her best foot forward for this fashionable young woman from the big city who was coming to their simple farm home, and shame for the snobbish feeling, she carefully arranged the set. "It really does add to the room, doesn't it?" she signed to Rose, who agreed, but without her usual enthusiasm.

Ethan and Hans had carried all the storage boxes downstairs to the woodshed. Now, gathering up the dust cloths and other cleaning tools, Larissa let Rose precede her into the hallway. Holding her candle high, she surveyed the room a final time and felt that it had lost the unused chill that had pervaded it when they went in. In spite of her weariness and irritation, she very much wanted everything to be right for Mac, for Amity, for all of them. *We can only do the best we can.* Too tired to worry about it anymore, with one last glance at the bowl and pitcher and the rose pattern, she followed her daughter down the hallway.

***

Morning came far too soon and definitely felt as much like it was still the middle of the night as it looked. Larissa stumbled through the breakfast preparations. The only thing that kept her going was the joy in her heart that the day she had waited for so long had arrived. Mac was coming home. Charity and Rose, still subdued, helped her, but without the joking and chatter that flew around the kitchen every other morning. Larissa, casting anxious glances at Charity, saw she looked as wan as she herself felt, and could only guess at her desolation during the night. Surreptitiously adding extra coffee beans to the morning's grinding, she hoped it would wake all of them up. Ethan's exhaustion showed clearly in his eyes, and he, too, made no effort to keep a conversation going. Hans, having put most of the pieces of the story together, retreated quietly to the background.

The coffee beans must have worked their magic, for once in the buckboard on the ride over to the Volker farm, Larissa finally came fully awake. But so did the resentment she had pushed aside last night as one too many feelings to cope with. Resentment that Amity was tagging along on this day of Mac's homecoming. Resentment for the hurt to Charity. And resentment for making her feel resentment about it all. Ahead of them, with Hans driving the team, Charity and Rose, riding in the back of the farm wagon among the rakes and other tools needed for the day's work, were too quiet. Undoubtedly, Charity was steeling herself for the coming reunion with Mac. That would have been hard enough in itself, but they had watched her over the last weeks as she quietly, determinedly wrestled her emotions under control so that now, if Mac's name came up in conversation with an outsider, she no longer blushed, or showed anything more visible than sisterly affection for him. And now this. All that silence coming at Ethan and Larissa just wasn't natural.

They arrived at the farm as Perry Sayers was pulling in with his wife and two sons. Larissa and the girls joined Lena Volker on the porch, followed by Ariana Sayers. With little discussion, the men gathered the tools and set off for the field. The women entered the kitchen, each starting a task without having to ask who or what. The days had quickly become routine. All the women were weary, and Larissa sensed they would be as glad as she to have to prepare only the noon dinner today for the harvesters.

Realizing she would have to tell the other women immediately about Amity's coming or risk censure for keeping it to herself, still she hesitated. Lena and Ariana assumed Charity's paleness was a result of the exertions of the past days. Larissa wished desperately that Charity didn't have to be in the room when she made the announcement. She also knew her daughter couldn't be sent away like a child. Flashing her a deeply apologetic look, she spoke in the sprightliest voice she could manage. "We received wonderful news last night." The women looked over at her expectantly. Good news of any kind was welcome in the community. Wonderful news to share was a rarity. "Just last night, we got a telegram from Mac."

Immediate concern washed across the women's faces. Telegrams were serious matters. "He's still coming home, isn't he?"

Smiling through stiff lips, Larissa even managed to laugh. "That's the surprise. Not only is he coming home, he's bringing his bride-to-be with him." She saw Charity close her eyes, but give no other sign of emotion. The announcement was enough to get the two women exclaiming and questioning so that they didn't notice Charity's shoulders slump for an instant, then straighten again. She had been signing the various comments to Rose. Now she turned, putting her back to the women's talk so that only Rose could see her face, and began signing busily.

Larissa, catching a glimpse of her flying hands, knew that she was not repeating the current comments. Since no one but Larissa could read what they were saying, it looked simply as if they were talking excitedly about the arrival of Mac and Amity. Charity was in fact telling Rose Part I of *The Rime of the Ancient Mariner. The guests are met, the feast is set* .... She saw Rose take up the third verse, *He holds him with his skinny hand* .... as if in answer to Charity. She turned quickly back to the women so that they wouldn't focus their attention on the girls. Memorizing the poem was one of Miss Sullivan's requirements before a student could graduate. Larissa didn't know exactly how many verses it contained, but from the weeks of reciting aloud it had taken them, she knew there were enough lines to keep them busy until next harvest. Her heart welled with pride in her daughters for their quick thinking, and, once again, she blessed Miss Sullivan's high standards.

In a short time the women returned to their work, for the noon dinner must still be made, but they continued to pepper Larissa with questions and comments. Charity's and Rose's assigned duties were to peel mounds of potatoes, shell peas and snap beans, and set the table. By the time they were finished, dirty pots and pans had begun to accumulate and they had to wash and dry them as fast as they were plopped to the counter under their elbows so that the women could use them again. With these activities, they could sign only occasionally, so it fell to Rose, for once, to do the talking and Charity the listening.

All through the morning's work, Larissa's heart was pulled in two directions: sharing Charity's grief and savoring the joy of Mac's homecoming. The meal it took all morning to prepare vanished in a few minutes under the men's enthusiastic assault. When they'd finished eating, Larissa rolled up her sleeves, preparing to attack the dirty dishes, but Lena, with Ariana nodding vigorous approval, shooed the girls and her away. "Go get your son. We'll finish here."

In the face of their determination, Larissa didn't resist, but gratefully hugged each of them. With their happy wishes following her and the girls down the steps, they found Ethan and Hans waiting. Apparently, Perry and Jens had enacted the same scene as their wives, for the horses were already hitched to the buckboard and farm wagon. With more friendly comments drifting to them, Ethan headed the team for home. Only after they were out of sight of the farmhouse, Larissa drew a deep breath of relief, which Ethan promptly echoed. That said it all for them, and apparently for the occupants of the wagon ahead, for they, too, were silent.

Before going in the house, Larissa remembered with a flash of annoyance that she had to pick a bouquet of flowers for Amity's room. Hans and Ethan promptly disappeared in the direction of the pond. By the time she had arranged the flowers and set the vase on the bedside table, she had to hurry to wash and dress if they were to be at the station on time to meet the train. Not that the train would necessarily be on time, but they would take no chances. They had finally sorted out the problem of transportation. Since the seven of them wouldn't fit in the buggy for the return home, they'd decided to have Hans drive the buckboard to ferry the travelers' luggage. The girls would ride back to the farm with him, leaving the backseat of the buggy free for Mac and Amity.

This solution solved two of Ethan and Larissa's concerns. It brought Hans with them, when he would have stayed at the farm so as not to interfere with the homecoming. It would also give Charity a space of time to regain her composure after greeting Mac and Amity together. Larissa suspected she would sorely need that opportunity.

As they neared town, Larissa's thoughts flew to the coming reunion. Try as she might not to, she still felt resentment toward Amity. She knew, as surely that August was peach-picking time, that she must not let a hint of her emotion show to Amity or Mac. Most especially not to Mac. She thought of what Charity was enduring in self-discipline, and knew she'd better practice what she preached. Determinedly switching mind-topics, she sent a small prayer of gratitude heavenward that travel times and transportation had improved considerably in the years since their trip to Philadelphia. Mac and Amity would not be spending as many long hours on the journey as Ethan, Larissa, and the girls had had to endure.

The railroad station finally loomed in front of them. The train had not yet arrived, but Doc was there, sitting in his buggy. The next few minutes were a whirl of confusion. Greeting Doc, whose usual grumpiness was fighting a losing battle with cheerful anticipation. Checking the tracks to see if the train was coming, which it wasn't. Going inside and finding Martha and Shawn standing by the door. Before Ethan or Larissa could get around their surprise to say anything, Martha was hugging Larissa and Shawn was shaking Ethan's hand. "We won't stay," Martha assured them. "We just came to tell you how happy we are for you that Mac's coming home." With another hug and handshake, they were out the door, leaving the little group blinking after them.

At last they heard the long, hoarse whistle announcing the train's arrival. They piled onto the platform where they'd said goodbye nearly five years earlier, and watched the black smoke come nearer, rather than fade away as it had last time. Completely unexpectedly, Larissa began to tremble. Ethan slipped his arm around her, drawing her comfortingly close to his side. "It's all right," he murmured.

And then the train was upon them, sliding past the station platform and the waiting group as if it had no intention of stopping, with its brakes squealing and hissing in reassuring denial of the possibility. Larissa's anxieties suddenly bolted, leaving only happy anticipation as she scanned the cars through the haze of smoke and steam. "There they are." Ethan's arm tightened about her waist for a moment, then relaxed.

She turned her head and found she had been looking, naturally, in the wrong direction.

CHAPTER FOURTEEN

Mac was assisting a beautifully gowned young woman to the ground, smiling up at her as he did so. They turned toward the station, their weariness evident. Ethan and Larissa could sympathize. They remembered that journey only too well. In spite of her air of confidence, the corners of Amity's smile held anxiety. Her arm was tucked under Mac's where he held it close to his side in what could have been reassurance.

It streaked through Larissa's mind that Amity might be just as uncertain about this visit as she was. After all, her presence was unexpected. Her parents had virtually thrust her upon them. She had to be aware of the awkwardness of the situation and worried about her welcome. Larissa lost the thought because, spying them, Mac broke into a big grin, and took off his hat and waved it. As the afternoon sun glinted off his auburn hair, she wondered when it had become so like her mother's. And then he was there, enfolding her in a bear hug so that her nose was buried against his shoulder, and she was laughing and crying at the same time.

He shook Ethan's hand with a firm grip and turned toward Amity, who was watching the reunion, her trace of uncertainty still evident. "Ma, Ethan, you remember Amity." He drew her forward, the blue of his eyes deepening as they rested on her. There was no mistaking the gladness in his voice.

Larissa's motherly instinct kicked in, and, before she thought about it, she held out her gloved hand to take Amity's in a firm clasp. She heard a voice—hers, she realized—saying, "Welcome, Amity." Whatever the young woman heard in her voice and felt in her handclasp, the uncertainty shadowing her blue-green eyes was replaced by relief.

Ethan took her hand in his. "Hello, Amity. It's good to see you again." His voice held nothing but pleasant welcome. "You remember Hans Druid." As Hans tipped his head politely to her, Ethan, in a natural movement, stepped back, revealing Rose and Charity.

Mac blinked. They definitely were not the young girls who had left Philadelphia four years earlier. The picture Charity had sent hadn't done them justice. They were two very attractive young women. Recovering, he grinned. "I was going to re-introduce you to my kid sisters, Amity, but it appears I can't do that because they've gone and grown up on me." Hans unobtrusively signed to Rose, so that she, too, could appreciate the compliment. "This is Rose." He signed as he spoke and Rose's eyes went wide with astonishment. His grin grew bigger. "Jeff and I have been practicing to surprise you," he signed off-handedly. "This way I can take up right where we left off, teasing you and making you mad as a wet hen."

"Oh, brother," she signed emphatically, but she was so thrilled by his signing that she couldn't even glare at him properly.

"Hello, Rose." Amity, too, signed the words, then blushed.

"You can sign, too?" The amazement and delight in Rose's voice were nearly equal.

"I've been practicing, but I don't know nearly as many words as Mac." She signed awkwardly, and her blush deepened.

"Thank you," Rose whispered.

Mac turned to Charity, saying to Amity as he did so, "You remember my other sister, Charity. Guess I can't call her a kid anymore, either."

If Charity flinched at the *sister* designation, Larissa, watching anxiously, couldn't detect it. All those weeks of practicing self-control had come down to this moment, and Larissa held her breath. Charity put out her hand. "It's nice to see you again," she said simply.

Amity took her hand in response, but before she could say anything, Mac let out an undignified yelp. "Doc!" Clasping Amity's hand, he drew her toward the old man who had been standing back out of the way of the family reunion.

Neither Mac nor Amity saw the pain that Charity could no longer conceal. Larissa took a swift step toward her, but Rose was quicker. She stood directly in front of Charity, thus shielding her from Mac's or Amity's notice. Her hands began moving. Charity stared blankly for a moment before a small smile touched her lips. Larissa breathed again, and felt some of her anxiety ease. Rose had picked up where they'd left off that morning with the *Rime of the Ancient Mariner. The ice was all around: It cracked and growled, and roared and howled ....*

Just as I'm sure Charity is wishing she could growl and roar and howl right now. Larissa sent up a quick prayer of gratitude for Rose's swift action, for her understanding, and especially for her ability to bring Charity a touch of humor when she most desperately needed it, all under the guise of innocent conversation.

Turning, Larissa caught the tail end of the handshake between Doc and Mac. For the space of a heartbeat, their eyes locked, Doc's sharply probing, Mac's direct and sure. Doc nodded once, and said in the gruffest tone he could come up with, "It's about time you got back here, my dawdling associate."

Mac laughed and drew Amity forward. "Doc, you remember Amity." Again the pride in his voice was unmistakable. Doc reached to take her hand as Mac continued, "Doc pounded medical knowledge into my head when I was knee-high to a grasshopper, and pinned my ears back a few times in the process." The laughter left his voice as he continued, "If it weren't for him, I never would have become a doctor, and I can't even imagine doing anything else."

"I'm very pleased to see you again, after meeting you in Philadelphia," she said gracefully. "Mac has told me so much about going out with you on your rounds and working in your office."

Doc observed the midnight-dark hair beneath the fashionable hat, the heart-shaped face, and the glow that seemed to come from deep within her. His steely eyes softened as he looked straight into hers. "When he was a young pup, I did my best to teach him to make wise choices. It appears he listened, after all. You put me in mind of a young woman I knew many long years ago." His eyes held hers for another moment before he growled, "When he left, I told this young doctor fellow that when he got back, he'd better still be wearing the same hat size or I'd personally perform the operation to make it fit. Looks like that particular procedure won't be necessary. But it does appear it's going to take a heap of thread to keep those coat buttons sewed on that threaten to pop off from pride every time he looks at you." Such gallantry coming from notoriously grouchy Doc stunned them all into silence.

"We'd best get going," Ethan suggested with only a faint catch in his voice. "We still have to check in with Shawn and Martha and make sure they're willing to keep Merry for a while longer. But while we're here at the station, Amity, would you like to send a telegram to your parents to let them know you arrived safely? They'll know you did, but, speaking from experience, it's nice to be reassured."

"Thank you. I would like to."

"Miles Painter will send one for you. He's been sending them for as far back as I can remember. Just don't be alarmed if he starts speaking to you in Morse code," Mac teased as he led her toward the station door.

The group on the platform watched them disappear inside, and a collective sigh seemed to escape everyone at the same time, but no one spoke. Ethan finally gestured toward the luggage at the end of the platform. "While they're doing that, we might as well start collecting their baggage."

Mac and Amity came back as they finished piling everything into the back of the buckboard and sorting out who was to ride in which vehicle. Through it all, Charity was very quiet, but suddenly everyone else was talking all at once, so that no one remarked upon it.

Larissa and Ethan insisted that Doc join them for supper, and after the requisite amount of grumbling, he accepted. He told them that he needed to check something at his office and put a note on the door, and would catch up with them out at the farm.

As the two-vehicle caravan wended its way to the parsonage, talk and laughter from the buggy drifted to the buckboard following behind. Mac was evidently pointing out to Amity some of the town's more distinctive features and regaling her with some of the more outlandish stories.

The three occupants of the buckboard were silent, partly because Hans couldn't talk and drive at the same time, and partly because saying anything would loosen Charity's death grip on her self-control.

At the parsonage, Martha's oldest son Garth, now nineteen, came hurrying down the path, ostensibly to greet them, but in actuality to help Hans take care of the horses. From a young age, he had had an affinity for animals, but particularly horses. As he grew older, his empathy had strengthened, not lessened, so that if someone in the community was having difficulty with a temperamental animal, they called on Garth. It was said that if Garth couldn't soothe a horse, no one could. After he politely greeted Ethan and Larissa, they left him and Hans, and they, along with the rest of the group, turned to see Martha waiting on the front step. She ushered them inside to the parlor where Shawn, with Noah and Camden beside him, greeted them warmly. Introductions were made and Shawn and Martha were hard put not to smile over Amity's glow and Mac's gladness.

"Where's Merry?" Larissa asked to get their attention off Mac and Amity, who clearly had no wish to be in the spotlight.

"She's with Gretta and Mara," Martha assured her just as the two girls entered the parlor without their small charge. Before Larissa could panic, Martha said in a stage whisper, "You're supposed to call out and find her."

Obligingly, Larissa raised her voice. "Where's Merry?"

A giggle from the hallway gave away her presence, but Ethan spoke up anyway. "I don't see her? Do you?"

Merry, still giggling, burst into the room. "Me right here!" She then looked to Gretta and Mara for approval that she'd done it just right. When they clapped their hands and cheered, Merry ran to her mother with outstretched arms. Before she reached Larissa, she skidded to such a sudden halt that she almost sat down on the braided rug. She recovered her balance, but remained poised in front of Ethan and Larissa. Clutching the material of her skirt, a shade of green that matched her eyes, she held it out to them. "See mine new d'ess? G'etta and Ma'a maked it." Having spent the first two years of her life in a houseful of talkative adults, Merry had developed a wide vocabulary, but she still had trouble getting her tongue around her R's.

"It's beautiful," Larissa assured her, bending to admire the delicate tucks in the bodice and sleeves. "You did a wonderful job," she added to Gretta and Mara, who beamed.

"We didn't do it all," Mara said in a burst of honesty. "Ma helped us fit it on her. She was awful squiggly, so we held onto her while Ma did the pinning and adjusting."

"You did an extra excellent job, then." Larissa couldn't keep the smile out of her voice. "How well I know that she doesn't like to stand still for very long."

Even then, Merry was on the move. She apparently decided that Gretta, Mara, and the dress deserved more praise, for she moved in turn from her parents, to Shawn, Martha, Noah, Camden, and Charity, stopping in front of each one and asking, "Like new d'ess?" twirling around so that the skirt fanned out and they could admire it properly.

She bounced over to Rose, stopped, and lifted her hands. "Like new d'ess?" she signed. In asking everyone else the question, she had used her voice, not her hands. From the earliest days of signing with Rose, Larissa and Ethan, choosing from the different types of sign language available, had decided that, in their particular circumstances, they should sign to Rose at the same time and in the same way as they spoke to one another. Rose had grown up speaking grammatically correct English, and by signing the words they were actually speaking, she would be totally included in the family circle. When Merry came along, they found their choice to be a good one in another way, because the little girl, listening as they signed, learned the sentence pattern being spoken around her. Now she showed that she had made the clear distinction it was for Rose that they signed.

Rose's eyes misted, and she bent down and hugged the little girl. "Yes," she signed back, "I like your new dress very much. It's beautiful."

Satisfied with the praise, and totally unaware that she had done something special, Merry continued her circle and abruptly came face to face with Mac and Amity. She had never seen these people before, and her eyes grew wide as she stared up at them and backed away toward her mother. Ethan picked her up and walked calmly back to Mac and Amity, who were obviously disappointed that she hadn't continued her game with them.

"Merry, this is your brother, Mac. He's been gone a long time, but now he's come home. And this is Amity. She's going to be your new sister."

Merry knew about brothers. Garth and Camden were brothers. She looked back over Ethan's shoulder at Charity and Rose, puzzled because she knew they were her sisters, not this strange woman who was smiling at her and saying, "Hello, Merry. I'm glad to meet you." Merry stared and then buried her face in Ethan's shoulder.

"It's all right, Merry," Mac said quietly. "Pretty soon you'll be used to us."

Neither one made an attempt to hold her or even touch her. Secure in

Ethan's arms, she relaxed a little as she peeked at them sideways, her green eyes solemn.

Ethan carried her back to Larissa and she reached out eager arms for her mother. "We really should be going," he said reluctantly. "Chores are waiting and it's going to be another early day tomorrow."

Larissa was wrenched from the contentment of watching her son to the reality that tomorrow would be another long day of cooking for the harvesters, and that it would be in her kitchen. She relinquished Merry to Gretta and Mara with special words of appreciation for their gift of the dress. They promptly chased the little girl into the next room, her delighted giggles at this new game drifting back to the parlor. With her daughter's attention thus diverted, Larissa expressed heartfelt thanks to Martha and Shawn for their care of Merry. Repeated assurance that they would be delighted to keep her for a few more days followed Larissa and Ethan down the path.

Once more, Hans and the girls followed in the buckboard. Once more, they sat silently as talk and laughter drifted back to them from the buggy ahead.

They pulled up by the kitchen path, Amity turning in an effort to see everything at once. "It's just like you described it," she murmured to Mac.

He gave a sigh of relief. "It looks the same. I was afraid that after a while I'd imagined how it was."

"Mac, you'll be sharing the cabin with Hans." Ethan moved to the back of the buckboard to begin unloading the luggage.

"Yes, and, Amity, we have your room all ready. You'll be upstairs with Rose and Charity." Larissa did her best to sound cheerful, but fatigue was dragging at her again after the excitement of the day, and there was much to do before she could sleep, preparing supper being the first on the list. As she stepped up onto the porch, she smelled something cooking. Wondering, knowing she hadn't left anything on the stove, she entered the kitchen behind the girls and stopped so suddenly that Ethan, Mac, and Hans, carrying Amity's luggage, almost crashed into her. The wonderful aroma filling the air was coming from a large pot on the stove. Raising the lid cautiously, she found bean soup. Bewildered, she watched Ethan pick up a piece of paper lying on the table beside a freshly baked pie.

"Welcome home," he read. "The soup only needs heating up. There is a pan of cornbread ready to go in the oven, and an apple pie for dessert. See you in the morning. Lena and Ariana."

"Bless them," Larissa murmured, and actually felt some of her weariness drop away. She took Amity upstairs, the men following with her luggage. They deposited the bags in her room and quickly retreated.

Amity stood just inside the door, taking everything in. "What a pretty room," she exclaimed. "The flowers are beautiful." She caught sight of the rose-patterned bowl and pitcher and flashed a delighted smile. "Thank you," she said softly, and Larissa knew it was not just for the room.

"You'll want a chance to freshen up. Supper will be in about an hour." She went out, closing the door, leaving Amity gazing out the window at the farm world she was now a part of.

Rose and Charity had prudently stayed behind in the kitchen when everyone else went upstairs, and they had a good start on finishing up the supper. The men had evidently taken Mac's luggage to the cabin. She glanced out the window over the sink and saw them disappearing in the direction of the hay field. Of course Ethan would want to show Mac what a good yield they were getting this year and give him a preview of tomorrow's work. Knowing they would do the barn chores before coming back in, she was surprised a little later to see Ethan hurrying up the path to the kitchen. Instant fear zipped through her. She couldn't see his face beneath the wide hat brim, but he wouldn't be coming back to the house this soon and fast unless something had happened. She reached the back door in time to snatch it open as he thudded across the porch.

CHAPTER FIFTEEN

"Ethan, what—"

He grabbed her hands and she finally saw his face. Instead of fear, he wore an ear-stretching grin. "Lizzie, if there's ever a contest for best neighbors, ours would win it hands down. Jens and Perry were supposed to take this afternoon off like we did. Instead, they kept haying. They must have gotten at least two loads into the loft. They never even gave a hint that they were planning it. You have to come see."

He was so exuberant that she couldn't refuse. Throwing a glance back at the kitchen, she saw the girls crowded in the doorway. Charity was so busy signing the news to Rose that she didn't even notice that Amity had also approached to find out about the commotion and was standing close behind them, her expression puzzled. Larissa got as far as, "Girls, the supper—"

"We'll tend it, Ma." Charity's assurance floated to her before Ethan, still holding her hand, started back down the steps. As her mind finally grasped the news, and its import, she caught his excitement and hurried along with him.

Hans and Mac were standing in the barn doorway, smiling reservedly, as became their young adulthood. Doc, just behind them, was old enough to let his emotions show in the form of tugging at his hat brim and drawing his watch from his pocket to study the hands as if fascinated that they moved. Larissa hiked up her skirt enough not to trip on it, and climbed the ladder to the loft to see for herself their neighbors' generosity. She already knew the answer; it had been made clear in the simple but filling supper that had been prepared for them so that they would walk in on a meal nearly completed, instead of having to start from scratch.

The men finally turned to their neglected chores. Larissa smiled all the way back to the house, basking in the warmth of friendship.

It was good she had those few moments to feel lighthearted, because when she re-entered the kitchen, the heaviness of the day's problems promptly came back to roost on her shoulders. Amity had changed her traveling outfit for a gown that was more elegant than anything Larissa would ever dream of wearing while preparing a meal. Charity and Rose were busily carrying out the supper preparations. It seemed, however, that they hadn't found any tasks for Amity, because she approached Larissa hesitantly, with a quick glance at them. "What can I do to help? I don't want to be considered a guest. I have every intention of helping with the work, not adding to it."

Larissa started to tell her that, no matter the circumstances of her arrival here, they considered her a guest, and to sit and relax, but apparently Rose and Charity had already conveyed this sentiment to her. She hoped Charity had been gracious and not aloof, but doubt joined the heaviness perching on her shoulders. Already tired, she couldn't dredge up the energy to confront Charity's bad manners. Rose's, too, when it came down to it. On impulse she said, "There's an apron in the left top drawer of the cupboard." She spoke as casually as if expensively dressed young women entered her kitchen every day and offered to help cook. She gestured to the counter where zucchini squash and cucumbers waited to be sliced and a vinegar and oil dressing made. "If you'll tend to that, it will be a big help. Thank you," she added. It crossed her mind to wonder if Amity knew anything about kitchens and cooking. This was one way to find out. She watched surreptitiously as Amity dealt quite competently with the vegetables.

Charity continued managing to avoid making eye contact with Amity, using the excuse of facing Rose in order to sign. Since signing was limited while their hands were otherwise busy, neither one said much. She also refused to meet Larissa' eyes, which meant that Charity knew she was sulking like a three-year-old.

To fill the silence that was fast becoming awkward, Larissa asked Amity about her parents and other people they had met and liked in Philadelphia. Rose and Charity had once more retreated to the corner, and, tired or not, Larissa's earlier spark of irritation flared into full flame. She'd sympathized with Charity ever since the telegram came; last night, this morning, and during the reunion at the train station. But at some point, Charity was going to have to accept the inevitable and face forward to life. Rose, too. Larissa had had to cope with many unbearable intrusions into her life, and she hadn't had the luxury of avoiding them.

Am I being too harsh? Perhaps, but life was reality, and that reality was standing at the counter, fixing the dish of vegetables. Charity couldn't avoid looking at or speaking to Amity forever. Besides, such rude behavior couldn't go unnoticed by either Amity or Mac. And he would make no bones about questioning the cause. It was already clear, just in the few hours they'd been home, that Mac would not tolerate any slights or insults to Amity. He expected, justifiably, nothing less than the family including her in their normal interactions. If he became aware of Charity's deliberate withdrawal, having to explain the reason to him would be infinitely more embarrassing and difficult for her.

Deciding, and speaking before her mind could back away from it, Larissa said conversationally, "Charity, you haven't even asked Amity about the girls you made friends with at the Terrills' dinner party. I know you've wondered what they're doing, and now's your chance to find out."

Larissa spoke in such a normal tone of voice that Charity automatically looked up at her. Too late, she tried to look blank, but Larissa's eyes stayed fixed with deadly intent on hers, waiting for a verbal response—a polite one. Receiving the message thus conveyed, Charity flushed from the roots of her hair to the collar on her dress and grabbed at the jar of pickle relish on the counter beside her. Her out-flung hand struck it and it skidded sideways. She tried to catch it, but it crashed to the floor, breaking the jar and spattering dill relish in a wide swath over the floor, Rose, and herself. Even Amity's apron got caught in the path of the green wave.

Larissa never afterward could make herself believe that Charity had done it on purpose, but it served perfectly to take the focus from her and her red face. Rose had missed her mother's unsubtly phrased command to Charity, and was honestly bewildered when the jar smashed at her feet. Charity ducked, effectively hiding her flaming cheeks. During the ensuing confusion, words flew in all directions as Amity dropped her knife and bent with them to clean up the sticky mess. Fortunately for the three girls, their aprons had taken the brunt of the splash. They removed them with delicate care, in order not to dislodge the clumps of green sticking to them like so many grasshoppers clinging to a milkweed stalk. Even without aprons, unfortunately, their dresses continued to exude an undeniably relishy odor.

Purposely or not, the episode served to bring Charity front and center into the conversation. She could scarcely continue her silent treatment after Amity had been down on her hands and knees, their faces inches from each other, scrubbing up the mess Charity had made. Larissa, hiding her smile, backed off in the middle of the cleaning up, leaving the three girls to finish while she continued the supper preparations.

They were making certain they had picked up all the broken pieces when the men came in from the chores, bringing Doc with them. Ethan and Hans had lived among these particular women long enough that they had become used to walking in on odd happenings. Doc blinked once, then maintained his usual crustiness. If Mac felt any shock about seeing his bride-to-be scrabbling around on the kitchen floor with Rose and Charity, his doctor's demeanor served him well.

The girls scrambled to their feet, their faces now equally pink, so that Charity's earlier blush escaped everyone's notice except Larissa's. Explanations were made, and, once everyone was seated, it was impossible for Charity to avoid observing Mac and Amity as they sat side by side across from her.

Supper was a mixture of conversation as Mac spoke of the diphtheria epidemic, sobering them all and catching Doc's attention. Doc forbore, however, to ask questions, other than to receive assurance from Amity that her parents were well.

The talk turned to tomorrow and everything that would need to be done to prepare for it. "What time do we start in the morning?"

Ethan looked up in surprise at Mac's question. "But aren't you going with Doc, tomorrow? I know he's been waiting for you to come back."

The old man stroked his beard. "It's true I've been waiting to see what magical techniques this doctor with his modern education possesses, but I've waited this long. I imagine I can wait a few more days."

Ethan accepted the offer with no more hesitation. "It'll be good to have your help, son. Jens' boys are willing workers, but they're only nine and ten. They simply aren't big or strong enough to do the job an adult can. Just remember, we'll be starting even before the birds are awake."

"I can guarantee that after all the odd hours I've been keeping these last years, getting up early won't be a problem."

Doc peered around Amity and nodded sagely. "The first rule of doctoring. If you ever get a full night's sleep, be sure to mark it as a red-letter day—or night."

"What are we cooking tomorrow, Ma?" Charity's voice was pitched higher than usual, but apparently Larissa was the only one who caught it.

She gave her daughter a genuine smile for her effort. "For starters, a turkey, with potatoes and gravy. Peas, green beans, fruit salad, doughnuts, pie for dessert. And coffee. Lots and lots of coffee."

"It's making me hungry already," Mac confessed. "I sure am looking forward to eating your cooking again."

"I'm sorry supper tonight is so catch-as-catch-can. I promise that after harvest, I'll do a better job."

"I guess, like Doc, I can wait a few days longer. You have been somewhat busy."

"I'll help however I can," Amity put in, "if you'll just tell me what needs to be done."

"I'm certain we'll find plenty for you to do. Thank you for offering." Larissa had one large reservation about Amity helping in the crowded, steamy room that the kitchen would become tomorrow, but knew it was not the time or place to address it.

Supper finished, the men went down to the barn so that Mac could get a good look at the blooded horses they were once again raising for sale. "How's Deneb doing?" he asked as they went out. The Morgan horse Deneb had been the pride of their stable before Zane joined the Union cavalry during the Civil War. Called upon to furnish his own mount, he had taken Deneb with him. As a result of the vagaries of war, Zane and Deneb had eventually ended up in far-off Nebraska Territory.

There, Zane became friends with Steve Jamison and Anne Clayton's husband Ben, who were serving with him. After Zane was killed, Ben and Steve had brought Deneb home to Larissa.

Her hands paused as the back door closed and cut off Mac's question, but she quickly resumed shaving pieces from a bar of soap into the dishpan. She had too much to do and too little time to do it in to spare thoughts on a past that would never change. While the three girls did the dishes, she was able to get some of tomorrow's necessary tasks out of the way. She still wanted to talk to Amity, but had no chance until she sent Rose and Charity down cellar for the potatoes, canned vegetables and other food items they would need.

There was really no way to approach the subject delicately, but Larissa tried. "Thank you for your help tonight. And another pair of hands will certainly make tomorrow go more smoothly."

"I'm glad to help," Amity said seriously. "Becoming a part of the family means just that, doing my part."

"Your dress is beautiful." Larissa gently touched the shiny smoothness of the green taffeta sleeve. "I know some of tomorrow's tasks will be quite messy, and may have unexpected results, as you saw tonight. Do you have any washable dresses that stains and spots won't ruin?"

She feared she was saying it badly, especially when Amity looked nonplused.

"Mother and I packed so hastily, we didn't take all possibilities into consideration. It simply never occurred to me that I'd be doing work that would require wearing such a dress."

Larissa bit her lip at the explanation suggesting that the young woman was accustomed to having servants do such drudge work. Amity blushed. "I didn't mean it to sound —" She floundered.

Fighting to smother her indignation, Larissa said crisply, "We'll figure something out. Rose and I are too short, but you and Charity are nearly the same height. She's not taking all her dresses to Wyoming Territory. Perhaps we can find something for you."

"Find what, Ma?" Charity, her voice still lacking enthusiasm, her apron full of potatoes, came from the cellar in time to hear the last of her mother's words.

"If we're going to initiate Amity fully into the fun of life on a farm, she'll need to wear something that suits the part. I was just thinking that perhaps she could borrow one of the dresses you're not taking to Clark's Valley."

Instinctive objection to the proposition flicked in Charity's eyes. It changed to a spark bordering on smugness as she realized that, in however small a manner, she suddenly possessed something that Amity, with all her elegance and city-bred ways, didn't have, and that only she could provide. As small a satisfaction as it was in the larger scheme of things, Charity grabbed it. Taking her time, she dumped the potatoes from her apron into a box on the counter. When she slowly turned, the smallest of smiles edged her lips. "I expect we can come up with something," she agreed pleasantly. "The dresses I'm leaving behind have seen plenty of kitchen work, I assure you, and certainly can't be made any the worse for wear. Luckily, we're close to the same height. We'll go find something after we finish up here."

All through Charity's coolness toward her this afternoon and evening, Amity, reading the situation as from one woman to another, had maintained her poise. Now she looked justifiably wary at the sudden display of cheery helpfulness. Glancing at Larissa, who was already busily sorting through the box of potatoes, she plunged into the murky waters of her relationship with Charity. "Thank you. I appreciate it," she said. In the face of her graciousness, a churlish response from Charity would stick out like a wart on a frog.

With her small victory to savor, Charity became more animated as they tackled the night's remaining chores. By the time she and Rose took Amity upstairs to show her the collection of dresses, some of her vim had reasserted itself. As small a shadow of her old spirit as it was, Larissa, watching them go, felt a large weight drop from her heart. Charity's soul-deep grief would not right itself for many days and nights to come. Mac was lost to her, but she had regained her dignity, and she would not put her pain on display for the world to see.

***

As forecast, the family was up and busy long before the first birds untucked their heads from their wings to twitter sleepily. After producing a hearty breakfast that would keep them going for the next few hours at least, Larissa marshaled her kitchen forces while Ethan, Mac, and Hans went out to finalize their strategy for the day's work.

The Volkers and the Sayers arrived. After a quick cup of coffee on the back porch, the men headed for the field and the women turned to the kitchen. But before they could begin work, Ariana and Lena had to be introduced to Amity, suitably decked out in a faded red dress of Charity's and a large and practical apron. They exclaimed over her and welcomed her and spent much of the morning asking questions about Philadelphia—a big city which neither woman would ever see. Then they asked more questions about Mac and her, how they'd met, and the upcoming wedding. Exciting events had entered their quiet lives, and they took great pleasure in this stretching of their world. With their hands as busy as their tongues, the time for the mid-morning break came quickly. Rose, Charity, and Amity carried freshly made doughnuts and coffee to the men in the field, to save them the time of leaving the work and returning. Mac, eyes lighting when he caught sight of her, introduced Amity to Jens and Perry, and endured their good-natured ribbing after the young women returned to the house.

When Amity rang the noon dinner bell, the men trooped to the pond to rid themselves of chaff and hurried into the kitchen, where the painstakingly prepared food disappeared like the morning mist over Mill Creek. The afternoon, too, sped by, with the men coming in for supper, congratulating themselves on how much they had accomplished, and deciding that with one more day in the Sayers' field, and one more day here, they would finish the job.

Larissa, intensely relieved because she had expected it to take at least three more days, smiled her pleasure at Ethan, who grinned at her and went on conferring with the other men about meeting in the morning. Only after the neighbors had departed did they have a chance to be alone. Rose and Charity, bone tired, had gone up to bed. Amity had disappeared onto the porch with Mac, where their murmurs and an occasional laugh, quickly hushed, drifted to Ethan and Larissa.

Ethan drew her into his arms and held her close. Tired as she was, the warm comfort of his embrace nearly put her to sleep on her feet. His soft chuckle against her ear roused her enough to raise her face for his lingering kiss.

"Guess we'd better get to bed before we both fall asleep and Mac and Amity find us flat on the floor when they come in." At his teasing statement, she straightened and hastily turned to look at the back door. Since it showed no immediate signs of bursting open and revealing them to Mac and Amity, she turned back to him with a smile that belied her weariness. As he glanced toward the bedroom door, the twinkle in his eyes that should have reflected only exhaustion, and the upward curve of his mouth, told her that her silent invitation had been received and wholeheartedly accepted

CHAPTER SIXTEEN

The next two days were a tiresome repetition of the previous ones, both in the kitchen and out in the field. Somewhere in the midst of the hard work, Charity's animosity toward Amity lessened to the point that Larissa no longer feared that Mac would see it and demand an explanation. It appeared that Amity had said nothing to him about it, preferring to wage her own battle in her own way. She so unobtrusively included herself in the preparation of the harvest meals that Larissa, without thinking about it, was soon giving her tasks to do just as she did Rose and Charity.

Finally, on the evening of the second day, the men forked the last of the final load of hay into Ethan's loft. For the last time, the women filled Larissa's table to overflowing with the food they had spent the day preparing and which disappeared in a matter of minutes. For the last time they washed the stacks of dishes, now saying little to one another, wanting to be done with the chore. For the last time, the men harnessed the horses to the wagons. And this time, when the Sayers and Volkers departed, deeply appreciative thanks were exchanged with no mention of meeting in the morning.

That night Larissa, preparing for bed, began a mental list as she always did of the tasks to be done the next day. Bring Merry home. Continue the preparations for Charity's leaving that had been put aside during … Her head touched the pillow and, list dangling, she sank into oblivion.

***

Mac awoke the morning after the harvest was completed and stifled a groan. He couldn't ever remember his muscles being this sore after doing farm chores, not even haying. He shook his head. A few years away from farm life and in the big city had changed him in more ways than one. As he had said when he and Amity arrived at the house that first evening, the farm looked as he remembered it, except that trees and bushes had grown taller. And somehow it seemed smaller than it had before he left. Was it his five-year experience with tall buildings and crowded streets that made the house, the barn, and outbuildings appear to have shrunk in the space around them?

The biggest change in him, of course, was Amity. She had brought a lightness and joy to his life that he had never experienced before. He remembered the first time he'd ever seen her. He and Jeff Kinsley, with four other medical students, had been invited to dinner at the home of Oliver and Matilda Terrill. When he and Jeff arrived, he didn't know which was making him more nervous, the fact that Dr. Terrill was the head of the department of the University of Pennsylvania's medical school, and one of his instructors, or the fact that this would be the most formal dinner he had ever attended.

Both worries had faded into insignificance when Dr. and Mrs. Terrill introduced him to their daughters, Amity and Mercy. Amity's soft cloud of midnight-dark hair, her eyes that were neither green nor blue but a beautiful combination of both, and her laughter had quickened his heartbeat from the first. Especially her laughter. She had sat directly across from him at the table, and, as if sensing his uneasiness in the face of so much cutlery and glassware, had unobtrusively indicated which piece was to be used when. Jeff Kinsley, who came from a well-to-do Pennsylvania family, sat at Amity's left, unfazed by all the elegance. By covertly watching the two of them, Mac had survived the dinner with no fatal or even mildly embarrassing mishaps. And from that evening on, Amity was a part of his heart.

It hadn't been a relationship he could pursue, of course. Revealing his attraction to the daughter of the head of the hospital, who, with his red pencil, held the power of life and death over Mac's medical career, would not be a wise choice. He was also too immersed in his studies for any kind of romance to succeed. But as time passed, Mac and Amity were occasionally brought together by the Terrills. Matilda, particularly, believed that young medical students should be exposed to the intellectual side of Philadelphia, as well as the scholarly. Through her influence, Mac attended concerts, literary readings, and dances, thereby introducing him to a world he had heretofore only heard of. Through it all, even though she must have had dozens of offers of marriage, Amity remained unattached and cordially happy to see him whenever the occasion presented itself. They were never alone; such a circumstance was unthinkable between a young woman of her social class and a just-beginning medical student.

There was the reality, as well, of his solemn promise to Doc Rawley that, when he completed his schooling, he would return to Fairvale and become Doc's associate, eventually to take over the practice. Would Amity be happy in a town as small as Fairvale, with its limited social events? In spite of her parents' presence at the far end of the room, the distance, he was sure, courtesy of Mrs. Terrill and not Amity's father, they had discussed it in depth, and she had assured him that she would be happy wherever he was.

Then had come the diphtheria epidemic and, out of it, Amity's return with him to Fairvale, and the unexpected blessing of not having to be separated for many weeks before his return to Philadelphia for the wedding. She'd confided that she was nervous about intruding on his family, but he had assured her they would welcome her with open hearts. And so his mother and Ethan had. He'd noticed that Rose and Charity had started by acting somewhat standoffish, but he put that down to the sign language barrier. The family did everything they could to include Rose completely, and apparently Charity was her main interpreter. Just to be certain she wasn't being snubbed, he had asked Amity and she had assured him that it was only a matter of them all getting used to each other.

In addition, Amity had immediately been thrown into the exhausting, temper-testing work of preparing harvest meals. When he had expressed concern that she was overdoing, that no one expected her to shoulder such a large share of the unaccustomed load, she shook her head and told him firmly that since she would soon be a part of his family—she smiled at her words—she would contribute just as all the other members of the family were doing.

She had a mind of her own, Amity did, and she wasn't hesitant to let him know her opinion. He grinned. *Life with her is certainly not going to be dull. She—*

He was rudely jolted out of his reverie by a pillow whacking him in the head. He rolled over and squinted against the glare of the coal oil lamp on the table. Hans was standing beside his bed, smiling innocently in spite of the fact that the edge of the offending pillow was plainly sticking out from behind his back. Mac grabbed for his own pillow but Hans, retreating, tossed his weapon onto his own bed and gave Mac a cheerful salute. Hans might not be able to express a verbal opinion, but he definitely had a way of getting his point across. He now began to sign, slowly enough that Mac could follow him.

"I was just letting you know that it's time to get up. On a farm, we don't spend all day in bed."

Mac switched his glare to the window, where the dark still pressed in, then shifted his scowl back to Hans, who was already dressed. "It appears we don't spend all night in bed, either." He signed his retort with gusto.

Hans grinned and brushed his fingertips upward against the sides of his mouth to indicate he was laughing heartily.

Mac grabbed for his pillow, but Hans backed out of reach, and with a cherubically innocent smile signed, "Ethan says the rule on this farm is that if you don't help with chores, you don't get breakfast. You must not be very hungry."

Mac threw back his covers. "I'm hungry enough to eat a bear—or a smart aleck medical assistant!"

His eyes sparkling with pride in spite of himself at the recognition, Hans made a royal gesture toward the washbowl and towel set out on the table.

"That's better. Time to show a little respect for your elders." Since Hans was only two years younger than Mac, that set him off again so that he failed to see Mac's pillow arc toward him. He dodged, but couldn't evade the whumping clout that landed against his ribs.

Having secured his victory, Mac tossed his feathered weapon aside and pompously turned to the bowl and pitcher. Hans gave a sweeping bow, either in acknowledgment of defeat or because he was laughing too hard to stand up straight.

Their horseplay nearly made them late. They reached the barn just as Ethan was sliding the door back. He raised a quizzical eyebrow at Mac's slightly disheveled and out of breath state, but greeted them, handed each of them a rake, and silently picked up his milk stool. Mac had long wondered what it would be like to have a brother. Growing up with Rose and Charity, he knew plenty—or as much as a mere male could know—about sisters. He and Jeff Kinsley, through their medical studies, had formed a bond of closeness that they would never find with anyone else. Maybe it was the farm setting, the home where he'd grown up. Maybe it was the two-year age difference, being the elder one, just as he had always been older than Rose and Charity, and had felt the sense of responsibility known only to the oldest child in a family. Whatever it was, whether Hans knew it or not, Mac had finally learned how it felt to have a brother.

During breakfast, the family sorted out their various plans for the day. Ethan and Hans needed to get busy with several tasks they had neglected during harvest. Mac offered to help, but Ethan smiled at Hans and shook his head. "Hans and I can handle it just fine. You've been here over three days and still haven't had your meeting with Doc. If you delay any longer, he'll think you've changed your mind and he'll start looking for another associate. Hans, here, can't fill in for you. He's already spoken for over in Delaware County. From what I've heard, Dr. Ingemar is busting at the seams to have him come." Hans grinned and held his head a little higher at the praise. His fears of not being wanted or needed had long since vanished.

"No worries there about changing my mind." Mac turned to Amity. "But if I go into town, what will you do?"

"While we were fixing breakfast, we were talking about what still needs to be done before Charity can leave. According to the list I heard, there will be plenty to do here."

"And first on that list is picking up Merry from the parsonage," Larissa put in. "Martha and Shawn will get their crowns in heaven for keeping her this long. I fear their patience may be wearing a little thin around the edges, though. So I'll be going in to town. I may as well go to the mercantile while I'm there."

"Ma, can't we go with you?" Charity's voice was pleading. "I've thought of a few more things I'll need to get to take with me, and there might not be another chance. We promise to be good," she added, her hands clasped piously in front of her.

Reading the apology and the promise behind the words, Larissa glanced at Rose and Amity. "If we're all going, we'd better get a hustle on. Once Merry comes home, this peaceful life we've been living for the past several days will be over." Since the last several days had been anything but peaceful, the family, well acquainted with Merry's rambunctious approach to life, wasn't sure whether that was a threat or a promise.

Mac decided to ride Cygnus into town. Although the Morgan was getting on in years, he had always been Mac's favorite and he swore Cygnus, nuzzling his shoulder, remembered him even if it had been five years. Before he headed out, he drew Amity aside. "I'll probably be gone most of the day. Are you sure you'll be all right?"

"I'm sure." Her lips curved up in the smile that always went straight to his heart. "Except I'll miss you being here."

"I might find time to check at the boardinghouse to see if a room will be available in September."

Her eyes glowed. "Do you think there will be?"

"I expect so, but I'll put our names in early, just to be certain."

"Our names," she murmured. "I'll be Amity Edwards. It has such a wonderful sound to it, doesn't it?"

"The most perfect name I've ever heard, and it fits you exactly right." None of the rest of the family chanced to be around at the moment, and he drew her to him. She returned his kiss with an enthusiasm that made his head spin. He let out his breath in a long sigh and rested his cheek against her hair. "I'm sorry for the epidemic," he murmured, "but I'm glad as the dickens you're able to be here with me."

Jogging along toward town on Cygnus a little later, he thought about how true his words had been. He had meant it when he told her father that he would be circumspect in his behavior with Amity, that he had no wish to destroy what he and she had, then or in the future. But on the train ride, and here, they were allowed a closeness that had not been possible in Philadelphia. Tiring as the trip had been, hectic as their first days on the farm had proved, they had been able to spend spaces of time alone, talking—often in the language that didn't require words—learning all the small things about each other that would seal the foundation of the relationship they were building.

He wanted very much to take her around the farm, to show her the world in which he'd grown up, that had shaped him to be who he was. He especially wanted to take her to the sitting seat, the rock that jutted out over Mill Creek. From his earliest days, that had been his refuge when he was troubled over the events of a day spent riding out with Doc Rawley, or when he simply needed to be alone to mull his private thoughts.

He reached town, guiding Cygnus over the little bridge that spanned Mill Creek, getting his first good view of the town after so long. He noticed, as he had at the farm, that the buildings—even with their false fronts, three stories high at the most—seemed smaller than he remembered.

Now used to bustling crowds, the few citizens he glimpsed walking along Main Street gave the place a deserted air, rather than making it seem populated. And the quiet. No cabs or buggies or dray wagons rumbling along the brick street. No shouts in foreign tongues blending into one cacophony. No flower stalls or newspaper stands. No aromas from vendor carts with their fruits and vegetables, pretzels, coffee, and hot sticky buns that warmed one's hands on a chilly afternoon. The only sound to break the early summer morning was an occasional harsh cry from one of the peacocks that Ham Tolliver kept to cut down on the rodent population at his feed and grain store. That intrusion was so much a part of Fairvale, had it been missing, something would have felt out of place.

For a long while he remained motionless astride Cygnus, while the Morgan snatched at the grasses along the edge of the bridge, the nearby creek keeping them a lush green even in the drying heat of early summer. As he watched, he fancied he saw a young boy in short pants, cap pulled low over his blazing red hair, hurrying along the street toward the doctor's office, and felt once again that boy's deep satisfaction at using his hands for healing.

He blinked, and the eager young boy was gone forever. But the deep satisfaction remained.

He spoke to Cygnus, and they started forward along the quiet street, taking the familiar path to Doc Rawley's. After stabling and watering the horse in the shed behind the office, he picked up his medical bag. Doc had given it to him, complete with glistening instruments, so that he "could practice medicine properly," as Doc had informed him in the most brusque voice he could manage, to hide his pride in his pupil. Scuffs now marked the leather, and the instruments had lost their shining newness, but they had taken on the polish of use, each one now as familiar to him as his own breath. He looked at the back door to the office, where he and Doc had come and gone a thousand times on their rounds, but veered and strode around to the front. He opened the door and stepped back into the world of healing he had left behind. He had gone away into that larger world, but he had taken with him the solid medical knowledge Doc had instilled in him.

Doc, hearing the door open, turned from where he was rolling pills at the scarred table. He had been doing just that the first time Mac had entered this office after Doc had agreed to teach him medicine. Mac set down his bag. The years ran backward as he closed the door, removed his hat, and clutched it nervously in front of him. "Thank you, sir, for taking me on so I can learn about being a doctor," he said in the squeakiest voice he could manage.

Doc raised his eyebrows, then drew them together in a fierce scowl. "I agreed we could try this, but I expect you to listen and learn with no nonsense about it or you'll be out on your ear. Understand?"

"Yes, sir," Mac gulped, then drew his shoulders back and looked squarely at Doc, except that this time he didn't have to tilt his head up because their eyes were on a level. "I understand."

"Then hang up your cap and get over here. If I'm going to fill your head with doctoring, there's no point in wasting time."

Mac grinned, hung up his hat as ordered, and strode forward to take Doc's hand in a firm grip.

Wrinkled and baggy at the knees, Doc's suit might have been the same one he had worn that long-ago first morning. The once gray-streaked brows were now snowy, his shaggy hair and beard a soft, luxuriant white. His hazel eyes, however, were as piercing as ever as he looked at the tall, broad-shouldered young man who stood in the place of the solemn boy whose blue eyes had been alight with eagerness to absorb all the medical knowledge Doc could impart to him. He cleared his throat noisily. "Come sit. I've got a fresh pot of coffee going. We have a lot of catching up to get busy on."

Doc poured two cups of coffee and settled into his creaking leather seat, while Mac took his old chair at the side of the desk.

"Did you ever want to throw me out on my ear?" Mac asked curiously.

"Even if I had, you would have bounced right back with more questions than before. Didn't take me long to figure out when I was licked."

"Looking back on it, you must have had a lot of better things to do with your time than be followed around by a kid watching your every movement and always asking 'Why?'"

"To tell you the truth, I thought you'd stick around for a few days, and that would be it. You'd quit pestering me about teaching you and I could get on with my medical business. Instead, you stuck like a burr on a saddle blanket. And the questions you asked!" Doc shook his head dolefully. "Made me realize how much I still had to learn, and I was supposed to be teaching you. I can tell you, I wrote more than one letter to the University Hospital to see if they could answer your questions. Sure made me feel better when they couldn't always explain something, either."

"I didn't realize for a long time all the sacrifices people made—my folks, you—to indulge me. Pa and Ma, Ethan, even Rose and Charity had to take up the slack of the work I was supposed to be doing on the farm. And you certainly could have done things a lot faster and more efficiently if I hadn't been poking my nose in at every step."

Doc tugged at his beard. "Your Ma and Pa had faith in you. As for me, I'd been going around tending patients for over thirty years. Thought I was thoroughly set in my routine. I didn't realize how drastically that was about to change. Pretty soon I started viewing what I was doing in a new way—through your eyes, instead of my own that had seen it all a thousand times and could tend to folks' ills in my sleep."

Mac studied the coffee in his cup before raising his eyes to Doc's. "I've wondered just why you did take me on."

Doc paused a long moment. The words came hard to him out of a lifetime of barring his deepest emotions from the world. "That morning you walked into this office, I saw in you the dedication that I'd had when I first started medical school. The need that came from within to help other people. Once you've experienced it yourself, you can see—or not see—it in someone else. You had that spark, and no matter what I threw at you, you took it. And you kept coming back for more." Thoroughly embarrassed at his revelation, he scowled. "Enough of that. You've more than proved that your folks' faith, and mine, was justified. It's time to get busy putting that justification to work. Now tell me about this diphtheria that's causing so much havoc in Philadelphia."

Mac had felt pride, elation, and simple old-fashioned relief when Dr. Terrill had handed him the certification officially admitting him to the medical profession. Only now he realized that his true graduation lay in the words Doc had spoken aloud, and even more in all those he had not. Mac had just had bestowed upon him something of more value than even his hard-won license: Doc's esteem, from one professional to another.

CHAPTER SEVENTEEN

Swallowing hard, Mac hastily accepted the change of subject and began to tell of the epidemic, how they had first become aware of it and its far-ranging, tragic consequences. He even found himself telling of Enzo and the revenge his sister had exacted, so that Doc pursed his lips behind his snowy beard, but could not keep the spark of amusement from his eyes. They slid easily into other topics as if the five years of separation had been no more than a day or two, and Doc listened with intense interest as Mac detailed new treatments that were proving effective for old ills.

Doc finally pulled his watch from his pocket. "Time to go out on rounds. Grab your bag and let's get to it," he said as if Mac going with him was the most natural thing in the world.

Without thinking about it, Mac took the seat in the left corner of the buggy, just as he had on so many other rounds with Doc. As he headed Bella south, Doc began telling him of the people they would see, some faces from the old days, and some new, births and deaths having about kept pace with each other.

Their first stop was at the Theron farm. Mac remembered it well. The death of the Therons' infant daughter had been the first time in his work with Doc that he had experienced losing a patient. After the baby's death, Doc had answered the question Mac, huddled miserably in his corner of the buggy on their way back to the office, had blurted out. *How do they stand it?* Doc's reply, as clearly as if it were yesterday: *It never gets any easier, no matter how many times you go through it. But they'll stand it because they have to. And so will you if you're to be of use to anyone.* He thought of all those children succumbing in such rapid succession to diphtheria, his efforts to save them futile. Doc had been right. *It never gets any easier.* He'd borne it, but only because he had to.

His thoughts were interrupted by Doc's, "Here we are." His knock on the door was answered by a dark-haired girl of about eight. Her large black eyes traveled in confusion from Doc's face to Mac's, and finally down to his medical bag. "Won't you come in? I'll tell Ma you're here." With one last curious glance over her shoulder at Mac, she disappeared into a room at the rear of the house.

Before Mac could wonder if he'd left shaving cream on his ear that morning, the girl returned with a woman whose lustrous black eyes immediately identified her as the child's mother. "Doc Rawley," she said, drying her hands on her apron before extending her palm. "How good of you to stop by." As had her daughter's, Adelpha Theron's eyes traveled to Mac questioningly. Before either Doc or Mac could say anything, she exclaimed, "Young Doc! It really is you." She tipped her face up to study him. "My, you've grown into a fine young man. Has it really been five years?"

"Hello, Mrs. Theron." Mac put out his hand and she clasped it warmly before she drew the little girl forward.

"This is Dorrie. It means 'gift from God,' but she came to us through you, the night she was born."

Realization snapped into place. Adelpha Theron's baby was the first one he had delivered without Doc there to guide him. He remembered laying the squawking infant, black hair hanging in her eyes, across Adelpha's stomach, and the light that had come into the mother's eyes was as if he had just introduced her to God. He bent toward the little girl, who was peering cautiously from the shelter made by her mother's arm around her shoulders. "I'm pleased to remake your acquaintance, Dorrie. You're a young lady, now." She smiled shyly, and he thought of death, and birth, and the courage it had taken for the Therons to have a second child, trusting that she would not die, too.

Warmed by the Therons' hospitality, they set out on their remaining calls. Along the route, in a more social than medical fashion, they stopped by some of the families who had known Mac at the time of his lessons with Doc. Recovering from their surprise at the adult version of the boy they remembered, they responded with genial congratulations to "Young Doc." The people who had moved to the community after Mac's departure for medical school greeted him politely, then ignored him and spoke directly to Doc. After the second such reaction, Doc wore a definite scowl as he climbed back into the buggy. Mac had long ago learned that such thunderheads were best acknowledged by silence and, their new professional equality notwithstanding, he sat back in his corner and kept his mouth shut.

Doc finally glanced at him. "We're going to play it a little different with the rest of our calls. I'll tell you the symptoms as they were first described to me, and you'll take it from there." Since Doc didn't lay out his plan with an option for disagreement, Mac nodded, unable to completely conceal his smile. If a horse could be led to water, for sure Doc was the one who could make him drink.

"Our next stop is the Denholm place. The five-year-old daughter Elsa has fever, a sore throat, and she's coughing."

Mac jerked upright, his mouth so dry he couldn't form the words.

"Listen to me," Doc snapped. "I'm telling you it's not diphtheria."

Mac slumped, unable to stop his sigh of relief, while at the same time turning red with embarrassment at his inability to maintain a professional calm. *Even a first year medical student knows better than to let his reaction show so.*

"You all right now?"

His heart finally stopped racing. "Yes. I'm sorry for overreacting."

"I've been in the middle of a diphtheria epidemic. It was years ago, but I've always been thankful down to my socks that I've never been caught up in one again. So many babies dying, and knowing that, even with all your medical training that you're powerless to save them, is hell on earth. You might as well face it, it's something you'll carry with you for the rest of your life, but it will ease in time. I expect this is the first chance you've had to process what was going on. Who better to understand than someone who's been there?" As he talked on, the red in Mac's face receded and his eyes lost some of the shadowed tautness that only Doc had seen as soon as Mac stepped off the train, a haunted look that hadn't lessened even during their earlier discussion at the office.

Mac exhaled a long, slow breath. "That helps a little. Nothing else has."

Doc nodded as he pulled the buggy into the farm yard. "Here we are." He gestured for Mac to take the lead to the door. "Remember, this is your call in every sense of the word."

At Mac's knock, a young woman holding a baby boy opened the door. She looked surprised, then past Mac to Doc. But Mac spoke before she could. "Good afternoon, Mrs. Denholm. I'm Dr. Edwards, Dr. Rawley's associate. You sent word that your daughter is ill. May we come in?"

The woman's glance at Doc switched back to Mac in some bewilderment, but she opened the door wider. "Yes, of course."

"I'd like to wash my hands before I examine her. I understand she's showing symptoms of fever, sore throat, and coughing."

In the face of Mac's professionalism, Mrs. Denholm responded without further questioning of his status. With Doc following, she led them to the kitchen and provided a basin of water and a towel. "Her cough's worse than it was last night and this morning. Her fever's gone up, too." Mac heard the catch of worry in her voice. As soon as he dried his hands, she opened a door off the kitchen.

Mac took a full breath of the sickroom air before he approached the bedside. As he had learned, each illness had its own peculiar odor. A little girl, cheeks flushed with fever, lay against the pillow. She appeared to be sleeping, but at her mother's voice, her eyes fluttered open. Mac set his bag on the table beside the bed. "Hello, Elsa. I'm Dr. Edwards. I just met your little brother. He told me what a good big sister you are, always helping your Ma take care of him."

Her fever-bright eyes widened. "He couldn't say that," she protested. "He can't talk yet." She choked with the effort of getting the words out.

"You're right," he admitted apologetically, listening to the cough, "but I bet he'd say it if he knew how to talk. Your Ma says that the last day or so, you just haven't felt good enough to help her. Will you let me take a look to see if I can fix that?" After another spasm of coughing, she nodded. He took her hand and felt the racing pulse. "Do you have grasshoppers in your pasture?" he asked causally.

"Yes, lots of them." She looked at him as if he'd turned into one of the raspy green insects.

"I bet you don't know why they live in your pasture."

She shook her head. "Why?" she added with a wan spark of curiosity.

"I'm glad you asked," he said seriously. "Once upon a time, a young man named Tithonus lived in a far away country." Having captured her full attention, he gently began his examination. "He hunted deer and sang and danced in the grassy fields the whole day long. Everyone loved him, but Aurora, the goddess who went out every morning at dawn to carry light and gladness to the flowers in the fields, loved him best of all. He and Aurora married, and were very happy." He paused. "Can you take a deep breath for me?"

She did so, but immediately began another coughing spasm. "Is that the end of the story?" she asked raggedly.

"There's more. Aurora became sad, because, as a goddess, she would live forever, but he was human and would grow old and die some day. So she asked the father of the gods to make him live forever, too. Her wish was granted, and Aurora and Tithonus lived happily for a long time." He paused again. "Can you stick your tongue way out for me?"

Clearly wishing he'd get on with the story, she complied with more than a touch of impatience.

Studying her throat, he continued. "Aurora had forgotten to ask the god king to make Tithonus stay young forever as well as immortal. So while Aurora stayed young, he grew old. It made both of them very sad. Finally, one day he asked her to let him go back to his old home and let him be a bird or an insect and live in the field where she first met him. Aurora sadly agreed. 'You shall be a grasshopper, and whenever I hear the grasshopper's clear, merry song, I shall remember the happy days when we were together,' she told him." He smiled "And *that's* the end of the story and of my examination." She lay back on the pillow with eyes now brightened by something besides fever.

During the examination and story, Doc had stood back, saying nothing, apparently listening, but closely following Mac's every movement. Mrs. Denholm had watched apprehensively, unconsciously swaying the infant she still held in her arms. When the end of Mac's story coaxed a small giggle from her daughter, she visibly relaxed.

"Young lady, I believe you have been bit by a grasshopper named whooping cough," he said finally. "Now here's what I recommend to get that fever down and have you start feeling better." By the time he finished describing and demonstrating the treatment of a cooling sponge bath, the child had perked up a little. Mac gave Mrs. Denholm instructions for administering the medicine he left on the bedside table. "This will help with the fever and coughing," he assured Elsa. "May I come back to see you tomorrow and find out if my magical cure has turned you into a grasshopper?"

"Will you tell me another story?"

He touched her cheek gently, and found it noticeably cooler. "I will, indeed. Do you know why a peacock's tail has a hundred eyes?" She shook her head, her own eyes widening. "Then that will be our story for tomorrow." She nodded, already drifting off into a more relaxed sleep.

Turning to Mrs. Denholm, he gestured to the baby staring solemnly at him from her arms. The little boy looked to be about eight months old, and Mac had a sudden sense of the very recent past repeating itself. He wondered fleetingly if the baby boy he had turned over to Sister Bernadette had escaped the diphtheria scourge. Even more quickly he wondered whether Sister Bernadette had recovered from his emergency diapering treatment of the infant. "It would be a good idea to check the baby for fever, since he's been exposed to Elsa," he said with careful casualness, not to alarm the mother.

She looked down at her son before realization hit her of the possibility that the baby, too, could be ill. "Where would be best?"

"On a blanket on the kitchen table will be fine."

Mac had been so absorbed in his examination that he had forgotten all about Doc Rawley, who, still without comment, followed them to the kitchen. Mac smiled as he completed his careful examination of the baby. "He's just fine," he assured the anxious mother. "Healthy and kicking," he confirmed and received her relieved smile in return. "When I come back tomorrow to check Elsa, I'll take another look at him, just to be sure."

He washed his hands, gathered up his instruments and bag, and Mrs. Denholm showed him to the door, pausing first to pull a coin purse from her apron pocket. "How much do I owe you, Doctor?"

It was Mac's turn to look startled, for in his work at the hospital, he had been totally unused to collecting fees, and hadn't thought to ask Doc what his current rates were or whether Mrs. Denholm could afford to pay them. "No charge just yet," he said smoothly. "When I come back tomorrow, we'll have a better idea of how she's doing."

Her grateful thanks followed him and Doc to the door. Once back in the buggy, Doc gathered up the reins and spoke to Bella. Safely out of earshot, he slanted a quizzical glance at Mac. "How long did you say you've been practicing medicine, Dr. Edwards?"

Mac shot him an apprehensive look. "Why?"

"Because that was one of the smoothest maneuvers I've seen in a mighty long time, what with Elsa's examination, finagling to check the baby, and the question of fees. Since we haven't discussed the payment angle, you must have had a fine teacher to come up with that reasoning so fast."

Mac relaxed at the unusual note of praise in Doc's voice. "I had some fine instructors," he admitted modestly, "but there's no doubt one topped them all."

Doc snorted, his unusual praise replaced by his more usual brusqueness, and Mac smothered a chuckle.

They followed the same procedure for the next two calls, which were also families new to the area, and thus to Mac.

By the end of the afternoon, a highly satisfied Doc Rawley and his new associate headed back to the office. Once there, Doc promptly handed Mac the journal he kept his medical notes in. "You made the calls, you record them, 'Young Doc.' I'll make the coffee."

Mac accepted the journal, knowing he had just received Doc's highest praise of all.

As he jogged Cygnus toward the barn that evening, Amity hurried down the porch steps and flew along the drive to meet him. He dismounted and she swooped into his arms with a cry of gladness. He bent his mouth to hers and met the eagerness of her response with his own flood of elation at their reunion. She nestled her face against his neck. "I'm so glad you're home. How was your day?"

He kissed the top of her head. "I thought my day was the best I'd had in a long time, but now I know better."

Startled, she raised her head and her eyes were suddenly wide and anxious. "Is something wrong?"

He drew her head gently back to his shoulder. "I never realized how a very satisfactory day could be improved a thousand fold by coming home to a greeting like this. I just might have to go down the road and come back so we can do it all over again."

Her smothered breath of laughter brushed his neck. "Silly! Why waste time going away and coming back when we can do it without all that interruption?"

He tipped her chin up. "Amity Terrill, soon to be Amity Edwards, you are brilliant as well as beautiful, and I am so very lucky that you have become a part of my life. I don't know what I did to deserve you, but please Lord, let me know so I can do it again!"

She slipped her arms about his neck. "Blessed is a two-way street," she murmured and pressed her lips to his.

Lost in each other as they were, neither one was aware that they were in full view of the house—and Charity as she started up the kitchen path with the egg basket. Neither were they aware that, as quickly as she averted her gaze, she could not stop the choking sob that escaped her suddenly tight throat. When she did not return to the house in a reasonable time and Larissa became impatient, Rose went looking for her. She found her behind the chicken yard, seated beneath the spreading oak that shaded the coop. She was staring into the basket full of eggs as if she had no idea what they were or how the container had come to be in her lap.

When Rose spoke, Charity jumped, putting the contents of the egg basket at grave risk of becoming scrambled long before tomorrow's breakfast. Seeing who it was, Charity regained a precarious one-handed hold on the edge of the basket, and with her other palm, scrubbed at her damp cheeks. Rose fell to her knees beside her. "Kinsee, what is it?"

With a sigh, Charity leaned her head back against the rough tree bark and closed her eyes. Rose prudently removed the basket from the one-handed grip, thus assuring that the eggs would not meet their intended fate before morning, and that Charity's hands would be free for talking. "I've tried so hard to be mature and accept that he loves Amity and not me."

"Of course you have," Rose said soothingly.

"And I've tried to be accepting of her, and not jealous."

"I know that, and so do Ma and Pa. You've been doing wonderfully well."

"It's just that she's so nice." Rose could not truthfully disagree with this assessment, so she kept silent.

Charity's voice quivered as her next words came out in a rush. "But seeing them together, kissing—"

"You saw them?" Rose couldn't keep the horror from her voice. "When?"

"Amity went outside. Ma had told me to gather the eggs. I didn't know Mac had come home and that Amity was running to meet him. They were down by the barn and I couldn't help seeing them." Her voice rose. "What am I going to do? I can't let him know how I feel. Or her, either."

Rose didn't tell Charity that she suspected Amity already knew, even if Mac hadn't tumbled to it yet. Rose couldn't hear what was going on around her, but she had long ago learned to compensate by sharp observation of other people's actions and reactions.

"She even makes my old house dresses look good," Charity wailed. "I want so badly to hate her, but I can't." She signed the words with such vigor and with such explicit facial expressions that her frustrated fury came across clearly.

"Charity, you can't let them know. You can't!" Rose couldn't hear the urgency she deliberately put into her voice. She could only pray that Charity would hear it. Something of it must have come through, for Charity stared at her with darkening eyes before jerking her head to the side so that she was no longer looking at Rose.

She grabbed Charity's shoulders and shook them. "If they find out, if Mac finds out, he'll never forgive you for resenting Amity. I know my brother. And so do you." Charity shook her head violently. The pang of dread that made Rose's stomach clench propelled her into words she might otherwise never have spoken. "Listen to me. You know what I'm telling you is true. You've lost him to Amity. Nothing is going to change that."

She still stubbornly refused to look at Rose, who could no longer keep the desperation out of her voice. "But do you want to lose him to you, too, for the rest of your life?"

CHAPTER EIGHTEEN

Charity remained rigid for another long moment before she once more slumped against the tree. "No." With the single signed answer to Rose's question, her hands fell to her lap as if she had no strength to hold them up any longer.

Rose had lived through many anguished moments in her life, but she couldn't ever remember feeling so much relief as she did at this dejected admission. Their arms went around each other. Charity bowed her head against Rose and cried all the tears still bottled inside her. Rose had grieved when her father went to war, and she had wept to the depths of her soul when he died. She had shed bitter salt tears when she knew that she would never hear again. Charity's grief soaked the shoulder of Rose's dress, and, one more time in her life, Rose cried for what would not be changed. In their sorrow and loneliness, they rocked and hugged, and shed tears that the rest of the world would never see.

Realization that Larissa would come looking for them, or, worse yet, send Amity or Mac to find them, made Charity jerk up so abruptly that she almost sent Rose sprawling backward. Glimpsing Rose's swollen features, ignoring the astonishment that swept across them, Charity clapped her hand to her mouth before signing in panic, "We can't go back to the house looking like this. What are we going to do?"

Charity was usually the one to come up with solutions to the scrapes they found themselves in, mainly because she was the one whose bright ideas most often landed them there. This time, however, Rose stood and grabbed Charity's hand to pull her to her feet. Clutching the basket of eggs, she headed toward the chicken yard. Instead of entering, she followed the fence to a spot about halfway along the back. Kneeling, using both hands, she began frantically clawing at the soil under the enclosure wire. "Dig on the other side," she gasped.

Charity stared open-mouthed before dashing around the fence. Kneeling opposite the rapidly enlarging hole, she began scooping at the dirt on her side, careful to push it all toward Rose on the outside. When the hole was big enough, Rose stood and heaved a rock into the area beyond the chicken yard. The stone thumped and crackled as it landed in the dry weeds. "Did it make a lot of noise?" When Charity nodded, Rose pushed a rock through the hole. "Throw it," she commanded.

After an enthusiastic windup, Charity lobbed it over the fence and beyond the one Rose had thrown. Waiting only long enough to see it drop, Rose turned and raced through the gate and inside the henhouse. The occupants had already retired to their roosts and watched with only vague interest and a few muttered clucks as Rose sidled to the far end of the room and suddenly made a flashing motion with her arms and the egg basket. A couple of eggs flew and splatted onto the floor. At first the hens didn't respond, but when Charity finally grasped the full intent of the plan, she, too, began to wave her hands wildly about. That got the hens' attention and they rose up, clucking biddy curses and batting their wings. Within moments, every resident of the coop was in fluttering, squawking motion, and the racket would have awakened the occupants of any chicken yard on the far side of Fairvale. Rose barreled past Charity out the door and into the fenced yard. "There he goes!" she yelled and raced for the gate, tossing a couple more eggs for good measure.

Charity, close on her heels, jumping wildly up and down, obligingly screeched into Rose's ear, "He's getting away! We'd better get Pa!" before she silently signed urgently, "Pa's going to ask. Before he does, shouldn't we decide just what got away, for Heaven's sakes? How about a skunk?"

"Fox," Rose panted. "No stink," she added succinctly.

Hollering for Ethan, they were halfway to the house when he came charging out with his shotgun, barrels pointed to the sky. He was followed closely by Hans, hefting the hunting rifle. Amity and Mac straggled behind Larissa, who was carrying Merry. Reaching the girls, Ethan cut through their babbling long enough to assure himself they were both in one piece before he demanded, "What in holy hell is going on?"

"It must have been a fox, Pa," Rose gasped. "Inside the chicken coop. We threw some of the eggs at him and he took off under the fence. Over there." She pointed helpfully. "We screamed and threw rocks. It was hard to tell, but maybe he took off toward the orchard."

Ethan, Hans, and Mac spread out to see if they could locate the culprit. Larissa handed Merry to Rose who, in an effort to cover up the dead giveaway of her shaking shoulders, began to bob the little girl up and down. With Amity dutifully following, Larissa entered the coop to try to soothe the thoroughly outraged inhabitants. Charity, biting her tongue so hard it was wearing tooth marks, trailed in their wake.

By the time the hens had settled down in an uneasy truce, the men came back to report that they'd seen neither tail nor coat of the rascally thief. Mac and Hans filled the hole with rocks and stamped it down to discourage any visitor from re-entering or departing that way. They also volunteered to stand watch, but Ethan declined the offer. "I'll take another look, but I suspect the hens themselves will sound a rousing alarm if anything comes within a mile of the place tonight."

Hans remarked dryly that the girls had made such a ruckus, he expected that, whatever it had been, by now it was most likely cowering in terror under a bush somewhere, and swearing off chicken dinners forever.

By the time they got back to the house, any telltale signs of Charity's and Rose's earlier weeping had become indistinguishable from the excitement of the supposedly attempted theft. Unable to suppress a twinge of conscience, Rose gravely relinquished the egg basket to her mother. Larissa's lips tightened at sight of the sadly depleted contents, but she didn't remonstrate, which had the effect of instantly transforming Rose's guilt from clustered bud to full-blown bloom. Over the long-delayed supper, they told their story again, adding a couple of small details to spice it up, bits which they naturally could have forgotten in their earlier excitement.

When Mac could get a word in sideways, he reached for Amity's hand. "We have some pretty fantastic news ourselves." Charity began signing to Rose, thus giving her the double advantage of not having to watch Amity's glowing smile or her fingers clasped in Mac's. "A room at Mrs. Orvin's boarding house will be available in September. I gave her our names, and she promised to hold it for us for after we're married." There was no mistaking his pride and elation.

Charity's hands wavered, completely snarling up her sentence. Fortunately, no one but Rose noticed, because Ethan and Larissa spoke at the same time, pressing Mac and Amity for details. Rose immediately began signing *It is an ancient mariner* ... so that Charity was able to smile with no one the wiser that it was for anything except Mac's news.

With the dishes finally dried and put away, Mac and Amity disappeared outside. Rose and Charity went upstairs, theoretically to sort out the purchases they had made that day at the mercantile. With the door to Charity's room safely shut behind them, they gave vent to the sputtering giggles they had been forced to swallow until now and that, unfortunately, were not entirely muffled by the hands clapped hastily over their mouths.

"I can't believe they actually believed us." Charity was shaking so hard with suppressed laughter that her signs were decidedly wobbly. "How did you ever make up such a good story? Even I couldn't come up with one that fast!" Her eyes sparkled with admiration as she gazed at Rose.

"It wasn't a lie," Rose said with all the virtuous indignation of one who knows full well she has fibbed. "We threw rocks, and there was a hole, and we yelled and threw eggs. It was shadowy in the henhouse. Are you *positive* that one of those shadows wasn't a fox?"

Unable to resist, both girls began to laugh. And their laughter, that the rest of the world would never share, became a healing balm for their earlier tears.

Whenever the family gathered, even though he had no doubt that he was fully included, Hans tended to sit back, listening, letting the conversation flow around him, so that when he did contribute, it got their attention. The next evening at supper, when the girls' prattling slowed for a moment, he jumped in. Clearing his throat, one of the few sounds he could make naturally, he signaled that it was his turn to throw his hat into the information ring. Surprised, everyone nevertheless turned to him expectantly. "Dr. Ingemar sent me a note through Doc and Mac. He's personally going to make the trip from Delaware City to here, and then back, to take me with him. He insists it's because he wants to start learning to sign as soon as possible. He said—" Hans shook with the laughter he could not voice and his hands wavered in mid motion, so that he had to repeat the signs. "He says if an old coot like Doc Rawley can learn to sign, then he can, too, so we'd better get started on it."

Ethan translated for Mac and Amity's benefit, and they all laughed with Hans. Ethan's eyes then met Larissa's. They both understood that Dr. Ingemar, in his enthusiasm to have Hans begin working with him, would not be making the thirty mile round trip solely because he couldn't wait to learn to sign.

Mac snapped his fingers. "Talking about Doc reminds me. You got a letter today, Speck. Al Thompson caught me as I was leaving town this evening and asked me to bring it out to you. I forgot all about it until now." He was fishing around in his pockets as he spoke.

Amity said curiously, "'Speck'?"

Charity's cheeks turned pink at the sudden direct attention from Amity. "Mac used to call me that when we were little, because I couldn't say 'expect' properly. It always came out 'speck' so he started calling me that, and it looks like I'm still stuck with it. Thank you so much," she said bitingly to Mac and stuck her tongue out at him.

He gave her a smug smile. "If the word fits ...."

Before she could make a heated retort, Larissa broke in. "Children! Behave," she ordered severely before she realized what she was saying—and doing—to her offspring who were no longer children to be admonished for bickering. One after another, like a row of dominoes falling, Rose, Ethan, Amity, and Hans lowered their heads to concentrate fiercely on their plates. As muffled gurgles drifted her way, Larissa's lips tightened. But her heart gave a little bump of happiness at the squabbling as, for an instant, the children were small again, instead of mature—well, mostly mature—adults.

Mac, still searching his pockets for the letter, smacked his forehead in disgust. "I remember now. I put it in my bag. It's over in the cabin. I'll get it as soon as we're done eating." He picked up his knife to cut his meat.

"Why can't you go get it now?" Charity demanded.

"Because I'm not done eating," he said with perfect male logic.

"Ma," she squawked. "I've been waiting for a letter from Mrs. Clayton. It's really important."

"It wasn't from Mrs. Clayton," Mac volunteered.

"Who, then?"

He chewed, swallowed, and shrugged. "I didn't recognize the name on the return address." He took a bite of pork roast and looked up to find all eyes on him expectantly, including Amity's, whose face held as severe a frown as she had ever been able to direct at him.

"What?" His innocent puzzlement didn't fool anyone. "Guess I'd better go get it, before you twist my arm all the way off," he said darkly.

"I guess you'd better," Ethan said. "Remember, son, the women still outnumber the men in this household."

Mac put down his fork, heaved a martyred sigh, and pushed back from the table. "Want to come with me?" he asked Amity, reaching expectantly for her hand.

She tilted her chin up at him. "No, thank you. I'll just stay here and finish eating." She smiled sweetly.

Silence reigned for approximately two astonished seconds before, fortunately not having to conceal it this time, everyone burst into laughter at her unexpected reply and the astounded look on his face. "I'll go do it myself, then," he mumbled with much the same tone the Little Red Hen must have used when no one would help her in her garden. With as much dignity as he could muster, he walked to the door, opened it, and bolted through.

Because Charity signed without thinking about it when she or others spoke, Rose had been able to follow the little drama and laugh with the others. "That was wonderful, Amity," she said when she could get her breath.

Amity slowly began to sign. "Thank you, Rose. It won't hurt him to be taken down a little. But I'm—" She looked at Charity for help. "Curious?"

Pinching the skin of her throat between her right thumb and index finger, Charity raised her eyebrows. Amity repeated both gestures carefully.

"About what?" Rose responded promptly, unable to mask her pleasure at Amity's effort.

"Did Mac give you a—" Again, she turned to Charity. "Nickname?"

Palms facing, Charity joined the index and middle fingers of each hand, crossed them right over left to make a T and moved them slightly forward. "'Name,'" she explained. She thought a second. "You could put 'fun' in front of it, to make it clearer." She demonstrated by brushing the side of her nose with her right index finger, then clasping her palms together. "If we don't have a word that fits, we make it up as we go along. Of course, you can always spell a word, but sometimes inventing one is more fun. Just like in voice talking. 'Speck' from 'expect.'" She wrinkled her nose. "It's just what I would 'speck' Mac to come up with."

Amity smiled in acknowledgment of Charity's dry humor, but if Mac had come up with a nickname for her, she didn't reveal it. Charity suddenly couldn't bear to ask. Hastily, she demonstrated her version of *nickname*. Again Amity carefully imitated her movements.

"He called me 'Shadow,'" Rose admitted, "because he said I followed him around as much as his own shadow did."

"Did you have a nickname for him?"

Rose and Charity looked at each other and burst out laughing. "We did," Rose confessed, "but we'd better not tell you in front of Ma and Pa."

Before Ethan and Larissa could pursue this interesting tidbit, Mac stomped back in and over to Charity. With an exaggerated bow from the waist, he extended the envelope to her. She was too impatient to find out who had sent it to rise to this new bait. "It's from Mr. Ezra Clark, the president of the Clark's Valley school board," she said breathlessly.

At that momentous news, Mac left off his teasing and quietly returned to his seat beside Amity. She smiled up at him, a genuine one, and slipped her hand into his as Charity removed the letter from the envelope. As she unfolded it, a paper fell out. She rescued it before it floated to the floor, then stared at it wordlessly.

"She's speechless," Mac said wonderingly. "It must really be something." Amity poked him with her elbow.

"It's made out to me and signed by Mr. Vincent Trumble. It says it's in the amount of one hundred dollars."

Before Mac could comment, Amity nudged him again.

"May I see it?" Ethan held out his hand, and Charity passed it to him. "It's a bank draft," he confirmed. "It means they'll give you a hundred dollars in exchange for it at the bank."

With shaking fingers, Charity turned to the signature page. "The letter's from Mr. Clark and Mr. Trumble, who signed it as the treasurer of the school board. It says:

"Dear Miss Michaels,

"As the representatives of the Clark's Valley School Board, we wish to express our pleasure that you have accepted the position as the school's first teacher. As you are aware through Mr. and Mrs. Clayton, we have been working for quite a while to realize our goal of a real school for our children. This is, indeed, a momentous occasion in the life of our community, and we are pleased that you have chosen to be a part of it.

"We understand that you will be traveling with Miss Sullivan, who has taught the school in your town for many years. In recognition of the service each of you is rendering, we have enclosed a bank draft to cover the cost of both of your train tickets to Laramie, the nearest rail station, and a return ticket for Miss Sullivan. Please let us know the date you will arrive, and we will be at the station to welcome you and Miss Sullivan.

"We have made arrangements for you to board around with the families of the children you will be instructing, and will let you know the schedule upon your arrival.

"We look forward to meeting you and welcoming you as a most important part of our community.

"With sincere appreciation,

"Clark's Valley School Board

"Ezra Clark, President

"Vincent Trumble, Treasurer."

Charity looked up to find everyone regarding her solemnly. "I guess it's really going to happen." She smiled, but her lips trembled.

The silence stretched until Ethan cleared his throat. "Well, *Miss* Michaels," he said briskly, to draw everyone's attention away from the pain that had flashed in Larissa's eyes, "it sounds as if you are on your way to a teaching career as illustrious as Miss Sullivan's. We'll be able to say, 'We knew you when.'" His voice suddenly husky, he continued. "And when we do, we'll be as proud as Ham Tolliver's peacocks," he said, referring to the glorious-plumaged, noisy-strutting birds that effectively cut down the rodent population at Fairvale's feed and grain store.

"Oh, Pa," Charity managed to laugh, not an easy task over the sudden goose egg-sized lump in her throat.

CHAPTER NINETEEN

The next few days were so filled with activity that, fortunately, there was little time to dwell on the individual changes that came nearer with each sunrise. Seeing Hans off with Dr. Ingemar to Delaware City, with the knowledge that he would be home only on weekends, created a new gap in the family circle that had only just become complete again upon Mac's return. The realization of how much a part of their lives Hans had become in the four years he had been with them reminded them forcefully that they should take nothing for granted.

Adjusting to Mac's being home after five years became Larissa's secret task. She kept in her own heart how much he was the image of Zane. She schooled herself firmly not to catch her breath when, in the midst of other thoughts and duties, she would come upon him. For a flashing instant, she would think that Zane had come home from the war after all, before catching herself and returning to the reality, and the contentment, of her life as it was now.

With quiet determination, Larissa tended to the hundred and two tasks that needed to be accomplished before Charity, too, would leave. She laughed and smiled, and tried not to listen to her heart murmuring that, unlike Hans, Charity would not be coming home on weekends.

It was not only the departures that were bringing clouds to their horizon, however. As Larissa and the girls completed the packing and sewing tasks required to send Charity off, Rose joined in the talk and laughter, but Larissa saw how the shadow in her daughter's eyes lightened whenever she was around Charity, and how it darkened when Charity wasn't there. Of them all, it was going to be the most difficult for Rose. She and Charity had been fast friends since they were five years old, from that springtime morning when Ethan brought his daughter to the farm for the first time. A bond had been forged between them that day, one that had only grown stronger with the years.

The bond had deepened after Rose lost her hearing. All the family learned to sign and to read the signs of the others, but it had been Charity to whom Rose turned most often in her newly silent world. With no fuss or drama, Charity had willingly become Rose's interpreter, and the girls had been able to retrieve much of the way of life they had had before Rose became deaf.

And Charity would be teaching, a dream the girls had shared and worked toward together for many years. Awareness that her own dreams were crushed, that she would never be a teacher, had to be dragging heavily at Rose, particularly with all the attention now focused on

Charity before she departed. Larissa remembered the afternoon Charity had gone to Milford Center to take her teacher's examination, and how she had come bursting into the house, proudly waving her newly acquired certificate. Rose had cheered and laughed and hugged her, giving her all the praise she richly deserved. Late that afternoon, however, Larissa saw Rose, sketchpad tucked under her arm, hurrying along the path to Mill Creek. With an aching heart, she knew that her daughter would lose herself in the peace of those particular surroundings, and seek consolation for her inner being in the most direct way that she possessed. Later, she would return to the house, a new drawing in her book, and her outward demeanor serene. She had had a lot of practice in that department, Larissa reflected caustically, her pain for her daughter's hurt more sharp than it could ever be for any of her own.

Larissa suspected that the loss of Rose's teaching dreams was warring heavily with her knowledge that she would spend the rest of her life quietly at home with the folks. *For her there will be no going out into the wide world as Charity is doing, as Mac did before her. As even Hans is doing....*

***

After consulting with Miss Sullivan, they decided that the departure date should be set for the following Tuesday. Privately, Ethan and Larissa had discussed whether Miss Sullivan should accompany Charity or whether Ethan should. With the demands of haying past, it was no longer necessary that Miss Sullivan be the one to go with her. But when they saw her at church on Sunday she was, for her, nearly bursting at the seams with excitement over making the journey. She even invited them to her room at the boarding house for tea and to discuss a few remaining details. She confessed that she had been to the dressmaker and had had two outfits made. One of course, was her traveling suit, the other — at this point a flash, nearly of shyness, if such a thing were possible, crossed her features. She said, as one admitting a large sin, "It's dark green and serviceable, of course, but it should be appropriate for any occasion that may arise."

Larissa was so stunned, she couldn't think what to reply. Then her natural sincerity came through and she said warmly, "That's wonderful. We made new outfits for Charity, too, hoping they will fill any occasion that her school waists and skirts won't."

Miss Sullivan nodded firmly. "Going into a new country requires that one be prepared for any situation."

On the drive home in the buggy, neither Larissa nor Ethan spoke for the first part of the trip. The night before, Mac had surprised Amity — and all of them—by coming in, not on Cygnus as he had gone out, but driving the finest buggy from the livery stable. Doc had told him he needn't go in to the office after church. This way, Mac had explained, he and Amity could attend services, and afterward take a picnic lunch and go for a ride so that he could show her the beautiful countryside that would soon be her home. If Larissa and Ethan had any suspicions about how deeply the two would concentrate on the countryside, however beautiful, they kept those thoughts to themselves.

Now Rose and Charity, with Merry scrunched importantly between them, were chatting in the backseat, and Ethan finally spoke in a low tone. "We can't do it to her," he sighed. "She's like a kid in the mercantile with her eyes glued to the row of candy jars. We can't take this opportunity away from her."

"Charity seems to assume that Miss Sullivan will go with her. She's never given any other indication since the night we first discussed who would accompany her."

"I've noticed that, too." He reached his left hand to cover hers. "I feel so guilty about not taking her myself. As her father, it's my responsibility to make certain she arrives safely."

Larissa tried to smile. "If anyone can be trusted to carry out her responsibilities on this journey, it's Miss Sullivan. If a suspicious character even looks at them sideways, she'll whap him over the head with her handbag so fast he won't know what hit him."

"She would, too. I have no fear of that." His voice was tinged with admiration.

"We're supposed to be letting go, so that Charity can make her own way in the world as an adult."

"I know," he said glumly. "Besides which, when she first suggested Miss Sullivan, it never occurred to me that the woman would even want to go, let alone that it would become the chance of a lifetime for her."

"I guess it means that we can't really see what's in the heart of someone who has always, to us at any rate, seemed reserved, even cold sometimes. We know she's not the icicle she pretends to be. If she were, she wouldn't have gone to all the effort she did to make certain that Rose would be able to keep going to school."

"Or learned sign language so that she could communicate the lessons effectively."

"Or taken an interest in Charity's future beyond the walls of the schoolroom."

"Or—" They spoke together.

"I guess what we're telling each other, and ourselves, is that we can't take this opportunity from her. We have a parental responsibility to Charity. We also have the parental responsibility to let her try her wings without interference from us."

Her fingers tightened around his. "If we have to be so parentally responsible, or irresponsible, we couldn't have been given a finer assistant to do it with, but … Miss Sullivan wearing a green dress? I've never seen her in anything but black and white."

"Dark green," he amended with a grin.

***

The remaining time seemed to pass by in jumps. The dwindling hours were filled with last minute laundry and packing, the final decisions of what to take and not take—re-decided several times—and the need to finish sewing Charity's traveling outfit. In spite of the many must-be-finished details, Ethan and Larissa found the moments to gather a few small items and tuck them in Charity's trunk for her to find later and be assured she was still a part of their hearts and their home.

In the midst of the bustling and confusion, Amity's presence turned out to be a blessing when she volunteered to keep Merry out from under their feet. The little girl had stoutly maintained her distance from Mac and Amity all through the first evening and night. They spoke cheerfully to her but made no attempt to force her to come any nearer than she felt comfortable. Her shyness—or contrariness—didn't last long. Soon her natural curiosity, not unlike Charity's, Ethan pointed out with a grin and a sigh, overcame her misgivings about the new adult, soft-spoken and pretty, who smelled like the violets in Ma's flowerbed. When she saw the lady sewing something small, she stood close to peek at it and, in so doing, unconsciously leaned against Amity's knee. She discovered it was a rag doll just for her, with strawberry-blond yarn hair and large green embroidery eyes, and the walls were breached.

Thus, when Amity offered to watch Merry so that the others could get their work done, Larissa gratefully agreed. It turned out to be a good arrangement. Larissa was relieved that she would no longer have small fingers rearranging her pattern pieces or a small figure prancing away with her tape measure wrapped around its head in imitation of a horse's flowing mane. Amity sang and played with Merry until the little girl was fairly on her way to becoming spoiled with the undivided attention.

It took a longer time for her to get used to Mac, mostly because he was not around during the day, as Amity was, and sometimes she was asleep before he came home at night. When he was there in the evenings, he loomed above her and spoke in a voice deeper even than Pa's. She finally accepted him because everyone else she loved and trusted did. She wasn't certain why, but he seemed in some strange way to belong to Amity, who by now had her whole-hearted admiration. Merry generously decided that Mac could join in their games and discovered he would give her pony rides on his shoulders. These galloping sessions allowed her, literally, to tower over all the adults she was accustomed to looking far up to, thereby vastly increasing her approval of her steed.

When Amity and Mac asked if they could take Merry with them on their after-supper walks, Larissa protested. "That's your time. Surely you don't need to be dragging a rambunctious toddler with you."

Amity spoke with eager assurance. "We really do like having her with us. We can always take walks by ourselves after she goes to bed."

Larissa glanced at Ethan, who shrugged. She shook her head, admitting defeat. "Just make sure she behaves herself," she said sternly.

"Why, Ma." Mac was all injured innocence. "We wouldn't dream of letting her get away with anything. Would we, Amity?"

"Well, of course not," she said, wide-eyed. "We're very strict with her."

"I've seen your version of strict," Larissa replied crisply. "If she wanted to fly off the barn roof, you'd think it was cute."

"We missed the first two years of her life. We have a lot of catching up to do." Mac said it casually, but his forthright admission brought a swift mist to Larissa's eyes. During the two extra years Mac had spent in Philadelphia, Merry had shed her infancy. She blinked back the film of tears, not sure whether they were for what Mac had missed, for herself, or for the babyhoods of her son and her daughters, a time that could never be retrieved.

She watched them saunter down the kitchen path, each holding one of Merry's small hands. She felt a touch on her shoulder as Ethan slipped his arm around her. Merry's delighted giggles drifted to them as Mac and Amity grasped her wrists and swung her between them down the walkway.

***

No matter how hard Larissa might push against it, the day of Charity's departure arrived. At breakfast, they attempted to speak lightheartedly and discussed at some length the logistics of getting Charity, her luggage, and everyone else to the train station on time. They finally worked it out so that Mac would take the buckboard, instead of riding Cygnus, and take Charity's trunk and cases to the depot. He would then transport Miss Sullivan's baggage to the station before going on to Doc's office. After giving Charity a bear hug and telling her not to terrorize her poor unsuspecting students too badly, way out there in Wyoming Territory, he left. They listened to the buckboard rattle along the drive and the faint jouncing of the trunk and bags in the back until the sounds faded.

Somehow, all the last-minute tasks were accomplished on time and Ethan brought the buggy, pulled by Lynx and Lira, the matched Morgan horses, to the kitchen path. He assisted Larissa into the front seat, then placed Merry on her lap. Charity, Rose, and Amity squeezed onto the back seat. No one spoke for the first part of the ride. All the days of rushing and planning had pooled into these fleeting minutes of sitting, idle hands clasped in their laps, while every spirited step Lynx and Lira took drew them closer to the train station.

Finally Rose, wedged between Charity and Amity, stirred and asked briskly, "Say, Charity, you know what having the three of us back here reminds me of?"

Charity had been staring out the right side of the buggy, as if memorizing the countryside that had been familiar to her since childhood. She looked toward Rose and, by default, Amity.

"No. What?"

Rose gave a breathy laugh. "With Amity here, it reminds me of when you and Mac and I rode in the back, just like this. Remember how he used to take more than his one-third share of the seat?"

"Tried to take," Charity amended. Rose couldn't hear the dullness of her tone, but her gestures definitely lacked her usual enthusiasm, as if her thoughts were elsewhere. "I remember how he'd step on our toes, to make us scrunch away from him and give him more room. He always insisted it was an accident."

Rose, her body angled toward Charity, felt swift motion from Amity on her other side and turned to find that she had abruptly withdrawn into her corner of the buggy. "Amity, what's wrong?"

"Nothing." But she looked troubled in spite of her denial. "I was just giving you more room." She signed the words carefully, using the gestures indicating a space in a house, such as a kitchen.

Seeing Rose's hesitation, Amity brushed her hand over the small distance separating them. "I didn't want to take more …."

"Area?" As Rose gestured and spoke the word, she felt Charity, pressed behind her, straighten ever so slightly as if her full attention had finally been captured.

"Yes. Like Mac." Embarrassment suffused Amity's face.

Rose couldn't help it. She laughed and reached to hug Amity to take away any sting her amusement might cause. "You couldn't ever be like Mac," she said reassuringly. "No one could be like Mac when we were growing up."

Whatever satisfaction Charity might have gleaned at the words didn't show, even though the deeper meaning was clear. Mac had shared their childhoods while Amity had not. "Compared to him, you hardly take up any room at all." Charity signed slowly so that Amity could follow her, and, with only the slightest of hesitations, added, "You fit right in."

Amity blinked, then reached across Rose to take Charity's hands. "Thank you," she said softly. Their eyes met for just an instant before each settled back in her corner and gazed steadfastly out her own side of the buggy.

Charity couldn't read Amity's thoughts, but her words had been clear. *Amity knew.*

CHAPTER TWENTY

When they reached town, Ethan, as earlier planned, drove directly to the train station to drop off the women before he went back for Miss Sullivan and the luggage she would hand carry on the trip. As he drew up in front of the boarding house, he saw a definite stirring of the lace curtain at the downstairs window. Mrs. Orvin directed him to the front parlor. Miss Sullivan was seated on the horsehair sofa. Her back straight, not yielding an inch to the slippery surface beneath her, she was deeply intent on the book in her hands, a valise and carpet bag placed carefully on the floor beside her. His quick glance at the lace curtain confirmed that it was still moving slightly.

"Good afternoon, Miss Sullivan. I hope we haven't kept you waiting long."

With great dignity, she closed her book. "Not at all, Mr. Michaels. I was so engrossed in Miss Austen's work, I didn't realize that it was time to leave. One finds new meaning with each reading." Before she slipped it into her handbag, he glimpsed the title: *Pride and Prejudice*.

"I've found it so with Charles Dickens' works," he said thoughtfully, and she nodded her agreement. "If you would like to wait in here, I'll take your pieces out." Carrying her luggage out and stowing it on the back platform of the buggy, he couldn't resist a smile at the care she was taking to conceal her excitement.

Returning to the parlor, he found her standing beside the sofa, in the process of draping a charcoal-gray linen duster over her shoulders. Before the cape obscured them, he saw that she was wearing a fitted jacket and a skirt drawn back over a bustle. The oval hat perched above her stiff gray bun of hair was actually adorned with a small black feather. It registered in his mind that she was wearing some version of the latest fashion, which he knew only because of the incessant chatter and modeling sessions that had taken place during the last several days with the sewing of Charity's new wardrobe.

Living in a houseful of women, he had had more practice than most other men in the appropriate phrasing of a compliment concerning feminine attire. He started to say, "That's a nice-looking outfit," but stopped at the rooster-crow of warning that sounded in his head. Literal Miss Sullivan might interpret his sincere observation as suggesting that the uniform of plain black skirts and white waists she had adopted at the beginning of her teaching career and had worn every day for nearly four decades was not nice-looking. He changed it hastily to, "Your new traveling outfit looks very genteel." To his ears, it sounded unbearably stiff, but it obviously struck the proper note with her.

She looked surprised, apparently because he had even noticed, and tipped her head in gracious acknowledgment. "Thank you, Mr. Michaels."

He mentally rolled his eyes, but put out his arm for her to take. "We should go." He assisted her into the buggy, and during the short ride to the train station she maintained her poker-straight posture, although he noticed that she clasped and unclasped her gloved hands in her lap. *Miss Sullivan nervous and excited? Jumping jackrabbits! This trip does mean more to her than we'll ever know.* He felt a sharp twist of shame for ever taking her feelings so lightly.

At the depot, he again offered his arm to escort Miss Sullivan into the waiting room. There they found Hans including his farewells as part of the family group. Ethan shook his hand in wordless gratitude, knowing that his coming over from Delaware County in midweek had entailed more than a little inconvenience. Ethan promptly enlisted his assistance in going out to unload Miss Sullivan's bags from the buggy.

When they went back inside, Ethan's eyes immediately sought Charity, who was holding Merry on her hip, heedless of the wrinkles the posture would inflict on the folds of her new silk skirt looped back over a bustle. With her departure now such a very few minutes away, he strove to paint this picture of her on his heart. An oval hat, with a blue feather the exact shade of her eyes, sat sedately over her pinned up, honey-gold hair. Her navy blue gown was patterned with a tiny black stripe that, he remembered hearing from countless discussions, was practical because it wouldn't show travel wear and stains as easily as a lighter, solid color. As she reached up to gently brush a wisp of strawberry blond hair back from Merry's eyes, the sleeve of her bodice jacket flared away from her elbow. Touches of lace and ruffles curved at the wrists and around the bottom edge of the jacket.

In the warmth of the June morning, Miss Sullivan had removed her linen duster. Except for the fact that her dark gray bodice and skirt were severely tailored, if she and Charity had put their heads together beforehand, they couldn't have come up with more similar ideas. Miss Sullivan, however, appeared to be oblivious to the resemblance. While everyone else was doing their best not to offend her by laughing, the station door swung open and Mac walked in.

"Train's coming," he announced. As their talk trickled off, they heard the far-off moan of the whistle. Larissa caught her breath at the significance of the sound, and Ethan slipped his arm about her in a hug that no one else noticed.

Charity's heart jumped when she saw Mac. She had already gone through all the emotions of parting from him this morning, and had thought it was over and done. He edged over to Amity and took her hand as they followed everyone else out the door. Charity wondered tartly if he had come to see her off or whether this was a chance to be with Amity. She stuffed the question down into a far corner of her heart and refused to contemplate the answer. The train was approaching and now all the goodbyes began. Charity gave Merry a final squeeze and reluctantly set her on her feet.

Pa's strong arms held her in a hug that would have to last until he saw her again, with no idea when or how long that would be. "My little girl, all grown up now," he murmured. "I'm so very proud of you." His silky brown beard tickled her cheek as, belying the sadness in his eyes, he chuckled. "For sure, Wyoming Territory will never be the same after you get there." He released her, as, in spite of his effort at cheerfulness, his voice snagged on the last words.

Ma took hold of her hands. "You'll be a blessing to them, the same as you've been to us all these years. Don't you ever think otherwise." Brushing Charity's cheek with her lips, she embraced her tightly and whispered, "Be happy."

Ordering herself fiercely not to let any tears fall in these final moments, Charity turned to Rose. As they clung to each other for those last few seconds, instead of signing, she spoke close to Rose's ear, and they said it at the same time, "Goodbye, Kinsee," so that they covered their parting pain with smiles.

Everyone—including Mac—was watching and listening, so she said, "Goodbye, Amity." *At least I don't have to wonder any longer about my rival—or see every day that you're as beautiful as I hoped you wouldn't be.* "I'm glad we met."

"I am, too." Amity looked straight into Charity's eyes as she said it.

She clearly understood that Amity, with knowledge of her feelings for Mac, was saying that she held no ill will against her. *She doesn't even see me as any kind of competition.* She broke off the forlorn thought. *Not here. Not now.* As with her earlier suspicion about Mac's sudden appearance, as much as the realization about Amity's awareness rankled, she shoved it as far inside as she could since she had no time to brood over it. The only problem was that it seemed to settle much nearer to the pit of her stomach than her heart.

Whether or not Miss Sullivan approved of so much unabashed emotion swirling around the station platform, she had nevertheless been standing back, letting everyone say goodbye without intruding. Now she stepped forward. "It's time to go, Charity."

Charity turned toward the train, but before she could take a step, she felt a firm hand on her shoulder. Startled, she looked back to see Mac. All his levity had vanished, and he said quietly, "I wanted to be the last one to tell you goodbye."

Charity couldn't have spoken to save her life. Mac's nearness, his seeking her out, and his solemnity, brought the tears she had been fighting all morning perilously close to spilling over. If he noticed, he didn't mention it. Instead, he put his closed hand, palm down, toward her. Automatically, she reached out and he pressed a small paper-wrapped packet into her gloved hand. "Don't open it until you're on the train," he said, sounding more like the bossy older brother she was accustomed to. She nodded and he pressed his hand over her closed fist as if to seal in whatever was there.

"I won't," she said with hopeless inadequacy. "Thank you."

He stepped back beside Amity as Miss Sullivan took firm charge and began hustling Charity toward the waiting passenger car. With the older woman on her heels, she couldn't look back, but as soon as they found seats on the depot side, she leaned toward the window, her nose nearly touching the glass. The train started with a jerk, knocking her off balance, so that by the time she steadied, she caught only one blurred glimpse of everyone waving before they were gone. Even craning her neck against the window in a most ungrownup fashion didn't help, so she sank stiffly onto the seat that faced Miss Sullivan.

Knowing how the older woman would strongly disapprove of messy tears, Charity kept her face turned to the window for a long time. However, she saw nothing of the rich, green-ripening fields flashing by, the long lines of trees planted as storm windbreaks, or the farmhouses, each with its gray-penciled chimney smoke rising into the cloudless sky. *I'm exactly where I've wanted to be for months. I'm really and at last on my way! So why in tarnation am I crying?* Using such a scandalous swearword, even in her thoughts, didn't dry up the flood, but as she pictured Ma's and Pa's probable reaction to it, she felt an unholy smile curve her lips.

She glanced at Miss Sullivan to make sure she hadn't honed in on these decidedly unfeminine thoughts and saw that the older woman had already taken her crochet project from her handbag. She was busily counting stitches so that, by accident or design, she didn't see and comment on either the undignified behavior—or mind wanderings—of her supposedly adult companion.

As Charity finally turned from the window, the tears for the past that she had so firmly banished were replaced, first by a trickle, then by a flood of anxiety for the future. *What have you got yourself into this time? Agreeing to travel to Wyoming Territory, a journey of hundreds of miles, and not knowing a soul at the far end! Whatever possessed you?* In spite of all her brave insistence that she was doing this for herself, that she wanted to do it to expand her horizons, reality was setting in, and all the sarcasm in the world wouldn't change it. *Well, isn't getting away from Mac doing it for myself?* Her horizons were undeniably expanding as, with every huff of the engine, Fairvale receded and Clark's Valley loomed.

She'd just have to be more like Miss Sullivan. *Like Miss Sullivan, who had been the terror of every Fairvale student for the last forty years?* Since Charity included herself in the equation, the irony of such a choice did not escape her. Miss Sullivan never backed down from anyone or anything. *She's also an old maid school teacher.* The words were so distinct that, startled, she looked around to see who had uttered them. No one, of course. She sighed. If she was going to make Miss Sullivan her role model, she at least had the teaching part worked out. *The old maid part will take much more practice, but it appears that I'm being given ample opportunity to perfect that trait, too.*

Banishing the probability, she forcefully gathered the sadly shredded remains of her dignity, sat straight, and with proud care arranged her skirts so that they draped gracefully over the shiny toes of her new black shoes. During the last hectic week, when they were frantically sewing her new clothes, she had actually stitched much of this skirt and jacket herself, with fitting and shaping assistance from Rose and Ma. With the thought, she remembered her new hat and reached up to assure herself it hadn't been dislodged while she had pressed her face against the window. *The window!*

She caught her breath sharply and turned to peer at the glass. Now that she was eighteen, why couldn't she remain dignified and not allow her maturity to fly out the door when she felt excited about something? *No nose prints, thank goodness.* The window gave only the reflection of a tall, slender young woman. The curls of childhood had disappeared into a French twist, a style significantly easier to cope with on a long train trip than the upswept ringlets that were so much more fashionable. In spite of all her efforts, escaping tendrils insisted on curling about her face. After fourteen years, she could no longer summon to mind her birth mother's appearance, but the way Pa looked at her sometimes, then got a faraway expression in his eyes, she suspected she resembled her mother a lot.

She clenched her hands tightly together over her skirt and something rustled against her lacy glove. Mac's gift, whatever it was. She had dropped it on her lap and forgotten about it. The tightly twisted paper was torn from a school tablet, and memory of the day Mac had left for Philadelphia to begin his medical studies stirred within her. At the last moment before he boarded the train, she had told him she wanted to be the last one to tell him goodbye, and had given him a tiny package wrapped in paper torn from her school tablet. Now, nestled in the paper torn from another school tablet, she found a shiny brown nut from a buckeye tree. Wonderingly, she smoothed her fingers over the marks strongly resembling a deer's eye that had given the seed its name. He had written something on the paper, just as she had written him a note. She carefully flattened the wrinkles.

Dear Sprite,

Someone once gave me a buckeye nut to take with me on my first trip away from home. She said it was for luck and friendship, and it certainly brought me both. So here is a buckeye for you. I found it in the trees between the cabin and the house. This way, you'll take a part of home with you, just as I did.

She cupped the seed to her cheek, remembering how torn with thirteen-year-old agony she had been whether or not to give it to him.

Your friend,

Mac Edwards.

He had signed both of his names, just as she had, as if she'd been afraid he would mistake her for some other Charity.

She wondered where he'd found a sheet of school paper to write his message on. She wouldn't put it past him to buy a full tablet at the mercantile, just so he could use a single page. Her heart lifted a little at the mental picture of him plopping a nickel onto the counter and the undoubtedly curious look Mrs. Wagner would have given him. Or he could have stopped by the school and bribed one of the students for a sheet of their paper. *I wouldn't put that past him, either.*

In the fading light, she saw that he had added something after his name, and she held the paper closer to the window.

P.S. By the way, Teacher, I suspect there will be mud puddles and bullies in the school yard in Wyoming Territory, so watch out for them. Or maybe someone should warn them to watch out for you!

The last sentence made her smile, as he had doubtless intended. She thought of her first day of school in Fairvale, the first time she had ever seen him. While everyone else stood staring open-mouthed, the young boy with blazing red hair and deep blue eyes had hauled her from the pond-sized puddle some older boys had shoved her in. She had been covered with mud and was screeching so loudly the folks in the next block over had heard her. Unfortunately, before he managed to fish her out, he had ended up splatting into the puddle beside her and becoming equally mud-drenched. She had given her five-year-old heart to him that day, and all the years that stretched between had only strengthened that first childish awareness of love. A love that, in the end, had brought her onto this train and into a seat opposite Miss Sullivan.

A love that was hurtling her along the narrow rails away from him, down the shining tracks that were the path to her future without him.

CHAPTER TWENTY-ONE

Albany County, Wyoming Territory
June 1871

Owen Corley finished harnessing the team to the wagon. Climbing aboard, he guided the horses toward the house. He was halfway there when the back door opened and his two children spilled down the steps. Catching sight of his father, seven-year-old Amos grabbed his sister Carolina's hand, preventing the five-year-old from dashing headlong into the path of the horses. She didn't appreciate his gesture and struggled, however uselessly, against his grip until Owen was near enough to speak without shouting and spooking the team.

"That's enough, Carolina." The words weren't particularly loud, but had the desired effect as she quit struggling, throwing her brother a bitter look as she did so. Even then, Amos kept his grip on her arm until Owen halted the horses.

Twisting free, she ran to stand beside the front wheel, big blue eyes turned innocently up to her father. "I wasn't going to run in front of the wagon, Pa. I know better than that. But Amos wouldn't let go of me!"

Owen swung down from the high seat and lifted her to the wagon box. "I know you know better, Carolina. But Amos was still right. Horses can be unpredictable. You remember that next time."

With a toss of the brown braids poking out from beneath her sunbonnet, lower lip sticking out so far she was in danger of stepping on it, she thumped herself onto the quilt folded over the wooden floor behind the wagon seat. Owen eyed her and the corners of his mouth tightened ruefully. She'd always been headstrong. Seemed like even from her cradle she'd been positive that she could do things without help or advice from anyone else, and she'd butted heads with anyone who didn't see things the right way—her way, of course. Other babies started talking by cooing "mama" and "papa." Some of the first words out of her mouth had been "Me do it!"

Owen suppressed a sigh as he lifted Amos's wide brimmed hat and ran a hand through the dark hair, pushing back the unruly lock that was forever flopping down on his forehead. "You did good, son." He plunked the hat back down. The boy's brown eyes sparked with relief and his anxious frown disappeared as he turned to scramble up into the wagon bed. Owen gave him an assisting boost on the seat of his britches before closing the wagon tail and turning toward the back door.

Callie was descending the steps, and he flashed her a quick smile, completely unaware of how it chased the solemnity from his gray-flecked green eyes and lightened his whole countenance. They made a good pair, he and Callie. Folks had contributed their share of words against the match eight years ago, what with both of them trying to outspeak the other, but it had worked for them. Not that it had always been easy, but he'd found he could talk and she'd listen, her own impulse to snap back put on simmer because she shared his dreams and plans. It had worked the other way, too, as he'd learned from her to curb his tongue to let her have her say. Now they each tried to outtalk the other only about half the time.

"I just wish I was going, too. I'd so like to meet Miss Michaels." The pensiveness of Callie's tone didn't escape him. With her fondness for books and learning, she had once been an excellent teacher herself. But society's rigid rules had forced her to decide between teaching or a home and family. She had chosen marriage to him. His only regret was that she had been obliged to make a decision at all. Watching her teach Amos to read, and now having started Carolina on her letters, he sometimes felt as if he had taken a part of herself from her. Not that she'd ever said anything or even hinted at it. But he'd seen her brown eyes sparkle with anticipation whenever discussion turned to the new teacher's coming. He couldn't give her back the missing piece, but he had worked hard to get the new school going, and he was glad the empty place wouldn't be quite so empty now.

He took her hands and shook his head in response to her wistful remark. "Now, Callie, we been over that trail. The bouncin' wouldn't be good for you or the little fellow right now."

A time past, she would have protested vigorously, with a hundred reasons to override his objections. Even now, he saw a dangerous glint in her eyes. But it faded as quickly as it had surfaced. Since losing the baby that had come too soon to survive two years ago, she had tempered her strong-minded impulses. It hadn't been her fault, hadn't been anyone's fault, but she had blamed herself bitterly.

When this new young one started up, Owen had feared that she would exaggerate her caution. She had a little at first, but with the passage of days had settled down to the business of fulfilling her part of the miracle taking place. He understood that she had worked through the blame and was treasuring the knowledge of this baby as she had Amos and Carolina, and the daughter who had not drawn a first breath. They had named her Aura. Callie had said that in Greek it meant "light breeze" and that was how she had come into and gone from their lives.

"I know." Callie's resigned reply to his reminder that she should avoid jouncing along the rough roads brought his meandering thoughts back to her wistful musing. "Daughter and I will just stay here and have a hot supper ready for you when you get back from the train station."

He cupped a hand to her glossy brown hair and kissed her gently. "If you and the *little fellow* fix a hot supper, that'll do the trick, no doubt about it." She wrinkled her nose at him and he grinned, his heart lightening because she was once more sparring with him, something she had done very few times in the last months, and which he had acutely missed. Releasing her hands, he climbed onto the blanket-padded wagon seat.

Her voice, low but distinct, followed him. *"Daughter."*

In spite of himself, he chuckled. As the wagon gave its first forward lurch, Carolina scrambled to her knees, clutched the side of the box with one hand and waved vigorously with the other.

"Bye, Ma!" Amos, too, was waving.

With the team settled into the pull, the wagon bumping along over the rutted road, Carolina remained on her knees, watching the passing scenery. "Pa?" Her sunshine had been restored as quickly as the thunderclouds had built earlier. That, too, had come to Carolina from Callie. Lucky for the young ones that Callie had more good sense than he in that department. Quick to anger she might be, but she was also quick to put it behind her and get on with the business of life. He was learning, but still had a tendency to cup a displeasure in his hands, to keep the sparks fanned until he succeeded in making his whole day miserable. He lifted his wide-brimmed hat and settled it more firmly onto his head. His normally shaggy brown hair had been tamed by Callie's scissors in anticipation of this trip, and the back of his neck still felt bare.

"Pa?" Carolina was tugging at the back of his coat and he realized he had failed to respond to her earlier attempt to get his attention.

"Yes, Carolina?"

"I forgot the name of the lady we're going to pick up."

"Her name is Miss Michaels. Now that we have a real schoolhouse, she's comin' to stay and teach because Miss Hartfield, who could only come out from Laramie once a month or so, is gettin' married next week."

"Why does she have to stop teaching just 'cause she's getting married?"

The same thought had crossed Owen's mind more than just the one time this morning, but he said firmly, "It's a rule. It just has to be followed. Everyone has rules to follow, and this is the one for school teachers." It sounded pretty lame to him, but Carolina apparently found it satisfactory enough. Or maybe she was just used to vagueness from adults. Her next question caught him off guard, however.

"Is she pretty like Miss Hartfield?"

"Why, I don't know. I haven't seen a picture of her. It's not important whether she is or not. What counts is that she can give you youngsters a solid education."

Amos had been silent, but now Owen heard him mutter, "Be lots nicer to learn from her if she is pretty." His father's sudden coughing fit interrupted the boy's frank observation. "Want me to pound you on the back, Pa?" The honestly well-intentioned question brought on a fresh attack, but Owen managed to wave his hand in a dismissing manner.

"I'm fine, son," he wheezed, sounding for all the world like a stove-up blacksmith's bellows.

"Pa, look." Carolina's scream in his ear startled him so he judged he jumped at least a foot off the seat. He whirled around to grab her, sure she was falling out of the wagon box on her way to landing in a heap in the dusty road, directly beneath the wheels that she was not even head-tall to. He missed catching her because he aimed too high. She was still kneeling, holding onto the edge of the wagon box just like she'd been instructed a thousand times. At least she was holding on with one hand. The other was waving frantically as she pointed to something off the side of the road.

Bewildered, he followed her gaze to a stand of weedy bushes. What he saw made him pull back sharply on the lines.

"A kitty, Pa. A kitty! Can we take him home?" The horses, having obediently responded to the tug on the lines, halted directly across from the "kitty." Sensing an alien presence, they rolled their eyes and drew back their ears.

"Lord a' mercy, child," Owen muttered, "that's not a kitty. That's a skunk. Looks like he's the granddaddy of all skunks, if the truth be told."

"I want to take him home," Carolina protested in a high-pitched squawk.

Owen was already signaling the horses to move forward at a bare crawl. Eyes riveted on the black-and-white form, he distinctly saw the critter's tail twitch. "Amos," he said out of the side of his mouth.

Hidden below the edge of the wagon side, his son was already wriggling on his belly across the rough boards behind Carolina. Before she figured out his intentions, he clapped his hand firmly over her mouth. She squealed again, but mercifully it was muffled behind Amos's palm. With expertise born of practice, he dodged the furious drumming of her heels, the potentially disastrous racket muted by the folded quilt beneath her. She struggled, trying to free herself with an elbow to his ribs, but he grunted and held on gamely. "Quiet," he hissed. "You want to get squirted and have folks think you're a skunk for the rest of your days 'cause you smell like one?"

She continued to writhe against his hand, but at least she did it silently. The wagon was creeping forward, inch by slow inch, until Owen figured they were out of shooting distance. He flipped the lines and the horses increased their pace. "All right, son. You can let 'er go, now."

Amos released his grip from Carolina's mouth and she instantly let out a screech that blasted across the plains. "Pa, Amos was hurting me!"

From behind them, a pungent odor wafted on the morning breeze. Owen increased the horses' pace. "You'd better be glad, Carolina. Your brother just saved you from a fate worse than a visit to the woodshed."

"So there," Amos jeered in her ear, rubbing his sore ribs. "If you don't believe Pa, just take a nice deep breath." With an *I'll-show-you* expression, she obeyed and started to choke. "See? Next time, do as you're told."

She flounced herself around so that her back was to him. Between coughs, she asked in her most wheedling tone, "Can't we go back and get the kitty now, Pa?"

Amos stared at her as if she'd lost her mind, and Owen flipped the lines again. The horses broke into a full trot. The odor trailed them for a long while before it mercifully faded.

Laramie was bustling this mid-June Thursday, and, just as they had smelled the skunk long after they left it behind, these children of the clean, windswept plains smelled the settlement long before the heaps of garbage carelessly piled on the outskirts came into view. Rough and wild as the town was, the two youngsters, wide-eyed at the enthralling sights, tried to see everything at once.

As the wagon traveled down the street that was dirt-clumped from last night's rain, they frankly gawked at the buildings with steep false fronts, every other one of which seemed to be a saloon. Some stores bore signs with gaudy examples identifying the business within. A ten-foot tall piece of footgear that would have had Homer's gigantic Cyclops friends gleefully tossing aside their Grecian sandals graced the boot maker's. The barrel maker's shop sported a wooden cask that would have made a dandy tree house—if there had been a tree in the vicinity to put it in. At the land office, a painted map of Wyoming Territory proudly covered the entire front window. As they passed a dentist's office, the children stared open-mouthed at a large set of false teeth that slowly opened and closed.

Amos and Carolina listened to the piano music spilling from the saloons that were doing a brisk business even at this hour of the day. They caught snatches of men's shouting, singing, and arguing voices, some cutting loose with words they had never heard before, but which they nevertheless suspected they'd better never repeat in their parents' presence. They watched the tangled mass of citizens—nearly all were men wearing the rough denim of miners, or the range garb and wide-brimmed hats of cowhands, with very few women present—striding up and down the rough boardwalks and plunging boldly into the unending line of wagons, horses, and pack mules jamming the street.

They passed a white square building that Owen pointed out as the schoolhouse. The children studied it intently. "That's a school?" Amos stared at it, perplexed. "Ours sure don't look like that," he said doubtfully. "Ours is lots littler. Pa, what if Miss Michaels don't want to teach us 'cause our school ain't painted a pretty white like this one?"

Owen almost laughed, but he turned his head in time to see his son's panicked face and the impulse promptly died. "Well, son, she could refuse to teach you young ones just because she don't think we built the school fancy enough. But that'd be kind of like us refusin' to attend church services just 'cause we don't have a regular church buildin' to hold them in. We know God hears us prayin' in each other's homes just as good as He does in a church with a steeple on it. It's what goes on inside that matters. Not whether the place is big or painted up pretty. And it's the same with a school. It's what's being taught and learned that's important. You understand?"

Amos, face shadowed by the flat brim of his hat, squinted at the school building. "You mean like Jesus teachin' outside by the lake and in the fields, and people didn't care 'cause they just wanted to hear what He had to say?"

A lump formed so speedily in Owen's throat that he had difficulty getting his words out. "Why, yes, son. I'd say that's an excellent example."

He reached back and squeezed the boy's shoulder, and Amos suddenly grinned. "Maybe if Miss Michaels don't like the school, she'll let us sit outside by the creek."

Owen yanked the boy's hat down over his eyes. "And let all that hard work we put into buildin' such a fine buildin' go to waste? Just so you can dream about catchin' the biggest fish in Willow Creek instead of listenin' to your teacher and gettin' a fine education?" He spoke over the giggles erupting from beneath the flapping brim. "I wouldn't count on it, son. I surely wouldn't!"

Owen finally pulled into the lot beside the train station. The train was not yet huffing and puffing into sight. A quick glance confirmed that neither Ezra Clark, owner of the Clark's Valley General Store, Cole Leverett, who ranched on Willow Creek downstream from Owen, or Vince Trumble, editor of the Clark's Valley *Clarion*, had arrived yet. He breathed a quick sigh of relief at having accurately gauged his time and travel distance. *For sure it wouldn't do to be late, today of all days.*

A democratic welcoming committee of two townsmen and two ranchers, they had agreed to meet at the depot in Laramie to greet the new schoolteacher and the older woman accompanying her. During early discussions, when the new school was actually becoming more reality than dream, they knew they must begin their search for a competent teacher. They had never expected, however, to find someone from all the way back in Ohio who would be willing to take the position on this still-raw frontier.

Ben and Anne Clayton had assured the school committee that Charity Michaels was the one they were seeking. Owen recalled the moment at the board meeting that, since the Claytons were greatly respected in the young community, their recommendation had been unanimously accepted. A strange gravity had fallen over the little group as if, having taken that step, a line had been drawn between the settlement's roughshod past and its brightening future.

With the others, Owen and Callie had studied the glowing reports of Miss Michaels' ability and character sent by the minister and the doctor in her hometown, in addition to the one sent by the schoolteacher who was accompanying her. Since the Claytons had never actually met Miss Michaels, however, other than communication by letter, their teacher-to-be was still coming to them as an unknown quantity.

One phrase in Miss Sullivan's recommendation, *Miss Michaels exhibits a tendency to high spirits,* popped into Owen's head. He recollected only too well Carolina's "tendency to high spirits." The dashboard in front of him and the rumps of his horses blurred for an instant as an unsettling picture formed. Five-year-old Carolina, in braids and a pink-checked pinafore, was standing at the front of the schoolroom, vigorously waving a pointer stick as long as she was, while bossily instructing the other students. He hastily shook his head to clear it. *Too late to backtrack now.* He forced his mind away from the thought, but the one that replaced it was scarcely more welcoming. The committee had learned that Miss Michaels was eighteen, not much older than one or two of the boys who might be attending. Owen knew there had been concern and discussion whether she would be able to properly handle the older students. He glanced along the empty tracks. *For better or worse, everyone's curiosity, along with any lingerin' doubts, will soon be answered.*

Hearing the rattle of a buckboard, he caught sight of Ezra Clark pulling into the station lot, followed by Cole Leverett in his own buckboard, with his grandson Griffin handling the lines. Owen noted with amusement that Cole, hat tipped over his eyes, slumped relaxed on the seat beside the boy. Cole and his wife Moriah had taken four-year-old Griff to raise after their son and daughter-in-law had died in a typhoid epidemic. Moriah had died of lung fever two winters ago. Against everyone's well meant advice, Cole had continued to raise Griffin, and, to Owen's way of thinking, he was doing a right good job. The boy, now ten, was well-mannered and quick to help his grandfather with both range and household tasks. The clattering tongues in the community, with their helpful suggestions, had long since fallen silent.

Jumping to the ground, Owen crossed to the back of the wagon and unhooked the tailgate. "You can get down and stretch the kinks out," he told the children. He reached for Carolina and Amos scrambled past him. "You stay put here by the wagon while I talk to Mr. Clark and Mr. Leverett." They looked disappointed but obeyed, probably with the idea in mind that jawbreakers or licorice whips might be hovering at the end of the shopping errands that would follow this meeting.

As Cole gave Griff permission to join the other children, Owen shook hands with the two men. Brown eyed, shorter than Owen at just shy of six feet, Cole pushed back his hat, revealing silver gray hair. His gaze swept the depot and surrounding countryside with a cattleman's necessity to know of any weather change.

Owen, too, was aware of the azure sky with only a few clouds drifting by, and the breeze that was always stirring something—the plains grasses, horses' manes, or dust along the street. He drew in a deep breath, but detected no smell of more rain coming after last night's storm.

"They picked a fine day to arrive," Cole said finally.

Ezra Clark, with his black, shoe-button bright eyes and gray-streaked hair, was of an age and build similar to Cole's. However, instead of the range wear the other two had come in, he was dressed in the "store suit" of long-sleeved white shirt, black coat, vest, and trousers he wore when selling merchandise—minus his apron, of course. Now he chuckled. "I'm sure Vince will record all the particulars in next Tuesday's edition."

As they spoke, Vince Trumble's wagon, bursting at the seams with his seven children, rolled into the lot. Brinna Trumble, perched on the seat beside her husband, always amazed Owen. She never seemed harried or ruffled or tired, yet her children all had the best-of-cared-for looks. She smiled and raised a hand in greeting to him now, and he touched the brim of his hat and nodded. Vince joined the group as the train whistle howled in the distance and they turned as one to examine the still-empty tracks.

"I believe this is a good move we're making," Ezra said with satisfaction. "Clark's Valley is growing. We're getting more youngsters all the time." He accompanied this good news with a sly look at Vince.

Vince grinned at his friends in recognition of the joke on himself. "Say, Brinna and I only contribute one every other year or so. Seems to me, with his four, and his flock of grandchildren, Ezra's no slouch in that department, either. And from what I hear about you, Owen, you're doing your best to catch up."

The train whistle, nearer now, drowned out Owen's reply.

"Be here in a couple of minutes." Vince turned back to his wagon. "Train's coming, Brinna. Ready to meet our new school ma'am?" He held up his arms to his wife, who edged off the high seat.

"You children mind yourselves now. Flanna, you're in charge."

"Yes, Ma." The oldest girl kept her eyes on the baby squeezing her fingers while standing on wobbly legs and grinning from ear to ear at the accomplishment. The other children were kneeling at the wagon side, leaning out to talk to Griff, Amos, and Carolina.

Before joining her husband and the other men, Brinna stopped beside Owen. "How's Callie doing? It's such a shame she can't be here. I know how long she's been looking forward to this day."

"She's doin' fine, thanks, but we just didn't want to take a chance with the rough ride."

Having given birth to seven healthy children, Brinna could have scoffed at Callie's extra precaution. Instead, she said sternly, "Most assuredly not. I'd have taken a hot branding iron to you, myself, Owen Corley, if you'd tried such foolishness."

Short and plump, she was a mother not only to her own brood, but to any stray, human or otherwise, that came within needing distance of her. Her mop of curly dark hair escaping the edges of her hat and blowing around her head like a halo, and her cheeks dimpling as she smiled could have lured the unwary into thinking her a pushover. The fire that lit her deep brown eyes as she admonished Owen immediately corrected any such erroneous belief.

His slow smile lit his eyes as he backed off, pushing his hands toward her in surrender. "You would, too," he said with conviction.

She fixed him with one last stern gaze before she said softly, "If she needs anything at all, you just let me know, and I'll be there quicker than you can say 'Jack be Nimble.'"

"Thanks, Brinna. I'll tell Callie." He had no time to say more because the train, with a great deal of squealing and clanging, huffed into sight and sighed to a stop.

The little group waited with varying degrees of patience for several passengers to disembark. Finally, an older woman wearing a charcoal gray linen cape, in spite of the heat of the day, appeared in the doorway. With a large cloth bag over one arm, she reached with the other hand for some kind of support as she cautiously descended the steps. "That must be Miss Sullivan." Since all the other passengers who had left the train were men, and she was clearly older than eighteen, Vince's guess was probably a good one.

They stood in front of the depot and down the track several cars from the one the woman was leaving. Vince took Brinna's arm, but before any of the men could reach the visitor to offer assistance, the porter put out his hand. Grasping it, she made her way safely to the ground. They caught a glimpse of her lined face and grim expression. Ezra muttered something under his breath. In deference to Brinna's presence, the only distinct words were, "Hoppin' horned toads!"

Owen didn't know what the others thought, but he silently agreed with Ezra's assessment. He remembered Amos's assertion that it would be much nicer to learn from the new teacher if she were pretty, and suddenly he clearly saw his son's point of view. If this woman had been his teacher when he was seven years old, he probably would have run howling down the road. Ashamed, he snapped off his rude assessment almost before it formed. If he even suspected Amos had such a thought, his boy would be eating standing up for a month. He swallowed and scrambled to collect his wayward adulthood.

As they approached, Miss Sullivan turned back to look up at another woman hesitating in the doorway. With her head tipped down to watch her step, and her hat shadowing her features, none of them could see her face. Brinna, however, took in with one fashion-starved glance from hat to toes the stylish outfit the woman was wearing. Her heart did a most uncommon flop at the realization that her best dress, which she was wearing today, was hopelessly out of style. She thanked her stars that neither she nor any of the other women in the community were still wearing hoop skirts, which had been the fashion when she and Vince came out from Virginia.

With only sporadic communication available between their rough frontier town and the bustling East, they might be—obviously were— behind the times in dressing out of Godey's *Lady's Book*, but at least they knew that hoops had gone the way of the dinosaur. A relief it was, too, because the morning-to-night duties they performed were impossible in a belled-out skirt. At the mental picture of herself and her friends on their hands and knees in an ocean of soap suds, scrubbing splintery wooden floors while their hoops sailed out behind them, she barely avoided laughing out loud.

They neared the passenger car and Brinna's thoughts went skidding. Fashion-musing forgotten, she desperately wanted to see the new teacher's face, which was still shaded by her hat. This young woman's coming meant so much to all of them connected with the school that, after all the months and years of delay, Brinna felt a sudden deep need to know *now* whether the choice had been wise.

Crude as the Territory might appear to outsiders, the Valley residents observed the amenities of polite society insofar as they were able, and etiquette demanded that they speak to the older woman first, no matter how eager they might be to meet their new teacher. Ezra, as head of the group, removed his hat, stepped forward, and put out his hand. "Miss Sullivan? I'm Ezra Clark, president of the Clark's Valley School Board. On behalf of the committee and everyone else connected with this fine endeavor, we would like to welcome you to Wyoming Territory and our community."

She touched his hand with gloved fingers. "Thank you."

Her black eyes regarded him levelly. She spoke as calmly as if this weren't one of the most important events in the growth of Clark's Valley. Her non-response left him standing there without a reply to further the conversation. He filled the unanticipated gap by shifting his hat from his left hand to his right. Upon successfully completing this brilliant maneuver, he remembered the group waiting just behind him. The natural act of turning to them masked his wry shrug. "These gentlemen are also members of the school committee." As he introduced and clarified each one's position on the board, Cole, Owen, and finally Vince stepped forward, hat in hand, to incline his head politely and welcome her.

Society having been properly placated, Vince drew Brinna to his side, and the touch of pride in his voice was evident. "Miss Sullivan, I'd like you to meet my wife, Mrs. Trumble."

She turned to Brinna and said with a formality that ignored his unseemly emotion, "Mrs. Trumble."

Considering that the trip had been exhausting, and hadn't exactly ended in the garden spot of the world, Brinna tactfully disregarded the response's austere tone. Important to remember, too, this visitor's presence added another female to a community whose population only three years ago had numbered just one woman for every six men. Even if she were here for only a short time, Brinna was confident their visitor would learn of the unspoken commitment the women shared with one another regardless of personal differences. Out here, survival depended upon such loyalty. On a practical note, Miss Sullivan hadn't been cut off from the more settled East and would be able to tell them details from "back home" that they yearned to know. Brinna put out her hand. "We're very pleased to welcome you. We hope your journey was smooth and that your stay is a pleasant one."

Miss Sullivan absorbed the sprawling depot, the clatter of the Union Pacific's nearby machine shops, the roughly dressed men hustling to one place or another, and the raucous town noise thrusting itself upon them. She returned her glance to Brinna. "I hope so, too." She quickly gestured toward the train. "I would like to introduce Miss Michaels." Catching the identically puzzled expressions on the men's faces at the unexpected, warm pride in the woman's voice in contrast to her reserved greeting, Brinna hid a grin and turned, at long last, toward the passenger car.

The young woman had paused on the bottom step to watch the exchange in front of her. The train lurched suddenly and, by some quirk of chance, she looked directly into Brinna's eyes. Brinna's heart seemed to stop in that moment of mutual questioning, then resumed a normal pace as if a life-altering exchange had not just occurred. Vince often said she was the best judge of character in the Territory. She'd picked him, hadn't she? He always winked when adding this last. He swore she had an uncanny sense of sizing up a person within the first moment or two of meeting them. She didn't know exactly where the knowledge came from, but it was handy. And this time was no different. Looking into the young teacher's eyes, she knew their sight-unseen choice had been wise indeed.

CHAPTER TWENTY-TWO

Feet glued to the bottom train step, breath stuck in her throat, Charity watched and listened to the awkward exchange between Miss Sullivan and the man who had introduced himself as Mr. Clark. She understood and was used to her teacher's apparent aloofness. It had taken years for her to realize it was the older woman's way of masking what she would consider unbecoming eagerness. Charity knew for a fact that Miss Sullivan was excited. But how could the head of the welcoming committee or any of the others watching know that?

Belatedly, she realized Miss Sullivan was beckoning to her and that she was still perched on the bottom step. As she reached her foot toward the ground of the community in which she had been invited to live and teach, the train gave a final lurch. The jolt flung her sideways, threatening to change her carefully planned, dignified arrival into a slithering on her nose at the feet of her welcoming committee. In that sinking moment of horror, she locked glances with the dark haired woman she'd noticed earlier. Which of them was more startled at the sudden eye contact, Charity wasn't given time to guess, because the men were already approaching her with questioning smiles. Somehow managing to remain upright, she reached the safety of the solid earth and forced her shaky legs to carry her forward. With all the grace she could muster, she joined Miss Sullivan, who put her hand on Charity's arm. "Gentlemen, Mrs. Trumble, may I present Miss Michaels, your new school teacher."

With the new teacher praying fiercely that no one had observed her near fall from grace, Mr. Clark, who Charity now saw was tall, with shoe-button bright eyes and dark, silver-streaked hair, held out his hand. "Miss Michaels, I'm Ezra Clark, president of the Clark's Valley School Board. We've communicated by letter, of course, but I'm most pleased to meet you and welcome you."

"Thank you, Mr. Clark." Her words came out slightly squeaky, but, looking a bit nervous himself, he appeared not to notice.

He turned to introduce her to the others, and she clutched at their names, determined not to mix them up later. Mr. Corley's and Mr. Leverett's attire indicated that they worked outdoors as Pa did. Since they were holding their hats in their hands, she could distinguish between them because Mr. Leverett was older, with gray hair, while Mr. Corley's hair was dark and had the shortened look of a very recent cut. Like Mr. Clark, Mr. Trumble was dressed in a town coat and trousers. He would be easy to remember because he was married to the dark-haired woman who had locked eyes with her.

When Vince introduced her, Brinna took both of Charity's hands in hers. "Miss Michaels, we are more pleased to meet you than we can say. This is indeed a special day for all of us." Charity could not doubt the sincerity in her voice and eyes, and some of the anxiety eased from her heart.

"We're the official welcoming committee," Mr. Clark put in, "but I can assure you that there are a lot of folks who are going to be really happy to make your acquaintance, including Link and Lillie Monroe. They ask special for us to convey their apologies that they couldn't be here today. Their young ones, Hannah and Jonah, will be attending school."

"We have a whole flock of youngsters who will be learning from you," Mr. Trumble added, and the others chuckled.

Before Charity could do more than wonder at their amused response, Mr. Corley said gravely, "Vince knows whereof he speaks, Miss Michaels. Amos and Carolina, the two younger ones by the wagon over there, are mine. The young fellow standing next to them is Mr. Leverett's grandson, Griffin. The other wagon full of young ones all call Mr. Trumble 'Pa.'"

Following the direction of his tipped head, she saw what appeared to her already apprehensive imagination a wagon with at least a couple dozen children clustered in the box and staring at her solemnly, as were the other three children Mr. Corley had pointed out.

"Oh, my." Her lips moved, but fortunately no sound emerged. Charity would have frozen to the spot, but "Miss Michaels" drew herself up and smiled, hoping fervently that no one noticed that it was a trifle wobbly.

Mrs. Trumble put her hand over Charity's. "It's true that we'll be making a larger pupil contribution than some families, but we've all been waiting for this day for a very long time." She smiled. "Waiting for you."

The butterflies that, for the past three days on the train had been doing acrobatic maneuvers in Charity's stomach, suddenly folded their wings and went to sleep. "Thank you," she said softly. "I'll do my best to justify your confidence in me." She could have bitten her tongue for sounding so insecure, but Mrs. Trumble only tightened her fingers around Charity's.

"I know you will, and we'll help you. That's a promise." She eyed each of the men in turn, and they all murmured agreement. "Come now, you and Miss Sullivan must be exhausted from your journey, and we're standing here in front of this dusty depot rattling on. As Mr. Clark and my husband explained in their last letter to you, you'll be teaching at the new schoolhouse out in the Valley. Town is about ten miles north of Laramie and the school is four miles north of that."

As they walked toward the wagons and the children who were solemnly scrutinizing Charity's every move, Brinna added, "Someday there'll be a branch train line from Clark's Valley to Laramie." She sighed. "But not yet. We do hope the ride won't be too wearing on you after your long trip."

Vince laughed. "Here we've been connected by rail to the rest of the country east and west for only two years, and already we're impatient to have train lines running wherever we want to go." He continued soberly, "It'll be a fine day when it happens. Then we'll be able to print the state and national news without the delays we face now."

Charity remembered that the Trumbles were the owners and publishers of the Clark's Valley *Clarion*. She had always taken the ease of Fairvale's communication abilities for granted, had never imagined it being any other way. She glanced at Miss Sullivan, whose expression clearly indicated her agreement with Mr. Trumble's assessment. Not only that, everyone else's reaction mirrored it. Charity's fears over being young and inexperienced flooded back, in spite of the fact that she had been so sure she had squashed them beyond resurrection. *Stop it! Now!*

Her scolding was so fierce that she looked at the others to make certain she hadn't uttered the words aloud. Apparently she hadn't, because Mr. Corley was speaking without any indication that he had been rudely told by the new teacher to shut up. She rubbed out the hideous vision as thoroughly as she had ever rubbed chalk off a blackboard, and concentrated on his words.

"…country's buildin' up." Owen stopped beside his wagon, removed his son's hat to tousle his dark hair and plopped the hat down again, gently tugged one of his daughter's light brown braids, and smiled at both of them. "That time will come before we know it. Until then, I guess we'll just have to rely on the same horsepower we always have. And pretty reliable horsepower at that."

"Owen, here, is a fine horseman," Ezra explained to Charity and Miss Sullivan. "He seems to have a distinct preference for the flesh-and-blood type over the iron ones."

Owen moved to the horses' heads to check their harness. "My offer still stands," he said mildly. "Anytime you want to challenge my warm-blooded horse against your iron one to see which one's better at cuttin' out cattle, I'll take you on."

"Don't let them get started on that subject," Brinna interrupted with a shake of her head. "We'll be here for hours while they debate the pros and cons. And still never reach an agreement. So let's tend to the important matters." She reached up as her oldest daughter lowered the baby over the wagon side into her arms. "Children, perk up your ears, now. This lady is Miss Sullivan, and this is Miss Michaels, your new teacher." Each youngster took in Miss Sullivan's no-nonsense expression before switching in wide-eyed silence to Charity's less formidable presence.

Vince stepped forward. "You won't be teaching all of them, Miss Michaels, at least not yet, but Mrs. Trumble and I would like to introduce our children." As he spoke, the children reformed their ragged line along the side of the wagon into a stair-step grouping, and Charity saw that there really were only six regarding her gravely, not the double-dozen she had first imagined. "Vincent, Junior, is our oldest. He's twelve." As his father spoke, the boy reached forward to shake Miss Sullivan's hand, then Charity's. "Flanna, here, is ten." She, too, shook hands politely. "Frederick is eight, and Garrett is six. These four will be going to school."

"I'm pleased to meet you," Charity said sincerely, carefully hiding her relief that they were so well mannered.

Brinna took up the list. "Serena is four and Bridget is three." She indicated two little girls who, apparently sensing their turns were coming, had shyly scooted sideways on the quilt to lean against Flanna. The ten-year-old slipped an arm around each one, holding them with a reassurance as natural as if she'd done it a thousand times. "And this one," Brinna turned the infant in her arms to face forward, "is our least one, Erin." The baby gave Charity a toothy grin that she couldn't resist returning.

Cole Leverett put his hand on the shoulder of the older boy standing by the wagons. "Miss Michaels, this is my grandson, Griffin. He's ten. I'm mighty pleased that he finally has the chance for a real education."

Charity noted the shock of licorice-black hair and steady hazel eyes as the boy extended his hand to shake hers. "Pleased to meet you, ma'am." Duty performed, with a barely audible exhale of breath, he retreated to stand beside his grandfather.

"Mrs. Clark and I have two sons and two daughters, but all above school age. It's our granddaughter Becky you'll be seeing in class," Ezra said. "Mrs. Clark is really sorry she couldn't be here, but we couldn't both be away from the store today. I assure you, though, she's really looking forward to meeting you ladies. We're making sure the next generation receives the opportunity our own young ones missed out on." His presence thus accounted for, Ezra stepped back to make room for Owen.

Owen tipped his head in silent courtesy toward both women and put his hand on his son's shoulder. "This is Amos. He's seven." The boy gave her a firm handshake. "And this is Carolina. She's five."

The little girl fastened Charity with an unnerving stare, different from the curious study of the other children. "Amos said if anyone is bad, you'll smack them with a ruler."

Amos reddened. "I did not!"

Breezily ignoring her brother's protest, she continued to stare at Charity. "Will you?"

From the corner of her eye, Charity caught Miss Sullivan's expression and knew she would get no help from that direction. Miss Sullivan was communicating as clearly as if she spoke the words aloud, "This is your first test as a teacher. Handle it."

Charity lifted her chin and returned Carolina's stare with a direct look of her own. "I have never used a ruler to punish a student," she said firmly. Carolina looked disappointed, Amos relieved. "That's the truth," she continued. "All my students were so well mannered and well behaved that I never needed to punish them."

Carolina didn't look impressed at this not-so-subtle warning, but the other children shifted warily. Surveying them, Charity gave them her warmest smile. "Meeting all of you today, I believe you will be very good students, and I'm looking forward to teaching you. We'll be reading stories about kings and knights and princesses. We'll find out what makes bees fly. We'll learn about countries where camels and kangaroos and monkeys live. Would you like to know about these things?"

Six Trumble heads, including shy Serena and Bridget, who would not even be attending school yet, nodded vigorously, along with Amos and Griff. Carolina was the lone dissenter, but Charity pretended not to notice. The oldest boy in the wagon raised his hand as if he were already in class. "Yes, Vincent?" she responded, proud she'd remembered his name.

"When does school start, ma'am?"

Charity looked to the committee, who were clearly gratified by their children's enthusiasm. Brinna gave her warm laugh. "My stars, Miss Michaels. If you're going to teach things as fascinating as that, I might just have to sneak in and do some listening, myself."

With masculine restraint, the committee members tempered their responses to solemn murmurs of approval. Ezra spoke for all of them. "We'd figured to give you a day or two to settle in, meet the other folks whose young ones you'll be teaching, and get a chance to see the town. We were thinking about Monday morning."

Today, what was left of it, was Thursday. Monday morning. *So far away—and yet so soon.* The butterflies in Charity's stomach woke up and did a series of vigorous back flips. "That sounds just right." Judging by the nods of satisfaction she received, she must have managed to convey pleased agreement without the acrobatic butterflies signaling their presence. Only Carolina continued to look discontented. Charity was starting to wonder if that was the child's habitual expression. She thought that, all things considered, she had weathered this initial meeting rather well, but she reckoned without Carolina's persistence.

The child searched her face appraisingly. "Amos says you're pretty."

"Carolina!" Mr. Corley and Amos uttered her name in a perfect duet.

Amos turned a deep purple. He lunged toward his sister, clearly intending to throttle her, but his father was faster. Owen took one long step forward and grasped the little girl by the shoulders. "Carolina, that's enough." He spoke so sharply that she gaped at him. "You will apologize to Miss Michaels, and to your brother, now." Her eyes promptly filled with tears, but he disregarded them. "*Now,*" he repeated, leaving no doubt about what would happen if she disobeyed.

She looked wildly around the group for sympathy, but found none. In fact, the other children were suppressing grins that told only too clearly that this was not the first time they had observed—or been victims of—her behavior. She burst into loud sobs but Owen folded his arms across his chest and waited, unmoved by her distress. Head down, she mumbled, "Sorry."

"That won't do," he said sternly. "Apologize properly to each of them."

His tone assured her that she had worked herself into a corner from which there was only one escape. She raised her head. "I'm sorry, Miss Michaels."

She sounded contrite enough, but, with her back to Owen, he couldn't see her face. Charity, on the other hand, had a spectacular view of Carolina's expression, and she figured that all the repentance there could be held in a teaspoon. It was their first skirmish and she strongly suspected it wouldn't be their last, but she was willing to call it a draw. She appreciated that Mr. Corley's disciplinary measures were fully necessary and not something to be put off until a more private or convenient time. However, having the episode take place in front of an audience made the scene all the more disconcerting.

Memory poked Charity with a vivid replay of a dramatic temper tantrum that she had once staged. She heard Pa's voice now as clearly as if he were standing beside her speaking, not back all those years ago when he had told her, "Unacceptable behavior reaps unpleasant after effects." In the end, her hysterical tears had reaped her nothing except unpleasant after effects at Pa's knee.

So it was with a hearty mixture of skepticism and commiseration that she now told Carolina, "Thank you for apologizing."

Carolina slanted a glance at her father, who tilted his chin toward Amos. With a heavy sigh, she crossed the necessary space to stand in front of her brother. She did not, however, put herself within arm's reach of him. "I'm sorry, Amos."

Still red-faced with embarrassment, he muttered, "I forgive you." *This time.* He didn't utter the last words, but they were clear as a bell to everyone listening.

Carolina looked at Owen again. He nodded and beckoned her to come to him. With dragging feet she did so, and he put a big hand on her shoulder in his own gesture of forgiveness before he turned to Charity. "Her Ma and I haven't decided yet whether we'll be sendin' Carolina to school or not. She just turned five last month, so she's still a mite young."

Accepting this revelation as his personal apology, Charity nodded, afraid to speak lest her voice betray her relief.

An uncomfortable silence followed, until Brinna finally broke it. "What on earth are we doing still standing here? Let's get our wagons and passengers sorted out, so Cole and Owen can get home before full dark."

While Owen had been dealing with Carolina, the other three men had tactfully made themselves scarce. Retrieving the baggage that had been stacked in front of the depot, they stowed it in the vehicles. They had earlier decided that Ezra, Owen, and Cole would, for now, divide the luggage among their rigs, since Vince and Brinna's wagon was already full of youngsters. Charity would ride in the wagon with Owen, Amos, and Carolina. Miss Sullivan would go with Cole and Griff.

"We're sorry we can't take you and Miss Michaels in one vehicle, but this will be easier on the horses." Cole gestured toward his buckboard where Griff was already making space for himself among the trunks and boxes in the back. "We had a whoppin' good thunderstorm last night and the roads are still a little sticky for the teams. When we get to Clark's Valley, we'll rearrange everythin', since Owen and I will be headin' on out of town. Providin', of course, that meets with your approval, Miss Sullivan."

Plainly enough, there was no help for it, even though Miss Sullivan was there in the role of chaperone to the younger woman. Cole intercepted the glance she darted at Charity. He could have made light of such concern when it was totally unwarranted. Instead, he spoke seriously. "We'll all be travelin' together to town. We'll probably stop a time or two to rest the horses. You wouldn't guess it from what you see right now, but we have some pretty spectacular country around here. I think you'll enjoy a few surprises along the way."

At the same time that he appeased Miss Sullivan's finicky conscience, he unwittingly tempted her long-denied desire to see more of the world than just that of Fairvale's settled regions. Miss Sullivan watched Owen guide Charity and the two children to his wagon. He was talking to Charity, probably giving her the same assurance Cole had just offered. "Of course, Mr. Leverett. That's perfectly understandable, and I'm looking forward to viewing your beautiful scenery."

Had Charity been listening to their conversation, Miss Sullivan's gracious admission would have pinned the new teacher in her tracks as securely as Lot's wife had been detained during her own long-ago journey. Fortunately for all concerned, she didn't overhear. The danger of a salty school ma'am thus averted, Owen assisted her onto the high seat while Amos, in normal boy fashion, scrambled into the back from over the wheel, instead of taking the easier path through the tailgate. Owen lifted Carolina up and over, where she retreated to the front corner opposite her brother. It was obvious he was still angry, and she had no intention of letting him prove it.

Owen settled beside Charity, and, with a last glance over his shoulder to make certain the children were seated, flipped the lines. The first several minutes of the ride passed in silence while they inched along the noisy, crowded street toward the other end of town. With their creeping pace, she had plenty of time to notice the mixture of building materials that had been used in the creation of the various businesses. Some were wood, either rough-planed or logs still retaining their bark. Others were constructed of lath covered with plaster and scored to look like stone, complete with false lintels. Around and among these grand structures, a few tents dared to poke up their canvas heads. Charity was glad speech was impractical at the moment, for she found herself as fascinated with the town as Amos and Carolina had been earlier. Of course, she reminded herself, she and Pa had moved from Applegate, Michigan, to Fairvale when she was small. She had also been to Philadelphia, so it wasn't as if she'd never traveled before. She had no memory of Applegate, but this place was definitely nothing like Philadelphia. *I can't wait to tell Rose.* With the realization that from now on she could only tell her in writing, a wave of homesickness crashed over her. *How can I possibly describe all this in just a letter?*

Through the din and clatter that was, minute by minute, a town emerging from the wind-blown plains, a yipping shriek slapped the air around them. Charity almost jumped out of her skin. As she stiffened in the rough wooden seat to keep herself upright, the unearthly yowl assaulted her ears again, and she caught sight of a man in range garb heading his galloping horse up the middle of the street. Even as her panicked gaze whimpered that he was charging in their direction, her brain seemed incapable of generating more than a single, ludicrous thought. *How can that horse manage anything faster than a snail's limp in all this human and animal madness?*

Alongside them to Charity's left, a cowman swerved his horse out of the way of the still yipping rider by squeezing into the small space between their wagon and Cole's buckboard up ahead. The swift, unexpected movement forced Owen to haul back on the lines. As her precarious balance shifted, Charity tightened her grip on the plank seat until she thought her knuckles would crack. She somehow managed to avoid toppling into Owen's lap, but had no time to dwell on the humiliation thus averted, because the galloping horse and howling rider were now barreling straight toward Owen's wagon.

Charity whirled to lean over the seat toward the children as Owen yelled for Amos and Carolina to lie down, and for once his daughter didn't need to be told twice. Owen shouted again, at her, Charity realized wildly. She didn't need to be told twice, either. The instant the children's heads disappeared below the edge of the wagon box, she dropped with a graceless thud into the well between the seat and the dashboard. The frantic pounding of her heart in her ears blurred lesser sounds as she crouched, waiting for the crash.

CHAPTER TWENTY-THREE

The horses reared in panic, jolting the wagon and flinging Charity toward Owen's booted legs. The team would have bolted from the oncoming menace, but there was no place for them to go. She grabbed sideways at the dashboard, clutching it so tightly the wood splintered under her nails. From her ungainly position, she couldn't see anything except the backs of the still-rearing team, and terror swept across her panic as she envisioned them overbalancing and toppling backward across the wagon.

Suddenly, the horse and rider who had earlier edged between Owen's wagon and Cole's buckboard found a fraction of space and swung in the direction of the crowded boardwalk to the right of the wagon. The still oncoming cowman, with a shrill yip of triumph, his horse inches from the hooves of Owen's stamping, plunging team, also shot toward the walkway, not a muzzle-length behind the first horse and rider. *They're going to run the animals right onto the boardwalk.* Charity's brain woke up and shouted the knowledge while the rest of her body stayed frozen in shock.

The crowd, obviously thinking the same thing, scattered like windblown leaves. The lead horse and rider sailed over the hitch rack edging the plank walk and kept going through the open doorway of the building on the other side. Somehow, the second rider managed to halt his horse in front of the log barrier he would otherwise have mowed down. As the man flung himself off his still-skidding horse, the mounted rider reappeared from the dim interior of the building. The fury on his face as he jumped from his saddle would have sent any other man hightailing it for the hills. His crashing right fist dumped his tormentor sprawling half on the walkway and half in the dirt of the street. Before the second man could grab a fistful of shirt, haul him to his feet, and punch him again, the man on the ground raised his head, shook it blearily, and rubbed his jaw. Then he held up the rough-edged stone he'd been clutching in his fist. The irregular shape glinted in the sunlight, effectively halting the fist-swinger in his tracks.

"Gold." Charity heard the word sigh among the onlookers, who began edging forward until they surrounded the man on the ground. Someone stuck a hand down and pulled him to his feet. In a clump, they moved toward the doorway of the building, and Charity glimpsed SALOON printed on a board tacked to a gallery post. The man was talking excitedly and gesturing, but his words didn't carry over the continued hubbub in the street and the louder questions being shouted at him. The other man removed his mount from the boardwalk, secured him properly to the still intact hitching post, and hurriedly followed the crowd into the saloon.

Charity let out the breath she hadn't even realized she was holding.

His team finally under control, Owen swung around to Amos and Carolina. "Are you two all right?" His voice choked.

"Yes, Pa," Amos answered shakily. He was sprawled over Carolina who, true to form, was protesting vigorously at the rough treatment.

This time, however, Owen took it as assurance that his daughter had come through unscathed. He held out his arms over the seat and the children tottered upright and stumbled into them. He held them tightly before cupping a rough hand to Amos's cheek. "You did good, son." Amos drew a deep breath and gave his sister a look that said more than words ever could.

Owen turned back to Charity who, assured the children were safe, had begun to peel her fingers from the dashboard. "You all right, Miss Michaels?" She nodded, and he put out a hand to help her back up onto the seat. She glimpsed Mrs. Trumble's pale face in the wagon behind and gave a weak wave to signify that she was all right. Some of the anxiety cleared from Brinna's horrified expression, but not all. In the press of other vehicles and horsemen, it was impossible for Brinna to get down from her wagon to take inventory of Charity's state. Clearly, however, only Vincent's restraining hand on her arm prevented her from making the attempt.

Fortunately, because of the normal chaos surrounding them, Miss Sullivan, in the buckboard ahead with Cole, hadn't seen or heard most of the spectacle. Alerted by the shouts and pointing gestures when the enraged rider had emerged from the saloon, she had turned in time to observe the recipient of his wrath crash to the boardwalk. By then, however, Owen had had his plunging team mostly settled. The horses' sidling and snorting conveniently blocked Miss Sullivan's view of Charity curled in the wagon well like a fuzzy caterpillar scrunching under the bark of a tree to escape the too-close scrutiny of a hungry woodpecker. Charity breathed a prayer of relief. If she'd seen the entire confrontation, Miss Sullivan would have them back on the train so fast everyone would think their arrival had never really happened. New panic burst through her. *Please don't let the others tell her all about—*

"That was Caleb Braden with the nugget." Cole's grim voice sliced through her heart's desperate plea. "He has a spread west of mine. He must think he's found a pot of gold. He's always schemin' somehow to make money quick. He comes up with lots of ideas that don't pan out, but that don't seem to faze him. When one idea fizzles, before you know it, he has somethin' new dreamed up and is rarin' to go on it."

That was more than Owen had said to her at one time since she'd stepped off the train. "But do you think he's really found a gold mine?" In spite of herself, her voice caught. She'd never seen a gold nugget before and Mr. Braden's had been dazzling. *What if—?* Dizzy with the sudden sparkling possibilities, she clutched the seat again.

Owen's mouth tightened. "All his deals wash out, which would be his own business, but he has a wife and son. Phebe and Will always seem to bear the brunt of his failures."

At his uncompromising words, a sharp pin promptly popped the bright bubble of her elation. As he urged the team forward in the wake of Cole's now slowly moving buckboard, they passed the doorway Caleb Braden had entered. In spite of the curious flatness that had settled around her heart at the loss of a gold-encrusted future, Charity couldn't resist peering around Owen. The first saloon she had ever seen was so dim inside that all she could make out was a press of men's bodies and a swelling of voices. She strongly suspected the loudest one belonged to Mr. Braden. "Will his son be attending school?" Despite her disillusionment, it wasn't a sarcastic question. She wanted to know the parents as well as the students. Apparently, this fellow wasn't the best of providers for his family.

"Yes. Will's nine. Caleb wanted to get him out on the range with the herd, but Phebe has been totally determined that he attend school. She gives in to Caleb on some matters, but not on this one. I expect on Monday you'll find Will on the school doorstep, polished to within an inch of his life." He added soberly, "What they don't have in the way of worldly goods, Phebe Braden makes up for in clean and well-mannered."

Charity's heart lightened at this information. Just because these people were living on the fringe of civilization, they weren't about to let rough ways become the norm.

Spotting a church, she turned toward it with a strange mix of curiosity and relief. Religious aspects had been mentioned in the letters of back-and-forth communication between the Fairvale farm and the Clark's Valley inhabitants. She knew that God was very much a part of the lives of those who had chosen this new country for their homes.

Seeing her interest, Owen halted the team for a moment. "Saint Matthew's Episcopal Church," he explained. "The first church constructed in Laramie. Before that, services were held in Ed and Jane Ivinson's general store. Clark's Valley don't have a regular preacher," he confessed. "We're still takin' turns makin' do with services in our homes. But we'll get there." His tone held such a mixture of determination and confidence that Charity actually pictured the steeple rising from the church-to-be. They passed the Baptist Church and her fingers itched for pen and paper to compose the description she would send Rose.

Led by Cole's buckboard and trailed by the Trumbles' wagon, they finally made it to the end of town. Passing the foul-smelling garbage heap, they emerged onto the grassy plains. Collectively, they drew deep breaths of the clean-scented air. When they exhaled, it sounded loud in the sudden quiet. Charity twisted to look at the town receding behind them and saw something fluttering in the heavens to the south. It was too large to be a bird and too wriggly to be a mountain. Mr. Corley, following the direction of her puzzled stare, waved his hand toward it. "Quite a sight, ain't it?"

"Whatever in the world is it?"

"Fort Sanders is off that way a few miles. You're lookin' at the garrison flag. It's a big 'un, all right. Some folks say it's at least thirty-six feet wide and twenty feet high, and the staff it's flyin' from is a hundred feet tall. Never went there myself to measure any of it, but I reckon I'm willin' to take the word of those who've been there and say so."

Belatedly aware that her mouth was gaping open, Charity closed it and folded her gloved hands in her lap, as befitted the attitude of a mature, newly-hired Eastern school ma'am, not an awkward, toting-butterflies-in-her-stomach girl so many miles away from her family's farm. She pulled her thoughts together, knowing that she should be carrying on a compelling conversation with her host to demonstrate her finely honed teaching skills. But completely awed by the vastness of the grassy plains surrounding her, the endlessly blue sky arching above, she, always the talkative one, could think of nothing more brilliant than a hushed, "It's so immense."

"That it is." As if appreciating her wonder at Nature's far-reaching bounty, Owen let her soak it in without throwing a bunch of distracting comments her way. As the wagon bounced along the rough dirt track winding through the green-grass sea, she realized with a start that, had she been running through them, those grasses wouldn't even have reached to her knees. Somehow, from the descriptions in the letters Rose's Pa had written while he had been stationed at Fort Laramie, she had imagined them to be so tall she could have stood straight and still been hidden beneath them. Of course, she had been considerably shorter then.

While Owen didn't intrude on her silence, he occasionally identified sites he thought might be of particular interest. "Off there are the Laramies." He pointed toward the nearly treeless mountains to the east, then gestured toward the western edge of the horizon, to forested peaks still white-capped this late in the season. "That's the Medicine Bow Mountains. Just so you won't be confused if you hear it mentioned, folks around here call the highest ones in the set the Snowy Range." With sudden awareness of just how much she had to learn about this new land

and the people who, for better or worse, were now her community, Charity felt swift gratitude at his casual teaching of the teacher.

As they rattled along, from her high wagon seat vantage point, she noticed dots of wildflowers completely unfamiliar to her carpeting the grass. "The light purple ones are fuzzy tongue penstemons." At the look she darted him, clearly revealing she thought he was teasing her, he raised his hand as if taking an oath. "Word of honor." His mouth twitched. "Just don't ask how they came by the name. The spiny one with the yellow flowers is a pricklypear cactus."

"I saw a picture of a cactus, once. I never dreamed I'd see one for real or that it would be so beautiful," she said.

Owen shook his head. "Might be pretty to look at, but it presents a big problem when it takes over grazin' land. The cattle ain't too partial to pokin' their noses into the spines on the pads while they're tryin' to get to the grass around it."

Charity twisted her head to look back at the plant with a new-found trepidation that overshadowed her personal insecurities. This was a different landscape, with different needs and expectations, but hindrances to healthy cash crops existed here every bit as much as they did for Pa and the farmers who fought weed infestations back home.

After several miles, she glimpsed a dark line ahead. It was so fine, Rose might have drawn it with one of her colored pencils. Charity leaned forward on the seat as if doing so would bring the distant smudge closer for inspection. Owen, catching her curiosity, tipped his chin toward it. "Willow Creek. Most of us have some rangeland frontin' it. It cuts back and forth and around through these parts, just like the Laramie River it branches off from, but it's considerably smaller, of course. We'll be stoppin' there to rest the horses and let 'em drink."

She found his words truly welcome. The day had turned hot and the warm wind did little to provide any cooling breath or to discourage the mosquitoes that seemed to find the exposed skin of her face and neck spectacularly appealing. As they approached the willow-edged water, the horses pricked up their ears at the scent. Dismay filled Charity as she recalled the scene in town with Mr. Braden. Turning toward Owen, she unconsciously reached her hand toward him. "Mr. Corley." At the urgency in her voice, he turned to her inquiringly. "Please don't mention to Miss Sullivan what happened back there with Mr. Braden." As his questioning expression deepened to perplexity, she felt her cheeks flame, but hurried on. "I'm sure she didn't see what happened. If she knew about it, she might get the idea that it's too dangerous for me to stay here."

As she stumbled to a stop, the beginnings of a smile creased his cheeks. "And she might get the idea that she should take away our new school teacher before she even has a chance to tell our young ones about bees flyin' and kings and knights?"

Charity didn't think it was possible to blush any more furiously than she already was, but she nodded ruefully.

Mr. Corley reached up, removed his hat and settled it more firmly on his head. "Well, Miss Michaels," he said slowly, "if the subject just don't come up, I reckon it can't be termed a lie not mentionin' it." He glanced behind him at the two children sitting in the wagon box, seemingly oblivious to their conversation. "I'll take care of any little pitchers with big ears ridin' with us. And I'll pass the word to Vince and Brinna. Once it's explained to them, I'm sure there won't be any waggin' tongues from that direction. Brinna's a force to be reckoned with when she makes up her mind to it," he said matter-of-factly. However, Charity got the distinct impression he was perfectly happy not to have Mrs. Trumble's "force to be reckoned with" aimed at him, and that he intended to keep it that way. Newfound maturity notwithstanding, Charity couldn't prevent the gusty sigh of relief that escaped her, and she saw the creases in his cheeks deepen.

Reaching the tumbling little creek, they pulled in behind Cole's buckboard. Before the Trumbles drew up to the meager but welcome shade, Mr. Corley walked back to their wagon casually, as if he'd just thought of something he wanted to mention to them. Charity never knew what he said, but as they passed her on their way to join Cole, Griff, and Miss Sullivan at the edge of the creek, Mrs. Trumble gave her a discreet wink and her hand a firm squeeze.

The children, released from the confining wagons and buckboard, scattered to play games that, Charity noticed, involved running. She secretly wished she could join them in their freedom, but knew she must content herself with a long drink from the sparkling creek and a leisurely stroll along the leaf shadowed bank with Miss Sullivan and Mrs. Trumble. The men watered and grained the horses and checked their harness for spots of discomfort.

They called in the reluctant children, and, about an hour later, Clark's Valley swam into sight through the heat haze. The town, consisting of one long street, made the village of Fairvale seem a metropolis by comparison. Skeletons of buildings under construction poked up from both sides. As in Laramie City, some buildings were rough-planed wood or logs, and others were plaster-covered. The canvas roofs and sides of numerous tents flapped in the stiff breeze. The thumping of hammers and rasping of saws echoed in the air, and the not-to-be-duplicated aroma of fresh cut wood shavings drifted to them. The throbbing activity gave ample evidence that the citizens had every intention of expanding their humble beginnings into a solid, prosperous community.

As they rolled along the dirt-churned street, folks on the boardwalks and on horseback hailed their arrival, moving along with them until the little caravan stopped in front of the Clark's Valley Store. "Ezra and Libby's place." Owen's explanation was broken off by the people who now crowded close to the wagon, dispatching greetings to him and welcoming smiles to Charity. A dozen hands reached up to assist her in alighting. Picking one at random, she was swung lightly to the ground. Looking up to say thank you, she met the gaze of a brown-haired man dressed in the same rough shirt and pants outfit as Cole and Owen wore. She noticed the Remington revolver strapped to his hip. Deducing that he was a rancher, her interest quickened. She knew for a fact that he wasn't Caleb Braden, who was probably still back in the saloon, entertaining the crowd. So this must be—

"Ben Clayton, ma'am, and more pleased to meet you than words c'n tell."

CHAPTER TWENTY-FOUR

Ben Clayton held his hat to his chest and shook Charity's hand. Blue eyes twinkling, he added solemnly, "And if you think I'm glad, just wait 'til you meet Anne—Mrs. Clayton."

She looked around expectantly, but he shook his head. "She didn't come with me. Eve was tryin' to follow the boys up a tree and fell. Got a good knot on her head. Anne didn't think she should get her brain whacked again by ridin' into town."

Before Charity could express her disappointment, other people crowded around, introductions flying like an uncovered pan of corn popping. She caught the names of Link and Lillie Monroe, and remembered Mr. Clark mentioning that their children, Hannah and Jonah, would be attending school. She also met Doc Fergus, who she guessed was in his late forties and had brown, gray-specked hair. As he shook her hand, the appraising regard in his hazel eyes reminded her of Doc Rawley's keen awareness of details.

A tall, thin, dark-haired woman, accompanied by a boy of nine or ten, stepped forward and shyly put out her hand. "I'm Phebe Braden, and this is my son, Will." She drew the boy forward as she spoke. He removed his hat and shook hands politely. "I'm sorry my husband couldn't be here today. He had urgent ranch business to tend to."

Phebe and Will Braden. Charity would have bitten off her tongue to keep from revealing that she knew exactly what the "urgent business" was and where it was taking place. "I'm very pleased to meet you, Mrs. Braden. I understand from Mr. Corley that you'll be attending school, Will."

He tipped his chin. "Yes, ma'am."

She thought of Caleb Braden, remembered Owen saying the man wanted his son out on the range, not in a school room. Deep respect for Phebe's resistance to her husband's edict filled her.

Phebe smoothed the shock of coal black hair from the boy's forehead, and it promptly fell forward again. "This is a day we've all prayed for," she said.

Charity was to hear that phrase over and over.

Ezra drew forward a woman in the process of removing a white store apron, which she hastily and unceremoniously thrust at him. "Miss Michaels, my wife, Mrs. Clark."

The gold flecks in Libby Clark's green eyes sparkled as she clasped both of Charity's hands in hers. Then their light muted. "I apologize for not being there when your train came in."

"It's quite all right. Mr. Clark explained. The committee was waiting at the station when we arrived. Miss Sullivan and I were greeted most cordially." With a guilty start, Charity realized that, caught up in the shower of introductions and comments welcoming her to the town, she hadn't even checked whether Miss Sullivan was being greeted with equal warmth or being ignored. She found she needn't have worried. From the group of women surrounding the older teacher, Charity caught enough of their words to discover they were admiring and asking eager questions about her traveling suit. For another woman, the faint gratification in her expression would have been unbounded pleasure.

Mrs. Trumble edged up beside them. "Libby, we really should get these ladies inside off this noisy street." Suiting action to words, she collected Miss Sullivan while Mrs. Clark led Charity toward the store entrance. The inside was cool after the hot, whipping wind outside. As her eyes adjusted from bright sunlight to interior dimness, Charity saw that the store, while not overly large, was stocked in such a way that every bit of available area was used to advantage. Shelves along the walls to her left held equipment and tools that she had never seen before, but guessed were indispensible to a successful cattle or mining operation. The shovels, ropes, and pitchforks intermixed with them she knew to be vital to the maintenance of a farm, and undoubtedly were to a ranch as well. Sacks of flour and cornmeal, bolts of material, patent medicines, coal oil lamps, blue and white speckled graniteware coffeepots, cups and plates, and barrels of pickles, crackers, and dried beans jostled each other for space. Mops and brooms hung from the ceiling like leftover Hallows' Eve accessories. The large red wheel of a coffee grinder arched imposingly over the far end of the wooden counter set to the right of the door. Mr. Clark, now wearing a crisp white store apron, stood discreetly at the near end, assuring that no one left without paying for his acquisitions.

With Miss Sullivan firmly in tow, Mrs. Trumble said briskly, "We know you'll be wanting to rest a little. While the men tend to the shopping, we'd like you to come to the newspaper office, just down the street. We can have some tea and let you sit without being choked by train ashes and wood smoke. Believe me, I know what your trip was like. Not one bit improved, I'll wager, over what it was when we came by train to Laramie City three years ago."

Libby went behind the counter and hung up the apron that Ezra had surreptitiously returned to her. At Brinna's questioning glance, she said firmly, "I was here this morning and missed out on the official welcoming. So it's Ezra's turn now to take care of the store. I'll get my hat and be right with you."

As they left, Owen was studying his wife's list while Amos kept

Carolina in line by warning her that she wouldn't get a peppermint stick, her all-time favorite sweet, unless she behaved. Knowing from past sad experience that he meant it, she was sticking close to her brother and keeping her mouth shut. Cole and Griff had their heads together, sorting out which items they needed to purchase. Vince, surrounded by a flock of little ones whose faces shone with anticipation, was discussing with Ezra the merits of the contents of the glass jars of horehound drops, caramels, and rock candy lined up on the counter.

Brinna eyed her children warily. "Hope he knows better than to let them pick black licorice again. Last time, they got more on the outside than they did on the inside." She swept away this rueful observation with a wave of her hand as they stepped once more into the heat and glare of the summer day. "The town started out small, but we're progressing by leaps and bounds."

"My, yes," Libby put in. "We've grown from the first four buildings—the store, the livery stable, the newspaper, and Doc Fergus's office—to over two dozen. Link Monroe, who owns the saddle shop, is also a boot and shoemaker. Most of the businesses here actually serve more than one purpose. As you may have noticed, the post office is in our store. In addition to shoeing horses at the livery stable, Sam McKnight, the blacksmith, turns out metal hardware, such as buckets or cook pots. Even Doc Fergus builds furniture and anything else of wood we need here. That man can craft a cabinet or a blanket chest as fine as you'd ever want to see, then turn right around and, gentle as can be, cure a sick child of a raging fever."

"We don't have a regular church yet," Brinna said regretfully, "but we meet every Sunday, either in town or out at one of the ranches. We might be a distance from God's House, but we certainly welcome Him to our homes. Here we are," she added, as they came to a building with a glass window across which Clark's Valley *Clarion* was painted in sweeping red and gold letters. "We'll just go around to the side. We live and work in the same building, of course. All the businesses in town are set up that way for right now. But I told Vince flat out that our family and our business were two separate enterprises, and that mixing little ones and printer's ink was not a wise combination. Fortunately," she smiled as she ushered them up the step and through the house door, "he agreed."

They entered to the fragrance of hot tea and what Charity's nose immediately identified as molasses cookies. She drew in a breath as enticing as stepping into the warmth and good smells of Ma's kitchen back home. Fortunately, before she could pursue the thought and the heart tug that came with it, Brinna seated them on straight-backed chairs that obviously belonged to a dining room set. The attached cushions, in a brown and gold leaf pattern, gave the comfortable, much lived in room an unexpected dash of elegance. Charity, glancing down to make certain her skirt was properly arranged, froze in awe at the hooked rug laid over the rough floor planking. Autumn bronzed and butter yellow trees dropped their leaves so convincingly that she almost put out her hand to scoop up one. The scene was worked in such detail and contrast that a wending path started at her feet and continued through the sunlight and leaf shadows of the glade. In the distance, the edge of a sapphire blue lake looked so cool and inviting, she wanted to stick her bare toes in it.

Seeing her bemused expression, Brinna laughed. "I'm so glad you caught the depth of it. As many times as I've stood on it, I still feel like I'm walking through the trees. I did it so the young ones would know what it's like to wander in a cool forest and know there's more in this world than just these grassy, treeless plains."

"It's beautiful," Charity said, wondering how the busy woman had found the time to create such a masterpiece.

"Very artistically done," Miss Sullivan added. From her, this was sweeping approval.

Brinna smiled, clearly gratified at this praise from the two stylish Eastern women. "I'll just go help Flanna with the tea things." She hurried through the doorway from which those wonderful smells were wafting.

Libby turned eagerly to the visitors. "Ezra and I originally came from Minnesota. Brinna and Vince are from Virginia. We do so want to hear about your town and people."

Her obviously sincere request was echoed by Brinna, bearing a Limoges teapot as she followed Flanna, who was carrying a tray of napkins, cookies, and cups with delicate pink roses encircling the edges. "Yes, please. We've missed the shops and atmosphere of a quiet, settled town. Could you tell us about your school?"

Miss Sullivan could, and did. The women and Flanna listened raptly as she described the exterior, the giant oaks, the forsythia and lilac bushes that bloomed in the springtime, and the chrysanthemums and sumac that blazed gold and russet in the fall.

"Could you tell us about your church, too?" Libby's wishful question brought them up short. "As Brinna said, we don't have a building, yet, or a minister, but we'd surely like to visit yours in imagination, if we may."

So Charity and Miss Sullivan took turns weaving a picture of daily life in Fairvale. The church and the Gallaways, Doc, Greg and Sally Wagner, who ran the mercantile, Alvin Thompson, the postmaster, and John Shearer, editor of the *Tribune*. As their audience listened, enthralled, it hit Charity, finally and truly, just how much she had left behind, what she had been so eager to escape from.

Vince, trailed by his bevy of young ones, who were mercifully free of black licorice stains but carried with them strong odors of molasses, wintergreen, and lemon drops, came in as Miss Sullivan was describing the town square. "Owen and Cole are ready to go. They'll need to push some as it is to get home before dark," he added apologetically.

Brinna and Libby's farewells followed them down the street, to Cole and Owen standing beside their horses' heads, and the children already seated in the buckboard and wagon. Charity and Miss Sullivan hesitated momentarily as the question occurred to them of who was to ride with whom for this part of the journey. Cole, however, neatly solved it by indicating his buckboard. "Miss Sullivan, I thought maybe you could ride with Griff and me again. We'd sure like to hear more about the county fair you were describin'. Wouldn't we, Griff?"

The boy nodded enthusiastically. "Especially about the pie-eatin' contest!"

Cole chuckled. "A ten-year-old boy and his stomach are never far apart."

"As you wish," Miss Sullivan said primly enough, but turned with such promptness that only good manners kept Charity from staring after her in surprise at such swift acquiescence.

"Cole thought it'd be a little less jouncin' for her than in the wagon." As if in explanation, Owen gestured to the height of the seat. Charity, settling once more onto the blanket-padded bench, saw that the children were already deep into the business of making their peppermint sticks disappear, rendering even Carolina silent during the first stretch of the ride to the ranch.

"I'm afraid we won't be able to stop off to see the Claytons today," Owen said with genuine regret. "It looks like you and Miss Sullivan will be spendin' the night at our place."

"It was my understanding that Miss Sullivan and I would be staying with the Claytons, at least for the first few days," she said hesitantly, not wanting to seem ungrateful with any of the arrangements.

"That was the plan, but it's gettin' on to late afternoon already and will for sure be dusk by the time we get home. Ben knows that if we aren't at his place by sundown, we'll be headin' for my ranch. We don't like to be out on the road after dark if we can help it."

He didn't mention specific reasons for this preference, but Indians, wolves, and the dreaded rattlesnake came immediately to Charity's mind. Not really wanting to know, she didn't inquire. "I met Mr. Clayton this afternoon, of course. I'm so looking forward to meeting Mrs. Clayton. It seems like they're family already, with Mrs. Clayton and my Ma writing to each other for such a long time."

"Ben told us he knew Zane Edwards in the War a few years back. That after Zane died, Ben and Steve Jamison stopped to see Zane's Missus on their way home after their enlistments were up, and that she and Anne have been writin' ever since. That's how we knew about you. From Ben and Anne. They've spoken right highly of you."

"It's very kind of them to recommend me for the teaching position."

"Ben and Anne are folks you can put your trust in. Their opinions are mighty respected around here."

She felt her cheeks turn pink at the implied compliment and resolved once more to be worthy of it. "What about the other students?" She could wait no longer to know. "How many will there be?"

He paused, as if calling the roll in his head. "Let's see, now. The Claytons are sendin' three. Their oldest, Jason, is eighteen, so he won't be goin'. He'll be out helpin' Ben with the cattle. Luke's thirteen, Matt's nine, and Catty's six. Eve is only three, so for sure she'll have to wait another couple of years." He slid a sideways look at her. "I'm not one for carryin' tales, but I am a member of the school committee, and you have a right to know what to expect. Matt and Catty will be fine, but Luke just might be a handful. He's big, and tall for his age, and he can be an ornery cuss. Ben and Anne have done their level best to settle him down, but it don't seem to have taken. They'll back you up in any trouble, but I just feel like you should know ahead of time."

She tried to hide her dismay. She'd been praying that her students would be well mannered and eager to learn. With the exception of Carolina, the children she had met today had seemed to answer that prayer. And if the little girl actually came to school, Charity felt certain she could handle a five-year-old. She had, after all, once been one, with a certain amount of orneriness tucked inside, to boot. A big, strong, obnoxious boy was another matter. She thought of Miss Sullivan, stilling with one hard-eyed stare any rebellion her own students might proffer. But she had had decades of practice. Charity pressed her lips together. She'd work it out, somehow. She absolutely was not going to let a thirteen-year-old bully destroy her first, long dreamed of teaching position.

Owen broke the silence she had unintentionally prolonged. "As for the other young ones, Cole's grandson, Griff, of course. He's ten. Hannah Monroe is eight, and her brother Jonah's five. Link Monroe has the saddle shop, so they'll be comin' from town, along with the Trumbles' four oldest and the Clarks' granddaughter, Becky. She's fourteen. Ezra and Libby were debatin' whether she's too old, but she really wants to attend."

"Of course she's not too old," Charity said emphatically. "No one is ever too old to learn, if she really wants to—"

"Pa!" An insistent tugging on Owen's coattail interrupted Charity's heartfelt assertion. He turned and came nose-to-nose with Carolina. "You forgot us, Pa. You forgot me and Amos. We're going to school, too."

Owen blinked at his daughter in astonishment, then broke into laughter. He reached back and tugged playfully on her braid. "I certainly did forget to include you. How could my two favorite pupils on the list have slipped my mind like that?"

"Oh, Pa!" Carolina giggled.

"Does this mean you've decided you want to go to school after all?" he asked cautiously.

"Yes, Pa. Amos has been telling me all about it. He says he was just teasing when he told me Teacher would be old and ugly and mean and make me stand in the corner with a funny hat on my head and everyone would laugh at me." She stopped for breath.

"And what does Amos say now?" her father asked gravely.

"He says that Miss Michaels isn't old or ugly—owwh!" She let out a wail as Amos grabbed for her and tried to drag her down into the wagon bed.

"Amos," Owen said sternly.

"And that she smells pretty!" Carolina finished defiantly as Amos pushed her face down into the quilt they'd been sitting on.

"Amos," Owen roared, hauling on the lines to halt the team. Beet-red, refusing to look at him, Charity nevertheless reached over and grabbed the lines. Hands thus freed, he turned to observe his son trying to smother his daughter in the folds of the quilt. She was shrieking and Amos was muttering. His words were mostly incoherent, but Owen got the general idea.

Swinging over the seat into the box, Owen waded into the scuffle and succeeded in hauling Amos off Carolina. He held them at arms' length as each one delivered a last, futile kick in the other's direction. "That's enough. Both of you stop, now!"

Amos, fiery red, sagged in his father's grip. Carolina, feisty to the end, stuck her tongue out at her brother and was promptly hauled up short by her father. "Carolina, what have you been told a hundred times about tattlin'?"

Her eyes were wide and innocent. "I wasn't tattling, Pa."

"What were you doin', then?"

"I was just—just—" Her shoulders hunched in concentration. "I was just letting Teacher know that she's not old and ugly, even if Amos said she was!" Her burst of inspiration caused Amos to lunge toward her once more. Only Owen's grip on his collar saved her.

"Whoa, Amos. Back off. Now." The authority in his father's voice brooked no argument, and the boy slumped once more.

"But Pa—"

The half furious, half beseeching tone caused Owen to let out his own breath in a heartfelt sigh. "I know, son, I know. But now ain't the time to go into it or into what you've been told about hittin' your sister." He gestured to the buckboard behind them. Cole had halted a discreet distance back and he and Miss Sullivan were waiting, undoubtedly curious, for Owen to continue the journey. Griff, on the other hand, looked as if he'd like to join in the fracas—on Amos's side.

"We'll talk about this later at home. That's a promise, Amos. That's a promise to you, too, young lady." His voice and look assured each of his children that the discussion might be put on hold, but it would not be forgotten. He released his iron grasp and watched as the children, scowling fiercely, arms folded defiantly across their chests, settled in opposite corners of the wagon box, not unlike two prizefighters biding their time.

With another sigh, inward this time, Owen climbed back to the front seat. Charity solemnly handed him the lines and, with a nod of thanks, he just as gravely shook them out. The horses started with a lurch. Mortified, Owen couldn't look at her, couldn't think of anything to say to break the silence between them. As it got to the stretched out point, he glimpsed her movement out of the corner of his eye. He blinked, sure he was mistaken, but saw it again. No doubt this time. Her shoulders were shaking with silent laughter, and she was biting her lips hard to keep any sound from escaping.

Astonishment whipped through him. What could she possibly find amusing in the shameful little scene just past? Then he saw it as she obviously had and mirth rippled through him. *Don't you dare laugh. Fine example for the young ones that would be.* If only those shaking shoulders weren't just within reach of his side vision. "Uh … what subjects you aimin' to teach, Miss Michaels?"

If she found the question as dumb as he did, she didn't let on. To her credit, he detected only a quiver of laughter in her words, and a slight breathlessness in her tone that hadn't been there earlier. "Reading, arithmetic, the usual disciplines." The last word hung in the air between them, fragile as a butterfly in flight, heavy as the Union Pacific train she had recently abandoned.

She shot him a startled look and found him returning it. Before he could unwind his tongue for a response, she bent over and buried her face in the traveling skirt that was supposed to emphasize her mature dignity. Before he could respond to that movement, she jerked upright and averted her face to the scenery on her left. "Look. What are those?"

The words came out half strangled, which he ignored in his haste to respond. "Pronghorn. You have 'em in Ohio?"

"No. They look a little like deer, except for the shorter horns. I guess I'm just used to the racks on deer and elk."

"We have elk and mule deer, here. Pronghorn's a cousin to deer, I reckon. Shirttail, maybe, because of the horns rather than antlers."

"They're beautiful. They hardly seem to touch the ground. And they're so fast. Faster than deer, even."

The awe in her voice startled him, so that he looked again at the fleeing herd, watching with new eyes as they floated past and dropped out of sight into a swale.

She turned to face him, all earlier laughter and embarrassment forgotten in her pleasure. "I came here to teach," she confessed, "but I think I'm going to be the one who learns about things I've never even dreamed of."

"Pa!" Because he'd been engrossed in the conversation with the new teacher, Carolina's piping voice in his ear made Owen jump a foot and a half off the seat as he hauled on the lines.

"What is it, Carolina?"

"My kitty, Pa. Can we take him with us now?" They were passing the spot where the skunk had reigned supreme. *Trust Carolina to remember.* Was it his imagination or was there still a faint, telltale aroma in the air?

"No." The strain in his tone was unmistakable. Charity glanced at him, puzzled.

"But Pa—"

"Carolina. No." Even at the tender age of five, his willful daughter recognized the flat, not-to-be-disputed finality of his words. Owen reflected that she probably also remembered that she was already in hot water for tattling on Amos, twice at that. Even so, he was surprised at her acceptance, without more protest, of his putting his foot down. When she got something set in her head, she could argue 'til the cows came home.

He made sure she had settled safely in her corner of the wagon before he once more faced to the front. "Her *kitty*," he said to Charity, "is black with a wide white stripe. And a very memorable odor."

Charity gulped. "You mean her kitty is a *skunk*?"

He tipped his head in solemn affirmation. "Not just a skunk. I think this one is the granddaddy of all skunks. This is where we passed him on the way into town," he added helpfully.

Charity clapped a hand over her mouth and nose. "Oh, my," she said faintly.

"Exactly so," he said tersely.

They rode in silence for a time before he finally broke the quiet. "Reckon our territory looks a tad strange to you after livin' in the East and bein' used to lots of towns and trees."

A "tad" different hardly covered it in Charity's opinion, but she nodded politely as he continued.

"Not much of anythin' here just a few years ago besides wind, buffalo, and Indians. Still lots of wind, but not many buffalo or Indians now. Clark's Valley was a wide spot on the plains after the War finished. When Ezra Clark went back home to Minnesota after the fracas, he heard that a group of fellows who'd served out here had decided to come out and raise cattle. Bein' a storekeeper all his life except for when he was solderin', he didn't know beans about ranchin', but he figured for those folks who did know, a store would prove mighty handy. Fort Laramie was already boomin' as a supply stopover for folks goin' west, but the men he'd heard tell of reckoned they wanted to be a little further from the metropolis. They'd all felt squeezed by bein' in such close proximity with a thousand other soldiers day and night, and wanted some breathin' room. It worked out mighty fine, too, with Ezra knowin' the mercantile business, and Hank Fergus joinin' the group doin' carpentry as well as havin' doctorin' knowledge. Obadiah Beldane was plannin' on bein' a blacksmith and farrier, but that didn't pan out. He decided to stick with the Army a while longer."

Now going full speed on his subject, Owen didn't see how Charity winced at his last words. She knew about Obadiah Beldane, knew only too well why he'd foregone blacksmithing for a longer stay in the Army. She could never erase from her memory the anguish-filled night he had returned to Fairvale and very nearly destroyed Ma and Pa's marriage.

"—figured that was enough to start a town."

She came dully back to Owen's explanation with no idea how much she'd missed.

"Ben Clayton and Steve Jamison came out at the same time and commenced to raisin' cattle. Steve and his wife Amanda were killed in an Indian raid in '65. Ben and Anne are raisin' their two young ones, Matt and Catty."

This time, Charity's nervous lurch bolt upright caught his attention. He frowned at her suddenly pale face as she scanned the surrounding countryside. "No need to fret," he said quickly. "There's still some Indians 'round about, but they don't give much trouble. Always best to be alert and aware, however." In attempting to bolster her confidence, he unwittingly confirmed her earlier suspicion that Indians were a good reason not to be on the road after dark. Knowing that rattlesnakes didn't slink about at night, she dared not bring up the possibility of bears attacking them.

"How near is the Clayton ranch to yours?" she asked instead, with what she hoped was proper enthusiasm.

"They're about three miles west of our place, over on this side of Willow Creek from us. It's not good to try to ford the creek in the dark."

She took this explanation as more inviting than bears, wolves, and Indians, but still had her doubts about the last two. Rather than think about the possibilities of any of them, she again turned her attention to the surrounding countryside.

A short time later, Owen gestured to a fringe of trees ahead. "When we cross Willow Creek, we'll be on Half Moon range. Another mile and we'll be home."

CHAPTER TWENTY-FIVE

Charity's visions of wolves attacking fled, and she looked eagerly ahead as the wagon bumped down into the creek. As they came up the far bank out of the water, he shook his head. "Goin' to have to build a bridge across there one of these days. Can't see the home place from here," he added, "but it'll show up just over that rise."

The wagon topped the gentle slope and Charity saw the dot in the distance that eventually became a house and outbuildings. Her first sight of a genuine ranch thrilled her so that she clasped her hands to keep from reaching out. It resembled the farm in many ways, but the scarcity of trees and the dust picked up and whirled by the unceasing wind gave it a lonely air. Her head had suspected such barrenness, but her heart felt a stab at the loss of cool greenness. It struck her that the house area seemed incomplete, somehow, then realized there were no fences to keep out the vastness of the land pushing in on it. She thought of Brinna's hooked rug and suddenly understood perfectly the reasoning behind it. She had no time to fret further, however, for as the two rigs rattled closer to the house, a woman descended the back steps. She moved carefully, and Charity saw the pronounced swelling at her abdomen.

"That's Callie, my wife." Owen's pride and love were evident in those four brief words. Mrs. Corley started toward them, and he chuckled. "She's anxious to meet you, no doubt about it."

"I'm really looking forward to meeting her." Charity observed her lustrous hair and dark eyes as the woman stepped away from the path of the wagon and stood waiting for them to come up. Her welcoming smile, even before they reached her, confirmed Owen's assessment of her eagerness and chased the last butterfly from Charity's stomach.

Owen jumped down and reached to take his wife's hands. "You all right?" Low-voiced as it was, his concern came clearly to Charity, and the last of the chill in her heart followed in the wake of the departed butterfly.

"Yes, I'm fine," she assured him. "I just couldn't wait any longer." Her rueful admission was interrupted by Amos and Carolina, who came barreling toward her.

The warmth and joy of the family's reunion, even after only a few hours' separation, caused Charity's throat to tighten. *Mac and I will never —*

Fortunately, that unproductive line of reasoning was cut short as Callie, hands outstretched, approached Charity. "Miss Michaels," she said simply, "at last." If Charity was any longer in need of such assurance, the glow in Callie's eyes confirmed the joy contained in her welcome.

Cole's buckboard pulled up beside them. Griff leaped nimbly down and Cole assisted Miss Sullivan to the ground. If Callie was taken aback by the older woman's stiff formality, she hid it beneath a warm greeting that left no doubt of her own sincerity. Introductions made, Callie gestured to the house. "Won't you please come in? I have chicken pie in the oven and hot coffee on the stove." Before Cole could decline the invitation, she smiled at the three children and continued innocently, "There's also fresh buttermilk and dried-apple muffins." Amos and Carolina looked as eager as Griff.

Cole's nose twitched at the unmistakable aroma of hot chicken smothered in bubbling gravy. "We really shouldn't, if we're goin' to make it home before dark," he said reluctantly.

"You'll have to eat there or here," Owen said reasonably. "Might as well be here where it's already cooked and save the doin' of it yourselves."

"I'm afraid we'd have to eat and run," Cole temporized, then grinned at Griff. "We don't do much chicken pie makin'," he admitted. Griff shook his head vigorously, and Cole gave in.

Callie led them into the room that served as kitchen, eating, and sitting area. The décor was as basic as Brinna's had been, but here, too, efforts had been expended to make not just a house, but a home. Among the simple furnishings, a framed watercolor on the wall at the head of the eating table caught Charity's attention. It was of a flower garden in the full bloom of summer. Scarlet roses climbed an arching trellis. Crimson and white snapdragons, lavender sweetpeas and purple columbine, orange daylilies, and blush-pink gladioli crowded together behind a white picket fence. Faintly visible in the background, a white house with yellow shutters stood guard over the riotous testimony to nature's abundance.

Callie followed Charity's gaze. "Just a reminder of what we will have here someday. We mustn't let ourselves lose sight of that."

Owen slipped his arm about her shoulders. "Faith and work will get us there," he assured her. Her lips curved as if she had heard him say the words a hundred times before. At the sudden determination in the woman's eyes, Charity wondered if it had become their family motto. She wasn't given time to wonder further, for Callie was turning to the stove, preparing to dish up the meal. She laughingly refused Charity's and Miss Sullivan's offers of help, saying they were guests and to sit and relax after their long journey. Amos and Carolina put the last touches to the table. With damp-combed hair and fresh-scrubbed faces and hands, Owen, Cole, and Griff returned from the wash bench beside the back steps.

Like iron filings to a magnet, conversation during supper kept returning to "back home." Answering the questions put so eagerly to them, Charity and Miss Sullivan provided bits of information that seemed trivial to them, but which their news-parched hosts drank in as if they were cool, reviving waters.

With dusk deepening, Cole and Griff left immediately after the meal, and Owen and Amos went out to the delayed chores. Callie smiled, a little shy now at being alone with the eastern ladies. "I know you must be exhausted. We've fixed it so the two of you can sleep in Amos and Carolina's room. Carolina will come in with me, and Amos and Owen will sleep out here." She might have been a bit awed by her guests, but the firmness of her tone left them no room to protest disturbing the family's usual sleeping arrangements. "Owen will bring in your trunks so that you can make yourselves comfortable."

Arguments thus firmly overridden, Miss Sullivan and Charity soon found themselves in a small, sparsely furnished bedroom. The two beds, one on either wall, were covered with bright patchwork quilts. A dresser stood between them, and a table holding a washbowl and pitcher was positioned against the opposite wall. Once again, Charity thanked Ma's ingenuity in recommending she pack a smaller bag with her night things and a fresh change of clothing. By doing so, she had avoided the inconvenience of not being able to retrieve items from her trunk during the journey. Miss Sullivan had packed similarly. The ability to freshen up at the various stops along the way had enabled them to feel less bedraggled on the long trip than they otherwise would have. Charity's relief now at being able to properly prepare for bed far outweighed the earlier nuisance of having to carry and keep track of the extra bag.

Surveying their sleeping arrangements, she felt a sudden awkwardness at the thought of sharing a room with Miss Sullivan. The woman had, after all, been the terror of her school years, and the thought of intruding on her spinster privacy filled her erstwhile pupil with the urge to run howling down the road. She didn't, mainly because in this vast empty land there was no road to run howling down. She couldn't tell if Miss Sullivan, heretofore the ever-stern instructor, was also embarrassed at the sudden intimacy of their relationship. Apparently, Miss Sullivan decided that the best way to get through it was to ignore the reality of what couldn't be changed. Her matter of factness enabled Charity to act likewise, and their sleep preparations were carried out with surprisingly little self-consciousness.

More grateful than she could admit, Charity slid under the covers of the bed that was obviously Carolina's. Somehow, she couldn't imagine that Amos would be partial to the rose-sprigged calico pillowcase beneath her head. Miss Sullivan blew out the candle, and Charity heard her small but profound sigh as she settled into the other bed. It was with that sigh she realized that, however straight-laced Charlotte Sullivan might act, she was, at the moment, every bit as grateful as Charity to have reached this end of their journey.

Her thoughts turned to her soon-to-be pupils and she began doing the mental arithmetic. Fourteen children from ages five to fourteen, including Carolina if it came to that, would be expecting her to impart her vast knowledge very early Monday morning. *I'll have to go over my age-suitable lesson plans.* She began mentally weaving a schedule but fell asleep before she'd even finished ringing the bell to call her pupils to class.

***

A shrill voice woke Charity. Swimming up from the depths of dreamless sleep, it took her a moment to identify the source. Carolina, just outside the bedroom door, was voicing her opinion to the world. "But Ma, why can't I go wake up Teacher? She must be really lazy if she sleeps this late every morning."

Charity gathered the comment was a version of one the child had heard her parents utter over the little girl's tendency toward reluctance to rise and shine in the morning. Since the windowless room was pitch black, she assumed she hadn't really overslept. This belief was bolstered by Callie, who spoke more softly than her daughter, but whose words carried through the thin wall.

"We've already explained to you that we got up earlier than usual this morning so Pa could tend to the chores he had to put off yesterday. Miss Sullivan and Miss Michaels had a very long trip to get here. Understandably, they are exhausted. You will be polite when they come out. Is that clear?"

Guilt shot through Charity as she realized how their arrival yesterday had disrupted the ranch's normal routine by taking Owen away from what would otherwise have been a work-filled day. She had lived on a farm too long not to know how one day's absence could double the next day's already overflowing list of chores.

A stirring from the other bed caused her to miss Carolina's reply. Although she could see nothing, she raised up on her elbow. Relief flooded her. Obviously, Miss Sullivan was being *lazy* also. She heard the scratch of a match striking, and the little room flared into soft gloom. The wavering shadows steadied as Miss Sullivan touched the flame to the candle on the dresser. Eyes crinkled to slits against the sudden brightness, Charity saw that Miss Sullivan was scarcely even blinking. *She must be used to waking in utter darkness and bringing forth light.*

Miss Sullivan glanced over at her and spoke in a voice too low to carry into the next room. "From the sounds, it appears we are derelict in our responsibility to know, from the total absence of light, that we were supposed to be up and doing at this hour. Whatever hour this may be," she added dryly.

Miss Sullivan making a joke? Charity was so bemused by the possibility that, once again, she was able to dress without undue embarrassment either for herself or for Miss Sullivan. Their morning preparations were carried out to the accompaniment of Carolina's observations on their tardiness and Callie's stern admonition to cease or she would do the ceasing for her.

"But Ma, I'm not being incorr—incorrdrigible." Carolina's protest held shocked hurt.

Charity, pinning up her hair—by feel, since there was no mirror in the room—caught Miss Sullivan's eye and saw her mouth assume its usual grim line. Even that evasive tactic couldn't, however, completely conceal the twitch of her lips. Charity looked hastily away, lest the laughter bubbling within her escape in a most unteacherly fashion. Suddenly remembering another little girl who had once upon a time used words almost as big as herself, an unwelcome thought skittered through her. *Did people smile at me, as amused by my large vocabulary as I am now with Carolina?* She quickly sobered and resolved that the child's accomplishment was something she would encourage, not belittle.

As they entered the other room, Callie looked up from the stove and smiled. "Good morning. I hope you slept well." Carolina, standing at the table arranging the silverware beside the plates she'd downturned to discourage the flies that persisted in believing they, too, were entitled to a share of breakfast, opened her mouth. The look Callie gave her speedily closed it again.

"We slept quite well, thank you," Miss Sullivan said smoothly. "What can we do to help? There must be something." She spoke in such a no-nonsense, stern teacher manner that Callie's emerging refusal changed swiftly to appreciation.

"There's milk to be strained and cornmeal to be set cooking. The water's just boiling." With one elbow she indicated the milk bucket on the bench, and with the other, the container of cornmeal on the counter beside her. Without pausing to discuss it, Charity took over the nearly full pail and Miss Sullivan reached for the spoon to measure the golden-yellow grain into the briskly bubbling pot.

Carefully pouring milk into the strainer, as she had done a thousand times, Charity looked up to discover Carolina staring open-mouthed at her. "You know how to strain milk?"

The little girl's blatant disbelief so startled Charity that she jiggled the pail and almost spilled the precious contents onto the floor. Recovering her aim in time, she said casually, "Of course. I can milk a cow, separate the cream, and churn butter, too."

The news of these abilities, which Carolina had obviously never considered that a teacher who had lived all the way "back East," wherever that was, would possess, temporarily silenced her. But when Amos and Owen came in from the chores, she waylaid her brother and announced, loudly and clearly, "Teacher knows how to milk and churn butter!"

Amos finally broke the echoing silence that filled the room after this pronouncement. "Well, shucks. I can do that stuff, too." His tone was so *what's the big deal?* that it actually momentarily deflated his sister.

Before she could recover, Owen said sternly, "Mind your tongues, both of you."

Charity hid her face by ducking farther over the strainer. She had long ago lost track of the miles she and Rose had accumulated riding the farm's blooded horses out to exercise. But this "incorrdrigible" child didn't need to know everything about her teacher just yet. Charity had a few other surprises she was holding back, too.

After Owen finished saying the blessing, into which he worked a large thank you for the presence of Miss Michaels and Miss Sullivan, they turned their plates upright and Owen began filling them in on the plans for the day. "We'll take you on over to the Claytons after breakfast. I'm sure Anne is as impatient to meet you as we were."

"We don't want to take you away from your ranch work longer than we already have."

"That's right nice of you to consider, but I was plannin' on goin' over anyway. Ben added a room onto the back of the house last summer. The south end's the kitchen, and the north end's a sleepin' area for the boys. With Jason turnin' eighteen, and Luke and Matt shootin' up like cornstalks, Anne said it just wasn't proper any more for them to be crowded into the main room like rabbits in a burrow." He took a bite of cornmeal mush. "But then she said she wanted a gallery—guess some folks call them porches, now—on the backside of *that* room. When Ben asked her what in thunder for, she said so she could stand and watch the sunrise without bein' blown clean away by the wind. 'Course now that she's gettin' one, all the womenfolks 'round here think they should have one, too."

"You gonna build us one, Pa?"

Amos's eager question was drowned out by Carolina. "What's a gal-a-ree?"

Owen flashed a grin in his wife's direction. "A gallery is a room that has a roof and a floor, but the only wall is the one that attaches it to the house. It's where fine ladies like your Ma can sit of an afternoon and drink tea and look out all the way to the horizon."

Callie laughed. "As if there's time of an afternoon to sit idly and drink tea." But she couldn't hide the wistful note in her voice.

Unmindful of the others watching, he reached out and pressed his hand over hers. "There will be someday, Callie. And just to make certain we're prepared when that time comes, when I finish helpin' Ben build his, he'll come this way and we'll do up one for you."

She gasped. "Owen, I never dreamed that we'd have one, too."

"I'm bein' sneaky," he confessed. "With Ben buildin' one first, he'll get all the kinks worked out, and then we'll proceed with ours with all speed and know-how. That is, if you want one." Her radiant smile gave all the answer he needed.

After breakfast, in thanks for the Corleys' hospitality, and to spare Callie at least a few chores, Charity and Miss Sullivan insisted on helping with the dishes and tidying up. Before they climbed up to the high wagon seat to make the trip to the Claytons, Callie embraced each of them. However surprised Miss Sullivan might have been to be included, she unbent enough to give her a stiff hug back. "I'm so very glad you've come here," Callie murmured. "It really is a dream come true."

"Even better than the gallery-porch?" Amos asked mischievously.

"Yes," she said softly. "Even better than the gallery-porch. And that's saying a lot." So they were all laughing when the wagon rattled away.

In some ways, this last leg of their trip seemed to take longer than all the days on the train put together. The three of them were scrunched literally elbow to elbow on the unyielding board seat, and the wind was gusting harder than the day before, so conversation was difficult. Charity was just as glad. It gave her time to sort out what had taken place so far and to anticipate the pleasant events to come. She was eager to see the new schoolhouse. Only then could she fit her already formulated ideas with the reality. But with both Mr. Clayton and Mr. Corley working on the porch today, Friday, she didn't see how they could squeeze in the time to take her there. The scarcely started lesson plans reared their heads again. She sighed. So much to see, accomplish, and experience. And she wanted to do all of it at the same time.

They topped a rise, and Owen pointed toward the bottom of the slope. "Willow Creek. The house is just the other side."

CHAPTER TWENTY-SIX

Charity stared in wonder at the green trees fringing the small creek. She thought she'd never seen anything so pretty in her life, and she'd only been in the midst of this tree-barren land for less than a day. Mrs. Corley and Mrs. Clayton had endured it for years. Once again she thought of Brinna's rug and Callie's painting. *The women who live here are far stronger than I could ever be.* Miss Sullivan stirred beside her, and Charity glanced over to find that the older woman's gaze, too, was fixed on the cool greenery in front of them. For the first time, it occurred to her to wonder how her former teacher would fare living in such an unforgiving country. The answer came with surprising promptness. *She has the spirit of determination these other women possess. If she had to, she, too, would make it work.* A new respect for prim, proper, unyielding Miss Sullivan, esteem heretofore unrealized from pupil to teacher, darted through her.

The horses dipped into the creek and the wagon followed with a lurch. Each clinging to the wooden seat with both hands, Charity and Miss Sullivan peered through the willow fringe ahead. Then they were out of the creek and rolling toward a house totally unsheltered from the blazing sun. They saw the corrals, larger by far than any she had seen in Ohio, and simple outbuildings of barn and chicken coop. Charity glimpsed another low building and wondered briefly about its purpose, but the sound of hammering snagged her attention.

A figure she recognized as Mr. Clayton was stretched up, pounding a nail into a post of the soon-to-be-finished porch. A boy of nine or ten was wielding a hammer near the man's feet. The new wood gleamed against the house siding already weathered gray by the relentless sun and wind. They finished driving in the nails, and, in the sudden silence, the jangling of the wagon traces sounded unnaturally loud. The shotgun resting alongside the flooring seemed to leap into Ben Clayton's hand as he turned, at the same time motioning the boy to stand behind him. Recognizing Owen, he lowered the barrel and the boy edged back into view. Ben called something toward the standing-open back door. A woman leaned out. When she caught sight of the visitors, her face lit up. A little girl about six years old and a toddler materialized on either side of the woman, who hastily smoothed the rich auburn hair caught in a bun at the back of her head. The older child was a towhead, the ends of her neatly braided light blonde hair brushing her shoulders. Sunlight caught the smaller child's hair which—there was no other word for it— glowed the shade of a just-peeled carrot. She, too, had stubby braids, but strands spiked defiantly from the tight weaving, defeating the intended neat appearance.

As they neared enough to make out features, Charity caught sight of the egg-sized lump adorning the smaller girl's forehead. Mr. Clayton had mentioned that his daughter Eve had tried to climb a tree and failed, netting her a hefty bump. He hadn't been exaggerating.

Ben, walking with the four, took off his hat and waved it in welcome. He assisted Miss Sullivan down, while Owen lent a hand to Charity over the high wheel. Along with the two little girls now clinging to her skirt, Ben drew the woman forward. "Anne, this is Miss Sullivan, and this is Miss Michaels. Ladies, my wife, Mrs. Clayton."

Anne Clayton closed the gap between them by reaching out her hands. "I'm so very glad to meet you at last." The lilt in her voice left no doubt of her sincerity. She clasped Miss Sullivan's hand warmly, her deep brown eyes sparkling. "Welcome to our home."

Miss Sullivan nodded her appreciation and drew Charity forward. "This is Miss Michaels," she said, and stepped back to allow the two women the full measure of their meeting.

Anne took both of Charity's hands in hers. The sparkle in her eyes became a glow of joy. "I feel like I already know you from your mother's letters, but to finally get to meet you takes my breath away." She stopped speaking and smiled, which told Charity more than a hundred words could.

"I just wish Ma could be here for this moment. She'd be so happy to see you and know that you're just the way your letters sound."

Wistfulness flitted across Anne's features, but was replaced with a quick smile. "Through our letters, we've become very good friends over the years. Now she and I have a chance to know each other even better, because you are here. I'm deeply grateful for that." She blinked away the mist in her eyes and quickly reached out to the boy standing beside Ben. "This is Matt. He's nine. He'll be one of your pupils come Monday."

The boy removed his wide-brimmed hat. "Pleased to meet you, ma'am." He put out his hand to shake Charity's, and she saw that his eyes were as gray as campfire smoke.

"Thank you, Matt. I'm glad you'll be joining our school adventure." He looked a little uncertain at her terming school an adventure, and stepped back beside Ben.

As if to urge them forward for their introductions, Anne had put an arm around each of the little girls still clutching her skirt.

"You must be Catty."

The child's face registered astonishment at Charity's knowledge, but at a slight prodding from Anne, she left the shelter of the skirt and stepped forward. "I'm Catherine. I'm pleased to meet you, ma'am." She bobbed a little curtsey before retreating to her mother's side.

"And this is Eve." Anne gently pushed the little girl forward, but the child took only the smallest of steps, the firm line of her clamped-shut mouth duplicating her resistance. "She's not used to being around people she doesn't know," Anne said apologetically.

"That's quite all right," Charity assured the child. "We've been meeting lots of new people, too, and sometimes it's a little scary." The toddler stared at her with the darkest blue eyes Charity had ever seen.

Catty stirred. "Are you really our new teacher?" The mixture of hope and uncertainty in her voice went straight to Charity's heart.

"Yes, I am. Are you excited to start school on Monday?"

"Will you read stories to us? Ma says you might."

"We'll do lots of things. But reading is definitely one of them. I brought books with stories just especially for that."

Anne's intake of breath made her look up and catch her own breath. The glow of joy had returned in full measure. "You brought books?" The wonder in her brown eyes was as if Charity had just announced that she'd brought the Book of Life from Saint Peter's desk beside the Pearly Gates.

"Yes. A volume of Wordsworth's poems. *Robinson Crusoe* and *Jane Eyre* for the older students. *Mother Goose* for the younger ones. *Godey's Lady's Book* and the *Farmer's Almanac.* A variety, to be sure, but all excellent reading practice and enjoyable, too."

With each revelation, Anne's expression became more wonder-filled. Ben chuckled. "My wife likes book readin'," he said in explanation of her silence. "I'm not much f'r it myself, but I've caught her readin' the labels on cans of horse liniment and bottles of castor oil at the mercantile."

This was obviously not the first time Anne had heard him tell this story on her, but she merely wrinkled her nose at him, the deep pride in his tone far outweighing his light teasing. She gestured behind her. "We're leaving you standing in this hot sun. Please, come to the house."

Ben and Matt joined Owen, who had been standing quietly to the side while the introductions were performed. "Guess we'd better get this baggage to the house and unloaded. Catty, Eve, do you want to hitch a ride?"

At his invitation, Catty hurried to the wagon and scrambled into the bed. Eve, not to be outdone, promptly abandoned the safety of Anne's skirts and followed closely on her heels. Unable to make the jump to the lazy board step to get over the side, her small face screwed into vexation. Ben caught her from behind and swung her up and in before she could begin a howl of protest. With the women walking to the side, out of the direct path of the horses, they approached the house.

The unfinished porch didn't possess any steps. Ben had placed a wide board from the ground to the porch flooring and their heels sounded hollowly against the improvised ramp. Entering the kitchen, it took a few seconds for Charity's vision to adjust to the dimness after the glare of outdoors. It wasn't perceptibly cooler, but at least the sun was no longer beating unmercifully on their heads. The room extended the width of the house. To the right of the door through which they had entered, Hudson's Bay blankets hung from a rod near the ceiling. The blankets were drawn together, shutting off whatever space was behind them. The black-striped scarlet background was a cheerful addition in the kitchen's muted light. A black cook stove stood against the far wall, to the right of a closed door, and opposite the stove a dry sink sat in front of a window with real panes of glass. A stout wood post jutting from the windowsill supported a square of heavy planking extended above the window.

At this point in Charity's survey, the two little girls came dashing through the outside doorway, Eve giggling wildly as Catty chased her. At the sight of the two strangers, her merriment died and she made a beeline for the safety of Anne's skirts. Catty pulled up abruptly and she, too, although walking decorously, slipped to her mother's side.

Anne's glance had followed Charity's. "Ben put in the window," she explained. "He was really reluctant because of the Indian scares we used to have." For the briefest instant, her fingers gently touched Catty's hair. Charity remembered that Owen had told how Matt and Catty's parents had been killed in an Indian raid and that the Claytons were raising the orphans. "He didn't want to provide an extra entrance to the house. After we discussed the situation—" her mouth curved up "—he agreed, as long as it could be closed off with an inside shutter. Now we don't have to keep candles burning all day."

Charity looked around the room that, even with the door open and window unshuttered, was still dusky. How could the inhabitants so casually shrug off the mental and physical gloom induced by the lack of sunlight at this late morning hour? She thought of the light, airy kitchen at home and once more sensed a depth to living in this edge-of-the-world place that she never could have imagined in placid Fairvale.

Anne turned to the stove and reached for the kettle. "Girls, please set out the tea things." Catty, trailed by Eve, immediately headed for a walnut cupboard on the left-hand wall.

Ben, bearing Charity's trunk, stomped into the room. Owen and Matt, close behind him, were gripping Miss Sullivan's cases. Anne hurried to push aside the Hudson's Bay blankets, revealing a narrow space carved out of the already limited confines of the kitchen. Two rope beds were lashed to the long side wall and a wooden dresser sat tucked between them. "We hope you don't mind sharing the room," she said anxiously as the men lowered their burdens to the floor.

"Of course not," Miss Sullivan said firmly. As usual not one to beat around the bush, she added, "But we don't wish to displace any of your family members. "These beds—"

Ben paused outside the blanket curtain. "It's all right, ma'am. Our sons Jason and Luke—they're out on the range now and will be in later— have moved out to the bunkhouse with Nightowl and Cork." Charity remembered the building she hadn't been able to identify as they approached the house. That had to be the bunkhouse, and was where folks lived and slept when there wasn't enough room in the main house. *Not unlike the cabin on the farm, then, just with a different name.*

"Rest assured," Ben said, as if reading her thoughts, "you're not roustin' anybody out that's not willin' to go."

"Heavens, no," Anne added. "Jason's been more than ready to go for some time, and Luke—" for the briefest instant a shadow crossed her face and was gone so quickly it might never have been there at all "—is determined to follow Jason's lead, at least in this. So it's all worked out perfectly." The kettle shrilled and she turned to reach for it, effectively bringing an end to the discussion.

Ben and Owen, shadowed by Matt, took their cups of coffee outside, ostensibly to discuss the important details of the progress of the porch, leaving the women in the kitchen to become acquainted over cups of tea. For a few minutes, all was peaceful inside and out. Then the hammering began again—in triple refrain this time. After a couple of minutes of attempting to lift her voice over the pounding, and unable to hear her guests, Anne set her cup into her saucer with a decisive clink. "That's enough," she said so distinctly that Charity and Miss Sullivan had no trouble making out her words. "Ladies, if you'll come with me, I think we can solve this problem before we all come down with raging headaches." She led the way out the door, striding past the three carpenters who finished hammering their respective nails before pausing to look up at her approach.

"Anne?" Ben clearly hadn't any idea why his wife looked so harassed.

"We're going down to the creek. We'll be back in a bit."

"Can we go, too, Ma?" Catty asked eagerly from the doorway. Eve, poking her head through the space between the door and her sister, peered at her mother silently, but her expression was just as pleading.

Anne shook her head and held out her hand. "You don't think we'd go and dip our toes and not include you?" The two girls rushed to her.

Ben said quietly, "You take care."

It might have been just a casual parting endearment, but Charity saw Anne's eyes meet Ben's and her sober nod. Then the moment was past and they were teetering down the plank walkway and turning in the direction of the green willows and the cool water, and Anne had shed her gravity. "I really don't mind the noise, since I know how wonderful it will be when the porch is finished. But right now, I want to hear all about your trip, and your town, and your family, and—"

Missing Ma and Pa and Rose as she was, to say nothing of Mac, Anne's anticipation brought warmth to the lonely spot in Charity's heart. She noticed that Miss Sullivan, too, looked almost animated. With the girls a little ahead, but, Charity noted, always clearly in Anne's sight, they approached the rippling little creek. Anne made Catty and Eve stand back away from the bank while she edged carefully around the stones in her path to the water. Noticing Charity's bewildered expression, Catty said concisely, "Rattlesnakes. She always makes us wait here while she looks."

Shaken with her old terror of snakes, Charity frantically scanned the ground at their feet. "Don't worry," Catty said soothingly, "if there are rattlers, they'll be down in the rocks sunning themselves, not over here." Determined not to reveal her fear in front of her new student, Charity could only hope that her face showed her normal color, not the grasshopper green she fully expected it was.

Anne, with a regal bow, indicated two smooth rocks just back from the water, but enticingly sheltered by gracefully slanting willow fronds. Miss Sullivan, with a glance at Charity that clearly told her to quit acting like an idiot, promptly joined Anne while Charity, inspecting the ground with every step she took, followed behind. They sat while Anne chose another rock close beside theirs, and the barefoot little girls headed for the water, still always within Anne's sight. Here, the hammer-pounding was only a faint background accompaniment to their getting-acquainted chatting.

"Tomorrow afternoon, we're having a get-together at the schoolhouse. The men all insist it's 'to break it in properly,' but we women know that it's by far the best way for you to meet the families around here, and more of the children you'll be teaching. The children always come to our parties," she added almost as an afterthought. "We aren't fancy by any means, but we always enjoy an opportunity to get together. We always hold these gatherings during the day, so that we can be home by nightfall." She didn't explain further, but Charity remembered Owen Corley saying the same thing. She thought about wolves and bears and Indians and couldn't prevent a shudder.

She realized that in her daydreaming—or nightmaring—she had missed part of Anne's explanation, but came back in time to hear the distinct touch of mischievousness in her voice. "It will also give you a chance to see where you'll be teaching." She smiled at Charity's quick breath of anticipation. "Sunday morning, church services will be held at

Cole Leverett's place. Then we have a potluck afterward. Monday, of course, school will start at nine o'clock." Her sigh of pleasure at the words left her listeners with no doubt that this was a dream come true. "We picked a little later starting time to ensure that all the children can arrive without undue rushing since some will be coming from town and others from the ranches hereabout."

She raised her face to the sun shining out of the endlessly blue sky. "I expect we'd better be heading back. All that nail pounding will have made the men hungrier than a snapping turtle with a stuck jaw, as Ben likes to say."

Charity started. "That's just what Pa says." Her tone held as much amazement at hearing the familiar words in this strange place as if she'd just found a gold nugget larger even than Caleb Braden's. She had no time to dwell on the coincidence, however, as Catty and Eve charged toward them, shrieking with laughter, wet dress tails slapping against their knees.

Once back in the kitchen, Anne tried to persuade Miss Sullivan and Charity to sit at the table while she prepared the noon dinner. "We're not guests," Miss Sullivan said firmly. "We know we've already disrupted your morning schedule, and we have no intention of putting you further behind in your work. We'll do whatever we can to help."

Anne glanced at their dresses, which were more elegant than her own work-faded calico. Intercepting her look, Charity felt a strange stab of recognition—and guilt. Amity Terrill had stood by Ma's table, not so very long ago, in a dress Charity and Rose had dismissed as too fancy for plain kitchen work, and so they had dismissed its wearer, too, and refused to assign her any chores. Charity felt her cheeks redden with embarrassment, which only deepened when Miss Sullivan looked at her oddly.

Before the silence could become awkward or Anne protest further, Charity said with a determination equal to Miss Sullivan's, "We have every intention of helping with the work, not adding to it." And found her words a strange echo of Amity's.

Anne gave in before their double insistence. After one direct look at each of them to ensure they meant it, she nodded. "All right. There's always more than enough work to go around. You'll find aprons in the cupboard."

So it was that Miss Sullivan was soon mixing a batch of cornbread. Charity was at the dry sink in front of the window, washing the Wedgwood cups and saucers they had abandoned earlier in Anne's haste to escape the noise. Charity's eyes went from the fragile blue and white cup in her hands to Anne, standing at the stove stirring a pot of bean soup. *This is her cool forest woodland, her flower garden bursting with color and fragrance behind the white picket fence.* Even as Mrs. Trumble and Mrs. Corley, Anne Clayton had found her own bit of beauty to treasure in this roughly-settled exacting land.

The afternoon was as filled with work as any typical day at home — with Charity discovering an inconvenience she had never given a thought to that added mightily to the burden of the chores. On the farm, she had always accepted the proximity of water for cooking, drinking, and washing of dishes and clothes. First it had been brought from the well near the back door. Then, several years ago, Pa had installed a pump at the kitchen sink, so that, with only a few maneuverings of the handle, abundant water flowed for any task necessary, requiring only heating on the stove if such luxury was desired. Here, water was hauled laboriously from the creek by bucket. Every precious drop was used to the utmost as even leftover dish and hand-washing water was carried back outside and carefully poured onto the garden patch at the side of the house. After volunteering innocently and cheerfully to make the trek to the creek, Charity quickly learned the value of restraint in any watery endeavors.

The afternoon passed in a haze of work. Miss Sullivan and Charity, whose firm insistence again won out over Anne's embarrassed protests, weeded the garden while Anne ironed the clothes she had washed the day before. Since the stove needed to be kept going to heat the flatirons, she mixed a batch of bread dough, setting it to bake while she tackled the stubborn wrinkles in dresses and pinafores. Those tasks completed, she gathered her sewing basket and a froth of material that was apparently a work-in-progress. She smiled at her daughters. "Would anyone like to go to the creek with me while I get some of this done?" It was now hotter inside the house than outside, so the little girls lost no time in chorusing their delight.

Since the children had not spoken to her unless she spoke first, Charity was surprised when Catty turned to her. "Ma's making a new dress for me to wear to school on Monday," she confided. "It's pink with little white flowers," she added with evident pride.

"I'm certain it will be beautiful on you," Charity said truthfully. "And you know what? Pink has always been my favorite color, too." Catty beamed, then, losing her bravery, retreated.

Anne turned to Charity and asked with sudden shyness, "Would you mind bringing one of your books and reading to us while we're down there?"

Remembering Ben's remarks about Anne's love of reading, Charity tried to hide her smile, but sharing the chores as they had this afternoon, she now felt comfortable enough that she couldn't resist teasing a little. *"Robinson Crusoe* or *Jane Eyre?"*

Before Anne, who looked as if either would be a small piece of heaven, could voice her preference, Miss Sullivan spoke up. "I also have *Pride and Prejudice*, by Miss Austen. It's handy in my traveling bag, and that way Charity won't have to dig into her trunk."

Charity, who had seen her reading it on the train and knew that she was well into it, felt surprise that Miss Sullivan would be so willing to go back to the beginning instead of speeding on to the end. But the older woman was already heading toward the Hudson's Bay blankets to retrieve her crocheting and the book in which, as she had told Ethan, she "found new meaning with each reading."

Back from the creek, they prepared the simple supper in the still-sweltering kitchen. Ben and Matt came in with the milk bucket, accompanied by a young man who strongly resembled Ben in build and mannerisms and a younger boy with flaming red hair and, Charity decided immediately, an attitude. As Ben introduced their older son, eighteen-year-old Jason stepped forward and shook hands politely. Luke, thirteen, under his father's watchful eye also shook hands, but Charity felt antagonism flow from his hand to hers, and her heart sank. Here was the trouble she'd been praying would not arrive.

After supper and the dishes were done, the family went early to bed. Charity collapsed gratefully onto her rope mattress, prepared to worry about what Luke's arrogant attitude would mean for the school. She heard Miss Sullivan's weary sigh. Before Luke's name had time to form in her thoughts, she fell into exhausted sleep.

CHAPTER TWENTY-SEVEN

A stirring outside the scarlet blankets brought Charity awake. In the darkness of the windowless alcove, she had no way of guessing what time it was, but the rattling of stove lids and the snapping of sparks emerging into flame were as familiar to her waking as any chiming clock could have been. She heard Miss Sullivan's rope springs creak as she, too, became aware of the time-to-get-up noises. They heard heavy footsteps across the floor, the back door open and shut, and booted steps across the unfinished porch, and knew that Ben had retreated from the kitchen for their convenience.

Refusing to groan, Charity got up and peeked around the blanket. The kitchen was indeed empty, but the shutter had been raised above the sink window, showing a sky still glittering with stars. A candle had been left burning on the table to light their way. Hearing stirrings from the other room at the front of the house, where Ben and Anne and the children had slept, she reached for her clothes.

Another work-filled day rushed at them, jammed with all the usual chores of tending the chickens and pigs, processing the milk, hauling water from the creek for the garden, preparing the meals, and cleaning house. Besides these tasks, Anne had Catty's dress to finish and a covered dish to prepare for the party at the schoolhouse that afternoon.

Yesterday, Charity had privately bemoaned the lack of easily accessible water. Today, she discovered a second inconvenience that Anne had to put up with—another one that Charity had never seriously considered. And the second lack was, to her, the more discouraging of the two. At home, the springhouse and icehouse had provided abundant coolness for storage of food prone to spoilage. Sometimes she had been annoyed at the time and effort necessary to retrieve eggs, butter, milk, and meat from their respective chilly abodes, but that afternoon she would have paid dearly to know that either one was just a short walk out the door and down the pathway. In addition to taking a covered dish to the get-together that afternoon, they would be taking one to the after-services potluck on Sunday. What Anne hadn't mentioned was the difficulty of keeping such contributions, of necessity prepared ahead of time, from spoiling in the unrelenting heat. With neither a springhouse nor an icehouse just down the path, Anne stored her milk, butter, and eggs in the cool, rippling creek waters, and her vegetables and other perishables in an earthen dugout Ben had constructed for her on the side of the creek bank. There was, of course, always the threat of their supplies being plundered by night-marauding animals, but so far the traps Ben had rigged had proved effective for the most part. All this preservation, of course, meant more trips to the creek.

For today's outing, Anne planned to bake a ham. As she explained to Charity and Miss Sullivan, for these events the women traded off providing vegetables, meats, and desserts. It was her turn to bring a meat dish. A ham would be a pleasant change from beef and would also feed a large number of people. For the next day's after-church potluck, she had decided that doughnuts would be easy to make, would keep overnight without spoiling, and would transport easily. Midmorning, while the ham baked, they took turns churning, dusting, and standing over the bubbling pot of lard and drawing out the golden circles.

They were so busy attempting to get everything done in the limited space of time that before Charity could really grasp that it was true, they were in the wagon, on their way to the party. *On the way to the schoolhouse.* Charity whispered the words to herself, savoring the knowledge that, after all this time, the building was only three miles away. As from a distance, she heard Ben explaining that she and the children would be walking and he hoped it wouldn't prove too tiring for her each day. She came down from her cloud far enough to assure him that she was used to walking such a distance, and that it wouldn't be a problem at all. Mature or not, she couldn't resist craning her neck at the last, when Ben announced that the school was just the other side of the next rise. They topped the incline and she saw it in the distance.

She had known from the beginning that it would not be the gracious brick building that housed Fairvale's students, but she felt a definite stab of surprise at the reality. The small wooden structure strongly resembled the cabin back home. The chinked logs stood darkly against the sunlit prairie. The sloping roof, so new that the shingles still gleamed golden, boasted a shiny pipe from which a plume of smoke rose and scattered in the strong breeze. Three buildings standing at the back, undoubtedly the boys' and girls' outhouses and the horse shed, had not yet begun to weather, thus also proclaiming their newness. A lone cottonwood thrust skyward near a line of trees indicating Willow Creek's flow toward the sea—and the school's source of drinking water.

Ben had stopped the team at the top of the rise, as if to give her a panoramic view of her new domain. They were all looking at her, as if gauging her reaction. The truth swept through her as cleanly as the wind gusting past her. *This is my school.* Pride of possession blazed within her and she raised her face to their waiting ones. "It's beautiful," she whispered. "Thank you."

Short as the speech was, they must have caught its heartfelt sincerity, for Ben laughed outright. "Well, then, let's go to a party!" He flipped the lines, starting the horses forward again toward the people milling about and the buggies and wagons already clustered near the front door.

The next few minutes passed in a flurry of greetings from Doc Fergus, Callie and Owen Corley, and Cole Leverett. Libby Clark and Brinna Trumble, seeming like tried and true friends in this push of strangers, stayed close beside her, as if to ensure that the community's evident eagerness to meet the new school ma'am wouldn't overwhelm her.

She tried to remember the names being thrust at her along with the hands reaching to shake hers in pleased greeting. She met Link and Lillie Monroe and their children, Hannah, who was eight, and Jonah, five. She was introduced to the Clarks' fourteen-year-old granddaughter, Becky. Remembering that they had been concerned that she was too old to attend school, Charity made a special point of telling her warmly, "I'm so glad that you'll be in my class." The anxiety in the girl's eyes vanished in a flash of pleasure. The Clarks then introduced her to their youngest daughter, Cora, who appeared to be only a year or two older than Charity herself.

Phebe Braden patiently waited her turn, then, accompanied by a barrel-chested, bearded man stepped up to her. "Miss Michaels, this is my husband, Mr. Braden."

He evidently did not recognize her from their recent near-miss encounter, but his face was firmly plastered in Charity's memory. He shook her hand politely, but as he stepped aside, she heard him mutter, "All this schoolin' foolishness! Blame waste of time—" Before Charity could hear the end of *that* fascinating dialog, Phebe, clearly embarrassed, hastily dragged him out of earshot, then looked back to see if the teacher had heard. Charity gave her a big smile filled with as much innocence as she could muster. It must have been enough, for Phebe returned it with one of her own that held distinct relief.

The children, temporarily freed from the usual restraints on their exuberance, darted among the adults, chasing each other and giggling at everything and nothing. During a lull in the introductions, Charity had a chance to study the room where she would soon be in charge of those energetic little bodies. She'd come in through the cloakroom where the children would hang their outdoor clothing and store their lunch buckets. A teacher's desk, temporarily decked with the evening's potluck offerings, sat at the front of the room. Each of the side walls boasted a window with real glass. Strung haphazardly along the four walls, the children's double desks were currently serving as seating for those individuals either bold enough to sit on the tops or slight enough to maneuver onto the seats. Assuming that they'd been moved from the center of the room for the party, she hoped they'd be returned before Monday morning. She was picturing herself vigorously swinging Ben's hammer, nailing them down while the children stood waiting for her to begin class, when a deep voice behind her thankfully released her from this appalling vision.

"Miss Michaels?"

She turned and found herself looking up into a sun-darkened face with lighter lines marking the outer edges of brown eyes. The fellow, who looked to be in his mid-twenties, had removed his hat, revealing shaggy brown hair—and a pale stripe across his forehead where his hat had done its job of protecting that strip of skin, at least, from the sun. He smiled and she saw the lines near his eyes fold into laughter-crinkles, so that she couldn't help smiling herself.

"Yes?" Realizing that this had come out sounding like a half-question, as if she wasn't sure she was Miss Michaels, she said quickly, "Yes."

"I just wanted to introduce myself, ma'am. I'm Cork Birkett. I'm Mr. Clayton's night hand. One of 'em, anyway. The other is Nightowl. He's over there, in case you haven't met him. The one talkin' to Mr. Leverett."

She glanced over to see a gangly man, probably in his late forties, in earnest discussion with Cole Leverett. She turned back to Cork Birkett. "It's nice to meet you, Mr. Birkett. Mr. Clayton mentioned that you both work for him, but I haven't met Nightowl, yet. Thank you for pointing him out. I'm trying to learn everyone's names, but—"

He chuckled. "There's a right smart crowd of us, for sure, but you'll get 'em all roped and tied down before you know it."

"I hope so." It came out more of a heartfelt sigh than she intended, and she said quickly, "Your first name's Cork?"

The pale lines around his eyes disappeared into crinkles again. "My first name's actually Corcoran. It was quite a mouthful for a fella only knee-high to a flea, and it came out Cork. Unfortunately, by the time I could pronounce Corcoran proper-like, the other name was stuck tight to me. You'll find most ranch hands have made up names, either by their own choice or courtesy usually of someone else's sense of humor."

"Like Nightowl?"

"I reckon he's been Nightowl so long he doesn't even remember any other name. He's a rare bird who actually likes night herdin' better'n day ridin', so the name's a good fit."

"And do you prefer night herding over day riding?"

Before he could answer, she heard her name called from the front of the room and looked up to see Mr. Clark standing near the desk—*my* desk—she corrected with a quick thrill. He was calling to her over the hubbub of voices and gesturing for her to come forward. As she wove her way through the clusters of laughing, chatting people, the voices quieted to murmurs. When she reached Mr. Clark, he drew her forward and turned her to face her suddenly silent audience. All she saw at first was at least forty pairs of eyes old and young, studying her intently. Mr. Clark's words seemed strangely far away, then abruptly became crystal clear as it sank in that he was talking about her.

"I would like to welcome all of you to our first—but by no means our last—social affair in our new building. It has truly been a community effort that has allowed us to gather here in celebration. Most of you have met Miss Michaels by now, I'm sure, and have let her know how pleased we are that she has come such a great distance to be our first teacher in our brand new school, here." Scattered clapping followed his speech, although whether it was for Charity or for the brand new school, no one was telling. Mr. Clark held up his hands and the room quieted again. "We searched extensively for just the right person to teach our young people, and I can say with deep assurance that we have found her. So it is with great pleasure that I present to you our new schoolteacher, Miss Michaels."

Charity felt her cheeks growing pink as she accepted the noisy approval of the community she had joined. She looked into the crowd and saw the children who would be her first students and the people who were, even in this short time, becoming friends. In a rush of gladness and relief, she clasped her hands. "Thank you. I am truly blessed that you chose me. I am looking forward to teaching Clark's Valley's young people and becoming a part of your community. This wonderful building is fresh and new now. But one day its walls will have stories to tell about the students, and the challenges, and the adventures they encountered in following the path of learning. All this is possible because your caring, your hands have created this space and given them this opportunity. Thank you so very much."

The applause began again, and this time it was clearly for her. She glimpsed Miss Sullivan standing to the side, and realized that her reserved, unemotional teacher was clapping as enthusiastically as everyone else in the room.

***

It wasn't until she was curled under her blanket on the rope bed that night that Charity had a chance to mentally review the day. The party at the schoolhouse had gone well. It had already been made clear to her that the people in this new country worked long and hard to wrest a decent living from the harsh elements surrounding them. Now it was also obvious that they enjoyed their leisure time every bit as much. It had been a simple gathering, nothing fancy or that different from Fairvale's standards, and certainly not in a league with Philadelphia's elite social affairs as she remembered them from the time spent there, but there had been a sense of togetherness greater even than she had encountered in

Fairvale. Beneath the surface ran knowledge of each other's strengths and dedication to the common cause of moving ahead, of becoming a thriving district in the Territory and, ultimately, sharing in the statehood that they were certain would one day come to them.

Charity had always felt that Fairvale was a close-knit locality. Whenever someone was in trouble, help and encouragement were always as close as the first person to learn of the difficulty. She recalled how the neighborhood's citizens had gathered when Rose became ill with the measles and lost her hearing because of the high fever that accompanied the attack. Pa and Ma had taken Rose, and Charity, too, to Philadelphia to determine whether her hearing could be restored and had remained there while Hans Druid taught them new communication through sign language. When they returned to the farm, they found that their friends and neighbors had finished adding to the house the extra room that Pa had begun building, but had not been able to complete before the trip. And she well knew that this instance was not one of isolated kindness. It was simply what people did. As if with fresh eyes, she recognized that same dedication existed here, but with an even greater depth and intensity. In this new country, such reliance was not just a social nicety, it was a necessity of survival. And it appeared that for many of these reasons or all of them, she had been accepted as a part of the effort that would transfer a raw frontier settlement into a solid, thriving community.

She snuggled drowsily into the pillow and pictured not Mac's auburn hair and vivid blue eyes as on every other night, but a thatch of dark hair and crinkling brown eyes. "You'll get 'em all roped and tied down before you know it," she heard a pleasant masculine voice saying as sleep claimed her.

***

The next morning, Charity and Miss Sullivan were pulled into the swirl of preparations for attending Sunday services at Cole Leverett's ranch. Before the party the day before, Ben and the boys had gone down to the creek to wash up and the women had heated water for bathing in the privacy of the kitchen. Anne assembled her family and made certain that faces, hands, ears and necks were scrubbed and shining. She mercifully did not include Miss Sullivan and Charity in the inspection, but they surreptitiously took extra care, anyway, with their own preparations.

Charity was twisting her hair into a thick bun and mentally putting faces to the names of her school-children-to-be when Miss Sullivan asked, "Do you think my new skirt and jacket will be too fancy for church services?" Charity turned around to see her wearing the dark green suit and holding out in front of her one of her black skirts and white waists of classroom fame.

Startled, as much by the concern in the older woman's voice as by her unexpected question—Miss Sullivan unsure of anything?—Charity dutifully studied the two choices. It was actually a query containing pitfalls, not for Charity at the moment, but for her future as well as Miss Sullivan's for the time she would be here. They had already seen on their arrival in town and at the gathering yesterday afternoon that the women of the community were starved for fashion news. They had also seen Anne's everyday work dresses and the undoubtedly "best" dresses of the neighboring women at the party, which were, by Eastern standards, sadly out of date. If Charity and Miss Sullivan wore their most fashionable outfits to church, would the other women conclude that they were showing off? After all, they had already arrived on the train dressed more elegantly than these women had been in a very long time. On the other hand, if they wore more simple clothing, would those same women think they were "coming down" to what they perceived was the level of the society they were now a part of?

Charity wanted more than anything to fit into the group of people she had come to live among. She would not, for all the gold in Heaven's streets, have them think she thought they were inferior. If she was to live and work and have her being among them, she would not go about it in a small way. In her own mind, she had never been a trendsetter, but she supposed there was always a first time. She took a deep breath. "The green suit," she said finally. "This one time, anyway. Then we'll see how it goes from there."

Miss Sullivan studied the black and white set and then peered down at the green skirt she was wearing. She nodded decisively. "Yes. That's my choice, too. We don't want to rub them the wrong way, but we should be allowed to show them what they can achieve in fashion."

Temporarily silenced at the thought of Miss Sullivan being a fashion plate, and at the realization of how closely their minds had worked toward the same solution, Charity gulped. *I'm a teacher now, just like Miss Sullivan. I've patterned my school outfits after hers. Am I starting to think like her, too?*

Before she could determine whether this was good or bad, there was a discreetly voiced, "Knock, knock," on the other side of the Hudson's Bay blankets, and Anne said softly, "May I come in?"

Charity pulled aside the blanket and Anne's eyes widened. "My, how lovely you both look."

Watching closely, Charity could detect no envy on their new friend's face, only wonder at the grandeur before her. Anne reached her hand as if to touch Charity's sleeve, then drew it back with an embarrassed laugh.

"Please. It's all right. I've always loved the feel of new material, too." Charity hoped she didn't sound as awkward to Anne's ears as she did to her own, but apparently it came out properly, for Anne reached eagerly to gently stroke the material.

She gazed from Charity to Miss Sullivan. "Could I see the backs?" she asked almost shyly, and they turned obligingly for her inspection. When they faced front again, Charity saw what she thought was determination added to the wonder in Anne's expression. "One of these days," she muttered.

Charity had been right. It was determination.

On the way to Cole Leverett's place, they joined up with several other wagons and buggies heading the same direction. The seemingly limitless horizon stretched in front of them, and Charity saw wonders of nature that made her heart dance. As they followed the rough road worn by teams and wagons, she saw to right and left foot-high craters of dirt thrown up around holes in the ground. She was familiar with the burrowing tunnels of moles—the pests were a never-ending source of frustration to Pa on the farm—but these mounds were several feet apart and each was surrounded by bare ground.

Matt, who had yet to speak to her beyond their first, polite introduction, saw her curious gaze. "Prairie dog town," he said briefly.

"Prairie dog?" she repeated, puzzled.

Seeing her confusion, he said quickly, "Not like a regular dog that lives at someone's house. This is more like a squirrel or a rabbit, but not exactly. You have to see 'em to know what I mean."

"I don't see any now. When will I be able to?"

Catching the eagerness in her voice, he said solemnly, "Prob'ly not any time soon. You see, as soon as they heard us comin', one of 'em gave a whistle signal and they all dove into their burrows—those holes in the ground—and they won't come out 'til we're gone."

She had to hide a smile at his apologetic tone. "Thank you for telling me. You certainly know a lot about them. We don't have anything like them in Ohio, and I want to learn all I can about my new home."

He looked around at the world familiar to him from babyhood, as if he were trying to see it for the first time, all new and interesting. It was clearly a leap for him, but after searching the landscape, he raised his head and triumphantly pointed up. "There!"

She followed his gaze toward the cloudless sky and saw the magnificent wingspread of a bird lazily circling on the currents of air that gusted past them on their own pinned-to-the-earth journey. "What is it?" she asked, awed.

"That's a golden eagle. He's got such good eyesight he c'n see rabbits and owls on the ground, and even little varmints like mice and such from clear up there. He's prob'ly huntin' a meal. He has real sharp talons f'r grabbin' stuff when he swoops down." As if suddenly realizing that this frank information might disturb the Eastern lady, he added consolingly, "Might not catch anything, though. See how his shadow sweeps over the ground? That warns the critters to hide from him."

Charity appreciated his young sensitivity toward her feelings, but before she could explain that she had grown up on a farm and was used to the ways of wild creatures, they arrived at the Leverett ranch. Although nearly everyone had been at the party yesterday afternoon, there were a few new faces to be introduced and the various potluck offerings to be arranged in the kitchen before the services began.

There wasn't room for everyone to sit, but benches were provided for those unable to stand for the necessary length of time. Almost as if they were guests of honor, Cole directed Miss Sullivan and Charity to be seated at the front. They hesitated, certain that others needed the space more, but, realizing that it would be an affront to refuse such hospitality, accepted with murmured thanks. A few moments later, Callie Corley eased down next to Charity and squeezed her hand. The unborn baby gave such a vigorous kick that Charity winced, certain she saw the shape of a little foot protruding before Callie, smiling blissfully, covered it with gentle fingers. Cole, officiating because it was his home they were gathered in, stepped to the front, Bible in hand.

The hour of services that followed was simple, with Bible readings and songs that Charity knew well, including "Abide with Me" and "Nearer My God to Thee." When it was over, she put her hands to helping the other women set out the potluck dishes.

After everyone had eaten and the dishes were washed, Charity left the women in the kitchen sorting out among their owners, with much laughter, the bowls and pans the food had been brought in. She was carrying the last bucket of dish water to pour over Cole's garden patch when she heard a pleasant voice behind her. "Howdy, Miss Michaels. Let me carry that for you."

She recognized the voice even before she turned. She had wondered if Cork Birkett would be here and how she'd feel if he was. She had her answer as her heart smiled.

"I was hopin' I'd get a chance to see you today. Sure was a nice party yesterday." He casually took the bucket from her and walked beside her to the upturned area where turnip, carrot, and beet leaves were pushing out of the earth. He poured the water carefully, giving each plant a share of the precious moisture. Task finished, he upended the bucket from which no further drops could be coaxed and gave her a mischievous grin. "Looks like they could use a bit more. We could get another bucketful from the creek. That is, if you don't have to go right back to the kitchen."

She glanced over at the house and then toward the creek. "Another bucket now would save Griff a trip later," she agreed, "but I really should be getting back."

He nodded. "Sure." As they walked slowly toward the house, he asked, "All set for your first day of teacherin' tomorrow?"

"Part of me is, and part isn't," she admitted, then stopped, appalled that she had voiced such weakness, and to someone she scarcely knew.

"That's only natural. The first day of anythin' is always the roughest. Then the second comes and things start smoothin' out. Then before you know it, it'll seem so natural, you'll feel like you've been doin' it forever."

They paused by the back step. "You'll do fine, Teacher." He winked and handed her the bucket. She took it and opened the door, aware that he was watching her go.

CHAPTER TWENTY-EIGHT

Charity knelt in front of the trunk holding her school materials. Ever since her arrival, they had been so busy during the day, and she'd been so tired at night, that she hadn't set her supplies in order for the first day of school. And now that first day was tomorrow.

She had worried that the Claytons would be offended if she attempted to work on Sunday, but Anne had assured her they would not be upset. On a ranch, caring for the cattle could not stop even for a Sunday. For herself, she tried to limit her tasks to pleasurable ones, such as finishing Catty's dress, which was what she intended to do today. Some might consider it to be ordinary work, and unacceptable, but for her it was a luxury to sit quietly and do something she enjoyed, while not worrying that there were a hundred other things she should be doing. Miss Sullivan had volunteered to read aloud to her from *Pride and Prejudice*, and Anne's eyes had shone with anticipation.

So, with a clear conscience, Charity eased back the trunk lid and gazed at the contents. A rush of homesickness almost overwhelmed her at sight of the neatly stacked books and school supplies as she remembered Ma and Pa helping her assemble the needed items. She hadn't known what the school board and the parents of the children attending would provide. Since there were no previous classes to fall back on for materials, Miss Sullivan had suggested that she start from scratch and provide extras of the basics such as rulers, writing pads, pencils, pens and ink for the older students, and slates and slate pencils for the younger ones. She had brought what she hoped was sufficient chalk for writing on the blackboard she had noted at the front of the room yesterday.

She lifted out a small bulky package she didn't remember putting in and carefully opened it. Her eyes widened at sight of the real blackboard eraser nestled in the cloth wrapping. She had heard of such an object, but never seen one. She'd fully expected to use old rags wrapped around her hand to remove chalk from the board as Miss Sullivan had done through the years of Charity's own schooling. The neatly shaped black eraser that fit so readily into her palm had been invented only a few years ago by a Mr. Hammett. After he discovered by simple chance how much better wool felt strips worked than a piece of cloth to erase chalk from a blackboard, he'd begun crafting and selling them. She hugged the eraser to her heart as she pictured Ma and Pa slipping it into the trunk for her to find later. Could they possibly have foreseen how much this simple object would cheer her spirits and lend her courage in her new venture?

She didn't see how that could be so, but she was deeply grateful to them.

After sorting through the trunk, she sat at the kitchen table and wrote out her teaching plan for the next day. Now that she knew the names and ages of her students, she was able to work out a rough schedule of the subjects she would cover. Her biggest problem, of course, was that she had no idea of how advanced the children were—or weren't—for their age groups. She realized that she would have to talk to each of them individually before she could arrange them into grades. And while she was doing that, she would have to make certain that the other children were sufficiently occupied to stay out of mischief. She didn't expect trouble from most of them. They had appeared polite and well-behaved when she had met them.

With two exceptions.

Her heart twitched with anxiety as she thought of Carolina Corley and Luke Clayton. She expected she could handle five-year-old Carolina if the child actually came to school. She remembered that the Corleys hadn't definitely decided that she would attend, although Carolina herself had expressed no doubt that she would. Charity would face that when and if it became necessary. But Luke was "a horse of a different stripe," as Pa would say. The boy was thirteen, and big and strong for his age. Charity was taller, but she suspected he weighed nearly as much as she did. She'd already seen him display a sullen temper and a large disregard for other folks' feelings and opinions, in spite of Ben and Anne's efforts. She knew that in bodily strength he could best her. But she didn't intend to engage in any physical showdowns with him. She knew there had to be other ways. The problem was she wouldn't know what they were until they jumped up in front of her. She picked up the black wool eraser and brushed it against her cheek. For the sake of the other students, for the school as a whole, for herself, she would find a way. She had to.

***

Morning came. Charity woke to the familiar noises of the stove lid rattling, booted footsteps across the kitchen floor, and the back door opening and closing. *Today is the day. Today I begin teaching*. The words sang in her heart as she dressed and helped Anne with the breakfast preparations. First day of school or not, Luke, Matt, and Catty had their customary chores to tend to. Luke did his with his usual sullen impatience. Matt and Catty did theirs with barely suppressed excitement. Matt, as befit an older brother, was more reserved than Catty, who was proudly wearing her new pink-flowered dress and pinafore, but even his eyes were bright as they joined hands for the before-breakfast prayer.

"Bless the work of our hands that it may prove pleasin' unto you." Ben's deep voice came out a little hesitantly, as it always did when he was talking out loud to the Almighty. So sure of himself at other times, he'd never lost his discomfort over speaking his deepest feelings in front of others, and thus usually kept his remarks brief. This time, however, he continued. "And please bless our new school and be with Miss Michaels as she begins her work of teachin' our young ones." Surprised at hearing her name, Charity looked up, but Ben had already rolled on to the next item on his agenda. "We thank You for providin' the means to build the school and for providin' the teacher to go with it. And we thank You most heartily for seein' to it that this day has finally arrived." Her head still raised, Charity saw the radiant smile Anne flashed Ben and knew that he had voiced aloud the words of her heart.

The after-breakfast flurry to get out the door and on the way to school had taken place in the Fairvale farmhouse so many times that Charity imagined the two kitchens could have been interchanged. Catty had charge of the dinner pail. Matt held on to the spelling book Anne was contributing to the educational effort. Luke, obviously indifferent about taking nothing to share, muttered, "Don't see what the hurry is. School can't start 'til the teacher gets there." Charity heard him, but chose to ignore his comment and concentrate on Anne's unabashed happiness. Instead of walking, Ben was taking them in the wagon so that they could transport Charity's trunk full of supplies. Miss Sullivan, Anne, and Eve followed the little group out to the edge of the nearly finished porch. Anne had to catch Eve by the dresstail as she attempted to follow the older children to the wagon. There was a slight scuffle which Anne won by dint of hoisting the little girl onto her hip and holding her securely.

Charity had expected Miss Sullivan to accompany her this first day, but the older woman had firmly declined. "This is your school. You must do things your way. You don't need me looking over your shoulder every minute, and you wondering if I would be doing things differently." At the faint flash of panic that crossed Charity's face, Miss Sullivan's lips had tightened. "You can do this. Remember, I taught you. I know that you're perfectly capable of doing an excellent job. So just go and do it."

This unemotional little speech, so like her old teacher, stiffened Charity's spine. The children piled into the wagon and Ben assisted Charity up to the high seat. Anne, eyes shining with joy and the tears she was trying hard to keep back, waved to the children with her free hand and admonished them to behave themselves and to listen to their teacher. Miss Sullivan didn't wave or call out. As Charity turned for a final look back, however, she saw the older woman nodding her head. The expression on her face was a curious blend of pride and confidence that Charity stored away for later taking out and examining that day if—

when—she felt an intense need for encouragement.

When they topped the last slope, Charity felt a fresh thrill at seeing her school, an emotion that was quickly dampened by a shiver of misgiving as she saw the children already grouped in the yard, waiting for her, clearly eager to begin their *real schooling*. She had asked Ben if they could arrive earlier than her pupils so that she could assemble her supplies, write a welcome to the students on the new blackboard, and make other pre-class preparations. The wished-for quiet bit of time was not to be. Ben pulled up to the front step and assisted her down. The children, who had been chattering like magpies, became totally silent as she made her way to the door.

"Good morning, children," she said cheerfully in as much of an unpanic-stricken voice as she could manage. While she admired and wanted to follow many of Miss Sullivan's teaching practices, she had determined that she would not strike terror into the hearts of her students to achieve results.

Murmured responses of "Good morning, Miss Michaels" and "Morning, Teacher" drifted to her as she unlocked the door and the children pressed in behind her. They paused to leave their hats, bonnets, and lunches in the cloakroom so that she was able to step by herself into the classroom and view her domain for a precious moment that she tucked into her heart. Then the children were pushing through the doorway and exclaiming at the sight of the desks that were, Charity saw with relief, firmly fastened to the floor in their proper places.

Ben, hoisting the trunk of supplies, broke the spell by asking, "Where do you want this?" and obligingly lowered it to the spot she indicated on the floor beside her desk at the front of the room. Straightening, he looked around to see if anything else needed to be done. The stove, crouching in the right front corner of the room, would not need to be lit today or for many days to come. Neither would they need to bring in the coal that would provide fuel for the fire. "I'll fetch a bucket of water," he mumbled and pushed through the children still standing crowded at the back of the room.

"Come in, children," she urged. "If the younger ones sit at the front, you older ones can take the desks farther back. We'll figure out permanent places in just a little while." The children shuffled forward and chose desks and seatmates, she was sure, based on friendship. Luke, with a scornful expression, chose a seat by himself at the very back. Charity suspected that suited the other children just fine. She looked around and discovered Carolina Corley had indeed come. The child was plopped down next to her brother Amos, holding onto the edge of the seat with both hands, and he was doing his best to unstick her so that Frederick Trumble could take the other half of the desk.

"Carolina," she called, "please come sit up front."

She wasn't certain the little girl would obey, but Amos hissed loudly enough for Charity and the rest of the class to hear, "Remember, Pa said if you want to come to school, you have to obey the teacher. If you don't obey, you have to go home and stay there and never come to school anymore."

Teacher wasn't certain how much of this particular speech was Owen Corley's and how much was Amos's invention, but it must have been close enough to her father's threat since the child peeled herself out of the seat and flounced to the front of the room. Charity gave her a big smile and indicated the desk directly in front of her own. She intended to keep an eye on this particular exuberant little body. Carolina slid into the seat, but her mutinous expression didn't bode well for future pleasant teacher-student relations. Charity sent up a short but heartfelt prayer that Owen's threat would hold at least through the day.

After confirming that fourteen-year-old Becky Clark could read, Charity set her to reading aloud to the other students from *Gulliver's Travels*. She realized the younger children wouldn't understand it, but figured they could happily relate to the six-inch-tall Lilliputians. With the class thus occupied, Charity was able to call each student up and determine how advanced each was—or wasn't—and thus could group the children by grades.

The time passed more quickly than she could have imagined possible as the students lost some of their shyness around her and began to respond to her guidance. She kept an eye on Luke and Carolina for signs of rebellion, but both seemed to have taken their parents' admonitions to heart. She strongly suspected it wouldn't be a permanent state of affairs, but she was deeply grateful that it had lasted for the day.

As she walked home with Matt and Catty—Luke had taken off on his own as soon as she had dismissed them—Charity listened to the children chatter as they unconsciously gave her their interpretation of the day's events.

***

The following days seemed to fly by. As Charity began to know the children, she found a fascinating mix of personalities and levels of learning. All of them, with the exception of Luke, and possibly Carolina, appeared eager to absorb what she could impart to them. She came to understand that in this new country where they had been denied the means to attend school, the reality was a treasured opportunity. She wondered at first, as in the case of Will Braden and his mother Phebe, if it was simply the parents' dreams foisted on the children. It slowly became clear to her that it was not. As her pupils' minds stretched and reached for knowledge, Charity found herself seeking new avenues to satisfy their varied interests, so that her mind, too, was forced to reach and stretch.

The new teacher's jury was still out on whether Carolina really wanted to receive an education or whether she just wanted to be a part of the other children's gathering each day, which she could only achieve by attending school. It quickly became evident that the other students were painfully wary of Carolina's attitude and tactics. They didn't shun her, but they didn't voluntarily include her, either. In the rare moments when she was free to mull the situation over, Charity tried in vain to come up with a solution, wondering as she did so whether Carolina even wanted a way out of the self-constructed corner she was in. Charity thought of discussing the matter with Miss Sullivan, to glean wisdom from the older woman's years of experience, but something held her back. This was *her* problem. If she were ever to be a successful teacher, she would have to learn to handle situations on her own.

Luke, in those first days, sat alone in his desk at the back of the room, rather as if he were surveying his kingdom from the rear. He didn't make any obvious trouble, but Charity had the uneasy feeling that he was merely biding his time, getting her to relax her vigilance before he flexed his muscles.

Never forgetting his potential for causing mayhem, Charity concentrated on the other children. Becky Clark, at fourteen, was the oldest pupil. At first, she seemed hesitant to intrude upon the other students' learning activities, as if fearing they would take offense at her imposing her age and knowledge upon them. She was short and rounded, with soft brown hair and rosy cheeks. Her mild blue eyes, fastening on Charity as she stood at the front of the room explaining the intricacies of fractions to Griff, Vincent, and Flanna, told of her desire to absorb and understand as much as she could as quickly as she could. Charity wondered if, because of her age, she feared that her time in the school room was limited. Charity certainly had no intention of having her removed in the foreseeable future. She meant what she had told Owen Corley that first day as they rode out of Laramie: "No one is ever too old to learn, if she really wants to."

Becky Clark wanted to learn, and Charity was determined to fulfill that wish. In the middle of one of those afternoons when the new teacher felt all fourteen of the students were requiring her time and attention at the exact same moment, she enlisted Becky's help. As on the first day when she had read *Gulliver's Travels* and kept the children occupied while Charity conducted her individual interviews, she proved to be a competent assistant. She helped the younger students shape their letters on their slates or add and subtract the numbers Charity had put on the blackboard. By the middle of the second week, Charity noticed at recess that the children were asking Becky to help them tie their pinafore sashes and showing her the prize bugs they had captured in the prairie grasses that surrounded the school yard. Far from taking offense at her new status, the children accepted her because she was one of them. And besides, she somehow made learning those pesky numbers and letters fun. Observing this from where she sat on the top step correcting the older students' essays on "A Person Who is Important to Me" during the noon dinner break, Charity couldn't suppress a contented smile.

***

The next day, Will Braden showed up on time for school as always, but he was silent and withdrawn. At morning recess, he didn't even participate in the marble competition that had sprung up on the first day of school. After the boys realized that they would be seeing each other on a daily basis instead of sporadically, they had enthusiastically entered into a friendly rivalry, continuing it from recess to recess. Sometimes one boy led in his possession of marbles, sometimes another. This day, Will, who was supposed to go nose to nose with Matt, shook his head and wandered off to stare into the depths of the creek. The other boys gaped after him, but Matt was the one who followed him over to the stony bank. Charity watched as Matt spoke to him. Will kept his head down but after several moments said something that obviously shocked Matt. They exchanged more words, then Matt joined Will in staring at the rippling water. When Charity called the end of recess, the two boys walked together into the building. For the rest of the day, they remained quiet and solemn, refusing Charity's attempts to draw them out.

At home that evening, Charity found out the reason for Will's uncharacteristic low spirits. At supper, Ben informed them that Caleb Braden had taken off from his ranch that morning. "He's cooked up another get-rich-quick scheme. Seems he plans to go to Texas, round up a herd of longhorns from the ones millin' in the brush there, and drive 'em to Abilene. Figures to make a killin' profit." He shook his head. "All that risk, in addition to leavin' Phebe and Will to fend for themselves. And knowin' Caleb Braden, it'll never work," he said grimly. "Somethin' will happen. With Caleb, it always does."

Charity remembered the dazzled look on Caleb Braden's face outside the saloon that morning in Laramie. Even more clearly, she saw Phebe's pride and determination as she introduced her son to the new teacher. What made two such unlike personalities merge their lives? Was it simply a matter of believing in the best, denying that the worst could ever happen to them? She looked at Anne, then Ben. They, too, from all outward appearances, were an unlikely match. Yet somehow they had made it work without either of them sacrificing their own deepest selves. *What makes it right for Mac and Amity but not for Mac and me?* She shivered. *I expect if I knew the answer to that one, I could bottle it and sell it.*

CHAPTER TWENTY-NINE

A few weeks into Charity's teaching, Sunday church services were held in town at the Trumble house, beside the newspaper office. She had learned that the congregation tried to alternate between assembling in town and in the country, so that distances members traveled from week to week were more evenly divided. After being at Cole's the first Sunday after she arrived, they had gathered in town at Link and Lillie Monroes' house beside the saddle shop. Last week, they had gone out to the Corley ranch. This warm morning, the Trumble house was crowded with all the folks who had come, so that some of the men standing at the back retreated into the newspaper office beside the printing press to gain a little breathing room.

In the close-packed sitting room, Charity, near the front, found herself standing on Brinna's marvelous hooked rug. When she looked down at her feet, she discovered that her toes were actually touching the edge of the sapphire lake, and she could have sworn that she felt an instant coolness. She looked up and got the distinct impression that the coolness hadn't come from the reviving waters of the lake beneath her toes. Cora Clark, Ezra and Libby's youngest daughter, was staring fixedly at her. Charity had spoken briefly to her when they were introduced and had hoped, since they were near in age to each other, that they could become friends. Since she'd been so busy with school, there'd been no opportunity to pursue any social contacts outside of church gatherings. She'd seen Cora the Sunday before at the Corleys' ranch, but the other young woman had never been near enough in the press of people for Charity to speak to her. She had hoped that she would see Cora today and that they could become better acquainted.

The first part of that hope had been fulfilled. Cora was indeed here. But the fish-cold stare she was giving Charity didn't appear to signal the beginning of a long and cherished friendship. Confused, Charity glanced at the woman standing to her right, who happened to be Phebe Braden. Following Caleb's abrupt departure for Texas, Phebe had held her head high around her friends and neighbors as one or another of them casually appeared each day to assist her and Will with the heaviest chores. She'd also continued to make certain that her son, his face scrubbed and his clothes worn but fresh-cleaned, was at school first thing in the morning. Charity strongly suspected that Phebe sat Will down each night and had him relay to her what he'd been taught that day.

Now, standing beside Phebe, their toes touching the edge of Brinna's sapphire lake waters, Charity could conjure up no earthly reason Cora would be directing such a deadly glare at the other woman. Phebe, blissfully unaware of the daggers winging toward them on the warm morning air, was earnestly singing "A mighty fortress is our God, a bulwark never failing," with the rest of the congregation, so Charity turned back to Cora. For a wild second, she thought she might have imagined the whole thing, because Cora had swung her attention back to Vince Trumble, who, with Brinna, was leading the singing at the front of the room. But she knew she hadn't dreamed it.

As they gathered informally after the services to partake of the potluck dishes contributed that day, Charity, glimpsing Libby Clark standing at the dry sink, took her filled plate and started toward her. She wanted to tell Libby how pleased she was with Becky's eagerness to learn in the classroom and how well the other children had taken to her friendly offers of assistance. Before she reached the other woman, however, she heard a remembered voice behind her. "Howdy, Teacher."

Her heart gave a little bump of pleasure as she turned to Cork Birkett. "Good morning, Mr. Birkett. Or is it afternoon now?"

He responded with his ready grin. "Since it's sure to be mornin' someplace in the world and afternoon some other place, I think we're safe in callin' it either way." He motioned with his full plate to hers. "Maybe we can find a spot out of the way where we won't have to risk gettin' poked by a stray elbow while we're eatin'." Since the conversation buzzing around them made using a normal speaking voice difficult, she nodded and followed him into the newspaper office where he found a corner not already claimed by other seekers of quiet. There was no place to sit, but at least the danger of being jogged while they had forkfuls of food partway to their mouths was greatly reduced.

"How's the teachin' goin'?"

"I believe we're getting set into a pattern, just as you said we would. The first day—actually the first week—was the hardest," she admitted, "but I'm getting to know individual personalities and making fascinating discoveries about the children." She felt her cheeks turn pink at acknowledging such personal feelings to a man she hardly knew, but he bent his head a little toward her as if waiting to hear more. Because he seemed genuinely interested, she related one of the more memorable moments of the week. Garrett Trumble and Jonah Monroe, only a year apart in age, after eating their noon dinners, had spent the remainder of the hour attempting to catch tadpoles down by the creek.

"Did they succeed?"

She flashed a wry smile. "They did. The only problem was that when they caught them, the only place they had to keep them was in their pockets. By the time they were back in the classroom, bursting to show us their treasures, and pulled them out, the poor tadpoles were rather the worse for wear. I have to give the boys credit. They felt really bad. They both said they hadn't meant any harm."

"So what did you do?"

She lifted her shoulders in a perplexed gesture. "What else could I do? Instead of a geography lesson about the Swiss Alps, the whole class held a double funeral."

"You did?" His surprise was evident.

She sighed. "We did. But instead of burying them in the ground, I had the boys wrap them in leaves and take them back to the creek. I explained that when sailors died on ships at sea, they were buried in the ocean as a way to honor their love of the water. And since the tadpoles had loved the water, it was only right to honor them by putting them back in it."

He made a peculiar sound between coughing and choking, and her already pink cheeks flamed crimson. "You're laughing at me?" She ducked her head in embarrassment. "I had to make it positive in some way for the children. The boys felt so bad—"

She broke off at his quick intake of breath and looked up to see his brown eyes, completely serious, fixed on her face. "I'm not laughin' at you. Honest. I think that was a dandy way to handle it. And to think of it so quick. What did you do then?"

At his apparent sincerity, a little of her mortification receded. She squared her shoulders and raised her chin. "We said the Lord's Prayer and sang 'Rock of Ages.' Then we went back into the schoolroom and had our geography lesson about all the different oceans in the world and the kinds of ships that have sailed on them." Her eyes met his as if daring him to laugh about her teaching methods.

"My Ma's highest praise was, 'You done good, son,'" he said quietly. "You done good, Teacher." There was no mistaking the admiration in his tone.

Before she could respond, she felt an urgent tugging at her skirt and a small voice said, "'Scuse me, Teacher." She glanced down to find Catty looking at her pleadingly, with Hannah Monroe hovering nearby. "Ma said to find you and Miss Sullivan and tell you Pa says it's time to leave."

"All right, Catty. Thank you for telling me. I'll be right there."

The child's face held a strange blend of entreaty and reluctance as she said, "I haven't found Miss Sullivan yet. Do you know where she is?"

Charity, who had a much better view of people's heads than the little girl did, spotted Miss Sullivan in the opposite corner, talking to Cole Leverett. "She's over there." When Catty visibly hesitated, Charity recognized the problem. She had a sudden, swift remembrance of another little girl, under strict orders from her father, having to face those stern, forbidding features and apologize for the wrong she had done. At the time, she had been older than Catty was now, and Miss Sullivan had, in some ways, softened in the years since. She realized, now that she thought about it, that Matt and Catty gave Miss Sullivan a wide berth whenever possible. Luke—the law unto himself—ignored her. Charity bent down to the worried little face. "Would you like me to tell her?"

"Oh. Yes," she breathed. "Thank you." Turning, she clasped Hannah's hand and they scurried away before Charity could change her mind.

Cork raised his eyebrows, but said nothing as he walked beside her to Miss Sullivan, who was nodding earnestly as she listened to Cole. When Charity relayed the message that the Claytons were ready to leave, some of the brightness in her eyes dampened, but, strangely enough, not all. Cole accompanied her outside, as Cork did Charity. The two men assisted the women into the wagon, then silently watched as it pulled away.

Curled up in her rope bed that night, Charity reviewed the day as she always did, at least until sleep overtook her. She remembered Cora's cold stare, but because she could do nothing about the problem, whatever it was, until she could confront the woman directly, she turned her thoughts to Miss Sullivan and the question that had been poking at her heart. How long was she planning to stay? The journey had been a long one, and once folks made such a trip, they tended to stay put for a time. Although Miss Sullivan said nothing about it, Charity knew that while she was at school during the day, the older woman plunged in, helping Anne with the endless round of chores living on a ranch necessitated. With the passing days, the look of exhaustion that had been stamped upon the young wife and mother when they first arrived had subtly faded. Charity discovered, quite by accident, that Anne was even able to sneak minutes out of the day to read from *Pride and Prejudice*—her greatest imaginable luxury.

Charity couldn't deny that Miss Sullivan's presence had been comforting to her, too. After her initial resolution to solve her teaching problems herself, she'd realized that it was a dumb thing to do. She had excellent guidance for the asking, and she was shunning it. So, in the evenings, she had begun filling Miss Sullivan in on her day. The older woman gave no advice unless Charity specifically asked for it, but she made a great sounding board. By being spoken aloud, some of the new teacher's questions answered themselves, and fresh ideas sprang to her mind as if by magic.

Her thoughts turned, irresistibly, to the magic she'd witnessed that afternoon. As she had approached Miss Sullivan and Cole Leverett, she had seen the distinct brightness in her former teacher's eyes, and had wondered if that was a faint trace of pink in her cheeks. *Miss Sullivan?*

And Cole Leverett? Stranger things have happened since the world began, but still....

Knowing that speculation about the older woman was useless, and that broaching the subject would be worse than futile, Charity finally allowed her thoughts to turn to the most important happening of her day. Cork Birkett. He was a nice looking young man, well-mannered and interesting to talk to. His attention was undeniably flattering to her bruised heart after so many years of Mac's "younger sister" attitude and his outright choosing of Amity over her. So how did she really feel about Cork? *You shouldn't even be asking yourself such a question. Nothing's going to come of it. Nothing can come of it. You came out here to teach, not fall all moon-eyed over the first man who pays you some attention. Wouldn't that set the school board on their ear, to have their long-sought teacher tell them her teaching days were over before they'd scarcely even begun?* She fell asleep and Mac's face and Cork's voice became strangely intermingled in her dreams.

CHAPTER THIRTY

It was during the next week of Charity's teaching that Luke made his move. In spite of telling herself to continue expecting him to do something outrageous, that he was deliberately lulling her into a false sense of security, she let down her guard. The day was hot. The never-ceasing wind gusted past the school, drying the prairie grasses and heating the interior of the little building as if the stove sulking coldly in the corner was blasting flames. The first flush of newness had worn off for teacher and students, and they were now settled in for the long haul. She turned from the blackboard, where she had been writing out questions for the older class's history test. The sight of her listless pupils struck an answering chord somewhere in the dullness of her own sluggish mind. She was frankly tired. Her skirt and petticoats weighed a ton as they pressed against her legs. The high collar of her waist chafed her neck and the long sleeves felt as smothering as the Hudson's Bay blankets that separated the alcove bedroom from Anne's kitchen.

It could have been desperation that sparked the impulse. Charity didn't bother to inquire. She simply picked up *Gulliver's Travels* from the corner of her desk and spoke with more briskness than she had dreamed she possessed at the moment. "Your attention, please, class."

Thirteen drooping heads lifted automatically. She waited until Luke, the lone laggard, finally looked up to see why she wasn't talking. The reason must have sunk in when he found her gazing at him pointedly. When the other children saw her clutching *Gulliver*, they perked up a bit. "Class, you've all been working very hard, in spite of the heat. I know how difficult it's been to stay focused and you've been doing a great job. I believe that effort deserves a little reward. How would you all like to go down by the creek where it's shady and listen to the next chapter of our story? We're getting close to the end."

The effect was as instantaneous as if a cool breeze had rippled through the room. The children brightened perceptibly as murmurs of pleasure circled among the desks. She gestured for them to file outside and led them over to the cottonwood near the creek where they settled down in a loosely grouped circle. Gulliver had escaped the Lilliputians and survived the gigantic Brobdingnags, including being the temporary pet of the nine-year-old girl who was small for her age since she wasn't even forty feet tall. The hero was now in Houyhnhnm country with the wise talking horses. As Charity had surmised, the youngest children didn't understand the plot, but they had been entranced with the tiny Lilliputians and the giant Brobdingnagians. Now they listened, fascinated, to the adventures brought on by the rude, semi-human Yahoos. Charity had just read, "'I had not been a Year in this Country, before I contracted such a Love and Veneration for the Inhabitants, that I entered on a firm resolution never to return to human Kind,'" when a loud splash interrupted her. She looked up to see that Luke had edged close enough to the creek to throw small stones into the lazily rippling water. "Luke, come back and sit down," she said firmly.

He looked over at her and threw a flat rock. It skipped three times before it sank below the surface. "Luke, come back and sit down with the rest of the class." She put another notch of firmness in her voice.

He stared at her. "I'd rather stand over here." To prove his point, he flipped another stone. It bounced five times before submerging.

As Charity realized that the day of battle had come, her foremost wish was that he had picked a cooler occasion. Already out of sorts, she wasn't certain she possessed the patience she knew would be necessary to get through this challenge. For challenge it was, and no mistaking it. The other children, sensing the battle lines being drawn, looked anxiously at her and warily at him. Sending up a silent prayer for guidance and strength, she slowly put the book aside and stood. At her movement, Luke let a grin cross his normally sullen features and braced himself as if he expected her to engage in a physical fistfight. She had no intention of going head to head—or fist to fist—with him.

Surprise crept into his grin as she stood next to him at the water's edge. "You consider yourself a good hand at skipping rocks?" she asked conversationally.

He shot her a cocky look. "Sure," he said as if it were a foolish question.

"What's your record?" she asked curiously.

"Done eight lots of times. If the creek was wider, it would of gone farther." He crossed his arms over his chest as if daring her to prove him wrong.

"Eight? That's a high number," she conceded. "I'd like to see that."

With a slight swagger, he bent and found a flat, rounded stone, flexed his wrist and shot the fragment over the water. It skipped six times before dropping out of sight. He looked disconcerted for an instant before protesting, "That wasn't a good stone." He searched carefully for a better one and flipped it. It shot out, skipped seven times and sank. He shrugged with large indifference. "That's still a good count. I don't see anybody doin' better."

"Seven is a good number," she agreed pleasantly. She searched the ground for a few moments and picked up a flat stone more triangular than round. "Do you think this one has possibilities?" He shook his head, his expression clearly pitying her lack of knowledge of the proper shape for such stones, but reached out anyway, expecting her to hand it to him. Instead, she faced the creek, cocked her wrist and sent the piece spinning out over the water. He watched it hit the surface and shoot forward, hit and shoot forward.

The children had gathered behind her, and not taking her eyes from Luke, she heard them counting off the jumps. "… eight … nine … ten!" They made no effort to conceal the admiration in their voices. "Teacher, you made it skip ten times! We didn't know you knew how to do that!"

Luke hadn't known she knew how to do it, either. With effort, he tamped his astonishment down to his usual indifference. "Your stone was flatter. If mine was thinner, it would've gone farther, too." Even the youngest children sensed that it was a weak boast.

Charity gestured to the pebble-littered ground, silently inviting him to try again, but he shook his head. "You was just lucky. I hurt my arm helpin' Pa yesterday, and my wrist plumb give out. Now if it was shootin' marbles, I could do that all year."

Charity didn't ask how the wrist too injured to flip a stone could shoot a marble. She looked at him inquiringly.

"Teachers can't shoot marbles," he said knowingly, grandly ignoring the fact that teachers weren't supposed to know how to skip rocks, either. He dug into his pocket and pulled out a leather drawstring-closed bag that clinked tantalizingly when he shook it.

The other children looked anxiously up at Charity to see how she would handle this new challenge. "May I hold the bag?" she asked mildly. When he surrendered it, she hefted it in her palm. "You certainly have a lot. Do you know how many?"

"I have fifty-eight." His superior tone indicated that no one else could even come close to claiming that number.

"Fifty-eight." She was suitably impressed. "I surely would like to try, but I don't have any marbles." She shrugged her shoulders.

"You can't have any of mine," he said, as if the very idea were preposterous. He looked around at the other children. "Anybody got some marbles Teacher c'n use?" His tone implied that he might as well have substituted the word "lose" instead.

The other boys traded glances, then Vincent drew a denim bag out of his pocket. "Here, Teacher. You can use mine."

"Thank you, Vincent, but I don't have any marbles to pay you back if I lose."

The boy squinted up at her in the bright sunshine for a searching moment, then apparently reached a private decision. "I have forty-six. I can afford to lose a few," he said with a shrug and handed her the bag, which was nearly as heavy as Luke's.

"Thanks." She gave him a brief smile. While Vince and Will drew a

circle and shooting lines, she inspected Vince's marbles and chose a
shooter. After determining the rules, including that each one's shooter
was not subject to capture, and that the loser of the shot to go first would
put out thirteen marbles to start, they knelt behind the shooting line. The
children crowded close until Luke protested that they were breathing
down his neck. He won the shot to go first. With exaggerated gestures, he
knuckled his first shot and missed every one of Charity's marbles by a
wide margin as his shooter flew over and out of the circle. "Golly," he
said in shocked disappointment, "I missed. I wonder how that
happened?"

Ignoring the snicker caught on the edge of his voice, Charity knelt
and knuckled her shooter. Two of the smaller marbles skidded out of the
circle while her larger one rolled gently to the edge and stopped just
inside. Luke's eyes widened in stunned surprise. The children gave a
gasp which they quickly stifled as Charity prepared to shoot again.
Minutes later, in silence so heavy it would have cracked if it had been
dropped, she had dispatched all thirteen marbles, leaving her own
shooter the lone occupant of the circle. She neatly scooped up the marbles
she had won and returned them to Vincent's bag. Picking up Luke's
shooter, she hefted it in her palm. "It has a nice weight," she conceded,
before offering it to the boy. "Shall we go again?"

Jaw gaping, he stared at her as if she had dropped out of one of the
willows fringing the creek, then turned beet red and snatched the marble
out of her hand. "Naw. Told you I got a sore wrist," he mumbled as the
other children crowded around her, crowing with glee.

She handed the bag of marbles back to a beaming Vincent. "Thank
you for lending them to me," she said politely.

Vincent's grin stretched from ear to ear. "Any time, Teacher. You just
say the word!"

She turned from her jubilant students to her affronted one. "Time to
go back to class," she said without satisfaction or censure.

Having blamed his defeat on his injured wrist, Luke had regained his
momentarily lost self-possession. "Not me," he said loftily. His gaze fell
on the four horses picketed near the creek. "Think I'll go f'r a ride." He
shot a glance at her as if daring her to argue.

She sighed. "Luke, you know you don't ride someone else's horse
without permission. Besides, it's time to return to class."

He gave her an insolent grin. "If I want to ride one of those horses, I
will." He surveyed the children grouped silent and watchful behind her
and snickered. "I don't see anybody tryin' to stop me." Griff and Will
each rode horseback from home. The town children came by cart and
wagon, switching off teams and conveyances so that all shared in the
trek. Today, the children had come in Luke Monroe's buckboard. "You

gonna stop me, Griff? You gonna stop me, Will? I didn't think so," he sneered. "Sure as owls hoot, Teacher from O-hi-o—" he drew out the word in a feminine lilt and fluttered his eyelashes with what he believed was a simper "— who can't ride ain't gonna stop me!" He flung her a contemptuous smirk and started for the horses.

Up to that point Charity had deliberately been keeping her irritation banked and her responses studiedly mature, as befit her schoolteacher status. But with his last bit of bald-faced rudeness, the temper she had battled all her life flared. Instead of grabbing him and shaking him until his teeth rattled, as every ounce of her was nagging to do, she rolled her eyes and sent up a silent prayer for—what, she wasn't certain. She only knew that it was heartfelt. "Luke."

Something in her voice made him pause and turn to look back at her. Whatever he saw in her face made his grin wobble, but only for an instant before he squared his shoulders. "I challenge you to a horserace!" He flung the words at her.

A sighing moan passed through the children clustered behind her. "Teacher." Catty pulled at Charity's skirt to get her attention, much as she had on Sunday at the Trumbles', and her voice quivered. "He's awful good at riding horseback."

"She's right, ma'am," Matt said, backing up his younger sister. "He gets on a horse, there's no catchin' him."

Charity looked into Catty's scared little face and up at the solemn expressions of the other children. "No one's ever beat him?" As if they were a wave, thirteen heads shook first one way, then the other.

She studied Luke, then the horses, then Luke again, so intently that he squirmed slightly in spite of himself. "All right. If the children give us permission to borrow their horses, I'll race you." His eyes went wide with astonishment and then he grinned so hugely she thought his face was in danger of splitting in two. "But," she said, forestalling his whoop of satisfaction, "this is the last contest. I mean it. Do you understand me?" Her voice was deadly quiet.

He was so excited he was rocking back and forth on his heels. "Sure, Teacher, sure."

She turned to the horrified children. "May we borrow two of your horses?"

Before they could answer, Luke pinned his glare on Will. "I want to ride Wrangler." It was not a question.

Will gulped and nodded reluctantly. "You be careful with him." The commanding firmness in his voice matched Luke's.

"You tellin' me how to ride a horse?" Luke asked derisively and turned away.

The children stared at Charity in stunned silence until Griff found his voice. "You can ride Storm. He's a good one, Teacher." In spite of his anxiety for her, his voice held only confidence in his horse.

She put her hand on his shoulder for a moment. "Thank you, Griff. I promise he won't come to any harm."

He nodded solemnly. "I'll go saddle him for you."

She turned toward Luke, who was already picking up Wrangler's saddle blanket. "Listen up." Her voice brooked no nonsense and she waited until he slowly turned to her. "We will have rules. It's too hot a day to be running the horses long and hard, so we'll make it easy on them." She ignored his snort of contempt that indicated he thought she was attempting to make it easy on herself. "We'll start at the front door of the schoolhouse and circle around back to the outhouses. We'll go behind them and come back to the front of the school." As he shrugged, she added, "We'll walk them around the course once first, to get the feel of it, then run them around twice. First one back to the front door the second lap we race is the winner."

Luke shrugged elaborately and resumed saddling Wrangler with practiced movements. While Griff tended Storm, Charity let the horse whiff her hand and then, murmuring to him, gently stroked his muzzle. Griff eyed this process and asked tentatively, "You know horses, Teacher?"

Her lips curved up. "Some." Taking Storm's reins, she led him to the front door where Luke was already mounted, his horse's hooves tramping over a long line the children had scraped in the dirt. Noting that he had taken the inside of the track, she raised her eyebrows and, without comment, moved to the outside position on his right. She let Storm get a last whiff of her hand, spoke quietly to him, and swung into the saddle. Her full skirts hampered her somewhat, but she adjusted them as best she could, praying that the unavoidable billowing would not spook the horse.

With the children strung out to the side of the starting line, Vincent called out, "Go!" and they began walking the horses along the path they'd take. Charity had had a good reason for walking the animals first, beyond that of inspecting the track. She also wanted to see what Luke would do. As she had suspected, he sat Wrangler as if he had been born on him, but he also made certain that his horse's head stayed just in front of hers. He also wasn't above leaning his mount into hers, trying to throw off Storm's pace. They rounded the outhouses, flanked by the children wheeling along the outer edge, and pulled up at the front door.

With Luke still defiantly on the inside, Charity nodded to herself. She had his measure now. She patted Storm's neck. He hadn't reacted to her skirts, so she figured he had been blanket-trained not to spook at coats and slickers fanning behind him. A definite break for her. Once more,

Vincent stood to the side. "On your mark, get set, go!"

Luke immediately jerked Wrangler into the lead. Charity let him stay far enough ahead that he couldn't ram her and cause Storm to stumble. She watched intently as he urged Wrangler forward, judging that he was running the animal harder than he should at the start. They swept around the outhouses and circled down to the front door, Luke triumphantly in the lead, the children yelling, cheering, and despairingly exhorting her at the top of their lungs to go faster.

As they rounded the outhouses on the final loop, he glanced back at her with a sneer. And as Luke turned and beckoned to her with an exaggerated sweep of his arm to catch up with them, Wrangler must have sensed the shift in his rider's carriage, for he slowed slightly in confusion. Charity promptly took Luke up on his invitation and, murmuring words of encouragement to Storm, urged him forward. They whizzed past Luke who, realizing his error, was trying frantically to correct it, which only confused Wrangler more. Charity and Storm were well in the lead when they zipped around the final corner and swept across the finish line.

The children, screaming at the top of their lungs, trailed Charity and Storm around the building as she eased him into a cooling trot and then a slowing walk, praising and petting him the while. When she finally dismounted, Griff took the reins, his smile wide. "You did right fine, Teacher."

Recognizing his sparse words for the high masculine praise they were, Charity's smile mirrored his. "He's a wonderful horse, Griff."

His grin widened. "I'll take him and tend him, ma'am." As he led Storm away, Charity surrendered to the cheers and hugs of the exuberant children surrounding her.

Horseman that he was in spite of his blunder, Luke had gradually slowed Wrangler to a cooling walk before dismounting and thrusting the reins at Will. Without a word, he stalked off to the creek. Charity glimpsed the exchange and Luke's retreat. She wondered if she should go after him, then encountered one of those not-knowing-if-she-was-right-or-wrong-but-it-must-be-made-instantly decisions she had heard Pa and Ma speak of. For the first time in her life, she understood how they must have felt. She stayed with the children and watched him go, wondering if she had made the right choice.

CHAPTER THIRTY-ONE

Luke didn't return to class. The other children, lively and alert, practically bounced into the room. The heat fatigue that had plagued them earlier had magically disappeared, and they obeyed Charity's instructions with a promptness that bordered on astonishing. She knew that they'd talk once they left the schoolhouse. There was no way to keep them from spreading the story of her victories over Luke, but before dismissing them for the afternoon, she tried. She called for their attention, not that it was really necessary, since they had been minutely following her every movement for the last hour.

As she stood before them and saw their faces lift attentively to her, it occurred to her how much she had come in these few weeks to care for these small persons entrusted to her charge. She'd been dutifully teaching them practical matters such as reading and arithmetic, but she realized now that she had also been shaping their minds and hearts and instilling in them the traits they would carry into adulthood. She wondered fleetingly if this was how a mother felt about her children, this sense of responsibility that she give them the very best of which she was capable.

She drew a deep breath. "Children, I know everyone is really excited about the contests Luke and I had today." They grinned and nodded eagerly. "Well, those contests are over now, and we mustn't give them more importance than they deserve."

Puzzled expressions crossed their faces, and a voice floated to her from the back of the room. "But Teacher, you won every time. Ain't you glad?" She recognized Will's voice and looked back to the desk he shared with Matt. Both boys were staring at her, their confusion evident.

"We can have contests with other people and win, but the winner doesn't necessarily have to feel overjoyed because he won. Sometimes, the winner can just feel relief that the contest is over without great harm being done." They looked at her blankly. She turned to the blackboard and wrote as she spoke. "A few years ago, at the end of the Civil War, someone said, 'With malice toward none; with charity for all ... to do all which may achieve and cherish a just and lasting peace among ourselves ....'" For the audible benefit of the younger children and the secret assistance of the older ones, she added, "Malice means acting mean toward someone else. Does anyone know who said these words?" She faced the class, waiting. At the back of the room, a hand timidly raised. "Yes, Becky?"

The girl stood and said softly, "It was President Abraham Lincoln."

"That's right. Thank you, Becky. Does anyone know what President

Lincoln meant when he said it?" A pause, during which everyone looked at everyone else and no one looked at the teacher for fear of being called on.

"It means that President Lincoln, after the Northern states won the War, didn't want to be mad at the Southern states, who lost. He knew it would be better for everyone if we all became one country, one family, and accepted one another, because everyone has faults and makes mistakes." The children, clearly not making the connection to Luke, waited for her to go on.

"We've all had contests with someone else, haven't we? Whether it's playing jacks or marbles or even the spelling bees we have in class. When it's a game or a contest, one person wins, right?" The children nodded. This they understood. "When a person wins, he doesn't make fun of the losers, does he?" A shaking of heads answered her. "Why do you think that is?"

This time Flanna Trumble raised her hand. "'Cause we're all friends, and it's not nice to make fun of a friend," she said earnestly.

"That's a very good answer, Flanna. We've all won sometimes, and we've all lost sometimes, so we know how it feels to lose. But it helps us feel better if no one makes fun of us because we've lost." The children again nodded their agreement.

"So should we talk about Luke and make fun of him? What do you think we should do?"

A resigned voice finally drifted from the rear of the room. "Be nice to him," it said on a long sigh. "Even if he did run my horse harder than he should of!"

***

Luke didn't show up to walk home with Charity, Matt and Catty, but that wasn't unusual. On the way to school, he stayed with them only as long as the ranch house was visible before taking off on his own. Charity considered it a mixed blessing that he appeared at school at all, and suspected that he did so only to avoid parental wrath if he stayed away. Charity couldn't remember a single afternoon when he'd accompanied them home, and felt secretly grateful, although a little guilty about that gratitude. Without his dampening presence, it was an ideal time for her to get to know Catty and Matt better, and for them to shed some of their shyness in being around Teacher. As they passed various displays of nature, both children eagerly shared their outdoor knowledge. Showing her how to creep quietly along in the grass, they found nests of ducks and geese along Willow Creek. Together they explained to her that the deep indentations in the prairie earth were old buffalo wallows, and pointed out bleaching bones of the buffalo themselves, killed when the railroad was being built three years earlier.

This afternoon, she wondered if either of them would bring up the subject of Luke, but they didn't talk about him, obviously preferring, as always, to avoid thinking about him as long as possible. She wondered what would happen at supper when Anne asked as she did each evening, what they had learned in school that day. Charity felt a little light-headed as she envisioned their probable response, and Luke's likely reaction, and wondered wildly if anyone would notice if she boarded the train and hightailed it back to O-hi-o.

When the dreaded moment came, Charity's stomach was in such a tight knot that Anne's face blurred a little and her voice sounded strangely distant as she eagerly asked the children to recount their lessons. Luke had come to the table his normal sulky, indifferent self, at least by all outward signs. Charity alone detected the forced nature of his attitude and his slightly red ears as he refused, as usual, to look at her.

When Anne asked, Matt and Catty exchanged a quick glance but didn't look at Charity. "We learned lots of different things today," Matt said slowly, and Charity waited for the full water bucket to slosh down on her head. "Teacher read more of *Gulliver's Travels,* and we learned about 'mal—malse'—" he looked at Charity for help and quickly away.

"Malice," she supplied and hoped her voice didn't sound as squeaky to the others as it did to her.

"Malice," he repeated dutifully. "It means bein' mean to someone," he added helpfully.

Anne looked intrigued. "What an interesting word. How did you come to be discussing it?"

Matt gulped. "Teacher was talkin' about Pres'dent Lincoln and how he didn't have none of that stuff for the South when he won the war."

In her enthusiasm, Anne didn't notice that his voice had trailed off. "My, you are learning so many wonderful things." She turned to Charity. "And the things I'm learning from what you're teaching them. It's a dream come true."

Anne, if you only knew. Charity was unable to carry the thought further without feeling even more light-headed. Luke's face was now as red as his ears and he was blatantly avoiding her gaze.

But Miss Sullivan was eyeing her with definite curiosity.

After supper and the dishes were done, the rest of the evening seemed to Charity to stretch interminably as they sat around the table, the children doing their homework, Anne and Miss Sullivan mending, and Charity working on next week's lesson plan. Ben had gone out to the bunkhouse to speak to Nightowl. Since Charity couldn't confess her clash with Luke without directly violating the standard she had set for her class, she spent the time in uneasy silence, wondering how and when she would be called to account for her decidedly unteacherlike conduct. In spite of her lecture to the children that afternoon, she knew it was inevitable that the story would get out. She spent a restless night and rose to a dawn that was strangely cheerless.

On the walk to school that morning, Luke took off as usual once they were out of sight of the house. Charity wondered dismally if he would even show up for class and how she could explain his absence to his parents and the board members. As they entered the school yard, she glanced quickly through the cluster of children already gathered. Luke wasn't among them. Her heart sank as she opened the door, even while she responded as cheerfully as she could to the children's greetings. She was just ready to call the class to attention when she heard the outer door open, then close. A very long moment later, Luke appeared in the main room doorway. He didn't look at her or the other students. Chin jutting out, he silently took his seat in the back of the room. The other children looked from him back to Charity, their eyes large with questioning. Ignoring Luke and everyone else equally, she said firmly, "We'll start our Bible reading this morning with verses from Isaiah, Chapter 40: *"He giveth power to the faint; and to them that have no power he increaseth strength. Even the youths shall faint and be weary ... But they that wait upon the Lord shall renew their strength; they shall mount up with wings as eagles; they shall run and not be weary; and they shall walk and not faint."*

She set the Bible aside. "Let's all bow our heads and say the Lord's Prayer." As the young voices rose in the old words, her eyes went to Luke. He wasn't praying. He was looking directly at her, his expression totally unreadable. *And what do you see in my face? Understanding, I hope. For a fact, if anyone knows about feeling rebellious, I do. Just ask Miss Sullivan!*

The morning passed in a drone of oral arithmetic problems and chanted spelling words. Luke didn't actively participate, but he didn't disrupt the proceedings, either. At recess, he remained aloof, but he didn't tease the younger children. Charity figured she could happily find gratitude in small blessings. The class had settled down to work after the noon dinner hour, and Charity had begun an explanation of the planets and their relationship to the sun, using the diagram she had drawn on the blackboard during lunch. The sudden peculiar creaking of the hinges on the outer door as it was pushed inward indicated that someone was entering the vestibule. The children's heads swung to the back of the room as Vincent Trumble, Ezra Clark, Ben Clayton, Cole Leverett, and Owen Corley filed in. The children caught their breath and Charity's heart sank to the last button on her shoes as the members of the school board removed their hats.

"Excuse us, Miss Michaels," Ezra Clark said solemnly. "We don't mean to disturb you, but we realized school has been in session nearly a month and we haven't paid you and your students a visit to see how the new building is working out." He gestured with his hat toward the side of the room. "May we stand over there? We promise not to interrupt."

Charity wondered frantically how all the air in the room could have evaporated between one breath and the next. Her lungs certainly seemed incapable of finding any. "Of course, gentlemen." She prayed the quaver in her voice wasn't noticeable to her sober-faced visitors or to her wide-eyed students. "Please make yourselves comfortable. We were just beginning a lesson about the solar system." The men filed silently to the right-hand wall, arranged themselves in an orderly line, turned toward her, and waited for her to resume her lesson. She would have been happy to begin if she could only remember even the first word of what she had planned to say. She opened her mouth and, incredibly, words began falling into the swimming-deep silence of the room. Her words, she realized with shock. With even greater shock, she realized that the words were making sense.

"This drawing shows our solar system. Away out here is the sun. There are eight planets that orbit—go around—the sun. As you can see, some of them have really strange names. We're going to learn the names of all of them and some downright peculiar facts about each one. For instance, the earth was formed about four billion, five hundred million years ago." She wrote the number on the board: 4,500,000,000. "That's a lot of zeroes, isn't it?" The attentively listening school board members nodded along with the children. "Now, there's a sentence that can help you remember the names of the planets and the order they are in from the sun." Once more she wrote on the board: My Very Enthusiastic Mother Just Sang Until Nighttime. "Mercury, Venus, Earth ..." As she talked, she actually forgot about the school board members, who were listening to her words with unabashed interest. So she was startled when, as she paused to let the children write the planet names in their school tablets, Mr. Clark cleared his throat.

"Thank you for allowing us to observe your lesson, Miss Michaels. This has been most interesting." The other men nodded their agreement. "Most interesting, indeed," he repeated, "but we must be going." Under the watchful eyes of the children, they filed out as solemnly as they had filed in. The outer door hinges creaked, and Charity and the children were left in the vast silence of the schoolroom.

Refusing to give heed to the thousand questions buzzing in her brain, Charity finished the day's lessons and dismissed the class. The children filed out as silently as the men had, but the moment they were out the door, their voices rose in excited conjecture, putting words to the very uncertainties Charity had been forcibly quashing for the last two hours.

The trouble was, she had no better answers than her students did.

That evening at supper, when Anne framed her usual query about the day's school activities, Matt and Catty looked at each other, but before they could respond, Ben cleared his throat. "I c'n answer that one for you, my Anne." She turned toward him, puzzled, and he grinned. "The board paid a surprise visit to the school today. Like Ezra said, we figured it was high time we checked to see if the new buildin' is workin' out proper. Miss Michaels, here, was tellin' the young ones about the sun, and the planets and a whole mess of interestin' stuff." Eyes twinkling, he nodded at Charity. "We decided that after all our effort, the schoolroom is workin' out just fine."

The knot that had been in Charity's stomach for so many hours unkinked so suddenly that she once again felt lightheaded. But this time, her lungs found more than enough air to breathe.

Miss Sullivan had been casting surreptitious glances at her since the evening before. As they were preparing for bed, she finally broached the subject on her mind.

"Mr. Clayton gave a pretty explanation for the school board's visit to you this afternoon. Are you aware of the true reason?" Leave it to Miss Sullivan not to beat around the bush, but to whack it head on and let the consequences fall where they may. This most unteacherish mixing of her metaphors gave Charity a moment to assemble her version of the events of the past couple of days. Before she could speak, however, Miss Sullivan continued. "Even a casual onlooker would notice that Luke is not the most genial of young men. Although you have not said as much, I suspect that he has been, to put it politely, a thorn in your side at school. You have not asked my advice on this subject and I, therefore, have not offered it. As a teacher, you must learn to handle situations that arise in the course of your teaching duties. That includes dealing with students who are," she paused significantly, "not inclined to follow the rules you have set forth."

Charity's memory of the day she had flaunted the rules in front of the whole class by refusing to answer Miss Sullivan's test question flashed before her eyes. Recalling those actions when she was thirteen, the age Luke was now, still had the power to make her cringe. When Miss Sullivan put it so bluntly into words, proving that she, too, remembered, Charity's cheeks flamed crimson.

Miss Sullivan didn't actually smile, but her lips twitched slightly. "I was, to put it mildly, surprised, and not certain what to do about it. I had never, in all my years of teaching, encountered such an attitude from a pupil whom I considered to be one of my best students. I only knew, absolutely, that I could not let you get the upper hand."

"You didn't," Charity admitted wryly. "You told me that by refusing to take the test, I had failed it. Then I had to take your note home to Pa and face his wrath. I never did decide which punishment was worse."

That faint tremor of Miss Sullivan's lips came again, but she said briskly, "As for Luke. I was fairly certain he was causing disruption, but not until this morning did the full truth come to light. Anne and I went into town to purchase some items at Clark's store. The Clarks' daughter Cora was there, supposedly for the purpose of helping behind the counter, but in reality enlightening the customers with a most vivid account of how you apparently challenged one of your young students to a series of contests which included skipping rocks, shooting marbles, and," she paused dramatically then continued in a scandalized whisper, "horse racing. In front of the entire class. And you beat him every single time." Charity started to speak, but Miss Sullivan didn't give her a chance to defend herself. "Cora was outraged that you should single out a mere child and cause him to be so totally humiliated because you couldn't resist the chance to show off your mannish skills. Her words, not mine. Her audience, who was quite spellbound, I assure you, naturally included Mr. Clark. With great presence of mind, he took Cora by the arm and removed her, protesting loudly, from the room and her fascinated listeners. When he returned, minus his vocal offspring, he immediately removed his merchant's apron and left the store. Anne and I had no idea where he was going or what he had in mind, until Mr. Clayton enlightened us tonight at supper."

Charity's mouth opened, but no words emerged. She had noticed Anne casting odd glances her way as they helped prepare the evening meal, but she had been so busy dreading facing Ben that she'd given little heed to the nonplused looks. Now understanding, she turned beet red to the roots of her hair. "Anne thought … Mr. Clark and the school board presumed I …." Her voice trailed off at the enormity of their assumptions.

Miss Sullivan nodded. "Apparently. However, you must remember that they gave you a chance to redeem yourself. Which, from Mr. Clayton's description, you did most admirably. 'My Very Enthusiastic Mother Just Sang Until Nighttime.'" It came out a bemused question before a sudden catch in her throat momentarily choked off her words. "You certainly put a loop in their lariats." Clearly, Miss Sullivan hadn't lived on a working ranch for a month without picking up a few of the finer details. "I suspect they'll be reconciling their past, present, and future impressions of you for quite some time to come."

CHAPTER THIRTY-TWO

The remainder of the school week passed quietly. Luke still didn't walk with them, but he did sidle in on time for class and stayed until afternoon dismissal. He sat silently at his desk in the back, his attitude still sulky, but he made no more trouble. Charity hoped he'd come to the same conclusion she had and that he, too, considered their clash to have been a draw. She didn't push him to active participation, particularly since, with a fine show of doing her a favor, he turned in his assignments on time.

She was dreading rather than looking forward to church services on Sunday, for she realized that her real test of acceptance would come not with the school board, but with the other women of the community. If they believed Cora's explanation of her motives, she was in deep trouble. She wasn't given a lot of free time to ponder the situation, though. Services were scheduled to be held at the Clayton ranch, and Charity devoted any spare moments she had to helping Anne give the house a top to bottom cleaning in preparation for the congregation's visit.

Anne herself made no mention of the clash between her son and the new teacher. For the first few days afterward, however, Charity noticed that Anne displayed an uneasiness bordering on embarrassment whenever Luke and Charity chanced to be in the room at the same time. This inevitable togetherness occurred at breakfast, supper, and in the evenings when they sat around the table with their various tasks. Charity did her best to distract Anne by talking about the farm, and home, and especially Ma. Anne never tired of hearing about the woman she had never met but whom she considered a close friend. Such discussions were a mixed blessing for Charity. Talking about them brought her absent family close, while at the same time it added to the homesick feeling she could not shake. No matter how hard she tried to persuade herself that her presence in this community, with a respectable job, proved that she was indeed grown up, she was not entirely successful. If it were true, why did she sometimes wake in the night wondering what on earth she was doing here?

***

Sunday arrived. On waking, Charity wildly considered claiming some annoying illness, such as typhoid fever, that would, with apologies, keep her from mingling with the other women who would, true to form, begin arriving long before the services were scheduled to start. Miss

Sullivan and Anne promptly and neatly foiled any such attempt by determinedly keeping her with them in the kitchen doing chores that they somehow kept dreaming up until it was too late for her to escape. Brinna Trumble and Libby Clark came first. Charity glanced apprehensively behind Libby, but Cora had not come in with her mother. Before she had time to really digest the implications, Charity was jolted by a strange sense, almost of being sheltered, as Anne stepped close to her. In a rush of knowledge that brought tears to her eyes, Charity realized that Anne was declaring her support of the teacher and her actions against all comers, including the women who were such a vital part of her community life. Dazed, she felt Miss Sullivan quietly press close to her other side.

Coming face to face with such unyielding solidity, Libby and Brinna exchanged startled glances. They must have come to an unspoken agreement, for they turned back to the wall of three. "Anne Clayton," Brinna said in the scolding tone that made her children sit up and take notice on the rare occasions she used it. "What do you mean, preparing all this food?" She gestured to the table and the full bowls and platters residing there.

"You know perfectly well the rest of us are supposed to supply the eatables when you supply the house," Libby indignantly chimed in. "That's what friends do," she added, as if Anne had forgotten.

After a second of silence, during which Anne looked from one woman to the other, she smiled and held out her arms. "I was just being silly," she confessed, hugging them. The tension broken, Brinna and Libby arranged their own generous contributions on the counter by the dry sink and turned to greet Lillie Monroe and Phebe Braden as they came in. Soon the kitchen was filled with chatter and laughter as the women joined in making the final preparations for the potluck that would follow the prayer meeting. For the first time since she had come to the community, Charity felt completely relaxed. She knew that, with the exception of Cora, she had been accepted.

The men came from the corrals where they'd gathered to talk of cattle and horses. The various discussions trickled off as Ben and Anne took their places at the front of the group and Anne began to lead them in the opening hymn. *"A mighty fortress is our God ..."* Charity had been standing to the side, keeping an eye on Eve, as she'd promised Anne. The toddler had finally come to accept Charity as a part of the household, whether by default or out of resignation for the situation, the acceptee wasn't certain. She was, however, glad. The little girl with flame-bright red hair, who was about a year older than Merry and possessed a heaping supply of mischievous moments, helped ease the empty spot in Charity's heart for her own younger sister. She was bending over Eve, retying the ribbon that refused to stay neatly attached to the child's stubby braid, when she felt movement beside her. Without straightening, she swung her gaze up to see who had nudged into the confined space.

Cork's impish grin greeted her.

Unaccountably, her heart started beating faster as her fingers, of their own accord, finished tying Eve's ribbon and gave it a final pat. Task completed, she unbent from her less-than-graceful position. If he noticed her embarrassment at being caught in such a pose, he didn't let on. He crinkled his nose at Eve, who rewarded him by scowling and clutching Charity's skirt. Lifting her, Charity settled the child on the hip opposite Cork, from where Eve continued to stare unblinkingly at him. With an expression of sad defeat, he turned his attention to Charity and joined her in singing the final words of the old hymn. " ... *God's truth abideth still, His kingdom is forever.*" He had a pleasant singing voice. As he continued to stand beside her, she strove dutifully to concentrate on the services. She raised her eyes to the front of the room, intending to look at Ben and Anne, and almost keeled over. Cora Clark, standing a short distance to the side, was glaring at her with a coldness that sent a shudder down Charity's spine.

Knowledge that Cora had been the ultimate cause of the school board's unannounced visit to her classroom didn't dispose Charity toward following her own name's instructions and invoking kind thoughts toward the young woman. Rather, she felt a flash of anger that caused a slight wavering of the dead-fish expression in front of her. She must have tightened her hold on Eve, for the child squirmed in protest, bringing her back to awareness of her surroundings. "Sorry, sweetie," she murmured, and bent forward to kiss the little girl's cheek. Her fury ebbed but didn't fade completely as she once more tried to listen to Ben, who was now reading from the Bible. Shame for her anger welled within her. *To have such an attitude in church, of all places!* Then she wondered briefly if that retort was aimed at Cora or herself.

Shaken and confused, when the services ended, she allowed Cork to lead her out of the crowd. Anne came to claim Eve, who reached out eager arms to her mother. With a quick glance at Charity and the young man standing beside her, Anne, praising Eve for being such a good girl during the meeting, retreated. Cork watched her go before he turned back to Charity with a thoughtful expression. "Say, before we go get somethin' to eat, I'd just like to tell you that I heard about your run-in with Luke."

No, Charity thought wearily. *Not you, too.*

Cork, not having heard her interior admonition, plodded on. "I have to admit, Luke isn't high on my list of fav'rite folks. His stayin' in the bunkhouse hasn't improved my opinion, either. He's got a smart mouth and a chip on his shoulder that'd break his foot if it ever fell off. One thing he is good at, though, is horses. He treats 'em right and he's real knowledgeable when it comes to handlin' 'em. They even seem to take to him." He shook his head as if admitting the unlikelihood of what he was saying. "Sure don't know where it came from, but it does make workin' with him a mite more tolerable. What I'm gettin' around to askin' is where in blazes did you learn to ride so well that you could beat him?" His tone was such a mixture of astonishment and admiration that she felt a sudden spasm of mirth well up and cascade over her lingering resentment of Cora's undisguised antagonism.

"Just because I've come all the way from citified O-hi-o—" she couldn't resist mimicking Luke's sneer "—doesn't mean I don't know my way around horses. I grew up on a farm where my Pa and Ma raised Morgan horses for sale. Those horses had to be exercised every day, and my sister Rose and I got volunteered to do a lot of it." Her face lit in a moment of happy reminiscence. "Rose and I used to race when we could get away with it. I'm sure Pa would have skinned us alive if he'd known we were being less than careful with his precious horseflesh. Lucky for us, he never found out." She flashed him a guilty smile that still held a hint of triumphant mischief in it. "Promise you won't tell him."

He grinned and held up his right hand. "I promise. Bein' the cause of you gettin' skinned wouldn't be pleasant at all. But what about the skippin' rocks and shootin' marbles? Heard tell you left the little maverick in the dust with those games, too."

She wondered briefly where he had "heard tell" and from whom. *Is there no one in the whole Territory who hasn't gotten wind of our clash?* She sighed. *If hearing all about it is difficult for me, what must it be for Luke?* Forcing herself to casual cheerfulness, she explained about Mill Creek, and how Rose's and her goal had been to beat Mac's boastful assertion that he had skipped a rock fourteen times. They hadn't actually seen him do it, but they'd made a vow that, just in case it was true, they intended to break his record.

"Did you?" Cork asked curiously.

She shook her head regretfully. "We practiced until we'd used up all the stones along both sides of the creek that we considered worth throwing. And there were a lot of them. Rose got thirteen once, and I made twelve, but neither one of us could hit fourteen—or fifteen like we had to do to beat Mac's record."

"Did you ever tell him you were workin' on it?"

"No. Fortunately, we were smarter than that. If we'd told him, we never would have heard the end of it."

"Maybe if you'd told him, he would have had to prove that he'd stretched the truth a mite."

Her eyes widened. "We were just so determined to beat him in something, we never thought of that. The sneak! I can't wait to tell Rose."

He burst into laughter at her unconcealed indignation. "And the marbles?" he prompted over her sputtering.

"That was mostly by accident," she admitted. "After Mac left home to attend medical school in Philadelphia, I found a bag of marbles he left behind. Since Rose and I had picked the creek edge clean of all skippable stones, we needed to find other worlds to conquer. The boys at school were forever challenging each other and boasting about their marble collections, so she and I decided that we'd learn, too. We knew we couldn't ever admit to practicing, but it made a dandy secret for just between the two of us. When the boys were bragging about capturing seven or eight or nine marbles in a turn, we could smile because we knew we could do lots better than that."

"It appears Luke did a lot of underestimatin' you that day," he said thoughtfully. "Remind me never to make the same mistake."

As he led her toward the kitchen to claim their plates of food, Charity laughed. Already she was thinking of how amused Rose would be when she described in her next letter Cork's astonishment—and his unconcealed admiration—of her besting Luke all because on long-gone hot summer days, two young girls had determinedly fulfilled their vows to beat pesty older boys at their own games.

And one boy in particular. The problem is, in the long run, I still lost.

***

While Charity was conquering Wyoming Territory, events of which she was unaware because Rose's letter had not yet reached her had been taking place at home. On a July day of sweltering heat, Doc and Mac had returned to the office after making their rounds. A knocking—or, rather, a kicking—at the front door startled them both, for patients usually just walked in without announcing their arrival. Mac had dumped his bag on the corner of the desk, pulled off his hat, and was in the process of wishing he could shed his suit coat. "I'll get it," he mumbled, and pulled open the door.

Garth Van Ellis, Martha's son, stood in the doorway, grinning and holding a covered bucket in each hand. "Hi, Young Doc. Couldn't get the door with both hands full."

Mac, amused, stepped aside and ushered him in. "Got a couple of sick buckets? Usually our patients walk in on two feet."

"I was under strict orders to bring this over without drinking any on the way. Your Ma and Miss Amity came to visit my Ma a while ago. Seems the three of them put their heads together and decided you probably didn't want to be drinking coffee on such a warm day, so they made this for you, instead."

Doc recovered sufficiently from their visitor's unexpected appearance to yank Mac's bag from the corner of the desk and put a newspaper down for Garth to set the two buckets on, one of which was suspiciously frosted with moisture. After removing the covers, Garth stood back with a grand gesture. The two medical men peered into the containers. "In my expert laboratorial opinion, that's lemonade," Doc said gravely. "And that one's ice."

"I concur, Doctor," Mac said with equal solemnity. "But shouldn't we analyze them to make certain?"

"An excellent suggestion. We just happen to have the proper test tubes here, clean and ready for use." Doc produced three coffee cups which Mac had washed earlier, and handed one to Garth, who had been listening to their banter in bemused silence.

After filling the cups with ice and lemonade, Mac lifted his in a formal toast. "To three extremely wise women."

Doc and Garth hefted their cups and drank deeply, clearly agreeing with Mac's diagnosis. When Doc offered him a refill, Garth shook his head reluctantly. "I have to get back to the livery. I went home for lunch and got recruited to deliver this. Mr. Wrade'll be wondering where I am." Garth had been employed at the livery stable for two years. His handiness with and understanding of horses made it a natural place for him to work. He was becoming so skilled at taking care of equine needs that he had virtually displaced Doc and Mac as the main source of any medical attention his charges required. His dream of attending veterinary college was one he had little hope of fulfilling, however. A pastor's salary could not be stretched to such limits, and he did not expect Reverend Gallaway and Martha to try to force it to do so. After marrying Garth's mother, Shawn Gallaway had raised Garth and the younger children in every way that a birth father would. Garth considered that more than ample.

After Garth left, Doc and Mac settled down to a second cup of lemonade, but they had scarcely drunk any when a pounding of feet on the board walkway and a scrabbling at the office door interrupted them. Mac sprang to his feet. This commotion portended a more serious matter than Garth's arrival had indicated. As he reached to pull the door open, it pushed inward and a young boy fell against Mac's knees. He was breathing hard and sweat was pouring down his freckled face. "It's Chris Painter!"

Mac grabbed him before he fell on the floor and led him over to the chair by the desk. "Take it easy," he said. "Take a minute to catch your breath. Whatever it is can't be so tremendously important that you should be rushing around in all this heat."

Doc was already wetting a towel from the moisture on the ice bucket. He handed it to Mac, who brushed it across the boy's wrists and lightly across the back of his neck, then, carefully, across his forehead and cheeks. As the ragged breathing eased, Mac said gently, "It's all right, Chris. Just tell us when you're ready."

The boy arched back and dug in his pants pocket. "Grandpa said to give you this." He held out a crumpled yellow envelope with Mac's name scrawled on it. A hard fist squeezed Mac's heart as he took the telegram Miles Painter at the train depot had received and sent to the doctor's office.

Doc poured a cup of lemonade and handed it to the boy. "Here you go, Chris. I expect you're cooled down enough to drink this. But maybe we should walk you like a horse for a while first to make sure you aren't still overheated after your long run. What do you think?"

Effectively distracted, the child giggled at Doc's comparison and paid no attention as Mac pulled out the sheet of writing. Schooled as he was to show no emotion over a diagnosis, Mac closed his eyes and stood utterly still for a moment after reading the message. Doc eyed him sharply over the boy's head, but said nothing.

Mac dug in his pocket, crouched down beside Chris, who was happily guzzling his lemonade, and handed him a nickel. "Here you are. You did a fine job of delivering this telegram. I'll be sure to tell your Grandpa next time I see him. But you'd better get back now so he doesn't worry about you being gone too long." The boy put the cup down and obediently headed out the door. "Just don't run," Mac called after him. Childish laughter floated back.

As soon as Mac shut the door and leaned against it, Doc said gruffly, "What's happened?"

He took a deep breath and wordlessly handed the telegram to the older man. Doc read it and drew in a sharp breath of his own. "All right. This is bad. But we don't know for sure it's bad enough to panic over. Garth said your Ma and Amity were at the parsonage. They may still be there. You'd better get on over and let her know."

Mac nodded, snatched up his hat and, out of pure habit, his medical bag. As he reached for the door knob, Doc's stern voice trailed him. "Don't run in this heat or we'll have to be treating you, too. As a doctor, you don't know that it's hopeless. Remember that when you tell her."

The words echoed in Mac's ears to the rhythm of his feet pounding on the boardwalk as he hurried toward the parsonage. *You don't know that it's hopeless. You don't know that it's ....*

Somewhere between the doctor's office and the little parsonage next to the white-painted church, his medical training sank in. *You don't know*

234

that it's hopeless. This time, the words held a glimmer of meaning. He ascended the steps and, resisting the urge to either pound on the door or walk right in, he rapped the knocker and waited. It seemed an eternity but was in reality only a matter of moments before Shawn Gallaway opened the door. Mac was certain he'd regained his professional demeanor, but Shawn had been ministering to other people's broken hearts and souls for many years.

His smile of greeting faded as he drew Mac inside, shut the door, and gestured to the telegram still clutched in Mac's hand. "Do you need to come to my study first?" he asked quietly. When Mac shook his head, Shawn gestured down the hallway toward a closed door from behind which the sound of feminine laughter floated to them. "Your mother and Amity are in the kitchen with Martha." He led the way down the hall and pushed open the swinging door. Another burst of laughter trickled off as he pressed the door wider, allowing Mac to enter. The merriment on the three women's faces changed to puzzlement as they caught sight of him, but he had eyes only for Amity, watched her perplexity change to dread as she read the expression on his face.

"Mac, what—?"

He had no words to tell her what must be told. He lifted the telegram. "This came," he said huskily and handed it to her.

She stared at it for a moment before taking it from him, and he slipped his arm around her as she unfolded it. She gave a choked cry and buried her face against his shoulder. He held her tightly, the telegram crushed between them. He murmured, "We don't know that it's hopeless, Amity-love. Keep remembering that."

Seeing the dread on his mother's face, and the bewildered worry on Shawn's and Martha's, he forced the words out. "It's from Amity's father. Mrs. Terrill has come down with diphtheria. Apparently, she became ill almost three weeks ago. They thought she was improving, but last night she took a turn for the worse. She's been asking for Amity and Dr. Terrill thinks it would be best if Amity goes home. He says the peak of the epidemic has passed, so there shouldn't be any danger to her if she returns to Philadelphia immediately."

Amity raised her head from his shoulder. Her eyes were glazed with shock, but her voice held only a faint tremor as she said quietly, "Father wouldn't ask me to come home unless he felt it was absolutely necessary. I have to go as soon as possible."

CHAPTER THIRTY-THREE

Ethan was out in the cornfield, inspecting the stalks that were, as he had jubilantly announced at breakfast, growing so fast he could hear the joints popping when he walked by. Hearing the rapid hoofbeats of a team approaching on the road from town, he hurried to the edge of the field. Lynx and Lyra were coming at a brisk pace, pulling the buggy with Larissa, Amity, and Mac crowded together on the seat. Tied to the back of the buggy, Cygnus, whom Mac had ridden to town that morning, was following valiantly along.

Ethan stepped into the roadway and Mac eased back on the reins, slowing the team as they came alongside him. Seeing the distress on their faces, Ethan moved to Larissa's side of the buggy and reached his hands to her. "What's happened?" he asked. "Are you all right?"

She gripped his work-roughened palms as if they were a lifeline. "We're all right. But trouble's come for Amity. She'll be leaving tomorrow to go home. We'll tell you as soon as we get to the house."

Reassured for his family, but heavy-hearted for the young woman who had become another daughter to him over the past several weeks, he nodded. "I'll ride Cygnus and meet you there."

As they halted by the kitchen path, Rose, holding Merry by the hand, came hurrying down the walkway to greet them. Fear flitted across her face as she saw their grim expressions. Reading her panic correctly, Ethan signed, "It's not Charity. Amity's got trouble at home. They'll tell us inside."

She couldn't suppress a sigh of relief for Charity's sake but dread tugged at her for Amity's problem, whatever it might be. In the lonely weeks since Charity's departure, Rose had come to appreciate Amity's quiet strength. It wasn't, could never be, the same as with Charity, but somehow, when Amity was around, the ache in Rose's heart was a little comforted.

Ethan led the horses to the watering trough, and then, for one of the few times in his life, guided them to the shady pasture without unharnessing them. He would come back to tend them as soon as he could, but for now, Amity's trouble took precedence.

When he entered the kitchen, everyone was already gathered around the table. Merry was cuddled on Larissa's lap, and Rose was pouring tall glasses of water; it had been a hot and dusty ride from town. He slid into his chair beside Larissa and reached for her free hand. Then he remembered Rose, squeezed Larissa's fingers in a quiet message of strength, and released them so that he could sign the discussion as it proceeded. The emptiness in his heart for his missing daughter welled painfully. How they had taken for granted her energetic signing of their conversations to ensure that Rose was included in the family give-and-take. Resolutely pushing the memory away, he concentrated on Amity's relating of what had taken place.

Once the details were laid before them, Mac shared that he'd already purchased her tickets for the train leaving at eleven o'clock in the morning. Clearing his throat, he turned to her. The fingers of her hand nearest him were already tucked into his. Now he reached for her other hand, too. "Amity, I'm going with you tomorrow."

Her eyes widened and, for the first time in two hours, some of the sorrow left them. But only for a moment. "Mac, you can't. You have your medical responsibilities here. I can't take you away from those."

"I have bigger responsibilities elsewhere. And Doc agrees with me completely."

"You talked to Doc? When?"

"When I went back to the office to pick up Cygnus, I told Doc that I intended to go with you."

"Just like that? What did he say?"

"He said if I didn't make the trip back with you, he'd go himself." The faintest of smiles touched Mac's lips. "He allowed that you'd probably much prefer my presence to his, however, so I'd better quit dragging my tail—" He coughed slightly. "Or words to that effect, anatomically speaking—"

He got no further for she leaned her head against his chest and gave a tremulous sigh. "You'd better do as he says, then, before he comes up with a whole new vocabulary—anatomically speaking, of course."

Engrossed in each other, they had forgotten Ethan, Larissa, and Rose, still sitting across from them. Since no translation of this part of the discussion was required for Rose's sake, Ethan took Larissa's hand again. Their eyes met and, as one, they nodded.

Rose went upstairs with Amity to help her pack, while Ethan and Mac went out to tend the horses. Supper was a silent meal, punctuated only by Merry's cheerful chatter as, too young to understand the heavy hearts around her, she contributed how she and Rose had baked cookies. Rose explained how helpful the little girl had been by stirring in the flour, dropping the spoonfuls of dough on the pan, and helping take them off when they were baked.

Amity roused herself to ask, "May I have one of your cookies, Merry? I bet they're delicious."

The little girl grinned. "Yes." She added in a loud whisper, "Wose not looked, I eated."

After everyone had finished their supper or made sufficient pretense of doing so, Merry served the cookies. She made certain that each person took a bite and assured her that they had never tasted anything so delicious before she went on to the next.

Merry's antics carried them through supper, but all too soon they were thrust back into the reality of fear and uncertainty for the future. While Larissa and Rose washed and dried the dishes, Mac and Amity went to the cabin so that he could pack for the trip. During all the weeks that she'd been living on the farm, she had not been inside the old log building. They had held to the agreement they'd made when she came home with him. Not that it had been easy. There were plenty of romantic, secluded places about the farm, and they had had ample occasion in their rambles over the countryside to indulge themselves without taking advantage of the privacy the cabin offered. Now, as he held the door for her and she slipped inside, her eyes widened in delight. "Mac, this is wonderful. This is where your father and mother lived when they were first married?"

He nodded. "There've been a few changes over the years, of course, but not many." While he spoke, he surreptitiously began to gather up scattered socks and the blanket and pillow he'd tossed on the floor that morning and neglected to pick up in his rush out the door.

"They must have been very happy here."

"Ma and Pa were happy when they were together. I never really thought much about it when I was growing up. They were just who they were. Then Pa went to war, and it was never the same. When he died, Ma— " His voice caught. "I don't mean that Ma and Ethan haven't had a good marriage. I think they're right for each other in every way. It's just that, sometimes, I wonder how it would have been if Pa had lived."

She reached out to him and he drew her into his arms. "I love you so much," he murmured against her hair. "Since I've known you, I've come to realize much better what Ma and Pa had together, and to appreciate it in a way I never really understood before."

She raised her head and he saw the shine of tears in her eyes. "Mac, what they had, we have now. And it will always be ours. That's why I'm so glad you're coming with me tomorrow. As long as I'm with you, I can face the future. I'm scared, so very scared for Mother. I've been a doctor's daughter all my life. If she's asking for me, and Father told me to come home as quickly as I can, I know it's bad. I'm terrified she'll die before I get there, and I'll never be with her again." Her voice broke and she once more buried her face against his chest.

All he could do was hold her close and tell her he loved her. He couldn't promise her it would be all right. On a bright spring day, Pa had hugged Ma, Rose, and him before riding away to war. The last sight Mac had ever had of him was Pa sitting erect astride Deneb's back and waving and smiling at them, before he rounded the turn in the road that had taken him out of their sight forever.

He couldn't promise Amity that the glimpse she'd had of her mother smiling and waving goodbye as the train pulled out of the station the day they left would not be her final one.

But he could promise her that he would be beside her, no matter what.

***

In the morning, Larissa put together a hearty breakfast that no one could eat. She wondered dully how many such meals she had already prepared in her life, and how many more lay in the future for her to make because someone was leaving the family circle. Except that this time two were leaving: the young woman they had taken into their hearts in the short time she had been with them, and the son Larissa had so joyfully welcomed back after his five-year absence. *It's too soon to lose him again.* But for all the rebellious protests of her heart, she knew that Mac could do no differently. Nor, could she have chosen for him, would she have wanted him to.

The ride to the train station took some extra planning to ensure that everyone, and all the luggage, would arrive at the proper place and on time. It made a good topic of discussion at breakfast when no one could find words for the one important subject, and no other topics mattered in the least. At last Mac said that since he was all packed, right after breakfast he would drive the buckboard and take the trunks and bags to the station. That way, they could all ride together in the buggy later.

Silence fell for a moment before Rose asked, "Mac, did you pack carefully or did you make a snarled mess by just throwing into your trunk whatever clothes came to hand and leaving them in whatever order they landed?"

Mac looked painfully guilty, as if Rose had been peering over his shoulder when he was doing exactly that. Nevertheless, he shot back with injured pride, "I'll have you know I packed very carefully. I didn't put in any wet towels and I put the socks together two by two, just like Ma taught me."

His triumph at this success was more than a little tarnished when Rose asked sweetly, "Paired up how? Brown to black and green to gray?"

His mouth opened but no words came out. Finally, he managed to intone with great dignity, "It was kind of dark in the cabin for making perfect matches. But I know I got 'em all because I checked and there were no strays lying on the floor."

According to plan, Mac left in the buckboard immediately after breakfast and was back in good time to change his clothes and join the family in the buggy for the trip to town. Amity came down the stairs dressed in the outfit she had worn on the trip from Philadelphia. She tried to smile at Larissa. "It still fits. I've been eating so much of your wonderful cooking that I was afraid I'd completely outgrown it."

"That's farm life for you," Larissa joked in return. "Our reward for working hard to produce all that food is being able to eat just as much as we want of it and still stay slim." She held out her arms. "You look lovely, my dear," she said as Amity hugged her back, both of them laughing so that they wouldn't cry.

Ethan and Mac came in together. At sight of the two women, their unplanned, simultaneous whistles of admiration, momentarily at least, squelched any further danger of tears.

By unspoken arrangement, Mac and Amity took the backseat of the buggy as Ethan assisted Rose and Larissa into the front. He started to swing Merry up to Larissa's lap, but Amity spoke quickly. "Please, may she sit back here with us?"

Larissa turned, startled. "Are you sure?"

Mac and Amity both nodded and reached toward the toddler. Larissa shook her head in mock wonder. "If it's what you want. She's a wiggler," she warned as Ethan lifted Merry to their outstretched hands.

They settled the little girl between them and she snuggled in, smiling in self-satisfaction at her mother as she did so.

Larissa was certain that the ride to the train station was the shortest she'd ever taken. In what seemed no time at all, they were pulling into the lot beside the depot. While Ethan and Mac tended to the baggage, Larissa, Rose, and Amity went into the waiting room, Merry holding firmly to Amity's hand. Larissa wondered if, somehow, the child sensed the separation that was coming, even if she couldn't understand it. Before she could dwell on the possibility, Shawn and Martha came forward to meet them.

Martha reached out her hands to Amity. "We just had to come and say goodbye, and tell you how very special it has been getting to know you this summer."

"Yes," Shawn agreed, putting his hand on Mac's shoulder, a definitely unministerial twinkle in his eyes. "We've watched you grow up, and admired the good choices you've made over the years. We've concluded, though, that your choice to bring Amity into your life has to rank right up there with the wisest decisions you've made." He turned to Amity and took her hands in his. "We will be praying for you and your family, that your mother will be quickly restored to health," he said, all laughter gone. "And we look forward to your speedy return here to take up the life you have been anticipating with this young man." Smiling, he reached for Mac's hand and joined it with Amity's. "God bless you both."

As he stepped back, the door behind them opened, and Doc strode in. "Good. I'm not too late. Sylvie Mayhew picked this morning to come to the office and tell me in detail about the pain in her jaw. And, no, I didn't tell her that if she'd quit flapping it so much, it probably would heal right quick." His eyes swept the attentively listening group as if judging whether they believed him. "I was tempted, I'll admit, but I resisted." He glared at Mac. "If you don't get back here right quick with this perfect-for-you young woman, I swear I'm going to wrap Sylvie and her flapping jaw in gauze and send her to you in Philadelphia as an early wedding present."

Mac was still holding Amity's hand, but he raised his other as if to ward off the horror of Doc's threat. "We'll be back just as soon as we can, Doc. That's a promise."

Doc took Amity's free hand. "Your mother has some of the finest doctors in the country looking after her, I guarantee you that. Your father and I have known each other since Hector was a pup, and sure as bees make honey, I'd trust him with my life. You hold on to that when you start feeling down."

She managed a faint smile. "Is that your special prescription?"

He assumed the sternest expression he could summon up. "To be taken in large and frequent doses. And if Young Doc here doesn't—" The train whistle blasted, cutting off his further medical orders.

As everyone hurried out the door to the station platform, Doc held Mac back for a moment. "I want you to keep me closely posted on Matilda's progress."

"I'll send a telegram every day, Doc. And if you know of anything to do—"

The old man shook his head. "Oliver'll tend the medical side. Amity will tend to her mother. You tend to Amity. She's going to need your heart's understanding like never before. You see she gets it," he said grimly.

"I will." Mac's eyes held Doc's for a long moment that sealed his solemn promise.

When they reached the others on the platform, there was time only for quick, final hugs all around, then Mac and Amity hurried up the passenger car steps. The train started with a lurch, was a smudge of gray smoke in the distance, was gone, leaving the group standing on the platform in a deafeningly loud silence.

Martha finally spoke into the emptiness. "It's nearly noon. Why don't you come to the parsonage for lunch? We'd love to have you." Before Larissa could raise any objections, she added, "And it won't be any trouble. I expect Gretta and Mara are putting the finishing touches on everything right now. If you don't come, all their hard work will be for nothing."

Her expression was so innocent as she added this sledgehammer incentive that Larissa had to smile. She looked up at Ethan, who nodded. "Sounds like a fine idea to me." *A pleasant way to put off the ride home and facing the emptiness there, at least for a little while.* So clearly did she hear the words he did not utter that she scanned the other faces to see if anyone else was aware of them. Apparently not, because the group was moving toward the side lot where the horses and buggies were parked. Rose was leading Merry away, and the little girl was looking backward in confusion. With a last glance down the tracks, now empty even of the smoke smudge that had marked the train's path of departure, Larissa turned to Ethan, who took her hand. His smile didn't quite reach his eyes, but it was the best he could do to send her a silent message of encouragement that she accepted gratefully.

Once in the buggy, Merry, ensconced on the backseat with Rose, started moving her fingers, conversing with the big sister who could only "hear" her when she talked this way. She didn't understand why it was different with Rose, but she accepted it.

Although she had every confidence in Rose, Larissa half-turned to the back to make certain Merry was sitting properly and not getting ready to jump out the side of the buggy. The little girl, short legs with buttoned black shoes sticking straight out in front of her, was half hidden in the depths of the leather seat, her upper body turned toward Rose. Her fingers were fluttering frantically and her expression was one of pure panic. Before Larissa could ask, Rose leaned toward Merry and put her arms around her. Over the noise of the buggy wheels, Rose's voice came muffled, but Larissa's heart heard the words and she had to press her lips tightly together to keep from crying out. *She's asking Rose. Let Rose answer her.*

Larissa strained to hear the words as they floated brokenly to her. "Merry, we didn't forget Amity and Mac. They went bye-bye on the train. It's all right, sweetie. You like visiting Gretta and Mara?" Merry nodded vigorously. "Well, Amity and Mac are visiting Amity's Ma. They'll come home after lots of sleeps. Until then, I'll need extra-big sister loves. Will you give me some?"

Grasping the idea that Amity and Mac hadn't been abandoned on purpose, and that they would come back eventually, Merry's panic subsided. She considered Rose's request for a long moment. Finally she nodded and gently patted her big sister's cheek. "Me give you," she signed solemnly and hugged her tightly.

Fortunately, the parsonage came into view and Ethan pulled the team to a halt beside the front gate. In the busyness of alighting from the buggy, and in the excitement of seeing Gretta, Mara, and Camden, who all came running to meet her, Merry forgot to be worried about Amity and Mac being left behind.

Larissa found a moment to whisper close to Rose's ear, "You did that beautifully. I know she understands lots more words and ideas than she can say. I'm just so proud of you for explaining it at her level."

Rose smiled ruefully. "Thanks, Ma. She seemed to believe me. Now if I could just believe it myself, I'd feel better."

Larissa hugged her about the waist. "Welcome to the pitfalls of motherhood. The important thing is that she accepted it. I don't think I've ever seen her so panicked, thinking we'd forgotten them. It's good to know she has a tender side, especially since it took her a while to get used to them when they first came." Larissa gave Rose's waist a final squeeze and released her as they went in the front door to be surrounded by the warmth and friendship that were a soothing balm to their hurting hearts.

CHAPTER THIRTY-FOUR

The ride home a few hours later was a silent one. Merry, worn out from playing tag and hide-and-seek with Mara, Gretta, and Camden, fell asleep on Rose's lap in the backseat. Neither Ethan nor Larissa could think of anything much to say, so they stayed quiet, too.

Ethan pulled the buggy up to the kitchen path, assisted Larissa down, then reached to take Merry from Rose. He cradled the little girl, still soundly sleeping, against his shoulder and carried her to her bed in the room off the kitchen. Larissa followed and together they removed the child's bonnet and small black shoes. It was still too hot to cover her with her favorite blanket, but Larissa compromised by putting it close to the curved-in-sleep fist where she could grasp it if she wanted. They stood looking down at her, so peacefully asleep, and treasured the moment of silence, the soft breathing, and the stillness of their high-spirited bundle of joy. Without speaking, lest they wake her, they tiptoed out and Ethan pulled the door nearly shut. Only then did he let out his breath. "She can be a handful," he admitted, "but I sure am glad she's ours." He reached out and drew Larissa into his arms. Words were no use against the bleakness of the too large, too empty house. She leaned her head against his chest and, for a quiet space of time, they shared the desolation in their hearts.

Ethan went out to tend the team and Larissa realized that Rose wasn't in the sitting room, as she had supposed her to be. She went upstairs, but Rose's room was empty, too. She heard a small noise from the end of the hall and moved toward the door of the room that had been Amity's. She found Rose standing in front of the commode that held the rose-patterned bowl and pitcher that Martha had given Larissa and Larissa had put in this room for Amity's use and pleasure. Knowing that Rose hadn't heard her pause in the doorway, Larissa stepped heavily enough to vibrate the floorboards as she walked across the room, thus signaling her presence to her daughter.

Caught unaware nevertheless, Rose jumped. Seeing her mother, she relaxed and turning back to the bowl, ran her fingers gently along the pink-flowered edge. "Amity liked this set so much," she said softly. "She was so pleased that you put it in here for her to use." She smiled faintly. "She said it meant even more to her because she realized it must have been hard for you to give it up to share it with her." The trace of a smile vanished as her face crumpled and she fell into Larissa's arms. "Oh, Ma, why does everyone else get to leave here and I just have to keep staying? Mac left, Hans left, Charity's gone, and now Amity, and Mac again." She drew back and covered her mouth with her hand. "I'm sorry. I know Amity didn't leave just for a pleasure trip. She has to be terrified for her mother. And of course Mac had to go with her. It's just that everyone else has places to go and things to do out in the world, and I'm here. Always here." She buried her face against her mother's shoulder, and sobs shook her.

Larissa held her close, her heart aching for this daughter who had lost so much more than just her hearing while she lay so ill with the measles five years ago. She and Ethan, Charity too, she knew, had done their best to provide her with the security of their unconditional love and impart to her how vital her place in the family circle was. She well knew that Rose had her times of despondency. They occurred particularly when she was in a group of hearing, non-family members who were visiting together and laughing, leaving her standing on the side, watching while they conversed and shared jokes in which she could have no part. And now, following so soon on Charity's leaving, this new departure. Rose had opened up to Amity in friendship, in the anticipation of a sister-in-law who understood her heart.

Larissa, her own pain compounded by the abruptness of Amity and Mac's leaving and the reason for it, had no words of comfort for her daughter. She could not reassure her because she did not know how long they would stay in Philadelphia or what the ultimate outcome would be for Amity's mother. She could only hold her close and pray for the thousandth — or was it the millionth — time that Rose would find her own special place in the world and the happiness she so richly deserved.

***

Leaving Rose upstairs to change out of her going-to-town outfit, Larissa went down in time to hear Merry protesting vigorously about being held captive in her crib. She rescued the little girl and set her to playing on the kitchen floor with baking pans and wooden spoons with which she could "help fix supper." Rose came downstairs in time to assist with the meal preparation. Her face was flushed and her eyes swollen, but otherwise she had, outwardly at least, regained her composure. As they stepped over and around Merry in their maneuvers about the kitchen, Rose spoke to the child and even got her to sing about "Mary Had a Little Lamb" so that to Merry, all was normal. She didn't even ask about Amity and Mac, apparently trusting that Rose knew what she was talking about in saying they would return eventually.

Larissa watched the interaction between the big sister and the small one, and the beginnings of an idea poked at the edges of her mind. She knew that she would have to talk to Ethan first, and that he might object, but she was determined to at least try out the possibility.

After supper and the dishes were finished, Rose volunteered to put Merry to bed and read her a story, leaving Larissa and Ethan in the kitchen. Larissa knew this was her opportunity and said a swift prayer for the right words to present her idea to him. He was sitting at the table, reading the Farmer's Almanac for its predicted weather forecast, when she sat beside him and put her hand over his. He smiled at her, then saw the gravity in her eyes and abandoned the expectation of continued heat.

"Ethan, Rose had a really hard time after we got home this afternoon." She explained briefly what had taken place in Amity's room.

He shook his head regretfully. "She's right, of course. Everyone has been leaving to put their marks on the world, and here she stays. I don't know what we can do to help her, though."

Larissa took a deep breath. "I had a thought, but I wanted to share it with you first." He waited, and she plunged ahead. "It didn't occur to me before this afternoon, but with Amity leaving, Rose is going to be all by herself upstairs. Especially after sharing the space with others all these years, I suspect it's going to feel rather vast and lonely."

Clearly, the thought hadn't occurred to him, either. Concern flashed across his features. "But what can we do? Her room's upstairs. There's no place for her to stay down here."

Larissa swallowed and her hand tightened around his. "Mac's room, that became Charity's room, is unoccupied and will be for the foreseeable future."

He looked confused. "You want us to move up into Mac's room?"

She shook her head. "Not us. Merry."

His confused expression changed to dumbfounded. "Take Merry out of our room and put her upstairs?"

"Yes. She's past two years old now. It's time for her to have her own room. And that way, Rose won't be all alone."

Dumbfounded became dubious. "That's a long ways away to move her. What if she wakes in the night? Rose won't hear her."

Larissa bit her lip. "I know. I've thought of that. But it's been a long time since Merry's awakened at night. You know she sleeps right through once she's down and out. And we can make her understand that if she does wake up, Rose will be right across the hall and she can go to her there."

He still looked doubtful. "From Rose's viewpoint, mightn't this be an imposition on her? She shouldn't have the responsibility that, as Merry's parents, belongs to us."

"But we wouldn't do it without asking Rose. If she feels she can't do it, we can assure her that it was just a suggestion. Ethan, we've always given Rose the benefit of the doubt about what she can and can't do.

We've always given her our trust. Can we do less now?"

He ran his fingers through his hair and sighed. "Is this one of those leaps of faith that Shawn works into his sermons every once in a while?"

She cupped her hand against his bearded cheek. "It just might be. For all of us."

When Rose came out of the bedroom, she saw them sitting at the table, looking at her, and she frowned, puzzled. "Is something wrong?"

Larissa held out her hand and Rose went to her and took it. "Ma?"

Since Larissa's hands were otherwise occupied, Ethan signed for her. "We'd like to talk to you. Please sit down."

Rose, still clasping Larissa's hand, sat next to her, but faced Ethan in order to see what he had to say. "Ma and I have been discussing a change that concerns you, so we've decided it's time to discuss it with you. Merry is getting old enough to have her own room. How would you feel about having her move up into Charity's room? It would be more responsibility for you, especially if she wakes up at night. Since you'd be the closest, she'd come in to you if she had a problem."

Rose stared at him as if she hadn't read his signs correctly. Seeing her hesitation, he quickly added, "We won't do it if it's not right for you. We just thought—"

The first real smile they'd seen from her all day lit Rose's face. "I'd like it very much. I was thinking it'd be really lonely up there all by myself. But will Merry like it?"

Larissa smiled and squeezed Rose's hands reassuringly while Ethan signed for her. "If it works for you, we'll make it work for her. It might take a little time and patience, but we'll get there."

It took time and patience both, but ultimately Merry became excited about sleeping in a "big bed" with only chairs enclosing her instead of crib rails. She also took to heart their praises of her for being such a big girl—not that she had ever doubted it herself—that the switch was accomplished more easily than they had hoped.

Larissa actually had a more difficult time adjusting than Merry did. For the first few nights she started awake, thinking she had heard Merry call or cry out. But for both Rose's and Merry's sakes, she determinedly made the adjustment and found, as a most pleasant reward, a new closeness with Ethan that was exceedingly satisfactory to them both.

***

While changes and adjustments were taking place at home, Mac and Amity's train chugged its way toward Philadelphia. It was a long trip, made more difficult because, with each passing minute, they had no idea whether Amity's mother still lived. When Mac took the baggage in to the depot, he had sent a telegram to Dr. Terrill, informing him that they were coming and the time of their arrival. There had been no time to receive a response before they left. There was little opportunity for satisfactory sleep in the swaying passenger car, and Amity was so worried that, even had the occasion presented itself, she was too keyed up to relax. Mac, in addition to his concern about Mrs. Terrill, feared that Amity would wear herself out completely before they reached Philadelphia. He persuaded her to put her head against his shoulder for short periods only by reminding her that if she didn't rest, she would be so exhausted she'd be of no use to her mother when they did arrive. He cringed inwardly at using such a harsh tactic, but the doctor's daughter saw the logic of not making a bad situation worse. After that, she sat quietly, eyes wide open, breathing in short, stiff, "relaxed" breaths for extended periods. Whether these sessions actually helped or not, Mac wasn't sure, but he had to give her credit for trying.

They arrived in Philadelphia late in the evening of the third day. As they approached the station, Amity gave up all pretense of unruffled composure. She gripped Mac's hand tightly and he returned the clasp, not certain she wouldn't fly down the aisle before the train properly stopped.

As they descended the steps onto the platform, the glare of torch lights and the unmoving floor beneath them momentarily caught them off guard after they had become accustomed to the dim interior of the jolting passenger car. As Mac took Amity's arm to steady her, he heard a familiar voice call his name. "Mac! Over here."

He swung around and caught sight of Jeff Kinsley making his way through the crowd toward them. Keeping Amity's arm tucked firmly against his, he held out his other hand and Jeff took it in a warm and welcoming grip. "Good to see you, my friend. Hello, Amity," he added, taking her hand. Seeing the large question in her eyes, he said hastily, "Your mother is holding her own. She knows you're coming, and wants very much to see you."

At his reassurance, the determinedly composed expression Amity had been maintaining crumpled and, in spite of the bustling passengers around them, she buried her face against Mac's shoulder. He held her tightly, feeling her shuddering breaths of relief after all the tension. "It's all right, Amity-love," he said. "It's all right." He felt Jeff grip his other shoulder from behind, a firm hold that spoke plainly of Jeff's understanding of Mac's own release of dread.

Amity raised her head. "I'm sorry," she murmured. "It's just … after all the unknowing—"

Jeff broke in. "Don't worry about it." He flashed a trace of his old grin and sketched a slight bow. "In my expert medical opinion, Miss Terrill, you're doing very well."

In spite of everything, she couldn't help a small smile at his familiar antics, a faint curving of her lips that brought an enormous rush of relief to Mac's heart.

Jeff guided them to Dr. Terrill's enclosed carriage and indicated the service wagon behind it. "Your father had Devin come along in the cart. He'll collect your baggage. That way you can get right out to the house without further delay."

The servant, who had worked with the horses in the Terrill stables as long as Amity could remember, came forward and bowed slightly. "It's very good to see you again, Miss."

"Thank you, Devin. It's good to be almost home again." She turned to Mac. "When I was small, I'd sneak out to the stables and Devin would let me feed apples to the horses."

A faint smile creased Devin's cheeks. "And a fine job you did of it too, Miss. Now if you'll be telling me which baggage to collect, you can be on your way."

Once they were settled in the carriage, Amity tensed again. She clutched Mac's hand and looked at Jeff, seated across from them. "How is she, Jeff? I haven't known what to think since we got Father's telegram."

Without evasion, Jeff said quietly, "It's been touch and go. She's been delirious part of the time. When she was lucid, she kept asking for you. When your father told her he'd sent for you, she seemed to rally. She's adamantly holding on so she can see you. She's one courageous lady."

Amity drew in a breath at his words of admiration. Mac's fingers tightened on hers. "So is her daughter," he said decisively.

At long last, the carriage pulled up to the Terrill home. Before Mac could help Amity to the ground, the house door opened and Oliver Terrill came hurrying down the steps. Amity flew toward him and he gathered her in a strong hug. Mac watched tensely and felt Jeff alight from the carriage to stand beside him.

Recovering his dignity, Dr. Terrill, one arm still around Amity, came toward them, his other hand outstretched. "Mac. It's good to see you again." Encouraged by the lack of formality in being called by his nickname, he shook hands with the older man. Mac saw the deep lines etched in his face, lines that had not been there a few weeks ago. He understood only too well. More than the usual sleepless nights encountered by any doctor during a siege of illness, fear for Mrs. Terrill had put them there—the dread that all his medical skills would not be enough to save her.

"Thank you for bringing Amity safely home." For just the briefest instant, as Dr. Terrill looked at him, Mac saw a glint in the older man's eyes that was gone before he could identify it. He had no time to ponder what it might have been because Amity's father, after greeting Jeff, urged them to come in and turned back to the house with Amity.

"Father, how's Mother? May I see her?" The anxiety in Amity's voice wiped any other thoughts out of Mac's mind.

"She's been waiting impatiently to see you." The gravity in his voice brought Mac's and Amity's attention sharply to him. "My dear, you must understand. This illness has been very difficult for her. It's taken a toll on her physical appearance as well as her health. She," uncharacteristically, the self-assured doctor searched for words, "she's very fragile. I say this not to alarm you, but you must be prepared when you see her."

The light of joy that had come to Amity's eyes as she greeted her father now quenched at his uncompromising words. "I understand, Father. I won't distress her, I promise." She turned to Mac. "Will you come with me?"

He hesitated. "Are you sure you don't want to see her privately this first time, mother to daughter, after being away from each other?"

She bit her lip and reached for his hand. "I'm sure. Please come with me."

He curved his fingers around hers. "Of course I will." He glanced at her father, who looked at him intently but made no comment.

"Is she in her room, Father?"

He made a motion as if to lead them upstairs, but checked it and nodded. "Just knock on the door and the nurse will let you in."

Amity tugged on Mac's hand and together they ascended the curving stairway. In spite of the urgency of the moment, it crossed Mac's mind that he had never climbed these stairs or been on the second floor of the great house. He wondered fleetingly what Dr. Terrill's honest opinion was concerning Mac's new position within this family's intimate circle, but discretion decided he'd better not pursue the thought at that moment. He forgot it entirely as they reached the landing and Amity turned left down a thickly carpeted, gas lamp-lit hallway that seemed to stretch forever into the distance. They passed oil paintings and portraits that he couldn't make out clearly but suspected were folks perched somewhere on the family tree branches above Amity. His one impression was that the faces appeared uniformly grim. He could only hope that it didn't indicate they'd already made a swift judgment about him.

Amity finally halted in front of a thick oaken door. Before knocking on the panel, however, she turned to Mac. "Hold me," she whispered.

He slipped his arms around her. She was still wearing her traveling hat, so he couldn't press his cheek to her hair, but he cradled her head against his shoulder and gently swayed her body with his.

She drew a deep breath, raised her face to his, and kissed him quickly and lightly. "I'm all right now to go in." He rapped on the polished wood and the door was swung open by a young woman neither of them recognized. Before the nurse could question, Amity said, "I'm Mrs. Terrill's daughter. This is Doctor Edwards. May we see my mother?" Mac made no effort to suppress his flash of pride at the calmness of her tone and the confidence of her bearing as she asked the long-awaited question.

With no more than a flicking glance at him—Mac assumed because of the slightly emphasized *doctor* designation in front of his name—the nurse said politely, "Of course, Miss Terrill. I'm Miss Howell. Your mother has been resting, waiting for you to arrive."

She led them to the bed and stepped aside. Mac, following behind, after a quick glance at Mrs. Terrill's wasted features allowed Amity and her mother their own private moment to meet again after all the weeks of being apart. He watched Amity's face as she took in the sight of her mother rather than Mrs. Terrill's as she realized that her daughter had finally come home.

Whatever shock Amity must have felt at that first glimpse of her mother's fragility, she hid it well. "Mother," she breathed and reached out to clasp the thin hands that were lifted to her. "Oh, Mother, I'm so glad to see you again." Once she had choked out this understatement, she laughed softly. "I've so much to tell you." She looked up at Mac then and gently freed one of her mother's hands to reach out to him. As he stepped forward, she caught his fingers. "Mac's come with me, Mother."

Matilda raised her eyes to his and he gently took the hand Amity wasn't already holding. A weight as heavy as the old medical books he used to dust in Doc's office settled in his stomach as he noted the blue tinge of her lips and skin and the iciness of her fingers. Summoning every last ounce of what Amity teasingly called his "doctor demeanor," he said steadily, "I'm very happy to see you again, Mrs. Terrill. And as for the things Amity has to tell you, I have a few bits of chitchat myself, when she isn't around, of course, that I'm sure you will find most interesting." He was rewarded by Amity's sticking her tongue out at him and her hand being feebly, but promptly, slapped by her mother.

Matilda's lips curved slightly and her eyes took on a momentary gleam. "I'll be waiting to hear." Her voice was faint, but edged with eagerness.

Mac glanced at Amity. "We don't want to wear you out. We'll have plenty of time to talk. You rest now, and we'll be back later."

Amity bent down to kiss her cheek. "I love you, Mother."

Mac gently pressed her hand and laid it back on the coverlet. "I'll be making a list of all the things I plan to tell you about your daughter. You sleep well, so you'll be ready to hear them."

"There just might be a few things I can tell you about her, too."

Matilda's voice came weakly, but with a spark of mischief that caused

Amity to exclaim, "Mother!" so that she and Mac were laughing as they left the room.

Once out in the hall with the door closed behind them, however, she wilted. "Oh, Mac," she whispered. All he could do was hold her close, while the shock of her mother's illness washed over her, and the harsh truth that Amity did not yet suspect gripped his heart like a vise.

CHAPTER THIRTY-FIVE

As they descended the stairs, Jeff and Dr. Terrill met them at the bottom. "We can speak in my study," Oliver said with no pretense at small talk. His eyes on Jeff, with a slight motion of his head, he indicated the second floor.

"Yes, sir. I'll go right up." Jeff paused beside Mac long enough to promise, "We'll talk, first thing in the morning." He put his hand on Mac's shoulder. "I'm glad you've come back, friend." Then he was taking the stairs up, two at a time.

They watched him go, and Oliver said in explanation, "We haven't left her alone since this began. Either Jeff or I have been with her, in addition to the nurse, of course, at all times."

Oliver led the way to his book-lined study, gestured to a leather couch where Amity could sit, and a chair beside it for Mac to take his place. Mac started to take the indicated chair. "Mac." Amity reached to him. "Please sit beside me. There's plenty of room." As proof, she tucked the skirt of her traveling outfit closer, leaving the cushion beside her available.

Mac glanced at Dr. Terrill, whose eyes darkened for an instant then cleared as he gave a brief nod. Mac eased down beside her. Taking his hand tightly in hers, she drew it beneath the silken folds of her skirt, unaware that, to him, her fingers felt nearly as cold as her mother's had. Beneath the concealing material, he gripped her hand, and in that limited motion tried to transfer to her all the comfort and warmth he could.

Dr. Terrill sat stiffly in the chair behind his desk. He eyed them for a moment as if searching for words. "I'm very glad that you were able to make it home so promptly, Amity. And thank you for bringing her safely, Mac."

Mac wondered if the appreciation expressed had a double meaning, but had no time to pursue the thought, for Oliver continued. "Now that you have seen your mother, my dear, you can conclude for yourself that she has been very ill. She's not out of the woods yet, by a very long way." As Amity's face paled, he said quietly, "I tell you this not to alarm you, but so that you will know the circumstances. Your mother and I have always been honest with you. You can trust that I will not be less so, now."

Harsh as his words sounded on the surface, Amity sat straighter and drew a steadying breath. "Thank you, Father."

Oliver's glance flicked to Mac. "You, too, have seen her. Were you able to draw any medical conclusions from your brief time with her?"

The vise squeezed more tightly around Mac's heart. "Yes, sir."

Amity turned quickly to him, but before he could explain his suspicions, Oliver spoke as if to himself. "You see it, too. I fought admitting it, but further denial is impossible." He closed his eyes for a moment then looked directly at Amity. During the exchange between Mac and her father, she had tensed again, and was leaning toward him, waiting to hear she knew not what.

"Amity, the high fever severely damaged your mother's heart."

The bluntness of his words made her gasp. Beneath the skirt folds, she clutched Mac's hand so tightly he feared she would break the bones. "Father," was all she could manage to say.

He came away from his desk and opened his arms. She stood, forgetting to release Mac's hand until he pulled it gently away. She rested her head on her father's shoulder and the first great wave of their mutual grief crashed over them. He murmured to her as she drew long shuddering breaths. Finally he released her and guided her to sit back beside Mac. His eyes glistening with unshed tears, he took her hand and placed it in Mac's before turning away to his desk. He stood with his back to them for a long moment before he drew a deep breath and straightened. He resumed his seat at the desk.

He told her then, in as straightforward a manner as he could manage, about the days of his wife's illness, her nights of delirium, her high fever that had finally eased. They had believed she was through the worst of it, but then the other symptoms had set in. During his long practice of medicine, he'd brought heartbreak to many other lives by speaking cruel words of truth about his diagnoses. In spite of his years of experience, regardless of all the words he had spoken to others, he had not this time been able to accept the truth of his own discovery about the health of his beloved wife. He had argued with Jeff, had accused him of jumping to conclusions. But in the end, just like the families of his patients, he had been forced to accept the truth. "As you must accept it, Amity," he said with a finality that would not allow her to do otherwise.

Mac had sat quietly during the revelations that were as much an unburdening of Oliver's own soul as they were an explanation to his daughter. Piecing together the medical details that Oliver had spared giving Amity, Mac realized how truly close Matilda had come to dying. He very strongly suspected, in spite of—or because of—Oliver's denials of acceptance, the doctor's exceptional medical skills and his refusal to give up had saved Matilda's life. Oliver and Jeff working—arguing—together had proved to be an unbeatable team.

***

The following days and nights blurred past for Mac. Already sleep-deprived from the train ride, he insisted on taking his share of the twenty-four hour a day watch on Mrs. Terrill. When he stated firmly that he would take the night shift, Oliver and Jeff gave in with little argument. They were far more exhausted than he was, sharing as they had been stretches of eight hours on and eight off around the clock for many weeks. Although it was more difficult to stay awake in the still hours of the night, Mac found an unlooked-for bonus in taking that shift: he discovered that Mrs. Terrill was often wakeful in those dark hours before dawn. At first, merely to soothe her restlessness, he sat and talked quietly to her of whatever came into his mind. He found that tales of his boyhood, of his apprenticeship years with Doc, and of his studies under her husband could bring a smile to her blue-tinged lips. He also discovered that she enjoyed it when he read to her. The library downstairs was well stocked, and when he learned that she liked Dickens almost as much as Ethan did, it was an added windfall.

Another reward he garnered from these still hours, when the rest of the world slumbered, was Amity's companionship. When she learned that he had volunteered to stay with Matilda at night, she added her quiet presence to her mother's room. She never interfered, but she became a most pleasant companion, enlarging Mac's audience of one to two when he read aloud from *Romeo and Juliet* and, later, *The Old Curiosity Shop*. He was a little reluctant to impart the tale of Nell and her grandfather, since the mood of the story was not spectacularly uplifting, but Mrs. Terrill requested it and he could not deny her the opportunity to lessen her own distress through hearing of the bad fortunes of others.

***

During the hours he was not with Mrs. Terrill, Mac spent as much time as he could with Amity. Besides the night sessions, if she had had her way, she would have stayed in the sickroom all day, talking or reading aloud or simply sitting close by if her mother needed anything. After the long night watches, Mac made certain that Amity rested in her own room in the mornings. He also insisted that she walk outside with him for a portion of every afternoon. She had protested at first, but he was adamant. He put it to her as his expert medical opinion that she needed the exercise and fresh air to keep her own health secure. She gave in with a wry smile, since she had heard "expert medical opinions" all her life and had long ago learned to translate them into "for your own good." While at first she'd been reluctant to be away from her mother for the length of time Mac prescribed, she quickly realized that their strolls through the gardens and grounds of the estate were a perfect time to be with him without being under the all-seeing eye of her father. They weren't isolated, by any means. The many windows of the house provided excellent viewing possibilities for anyone passing by inside. Gardeners tending the lawns and flowers maintained a diplomatic distance, but both Mac and Amity were aware of the possibility of eyes and ears nearby, no matter how discreetly camouflaged. Dr. Terrill made no objection when he saw that the rosy cheeks and smiling demeanor that had been so much a part of his daughter's nature before her mother's illness returned with her from these outings.

Within a few days, Amity had also taken over supervision of the household. The servants knew their jobs well and were deeply devoted to Mrs. Terrill. They had carried on faithfully with their work during the time that she lay so ill. But someone needed to direct the domestic establishment, and, as the oldest daughter, the responsibility fell to Amity. Under her mother's guidance, she had been training for just such a situation for years, so it was not a complete upheaval for her already battered emotions to step into the position. It gave her something to focus on besides her mother's frailty, and, as she confided to Mac, "The hardest part is accepting that I'm doing it because Mother no longer can."

Mac, seeing her carry out her new duties with confidence and obvious expertise, discovered a facet he had not realized was part of this woman he very gladly intended to spend the rest of his life with.

While Amity was resting or involved with household responsibilities, Mac had time to talk with Jeff. They slipped into the ease of their old friendship as if Mac hadn't been away at all. Jeff filled him in on the diphtheria epidemic and its aftermath. Many had died in spite of the doctors' efforts. The lives of a great number of young ones had been cut short before they had really begun to live. With a gravity in his demeanor that had never been there before, Jeff asked the unanswerable question: "Why?"

Watching his friend's features, so much older than they should have become in the time Mac had been away, he comprehended in Jeff the same desolation, the same sense of futility of all their efforts that he himself had struggled with. He remembered Doc's words when Mac was telling him of the devastation of the diphtheria epidemic, and even farther back all those years ago when the Therons' year-old daughter had died. *It never gets any easier, no matter how many times you go through it. At least you better hope it doesn't.*

Aware that he was stepping into a deeply private place of his friend's heart, Mac quietly told him about the Theron baby. He had never spoken to anyone except Doc about the experience that had embedded itself into his soul. He'd never even told Amity. Jeff listened in silence, not realizing that the pain in his eyes was speaking louder than any utterance could have. Mac slowly repeated Doc's words. "'They'll stand it because they have to. And so will you if you're to be of use to anyone.'"

The words hung between them as Jeff sat motionless, his eyes closed. Finally he opened them and met Mac's gaze directly. "Have you learned to stand it?" he asked with a fierce intensity.

"I've never gotten used to it. And I stand it only because I have to. Doc was right. We can't let a failure we had no control over allow us to fail someone else we can help."

Jeff drew a ragged breath. "I've never wanted to be anything but a doctor. As long as I can remember, my instinct has been to save lives."

Mac said ruefully, "I know the feeling. You should have seen some of the bedraggled critters I practiced my budding doctoring skills on when I was six years old. Looking back on it, I don't know how my folks kept their patience—or sanity."

Jeff allowed himself a small smile. "Did you ever doctor a snake? I think that one came the closest to being my mother's undoing."

As they talked on about their childhood escapades and misadventures, the two friends relaxed, unaware that the bond for a lifetime of friendship had been indelibly sealed.

***

At long last, Rose's letter telling of Mrs. Terrill's illness and Mac and Amity's subsequent departure to Philadelphia reached Charity. Ben had brought the letter home from town and she had gone to the creek to savor it, delighted to be hearing from Rose, never suspecting the distressing contents. When she finished reading, she let the letter drop to her lap and stared across the rippling creek. In the days that she'd been here, she had kept busy from morning to night. In addition to her teaching and the always present necessity of preparing the next day's lessons, she helped Anne as much as she could with the never-ceasing chores about the house and garden. Such constant activity had left her no time to brood over Mac and Amity's happiness or her own sense of forlornness. By the time her head touched her pillow at night, she was so tired that she fell asleep before depressing thoughts had time to form, let alone take root.

But now, in this quiet time, alone with Rose's news, there was no tamping down of her emotions into that arid corner of her heart where she fondly imagined she had successfully buried them. As if on butterfly wings, her mind flitted from one thought to another. Her preconceived notions that, from their first meeting, she would dislike Amity. How that mind-set flared in the days that followed as she observed the devotion Amity and Mac shared. Her refusal to completely abdicate to Amity. She had not yet come to believe that was something she would ever do. Now this new trouble loomed. At the time of writing the letter, Rose hadn't known how Mrs. Terrill would fare. She could only stress that it must be bad or else Dr. Terrill wouldn't have urged his daughter to return home as quickly as possible. All of which Charity's own instincts agreed with.

As she sat with the letter in her lap and gazed across the rippling water, a pin-sharp jab penetrated that dust-dry corner of her heart. *Can Amity's mother be dying?* And then the second thought followed on the heels of the first and it was no longer a pin-sharp jab, but a sword thrust. *Has her mother already died?* Much as she might not be adverse to small woes striking Amity, such as spilling dill pickle relish all over her apron that first evening at the farm—*It was an accident, honestly!*—she, who knew so well from personal experience, would never wish on Amity the heart-ripping pain of losing her mother.

So where does all this thought-chasing leave me? She wasn't entirely certain. She would have to wait for the next letter from home to learn the outcome. She looked at the postmark date on the envelope. Rose had sent it two weeks ago. *So much could have happened in two weeks.* Then she did something she never would have dreamed that she would do for Amity. She bowed her head and prayed.

Because she could do nothing to speed up the mail process in order to hear sooner what was happening at home and in Philadelphia, Charity forced herself to accomplish additional tasks that left her no time for thinking or grieving. She was unwittingly assisted in this effort by the members of the school board, who advised her that since it was the end of July, her term of boarding with the Claytons was at an official end. She had been with Anne and Ben for six weeks instead of the standard four. Because she had come in the middle of June, rather than roust her out after only two weeks, she had been allowed to stay on with the Claytons. But now it was time to take up residence with another family, this time with Luke and Lillie Monroe, whose home adjoined the saddle shop in town.

Charity hadn't realized how big a hole it was going to put in her heart to leave Anne. An understanding had sprung up between the two women that was not solely linked to Larissa and Anne's connection. Quite without conscious endeavor, the older woman and the younger had become friends in their own right.

Charity had feared at first that her confrontations with Luke over school matters would alienate Ben and Anne. She'd breathed more than one prayer of thanks that it had not happened. Luke's parents disciplined him at home, but made it clear that discipline at school was to be left in Charity's hands, unless she asked for help. Sticking to her first resolve that she would handle her students in her own way, without involving any parents or school board members unless absolutely necessary, she had not gone to them with tales of Luke's escapades. She was certain, of course, that they'd heard. Her other students were not compelled by her particular code of determination to keep such stories to themselves, and the details had almost certainly circulated among the town and country families.

Luke seemed to have reached a "blood having been shed on both sides" draw with her. He still sat in the back of the room, not actively participating, but not being disruptive, either, at least not too often. Once in a while he'd drop a book with a bang that caused the unsuspecting students sitting in front of him to jump and smack their knees resoundingly against the undersides of their desks. Or he'd fire a spitball with unnerving accuracy onto the blackboard an inch from Charity's nose. She would then send him to stand in the corner or to write on the hapless board a hundred times: I will not disturb the class. He went to his punishment, not embarrassed, but with a ramrod straight spine and a gleam in his eyes that plainly said he was obeying because he chose to, not because he believed he had to.

All things considered, Charity was able to breathe a heartfelt sigh of relief at the end of her first six weeks of teaching. Her students were alive and thriving under her guidance. She had conducted her first tadpole funeral service. She had not been fired. *What would the next six weeks bring?*

Charity's moving into town to stay with the Monroes for the allotted month presented an unlooked for problem. Where would Miss Sullivan stay? Although their sleeping accommodations had been crowded at the Clayton ranch, they had all managed, with minor modifications, to make it work. Miss Sullivan had bountifully repaid their generosity by assisting Anne with the household chores, so that it had worked out satisfactorily for all concerned.

The Monroe home was, as Ethan would say, "A horse of another stripe." Link Monroe had built it sturdily enough and Lillie had furnished it in the most inviting way she could, given the limited resources available to the settlers of the new town. It was, however, so small that it could accommodate only the four family members. Attached to the side of the saddle shop, it contained a cooking and eating room, a bedroom for the adults, and a room that Hannah and Jonah shared.

Realizing that her presence for four weeks would further squeeze the already crowded family, Charity had offered to stay elsewhere. Lillie, however, had assured her that there was room for her and that they were looking forward to having her for "their" time. Sensing that it would hurt the Monroes' feelings deeply if she declined, she accepted graciously and was rewarded by Lillie's smile of unconcealed pleasure.

The problem was that there was simply no room for Miss Sullivan.

Charity wondered if the older woman would decide to return to Fairvale now that her mentoring of her former pupil was, in reality, finished. Charity was startled at the realization of how much, if Miss Sullivan went home, she'd miss her. *How did a companionship such as ours ever sprout?* Charity couldn't answer the question with certainty. Somehow, as her own feelings of confidence in her teaching blossomed, Miss Sullivan had taken less of an older, more experienced advisor role and more of one as an equal. *And friend?* The words sounded almost as strange as a foreign language, but one that, she was surprised to acknowledge, she just might enjoy learning.

Perhaps it was recognition of this new role between them that caused Charity to realize that, as difficult as it would be to broach the subject with Miss Sullivan, her new maturity would not let her dodge it. She practiced several openings but was not satisfied with any of them. *How would Miss Sullivan approach it if the situation were reversed?* Finally asking herself the obvious question, she received the obvious answer. *She would contend with it directly and without evasion.*

In the end, after all her fretting, she was saved by Miss Sullivan's raising of the issue herself. At supper one night, Charity announced her final, firm acceptance of the Monroes' hospitality and passed on the information that they would help her move to town on Saturday.

Some of the light went out of Anne's eyes, but she said sturdily, "I know it's time for you to go, but we'll really miss having you here."

"It for sure has been good havin' you stay," Ben added, "and givin' all of us a chance to come to know each other better than just in letter writin'."

Matt and Catty looked solemn. Only Luke glanced at her with a smug expression. What he meant by it, she had no idea.

After letting the others speak their regrets, Miss Sullivan cleared her throat. "I, too, have an announcement. I didn't want to say anything until Charity had finalized her plans. I have been offered a position. At the Corley home. Mr. Corley asked me if I would stay on with them for a while to assist Mrs. Corley with household duties and such. Since school won't start in Fairvale until after the September corn harvest, my presence will not be needed there for several more weeks. I indicated to him that when Charity's plans were completed, I could comply with his request." She didn't go so far as to smile, but tipped her head once, as if cementing her personal approval of the agreement.

As they were preparing for bed that evening, Miss Sullivan paused in the application to her hair of her one hundred nightly brush strokes. "You have taken quite admirably to your teaching experience." Charity, loosening her own bun, was so startled at the compliment that her fingers jerked, stabbing the pin forcefully downward into her scalp instead of pulling it out. Miss Sullivan, oblivious to her pupil's pained gritting of her teeth, continued, "You have done so well that I wasn't expecting to stay on in Clark's Valley after it was time to leave the Claytons. But I have come to enjoy being in this new country and experiencing the way life is carried on here. There are many fine people in the community." The flush of pink across her cheeks was so fleeting that Charity wasn't certain it had even been there. Before she could pursue the thought, Miss Sullivan continued hurriedly, "When Mr. Corley presented me with the opportunity to remain here a while longer, I took him up on it. Mrs. Corley is a very pleasant young woman and I shall do my best to assist her in the coming weeks." Even in their polite society of two, Miss Sullivan would not directly mention Callie's advanced pregnancy, but Charity was certain the Corleys would much appreciate the extra pair of hands.

Curled in bed a little later, sleep was overtaking Charity when she was momentarily roused by remembrance of Miss Sullivan's faint blush as she spoke of "the fine people in the community." *Has she found a certain one to be finer than the others? Miss Sullivan?* Charity dismissed the thought as preposterous and fell asleep even as her brain formed the picture of Miss Sullivan and Carolina Corley existing under the same roof for the next several weeks.

CHAPTER THIRTY-SIX

Saturday was a blur of emotion as Charity prepared to leave the Claytons' country-situated ranch and take up town life with the Monroes. Fortunately, there was little time for parting regrets. Owen Corley, coming in his wagon with Amos and Carolina to get Miss Sullivan, arrived at the same time that Link Monroe, with Hannah and Jonah in tow in his wagon, pulled up to the finally-finished back porch. In the midst of making certain Charity's trunks went into Link's wagon, and Miss Sullivan's into Owen's, Charity was able to shut her mind to the reality of the moment. *I'm leaving a place and family where I've come to feel I'm truly at home, and am setting out for a new site where I'll have to begin all over again to fit in.* Then she scolded herself roundly. *Isn't this why you wanted to come to Clark's Valley—for the adventure of it?* The small voice inside her that answered *yes* was nearly drowned out by the larger one that protested it would much rather be adventurous some other time—or year.

She hugged Anne tightly, knowing she could never thank her adequately for the many ways the older woman had helped her fit into her role as new teacher in this new community. Ben shook her hand formally, but his dark blue eyes twinkled as he said gruffly, "Just 'cause you're becomin' townified don't mean you can't come back and visit. We hope you will, right often."

Silly as they were, the tears she was holding back threatened to spill, but just then Catty flung her arms about her teacher's waist. "I'll see you on Monday morning, Catty. I'll miss our walks to and from school, though," she admitted. She turned to Matt, standing gravely beside Ben. The boy solemnly shook her hand. "You've taught me so much about your wonderful countryside. Thank you." She turned to go down the porch steps. Three-year-old Eve, apparently finally figuring out she was going somewhere that Matt and Catty weren't going, too, launched herself at Charity's knees and glared up at her with Ben's dark blue eyes. Anne, during the process of detaching her and assuring her that Miss Michaels would come see them again, balanced the child on her hip. Faces close together, Anne smiling, Eve scowling, her stubby red braids sticking defiantly sideways, they waved goodbye. Presented with such a picture, Charity, too, was genuinely smiling as she descended the steps. Since she and Miss Sullivan had said their farewells the night before, she gave the older woman a hug, which was stiffly returned, and accepted Link's assistance up into the wagon while Owen helped Miss Sullivan up into his. As the wagons turned to go their separate ways, Charity couldn't help noticing that Jonah and Hannah looked much happier than Amos and Carolina did.

The ride to town was accomplished in silence for the most part since Link Monroe, unlike Ben Clayton, didn't say much unless he really had something to say. As he guided the wagon around to the back of the saddle shop, Lillie came hurrying out the door. She gave Charity a warm hug and ushered her inside to the start of her life for the next four weeks.

As welcome as they made her feel, Charity was secretly dismayed to discover that she would put Jonah out of the room he shared with Hannah. The little boy himself made light of it, however, when the plans were explained. "I get to sleep *on the floor by the stove* in the main room. Almost like campin' out." He was clearly excited by the novel prospect, even though the stove, by the failure of being unlit these hot summer nights, would not provide the glow of a true campfire. Charity, relieved by his obvious enthusiasm, didn't have the heart to protest further. Besides, the only other option was for *her* to sleep on the floor in the main room, and that opportunity didn't appeal to her nearly as much as it did to him. She just hoped he wouldn't regret it after a few nights of his young backside coming in contact with the unyielding floor.

In the days that followed, Charity came to know and like Lillie Monroe in a way that would have been impossible had they not shared a roof. As she had with Anne, Charity pitched in as much as she could to help with the endless household chores. Even though they were living in town, those tasks didn't prove to be that much different from those on a ranch—or a farm. Lillie, too, had a large garden, and chickens to tend, a cow to milk, butter to churn, bread to bake, and clothes to make and mend. One aspect of this new living arrangement turned out to be very pleasant, however. Because of their close proximity, the town women found some excuse to stop in to see one another during the course of the day, if for no longer a time than to say hello and assure each other that all was well in their lives.

Clark's store was a favorite gathering place for the town's feminine citizens, under the guise, of course, of running errands. Charity would have enjoyed the casual encounters and her growing friendship with the other women if it hadn't been for Cora Clark's continued cold shoulder toward her. Not being totally dense, early on she had realized that Cora always did her best glaring whenever Cork was beside her. Either he never noticed or he simply chose to ignore it. At first Charity had felt some sympathy for her rival, but it had become increasingly difficult to maintain because she immensely enjoyed being with Cork.

Since Cora worked in the mercantile, helping her parents, her presence was nearly a notarized guarantee whenever Charity needed to go there. The one salvation was that Cora, apparently unable to bear waiting on her when she took her purchases to the counter, managed to be extremely busy in some other part of the store. Since either Mr. or Mrs. Clark was always there, this distaste, fortunately, was not a particular hardship for Charity.

Not that she had a lot of time to loiter there. The daily trips to and from school began early and ended late, accomplished in the wagon behind whatever team had been selected for the day from the townspeople's contributions to the cause. As the presiding adult—and the teacher who had the power to pass or fail them—Charity was given the seat of honor during these trips. Instead of riding in the wagon box with the other children, she was enthroned beside whichever boy was driving the team that day, usually the son of the owner of the rig. This gave her a priceless opportunity to converse with him. To even things out, she invited one of the girls to sit up front, too, turn about each day. In this casual fashion, she learned much about her students' hopes and aspirations. As she had said to Miss Sullivan on a day that now seemed a lifetime ago, she was learning what motivated them to act as they did in striving for goals and achieving or failing to reach them. She was discovering all the small details that made up their personalities and emotions to better understand them and the people they hoped to become. She sighed because there was nothing at that moment—or for many moments to come—to let her know whether she would succeed or fail.

***

On Monday morning two weeks into the new living arrangement, Charity, announcing that class would begin, noticed that neither Matt and Catty nor Amos and Carolina were in the group of students taking their seats. Anxiety poked her midsection with a sharp fingernail. Both sets of children were unfailingly prompt, and none of them had missed a day of school so far. Luke was slouched in his seat, which made the absence of the others even more puzzling. She saw Will and Fred, who shared the double desks with Matt and Amos, looking quizzically at the empty spaces beside them. Because Catty and Carolina were the two youngest girls, Charity had had no choice—with silent apologies to Catty—but to seat them together. Their desk now remained starkly empty. Knowing she was taking a chance, Charity asked the question anyway. "Luke, do you know where Matt and Catty are?"

Luke shambled to his feet, peered at the empty desk spaces with gaping surprise, and drawled, "Not here, that's f'r sure." He smirked at her and slumped back down into his seat.

Frustrated, but refusing to give him the satisfaction of showing it, she glanced around at the other children, who all dutifully and solemnly shook their heads. Imagining the four small bodies crumpled beneath the hooves and wheels of a runaway team and wagon—which was ridiculous because none besides the one bringing the town children traversed that path—Charity took a step forward. With the wild idea of racing out to find them, she actually opened her mouth to put Becky and Vincent, the two oldest pupils besides Luke, in charge.

A scraping at the entryway door, followed by the squeaking of hinges, indicated someone was coming in. Before she could react, the four missing children burst into the room, all talking at once. Her darting inspection revealed no blood and no broken bones. Such enormous relief swamped her that she almost followed Luke's example of slumping down in her chair. It took a moment for their wild words to penetrate her giddy awareness. "Children, please, one at a time." She heard the words, but would not have believed she had spoken them if she hadn't recognized her own voice.

The four youngsters fell silent, then Amos and Carolina both spoke at once. Before she could reprimand them, Amos jabbed his elbow into Carolina's ribs so that her breath whooshed out. In the limited time thus gained while she, in a sharp reversal of their usual roles, tried to recover from the well-placed blow, he spoke rapidly. "Ma's havin' her baby." Something flashed in his eyes and was swiftly gone as he continued. "Pa dropped Carolina and me off at Matt's house on the way to town to get the doctor. By the time he 'splained everythin', we was behind time leavin' for school, and then Matt's Ma made us eat breakfast before we could leave. We're sorry for bein' late, Teacher. We ran, but Carolina couldn't keep up." He glared reproachfully at his sister, who, fortunately for all concerned, still lacked enough breath to answer, although her eyes spoke volumes.

Charity drew an admirable amount of air into her own lungs. "What an adventuresome morning you've had. How exciting that you're getting a new brother or sister! We'll be waiting to hear which it is when you come to school tomorrow morning, and what name your folks have chosen. For now, please take your places so class can begin."

Four pairs of wary eyes fastened on her. "We ain't goin' to get in trouble for bein' late?" Matt sounded incredulous but hopeful.

"Not this morning," she assured him. "Just be on time from now on," she warned in her most teacherish voice as the children sidled to their seats.

When Charity, Hannah, and Jonah arrived home that afternoon, Lillie sent the two children to change out of their school clothes. With them thus out of hearing, she related to Charity that Doc Fergus had not yet returned from the Corley place. She added that Brinna, for a certainty experienced in childbirth matters, had gone with him but that she hadn't returned, either. Charity had heard bits and pieces murmured among the women about Callie's pregnancy following Carolina's birth, and that the baby girl had died, but no further details. Naturally wondering about the circumstances, she had discovered that the women in the community, deeply involved in each other's lives out of the necessity for survival, did not gossip behind their neighbors' backs. She was startled, therefore, when Lillie asked her directly if she had heard the story. When Charity admitted that she hadn't, Lillie's hands stilled over the bread dough she was kneading.

"I'm not surprised," she said finally. "We don't pry and we don't spread tales about each other. That's just the way it is with us. But I'm thinking that since you're such an important part of this community now, knowing will help you understand Callie and Owen better, especially in the next few days when memories might go hard with them. Why Callie's taken more precautions than maybe necessary with this baby and why Owen's gone along with them more than husbands usually do."

Charity's thought processes had momentarily stalled on *you're such an important part of this community now* and had to hurry to catch up with the unfolding story.

"It was one of those gray, drizzly days that makes a body glad to be able to stay warm and dry inside the house," Lillie began. But shortly after Owen had ridden out to the herd, Carolina had, with no warning, become messily sick all over herself and the floor. As he did every morning before leaving, Owen had brought water from the creek so that Callie wouldn't have to lug it herself. With care, the supply was adequate, usually with some to spare, until he returned and fetched more. But that morning, without time to get a pan under Carolina's chin, the resulting upheaval had spread far and wide. Callie had used all her supply of water to mop up the child and the floor, but needed at least another full bucket. She put Carolina to bed and stationed Amos beside her with a large pot and firm instructions to stick his sister's head in it if she so much as twitched.

"She bundled up in her cloak and pulled up the hood to keep her hair dry, grabbed the bucket and headed out into the drizzle." By the time she reached the creek, crouched, and dipped the bucket full, the rain had become a pounding force. As she straightened, her foot caught in a fold of the cloak and she overbalanced. Unable to stop, she tumbled forward into the creek. As she went under, her abdomen struck a mossy boulder, but the water was so cold, it took her breath away, and the impact with the jagged rock felt like a mere scrape. Forcing back panic as the cape, already rain-soaked, pulled her down, she somehow managed to struggle free of it and regain the edge of the creek. Shaken as she was, the only awareness she could pinpoint was the necessity of tending to Carolina's mess. Shuddering with cold and reaction, she'd managed to partially refill the bucket and drag it back to the house. Once inside, she put down the pail, shut the door, and leaned against it, trying to regain some composure before going in to see how the children were doing — or more to the point, to see how Amos had fared with Carolina.

"Callie said he'd eyed her drenched hair and dress, and her mind had scuttled for a way they could laugh off her mishap together. A rancher's son to the core, he asked worriedly if it was raining hard enough to spook the herd." Lillie paused momentarily at this revelation of a boy thinking like the man he would become, then went on.

Still frightened, her ears roaring, Callie was sure she hadn't heard him correctly. Then it hit home to her how he took it for granted that nothing, most assuredly not a simple walk to the creek to fetch a bucket of water, could best his independent mother. But now, she'd decided, was not the time to dissuade him from this rosy concept. She'd patted his hand, hoping he wouldn't notice how hers was still trembling, and told him it was coming down a good one. Young as he was, Owen included him when talking of the herd. Amos was already developing a stockman's instinct for weather change, and she would not lie to him in this. So she'd assured him that she was betting his Pa and the herd would be just fine.

His confidence restored, he'd reported that he hadn't had to shove Carolina's head in the pot. In spite of her own distress, Callie had detected a definite note of disappointment in his voice. Numbly, she'd changed out of her wet dress and tended to the rest of the cleaning up. While she was scrubbing the floor, her back began to ache, but she put it down to the clumsy position she had to assume to work around the baby. By the time she finished, pain was zigzagging around her spine.

Belatedly, she'd realized that she was having labor pains, although it was much too soon. With no way to stop them, and no way to get help, she had waited as long as she could, then directed Amos to stay with Carolina, to watch over her so that she didn't try to get up and perhaps be sick again. She'd scarcely known what she told him, but he was used to obeying and didn't question her.

She was alone in her room when the baby came late that afternoon, and her terror was confirmed when the infant didn't draw even a first breath. Owen had found her there when he got home a little later. He'd blamed himself for being away, but she'd refused to hear it — he'd been out doing his job. She'd blamed herself for being careless, but he'd refused to hear that — she, too, had been doing her work, tending to one of any dozens of catastrophes that could strike in the course of a day.

"As far as the rest of the world knows, Callie and Owen have worked it out," Lillie said softly, "but it's easy to see that the unfilled spot in their hearts still weighs heavily at certain times. The baby's birth day, Christmas, family days when she should be there. That's what I meant about understanding where Callie and Owen have been and how the next few days might go hard with them for remembering. Neither Carolina nor Amos, of course, knows what happened. Beyond being told that they had a baby sister who died, Callie and Owen would never put the burden on them of *why* she died."

Charity remembered that flash of something in Amos's eyes when he'd said his mother was having her baby. He was an intelligent little boy. *Does he know more about what happened than they think he does?*

Lillie sighed. "Link and I have been most fortunate. We only have the two children, but they're healthy and happy. We ask for nothing more in this life than that they stay that way."

Supper that night was a subdued meal as they waited for word that Doc Fergus and Brinna had returned and that all was well with Callie and the baby. They gathered around the table after supper and the dishes were done. While the children did their homework, Charity graded arithmetic papers, Lillie sorted a pan of dried beans for soup, and Link bent his head over the shop's ledger book. The knock from the back steps startled the adults, even though it was the sound they had been waiting for.

Link pulled the door open to find Vince Trumble holding a lantern high against the blackness around him. "Come on in, Vince. Any news, yet?"

Vince turned down the wick on the lantern. "Can't stay. Just came to let you know Brinna and Doc are back." He grinned at the intent faces around him. "Callie had the baby about five o'clock. A boy. Callie and Christopher John Corley are doing just fine. Owen's a tad frazzled, but Doc expects he'll make a full recovery."

A sigh of relief rippled through the adults, even as Lillie asked anxiously, "Everything's really all right?"

"Right as rain. Brinna says the baby weighs eight pounds and came with such a good set of lungs she was surprised we didn't hear him howling all the way here in town." He turned up the wick on the lantern. "I'll be on my way. Want to stop by the store and give Ezra and Libby the news."

After his lantern flickered into the darkness, Link shut the door and Lillie sank onto her chair, the brightness of her smile needing no words to express her joy.

Charity rejoiced with the young community over their population expansion. It was, she thought, as if a bright thread had been woven into the fabric of their living after the dark strand of the death of Callie and

Owen's baby had crept in two years earlier. Another dark cord had zigzagged in with Caleb Braden's get-rich-quick scheme and departure for Texas. But hadn't her own coming here to teach added colorful highlights to the emerging picture? She deeply hoped so. *When the weaving is one day finished, will there be more light than dark? Or will the light and dark balance each other out?* She had no way of knowing, of course. She thought of Brinna's hooked rug with its glowing and muted colors and how the shadowed places made the sunlit ones still more dazzling. She was completely unaware that dark strands were even then being woven into the fabric of her own life, threads that would enmesh her more tightly than the finest-woven spider's web holds an unwary creature.

CHAPTER THIRTY-SEVEN

On a sweltering August afternoon, the door to Dr. Terrill's study opened just as Mac reached the foot of the stairway. Catching sight of him, Oliver waved an envelope. "The mail just came from town. This is for you."

He handed the letter to Mac, who glanced at the scrawled address and smiled. "It's from Doc Rawley."

Oliver nodded. "I recognized the writing. I don't think Abe Rawley ever took top honors in penmanship."

"When I was studying with him, he used to have me put the notes in his case journal. Said I wrote a clearer hand than he did. Come to think of it, when I went home this summer, the first day we got back to the office from our rounds, as soon as we set foot inside, he handed me his book and pen."

"Sounds like Abe. It's just a good thing his doctoring skills and his handwriting aren't equally dependent on each other."

Mac was still smiling at the mental picture as, Doc's unopened letter in hand, he took his leave and wandered outside. During his stay, Mac had come across a place on the extensive grounds where he could retreat and regroup his thoughts. It was nothing like his "sitting seat" rock overhanging Mill Creek at the farm. It didn't resemble the old hideaway beneath the sheltering cedar trees he had frequented during his first homesick months as a student at the University. It was actually a wide wooden seat circling the trunk of a maple tree that Amity had told him was nearly a hundred years old. He sank down onto the bench beneath the cooling shelter of a million leaves rustling above him and closed his eyes.

When talking to Oliver, he had made light of Doc's letter, but the truth was that receiving it stirred the anxiety he had been harboring for several days. He hadn't even opened it and guilt and concern were already swirling through him. Not that Doc had, or ever would, deliberately cause such feelings. Mac knew this for a certainty as he slit the envelope with his pocket knife and withdrew the folded sheets.

He deciphered the scribbled contents and knew his instincts had been correct. As usual, Doc told of the situations he had encountered on his rounds and his diagnoses and treatments prescribed. He remarked on the patients who had come to the office, the teeth he had pulled and the broken bones set. He mentioned that he had stopped by the farm the other day and that everyone there was well and hearty, except that Merry had attempted to "mother" one of the barn cats who had taken exception to her compassionate efforts. Merry was fine. The scratches on her hands were healing nicely. "From what I gather, though, the cat hasn't completely recovered yet. Apparently Merry let out a screech that would have done credit to the last trump on Judgment Day. Now whenever she goes into the barn with your Ma or Ethan or Rose, at the very sound of her voice the cat heads for the hills." Mac couldn't help chuckling at the description—and feeling a sneaking sympathy for the barn cat. Merry was a scrapper. No doubt about it, Ma and Ethan had their hands full with her.

"Here you are." He looked up as Amity paused in front of him. "Father said you'd come outside."

He gestured to the bench, and she dropped a kiss on his cheek as she settled beside him. He lifted the sheets of paper. "I got a letter from Doc."

She studied his face. "Is everything all right?"

"Of course. He just talks about the aches and pains he's treated. Nothing serious. Except for Merry's latest adventure." He read the paragraph aloud, and she laughed with him. He finished reading and gazed out over the wide lawn.

"Mac." She laid her hand over his. "What's wrong?"

He sighed. Her perceptiveness was one of the many things he loved about her, but it did get him into trouble sometimes. "I've been thinking. I've been here for over six weeks. Your mother is doing much better. The worst danger now, thank God, is past. The diphtheria itself is no longer a threat to her life. Her heart is still weak, and she'll continue to need care. But—" He stopped, unable to voice the words that must be said.

She took a deep breath and her hand tightened over his. "But you need to return home, to keep your promise to help Doc with his practice, as you agreed you would do when you finished school."

He looked into the beautiful eyes that were neither green nor blue but the color of the quiet places along Mill Creek where the water lay in still pools. "Yes." A small word to hold so much pain. "If your mother were still in danger, I wouldn't even think of going. You know that. Nothing could make me leave her—or you. But her condition has stabilized. She will need care, indefinitely. There is no doubt about that. Her heart has been severely weakened. With rest, and gentle exercise to strengthen it, it may improve to the point where she can take care of herself. But that may be a very long time." The desperately honest words were torn out of him, but he would not lie to her to ease his own anguish.

As he had done earlier, she gazed out over the wide lawn. "I can't leave her," she said softly. "Not yet. She's still much too fragile."

He closed his eyes and swallowed hard. "I know. I would never ask you to. She needs you here. She needs your strength and courage." *I need them, too. I need you with me.* He wanted to fling the words at her but could not.

She drew a quivering breath. "When will you go?" No protestations. No pleading with him to stay for her sake. The doctor's daughter knew the meaning of duty, whether it was her own or someone else's.

"I'll have to let Doc know I'm coming, make the necessary arrangements to catch the train into Fairvale." He tried to smile. "It still doesn't make the run into town every day. We're a progressive city, as you've seen. But not quite that progressive." His attempted lightness faded. "This is Monday. I should probably plan to leave by the end of the week."

She raised her face to his. "I'm sorry, Mac. If there were any other way—"

He cupped her cheek with gentle fingers. "I know, Amity-love. I know."

***

The rest of the week blurred by. His telegram to Doc was answered by return wire. With characteristic straightforwardness, Doc told him that he would welcome the assistance, particularly on night calls, but not to let such a consideration in any way affect his decision to return. It was the final sentence that put into words what was in Doc's mind—and heart. "Don't show up here unless you are absolutely certain your presence is no longer required there." Telegram fees were charged based upon word count, and Doc had not left out a single syllable to shorten his message or the price of it. Mac caught the significance, loud and clear, and his sorely bruised heart did not beat quite so painfully.

When he discussed his decision with Dr. Terrill, Oliver sat silently for several moments. Amity's father had aged more during the past weeks than in all the years Mac had known him. There was a new gravity to his bearing, one far different from the solemnity incumbent on him as the head of the medical school and responsible for the transmitting of knowledge into the heads of sometimes flighty doctors-to-be. Mac suspected that never again would the formerly unflappable man of medicine look upon death and dying in quite the same way.

"You and Amity have discussed this, of course." He said it as statement, not question.

"Yes, sir." Even now, Mac could not shake the ingrained habit of regarding their conference as from young doctor to his superior.

Oliver nodded. It seemed it was as difficult for him to shake the longstanding rule of superior to younger and speak on equal terms as it was for Mac. But he tried. "Your coming here with Amity, staying to assist in treating her mother, there are no words to express our deep gratitude. Not just for the medical skills you shared without reservation, but for the compassion you have extended to Mrs. Terrill, and to the rest of the household as well. I will not willingly see you go back to Fairvale, but I understand the necessity for it. As medical doctors, we both know that Mrs. Terrill's recovery will be long and difficult. There is no way to sugarcoat that reality."

He paused for several moments before resuming. "I have talked to Amity about her position here and what she views as her responsibility, as the older daughter, to take over the household duties until such time as her mother can once more resume them. Our younger daughter Mercy cannot, of course, assume them because she is approaching her time of childbirth. I have not been able to persuade Amity that she does not need to undertake such a course, that we are financially able to secure whatever assistance is required. She has her mother's—shall we say— independence of spirit. In other words, she can be as stubborn as an army mule."

He raised his eyebrows in the briefest of lightings as his gaze met Mac's squarely and quickly sobered again. "I may be considered an old codger to certain younger minds, but I do understand the meaning of forgoing one's plans and dreams for the future. At least in the sense of delaying them for an unknown length of time. You and Amity are both adults and as such must make your own decisions. I do not know what the future holds. It is, however, my fervent hope that, in that future, your place and hers is together."

More than once, in the dark hours that followed as Mac completed his plans for departure, he remembered those words. He found a strange comfort in them, as if they held reassurance that his parting from Amity would be brief and temporary because, finally, Oliver had spoken aloud his blessing on their marriage.

When he told Mrs. Terrill, as gently as he could, that he would be leaving, her eyes clouded. "I'm so sorry, Mac, to have come between your happiness and Amity's."

He started to protest, but she continued. "I know it's because of me that Amity will be staying here, instead of going with you, where she belongs. If only I hadn't insisted on going to take care of my sick friend, so that I got sick, too." Her frustration was so plain that his heart twisted at the resulting clash of duty and loyalty that she could not possibly have foreseen.

He could not lie to her about the consequences, but he made as light of it as he could. "It won't be for very long, you'll see. And as for blaming yourself for becoming sick, just remember, your friend has recovered. Would she have survived if you hadn't been there to help her?"

She drew a long breath and patted his hand. "You remind me of another young man, not so many years ago, after all, with just the same dramatic powers of persuasion. It makes me more determined than ever to get better. I intend to dance at your wedding to my daughter."

***

All too soon, Saturday morning came. He and Amity went up together when he took his leave of Mrs. Terrill, whose weak hug contained a startling amount of fierceness. "I'll be ordering dancing shoes in no time at all," she promised him.

He pressed her hands in his. "The same color as Amity's eyes?"

Her fingers returned his squeeze. "The spittin' image."

Back out in the hallway, the door closed, Amity asked, "What did she mean?"

He drew her into his arms. Pressing his cheek to her hair, he said simply, "Her wedding gift to us."

Jeff and Dr. Terrill met them at the foot of the stairs. "The carriage is ready," Oliver said. "We'll see you back here before you know it." He held out his hand and grasped Mac's firmly.

Mac took Amity's arm and they walked outside together and down the steps. *For the last time until when?* Refusing to dwell on the answer, he assisted her into the carriage. Jeff, who would accompany her back to the house from the train station, climbed up beside the driver, giving them their last moments of privacy.

They held hands tightly and said very little on the all-too-swift trip to town. What was there, after all, to say with their voices that their hearts didn't already know?

On the station platform, Mac and Jeff's hands met in a grip that said more than a hundred words could have. Jeff put his other hand on Mac's shoulder. "Take care, my friend," he said and stepped discreetly away so that Mac and Amity could say good-bye.

Holding her against his heart, Mac breathed in the soft fragrance of her hair. Their lips met as the whistle wailed, warning of departure. The tremble she could not conceal vibrated through him as steam from the wheels hissed toward them, giving final notice of the train's imminent disappearance. Releasing her, he cupped his hand to her cheek and looked deep into her eyes for a precious moment before he turned away to board the passenger car. He found a seat, leaned to the window, and caught a glimpse of her as she looked toward him, her hand raised in farewell. As the train gathered speed, the whistle gave a last long howl, but it was no louder than the wail that rose from deep within his soul.

***

They met him at the station when the train pulled into Fairvale three days later. Seeing in their faces the mingled gladness to see him and anxiety for the circumstances bringing him home, he had no words to tell them how little joy he had in seeing them. How he'd wished, before the train stopped, that it could have just kept on going, taking him with it until it eventually circled back to Philadelphia. Larissa hugged him. Ethan shook his hand. Doc had nothing to say in greeting, just looked at him keenly. After they had gathered Mac's baggage into the buckboard for the trip back to the farm, Doc said decisively, "My young associate and I are going back to the office right now. We have a few medical things to discuss. I promise to have him back to the farm in time for supper."

Since his tone left no room for argument, Larissa and Ethan, although clearly bewildered, departed for home, leaving Doc and Mac standing in a suddenly loud silence. Side by side in the buggy, Mac on the left and Doc on the right just as on so many other occasions in their lives, neither one spoke on the short ride to the office.

Once there, Doc rattled the coffeepot while Mac slumped into his old chair. Doc, while sending speculative glances his way, said nothing until he thrust a cup of fresh coffee under his associate's nose. "All right, Young Doc, you've had a three-day train trip and a half hour since arriving in town to sit and brood. You can go on being gloomy-dark as a thunderstorm in July and worry your folks into a tizzy fit, or you can unload to me. Which do you think is the preferable option?"

Mac stirred and let out a shaky breath. He eyed Doc, now sitting back and waiting for an answer, clearly prepared to wait, if need be, forever. "I'm scared, Doc." The words came low and despairing.

Doc nodded. "That's honest. Might as well put into words what you're scared about. Letting it fester won't help you or anyone else."

The words were spoken with Doc's usual uncompromising bluntness. Mac found to his surprise that by responding in the same way, he was able to give the details as if he were relating the facts of an illness. Which, in a way, he was. *My own illness.* He pushed the thought aside even as it wisped through his mind because, for a certainty, all in his own good time—and way—Doc would nose it out.

He told of the fear that had taken up permanent residence within him, that Mrs. Terrill would never recover enough to manage without someone to care for her, and that that someone would be Amity.

Doc eyed him. "And if that happens, what does that mean for the two of you?"

Mac stared at the wall beyond Doc's shoulder. "It means," he said slowly, "that Amity will never be able to come here to live." His voice dropped to a whisper. "That we'll never be married."

"Never's a long time," Doc pointed out flatly. "Besides, if she can't come here, what's to stop you from going to her? As I recall from a couple million years ago when I was learnin' the medicine trade back there, folks got just as sick and needed doctors just as much as they do out here."

Mac stared at him. "But, Doc, my place is here, with you. To eventually take over your practice. That was our agreement for you putting me through school. I haven't forgotten that, and I don't intend to."

Doc stared straight back. "Times and circumstances change. Folks have to change with them. I know that. I hope you do, too."

"That was one of the things Pa drilled into Rose and me, almost from day one. Your word is your bond and not to be gone back on. I gave you my word, Doc," he said dully. "I intend to keep it."

"Even if I release you from it? And where does that leave me in this little guilt saga you've dreamed up? Would you really expect me to sit quietly by while you slouch martyred through life, and me the cause of it?"

Mac's mouth fell open. "I never thought of it like that."

"Seems to me your thinking processes are lacking in a lot of ways right now. That finicky conscience of yours demanded you come back here. All right, you're here. But let's get one thing straight. I'll not have you glooming around our patients. Folks pick up on our moods. If you're worried and fretful, they will be, too, without knowing that it doesn't have a blessed thing to do with them or their situation. So if you're going to be my associate, you damned well better be a cheerful one. Understood?"

Mac's eyes met the older man's glare, and memory stirred. Doc hadn't chewed him out so thoroughly since the long ago day when Mac had confessed that he wasn't sure, after all Doc's painstaking training of him, that he wanted to be a doctor. Doc's comments on that occasion had all but skinned the hide off him. He'd made up his mind then that he never wanted to be the cause of a repeat performance of that ferocity. Yet here he was again, several years older but apparently not one wit wiser, because a distressingly familiar gleam was building in the hazel eyes pinned on him like the Three Furies come a-calling.

He lifted his chin. "I understand, Doc. You'll have no cause to regret me being in practice with you."

Doc's eyes continued to bore into Mac's, as if scouring the very surface of his interior to see whether he meant it. Finally he relaxed a little. "All right. We'll leave it at that for now. With just one last thought to chew on," he amended. "Maybe, just maybe, Matilda will get better and all this cussed worry will be for nothing. If it was my choice, I'd hang my thoughts on one that's positive, not one headed for doom and gloom. It'll get you just as far at the end of the day. Farther, when it comes right down to it, because then you won't be infecting everyone around you, including the young woman with whom I am presuming you will be communicating frequently by letter. She's going to need cheerfulness from you, too. For better or for worse. I recollect those words from somewhere. Won't hurt a bit to start practicing now to see that she gets every bit of the 'better' that you intend to give her later on."

CHAPTER THIRTY-EIGHT

As Mac was coping with the reality of Fairvale without Amity, Charity was experiencing a very different kind of upheaval. Her month of boarding with the Monroes would soon be over. She was surprised to discover just how reluctant she felt to leave their home and face the process of settling in with a different family. She had expected to experience hesitation upon leaving the Claytons to come here. Anne and Ben were, after all, connected to her past life with longstanding ties, enabling her to feel as much a part of their family as the one she had left in Fairvale.

During the weeks she had been living with the Monroes, however, an odd thing had happened. She had become close to them also. Link, unlike Ben Clayton, was a quieter sort whose actions, rather than his words, conveyed his feelings, but she had soon grown as comfortable with his silences as she had with Ben's talkativeness. Lillie had, at first, exhibited a shy awe of her new boarder that had been disconcerting until Charity realized it stemmed from the fact the school teacher was far more educated in some subjects than her hostess.

Charity tried hard not to flaunt her book learning with any of her new acquaintances, although she didn't hide it, either. When she discovered that Lillie tatted the beautiful lace that edged Hannah's petticoats, she asked if the young mother would teach her how to do it. Lillie was shocked to find that her houseguest, who knew so much about so many other things, didn't know how to tat. Charity explained that, early on, Larissa had made certain she could knit and crochet, but confessed wryly that her lumpy results had never been nearly as attractive as those her sister Rose created with such ease. Lillie, who in her spare time effortlessly produced handmade sweaters, socks, mittens, and scarves for her family, didn't allow even the hint of a smile to escape at this admission. She was unable, though, to conceal the light that flickered in her eyes as she gathered thread and tatting shuttle and assured Charity that she would soon be able to do it in her sleep. Charity had a few mental reservations about such swift success, but didn't voice them then, as Lillie cheerfully set about instructing her, or later, when her tutor continued the lessons with dogged resolve.

It was her last full Saturday at the Monroes before she would return next week to the country for her scheduled stay with Phebe Braden and Will. Caleb had not yet returned from his finding-the-pot-of-gold adventure, and although no one said anything, Charity suspected that folks were wondering why Phebe had had no word at all from him.

Charity didn't know him well enough to speculate. Other than glimpsing him the day she arrived in Laramie, she'd seen him only briefly at the party given in her honor at the schoolhouse and at church services. To her, he had seemed loud-voiced and somewhat crude, even without considering the gold nugget episode.

Charity was in the kitchen half of the main room that morning, helping Lillie and Hannah make pickles from the latest round of garden cucumbers. As the women worked, they chatted about the church services scheduled for the next day out at the Braden ranch. They were filling the last crock when they heard a rush of feet outside and a frantic pounding on the door.

Lillie jerked it open to find young Vincent Trumble standing there. "I'm lookin' for Mr. Monroe," he gasped. "Pa sent me to get him, but he's not in the saddle shop."

"Take it easy, Vince," Lillie urged. "Come in and catch your breath. It's way too hot today to be running so hard." Charity was already bringing a cup of water, but the boy shook his head. "I got to find Mr. Monroe. Pa just got word about Mr. Braden, and he said for me to bring Mr. Monroe to the newspaper office where the other men are waitin'."

Over Vince's head, Lillie's eyes met Charity's in unspoken dismay. Both women realized that if the news were good, it wouldn't be announced in this fashion. Lillie put her arm around his shoulders. "Now you drink this down. I'll find Mr. Monroe and bring him over there." She handed him the cup and he gulped the water. "You go on back now and tell your Pa that Mr. Monroe will be there as quick as he can." The boy turned to scurry off, and she called after him, "Pace yourself, Vince. Walk fast, but don't run." She watched as he obediently slowed a fraction, even though she was certain he would speed up again as soon as he rounded the corner.

Lillie turned to Hannah, who had been standing back, listening in frightened silence. "Go fetch your Pa. He and Jonah are out behind the stable. Tell him I need him here in the house." The little girl flew out the door almost before her mother had finished speaking. Lillie unpinned her apron, tossed it onto the table, and reached for her bonnet. "I'm suspecting that Phebe's going to need all the support we can give her." Her grim tone mirrored the unspoken fear in Charity's heart as she snatched her own hat from its peg.

Link came hurrying in, Jonah and Hannah close on his heels. "Hannah says there's word about Caleb." Before Lillie finished her brief explanation, he was reaching for the door knob.

"You children stay here," she ordered. "Hannah, bank the fire in the stove."

The three adults hurried around the corner to the main street, where they joined Doc and the Clarks as they emerged from the mercantile. Reaching the newspaper office, they found the other townspeople already gathered. With Brinna standing close beside him, Vince uttered the dreaded facts. "Word just came in from Laramie. The herd Caleb rounded up and was driving to Abilene got caught in a terrific thunderstorm two weeks ago. The critters spooked and bolted. Caleb was trying to turn them, but running his horse in the dark, he never saw the cliff in front of them and went over, along with the entire herd. It was a long steep drop. He never had a chance." He stopped speaking. All the words in the world weren't going to change the cruel truth. Brinna reached her hand to him and he slipped his arm around her, drawing her close to his side, while his listeners stood in stunned silence.

Doc Fergus finally stepped forward and broke that awful quiet. "Phebe doesn't know yet. I'm going out to tell her."

Charity had been standing, eyes closed, as if darkness would somehow blot out the reality. She raised her head in time to see Vince exchange a look with Brinna and her nod in answer to his unspoken question. He said quietly, "Brinna and I'll go with you, Doc, for whatever support we can give."

Doc Fergus tipped his head in silent acknowledgment, but Charity saw the flash of gratitude in his eyes. She well understood his relief. If any comfort in the world could be offered in this horrific situation, it would come from Brinna Trumble.

The young community had heretofore been boastful of every expansion that caused it to experience growing pains, much like an adolescent boy's creaking joints gleefully confirm the increase in his stature from one day to the next. Stunned, it now had to absorb the unreal loss of one of its own.

This was not the first time in Charity's life that death had reached out his bony hand. Just four years old at the time, she had only a faint recollection of the night her mother died after being bitten by a rattlesnake, a recall that had more to do with sensations than with actual physical remembrance. To this day, she was terrified of any kind of snake, even the most harmless garden variety. Her father's grief at her mother's death had been a reality that had stayed with her for a much longer time. Zane Edwards' death in the Civil War, when she was ten, was imprinted on her heart because she had been old enough to grasp the anguish of those around her. She had also been old enough to understand that all the words of comfort in the world, no matter how heartfelt the speaker's intention, may numb the agony of loss, but they do not erase it.

After the Trumbles and Doc Fergus hurried away, the people left behind stood in awkward silence for several moments until Ezra Clark edged his way to the front of the room. He rotated his hat in his fingers and cleared his throat. The crowd, clearly relieved to have someone take charge, eyed him expectantly. "This is going to be fearsomely hard on Phebe and Will," he said gruffly. "There's nothing we can do for Caleb, but we can all give every drop of support in us to help his family. We men have been taking turns going out to the ranch to make sure the roughest outside work gets done. The women have been visiting Phebe regularly to help. We'll continue doing that, according to the schedule already set up. At least until she decides what she's going to do for permanent."

Link, heretofore so quiet in the midst of others, motioned with his hat to catch Ezra's attention. "We're supposed to go out there for church services tomorrow. What about that?"

Ezra studied the faces turned up to him. "Rough as it sounds, I think we should still plan on going out. It's all set up. Phebe was expecting us—at least until this." His voice dropped, but he took a deep breath and resumed. "On their way out, Doc and the Trumbles are going to spread the word. But it might be some folks won't hear until tomorrow. We don't want them showing up expecting a normal Sunday service when it'll be anything but normal for Phebe. And for young Will, too. If we're all there, same as planned, it'll maybe go easier on her." He shifted his feet and inspected the hat in his hands. "Nothing can ever be the same for them, losing him like that. Nothing can be the same for the rest of us, either. We've lost one of our own. But one thing I expect to never be lost or changed is our pulling together as a community." At the hard resolution in his voice, the women exchanged glances and nodded their mutual support. The men, floundering in the murky depths of responding to the heartbreak of a woman they were not married to, squared their shoulders. Giving Phebe the physical strength of their hands and backs was solid action they could undertake, even if they could not bring Caleb back to her.

Since they didn't know how long Vince and Brinna would be gone, Libby and Lillie agreed that it would be a good idea for the Trumble children to stay with them. They reckoned without young Vince and ten-year-old Flanna, however. The oldest siblings expressed their strong doubts about anyone else taking care of the younger children. "Ma and Pa will expect us to watch over the little ones," Flanna said, not rebelliously, but with a firm assurance of responsibility. Vince nodded his strong agreement.

Libby listened seriously to the objections, then suggested, "You're right, of course. The young ones know you best and will feel much more secure being with you. The problem is that we don't think you should stay home without your parents here. What we're considering is that you, Flanna, with the three little girls, could come and stay with Mr. Clark and me, just for tonight. Vince here, with Frederick and Garrett, would stay with the Monroes. Don't you think Jonah and Garrett would have a lot of fun visiting, since they're such good friends? It would be a good way to keep your folks from worrying about you."

Vince and Flanna looked at each other, and he nodded. "I guess that would be all right," Flanna said finally. She and Vince insisted on helping gather the clothing the younger children would require both for the night and for church the next day. When they were ready to leave, Flanna stopped suddenly. "Wait. In case Ma and Pa don't come back in time, they'll need their Sunday clothes, too." Only after she was sure they hadn't forgotten anything, Flanna, taking her responsibility seriously, gathered the little girls together and calmly explained that they would be staying with the Clarks tonight. The children looked doubtful, but were clearly used to accepting their big sister's authority. Frederick and Garrett, old enough to have no misgivings, were already out the door.

With the four boys "camped out" beside the unlit stove that night, the three adults sat around the table at the other end of the room. They talked in low voices about the day's events, and waited, but no word came. Link finally prevailed upon Charity and Libby to go to bed, reminding them that the next day would be long and exhausting. He would stay up for a while longer, perhaps go down to the Clarks. If there was any news, he'd come right back and tell them.

In the morning, neither Doc nor the Trumbles had returned. The town vehicles made a slow procession out to the Braden ranch, where they found Phebe exhausted but strangely composed, as if she had long feared that disaster would strike, and, now that it had, she no longer needed to dread its coming.

The next days crept by, each in its own time. Will showed up for school every morning, a little early, as always. He was very quiet, not contributing to the proceedings unless Charity specifically called on him. But he handed in his homework, and Charity found that he had done it correctly. Without knowing for certain, she suspected that Phebe was using the school lessons as a light that she could focus on in the midst of her appalling darkness. It crossed the teacher's mind to wonder if Phebe were actually doing the work for her son. Charity was reassured, however, that was not the case when she asked Will questions and he answered them promptly and correctly.

Charity was not certain that she should impose on Phebe when, at the end of the week, it was time for her to leave the Monroes and go out to the Braden ranch for her month of boarding. She put it to the grieving woman as gently as she could.

Phebe, however, made it clear that she was expecting Charity to stay with her and Will, that she wouldn't dream of changing the plans now.

Then she hesitated. "Unless you'd rather not stay with us?"

Charity saw the shadow behind the dark eyes and heard the doubt behind the unasked question. Her heart went out to the woman who had endured so much that she even now silently wondered whether Charity wanted her friendship. She threw her arms around her and hugged her tightly. "Phebe! Of course I want to come. I've been looking forward to getting to know you better. I just don't want to intrude." She stumbled to a stop, unable to phrase the words delicately enough.

Phebe's arms tightened around Charity in a surprisingly desperate response. "Please do come. It would mean so very much to me."

Charity drew away enough to smile over into the other woman's face. She and Phebe, she had just discovered, were very nearly the same height, a most unusual occurrence in Charity's history. "I'll be there. But you'll probably have to throw me out when the month is up," she warned.

For one of the very few times since Charity had met her, Phebe laughed.

The first two weeks of Charity's stay with Phebe and Will sped by. As she came to know her hostess better, Charity found her to be warm and generous, with a deep hunger to draw from Charity all the learning she could. In the evenings, after Will finished his homework and Charity's papers were graded, Phebe read aloud from her volumes of Shakespeare, thus exposing her son to a world beyond the windswept ranch and their hand-to-mouth living conditions. She also had a dry sense of humor, although she didn't laugh or joke often.

Charity, with her own knowledge of having lost Mac without ever being married to him, could only sense the enormity of the burden of grief the woman who had lost her husband was carrying. She marveled at Phebe's ability to joke or laugh at all, and slowly realized that it came from deep within her love for her son. For Will's sake, she drew their mutual heartache into the open. She talked of happy times she remembered and acknowledged her own sorrow, thus allowing him to speak of his father when he might otherwise have kept his pain and inevitable anger silently within himself.

On a Saturday near the middle of the month, Miss Sullivan stopped by the ranch. Charity greeted her as warmly as her former teacher would allow. It didn't take her long to realize the older woman had come visiting with a purpose. As Phebe served tea in her best china cups, Miss Sullivan, who didn't know the meaning of the phrase "beating around the bush," faced Charity directly. "I came to tell you that on Monday, I'll be leaving to go back to Fairvale. School is scheduled to begin in two weeks."

Charity winced. She had known this parting was coming and thought she had prepared herself for it. But the realization that her final link with her family back home was about to snap made her swallow hard. She searched for something wise to utter, wishing for at least the hundredth time that she could abandon her pesky maturity. The words that came out surprised her almost as much as they did Miss Sullivan. "I'll miss you."

The older woman blinked. "I'll miss you, too." She stated it calmly, but Charity, seeing something flicker in her eyes, felt a stab of awe. She was not left to wonder long what the flash indicated, for Miss Sullivan continued, and her words took Charity's breath completely away. "You, of course, will be in school when the train leaves Monday morning, so you will not be able to accompany me to the station in Laramie. Mr. Leverett has graciously said that he will take me there." A sudden faint pink that on anyone else would have been a blush appeared on Miss Sullivan's cheeks. She drew in a deep breath of the air Charity seemed unable to find. "He has stated the wish to write to me in Fairvale and asks that I write back to him." She paused, as if waiting for Charity to say something, but her listener was momentarily stricken incapable of speech. "I wanted to tell someone, and you seemed to be the appropriate choice."

Charity finally got her breath and her tongue into proper working order. "That's wonderful!" Her voice was squeaky, but the words were totally sincere. She had seen Mr. Leverett talking to Miss Sullivan at every neighborhood gathering and church service, but had dismissed any deep mutual interest as unlikely as the reappearance of dinosaurs.

"We're just going to be writing," Miss Sullivan said sternly, as if to ward off any thoughts of wedding bells that Charity may have had. "During my time here, we have discovered that we have many things in common. So we will correspond. He will tell me of his world here, and I will share the excitement of Fairvale village life with him." She said this last with what Charity's reeling brain recognized as a grain of humor.

Phebe had been sitting quietly during their exchange as if reluctant to interfere, but now Miss Sullivan turned to her. "Please keep this between you and Charity. I don't mind if the two of you talk about it, as I know you will, but I don't want to give Mr. Leverett any occasion to be embarrassed by it."

Phebe, who knew the meaning of the word discretion if anyone did, solemnly agreed. Only after Miss Sullivan drove away, did Phebe and Charity look at each other and break into smiles as delighted as if they had just heard that Christmas had come early this year and Saint Nick himself was knocking on the door.

But the day came when even the deep well of Phebe's strength was drained dry.

CHAPTER THIRTY-NINE

On Tuesday afternoon as Charity and Will, coming from school, approached the house, they heard a sound that was unmistakable, even muffled by the closed door. Charity saw the shock that flashed across Will's face, followed by a dart of fear. He slammed open the door and bolted inside. "Ma? Ma, what's wrong?" He leaped around the work table, headed for the closed door of Phebe's room, from behind which the agonized wails were coming. He flung open the panel and raced inside, Charity on his heels. "Ma!"

The bedroom was darkened by the curtains pulled across the single window, but Charity heard Phebe's sob slice off in the middle, replaced by a gasp of shock. "Will!"

The boy was in front of Charity so that at first she couldn't see Phebe, then he moved, launching himself at the bed as his mother's dark shape lifted from it. Which one grabbed the other first, Charity couldn't tell, but they clung together while Will asked frantically, "Ma, are you all right? What's wrong?"

It was clear to Charity that Phebe wasn't hurt physically and Will, terrified as he was, must have realized this, for he repeated, "What happened? Tell me!"

Young as he was, he didn't grasp the supreme effort with which his mother fought to overcome the emotion tearing at her. She tried twice to speak but all that came out were sobs. Charity stepped forward at this point. "Will, your mother will tell you what's the matter, but we need to give her a chance to calm herself a little. Right, Phebe?" She put her hand gently against the woman's hair. Phebe nodded and drew another quivering breath. "Will, she isn't hurt like she's cut herself or anything. She's all right that way. What she needs is a drink of water to help steady her. Can you please get her one?"

Swift rebellion replaced the terror in Will's face. He started to protest, but Phebe said haltingly, "Please, son. It would be a big help to me." Reluctantly, he let her go and shot a wrathful look at Charity before darting from the room.

She sat down beside Phebe and put her arm around her. "He'll be back in a minute. You can tell us then what's happened." Not really sure what words to say, she hoped that her soothing tone would help the woman regain her composure.

Will came dashing back into the room, the outstretched cup of water he was carrying sloshing over the sides in his haste to return to her. "Here, Ma." He thrust it at her, not noticing in his eagerness to help that he succeeded in spilling some on his mother and on Charity.

Phebe took it with a shaky hand and sipped some. "Thank you, son. That's a big help."

"Would you like to come out to the other room? We could sit at the table and you can tell us what happened." At this suggestion, Phebe turned her face to Charity's and nodded.

She started to rise and Will gripped her arm. "Here, Ma. I'll help you." Letting him do it, Charity stood back while he awkwardly and carefully guided his mother to the table and pulled out the chair for her to sit.

She sank down. Tears were still trickling down her cheeks, but she had regained a measure of self-control. "Thank you, Will." She gave him the barest of smiles. "Could I have another cup of water, please?" Whether she was asking because she, Charity, and the floor were wearing most of the contents of the original offering or whether it was to give her son more chance to be helpful, Charity wasn't sure. Will came back from the water bucket, this time carrying the cup carefully. As he handed it to his mother, Charity saw that the terror in his face had been replaced by a stamp of deep anxiety that was much too old for his nine years.

As Will and Charity sat, Phebe put the cup on the table in front of her without drinking any. She set it down very carefully and precisely, then she reached along the table and took Will's hand. It crossed Charity's mind to question whether she should be here for what was obviously going to be a personal discussion, but before she could voice her uneasiness, Phebe reached across for her hand, too. She gripped their fingers. "A Mr. Henry Archer came here today. He's from the bank in Laramie." Her voice faltered, but she squeezed their hands tightly and continued. "He said that before Pa left on the cattle drive, he took a loan out on this house and property to finance the trip. 'Collateral' Mr. Archer called it. Since Pa's not coming back, I have to pay the money back or else he'll take the house and land."

Will had sat listening with growing horror. He didn't understand all the words, but he fully understood the intent. "Ma, no," he yelled. "They can't do that!"

Phebe blanched but said firmly, "Yes, Will, they can. Mr. Archer showed me the paper Pa signed. It's all legal. And I have no way to pay back the money."

***

Charity scarcely knew how she stumbled through the next days, and she wondered how Phebe endured them at all. Once it was known that the bank intended to foreclose on the property, other men from Laramie and Cheyenne came forward with the documents to prove that they, too, had loaned Caleb money to finance his "couldn't fail" scheme. The Clark's Valley community, learning of the newest disaster and its tentacled offspring, gathered around the Braden family. They offered to help Phebe pay the debts, but she declined, knowing that she would be taking money many of them could not spare. She insisted that Will continue to attend school and sent him off each morning with Charity. When they arrived home in the afternoon, she quizzed him about what he had learned. She refused to allow him to give any answers that she considered to be less than complete. In the evenings she went over the lessons with him. It struck Charity again that Phebe, encouraging her son to focus, rather than allow him to slip off into his own troubled world, was also preserving her own sanity.

Word came down from the Laramie bank that since Phebe couldn't pay the debts, the house and property would be sold at auction on the second Saturday in October. What she and Will would do then, Phebe had no idea. By that time, Charity would have moved into town to board with the Clarks for the month. Phebe, however, pleaded with her to stay on with them at the ranch. Neither she nor the Clarks were able to refuse.

Charity, while more than willing to remain with Phebe and Will for their own sakes under the circumstances, also felt a sneaking, vast relief. Boarding with Ezra and Libby Clark wasn't a problem. They were ready to welcome her as sincerely as had the other families she had stayed with. The snag was that she would be staying in the same house as their daughter, Cora, who had continued to treat her coldly whenever an ill-tempered Fate brought them together. These meetings generally took place at church services or during Charity's infrequent shopping trips to the Clark's Valley Store.

She suspected that Cora also talked behind her back, spreading little half stories and insinuations about Cork's attentiveness. This had worried her, not for the tales themselves which were totally untrue, but for her position as the school teacher. Women doing her job had to be totally circumspect in their behavior. And she was. But how were the parents of her pupils to know this unwaveringly? Her showdown with Luke had brought the school board out in force to check on her interactions with her students. Convinced that she was behaving properly, they had made no further issue over it. Was it the same with Cora's gossip? She had to believe that it was, for she couldn't come right out and confront Cora. She understood only too well that such an action would only bring out the total innocence in Cora's big blue eyes and a tearful amazement at such an accusation. Neither could she ask Anne or Brinna "What is she saying about me? Whatever it is, it isn't true." So she avoided Cora when possible, and when not possible made certain to be polite, cheerful, and to appear totally ignorant of the other woman's motives.

Chance, however, apparently in a particularly cranky mood, had arranged for them both to be at the community's gala Harvest Moon dance held in town at Sam McKnight's livery stable the last Saturday of the month. The full moon actually occurred two nights before, but the Clark's Valley celebrants weren't being fussy. This was one of the few times during the year that both the town and country folks laid aside their dislike of being out at night. Everyone arranged to be at the dance before full dark, and no one would think of leaving before dawn.

Cork Birkett had stopped by the school one afternoon as Charity was bidding the children good-bye. Her students, particularly the older ones, had watched with bright eyes. He'd dismounted from his sorrel gelding and sauntered over to greet her, where she was assuring herself that the town children were sitting securely in the wagon bed for the trip home. She did her best not to blush as she waved young Vince Trumble, who was in charge of driving the team that day, off down the road. As it lumbered away, every head in the wagon box—thankfully, Vince, on the high seat at the front, kept his eyes on the path ahead—turned back to observe the meeting between Teacher and the cowman.

He'd waited until the team, wagon, and children had rounded a bend in the road before he grinned at her. "Guess I didn't time that very well," he'd said wryly, "but I wanted to see you before you left." Charity, envisioning the talk that would circulate at the supper tables that night, had felt her blush deepen, and counted it fortunate that Will was in the shed behind the school, saddling his horse, Wrangler. But when Cork asked her to go to the Harvest Moon dance with him, she happily accepted his offer.

Only later did she wonder if, in society's rigid rule book, it was proper for the school ma'am to do so. When she had hesitantly asked Phebe her opinion that night, she had straightened away from the pan of dishes she was sudsing, and, with drippy hands on her hips, said emphatically, "If you don't go with him, you'll have to answer to me—and to every other woman in the community, I assure you!" Charity had sighed with relief at Phebe's loyalty. When she was preparing for bed, however, she realized the deeper meaning of the supportive words. *Cora is indeed gossiping behind my back for all the world to hear. But Phebe and the other women are on my side.*

Charity treasured every minute of that dance evening, except the several that Cora spent glowering at her. She enjoyed being with Cork. He was fun. He was articulate. When together, they discussed many subjects, but whether serious or lighthearted, she found that she was learning about many things she had never been exposed to. She had never given much thought to cattle, whether singly or in herds. Milk cows, of course, were important for their various contributions to the enjoyable pastime of eating. They had big, soft brown eyes. They were civilized. When Cork took her out to Ben's Arrow A herd one Saturday afternoon to show her the contributors to beef steak, she found the fabled animals to be much like those on the farm. Except that they were larger, carried a significant group odor around with them, and were extremely attractive to flies.

In the dark hours of the night as she stared up toward the ceiling, her heart acknowledged that when she was with Cork the cold spot put there by Mac's brotherly indifference was warmed. Cork listened to her. When she had something serious to discuss, he discussed it with her seriously. She had even told him about her terror of being near a snake, whether rattler or garden variety, and her mother's death from the bite she had received in the sheep pasture when Charity had been alone with her. Other people knew the story, naturally. But she had never discussed it, beyond the basic facts, with anyone except her father and Rose. *How could I tell Cork and feel no regret over sharing the emotions I've kept to myself all these years?* Clearly, he enjoyed being with her. He made her laugh. *Are the citizens of Clark's Valley wondering about our friendship?* She would not put a stronger name to it. Not yet, anyway. *But maybe in the future.*

The morning following the dance, church services were held at the Clarks' two hours later than usual to allow everyone a chance to get home, do the chores, and freshen up. After the notes of the final hymn died away, the congregation, instead of drifting toward the kitchen where the potluck lunch was waiting, stayed in their places. Ezra and Libby, officiating since the service was at their home, and still at the front of the group, called Phebe forward. Puzzled at the summons and clearly embarrassed to once again be the center of attention, she edged her way to the front, Will firmly beside her.

Libby reached for her hands and smiled reassuringly. Ezra put his hand on Will's shoulder. "We've called you up front," Ezra said, "because we have a very special announcement to make. We know that you've been experiencing tremendous difficulties these past days." Phebe's cheeks grew pinker and Will's expression turned to a scowl at the public airing of their heart hurt. "We know that you've been struggling to make some life-changing decisions that possibly involve moving to Laramie. Phebe and Will, we are all your friends here. We can't change any of what's happened, but we, all of us, want to share in your future. We know your plans are up in the air. We have some ideas that might bring those plans down to earth, if you're willing. Libby and I would like to hire you on at the store. Not as a clerk," he said hastily. "Libby will explain it all to you."

As he gestured to her, Libby tightened her clasp on Phebe's hands.

"We'd like to have you come to the store as a seamstress. Your stitches are so fine, the rest of us are frankly envious. We'd like to set you up in a space where you could sew dresses, hats, other things —" she cleared her throat delicately — "for the rest of us that are as lovely as the ones you do for yourself. You would be paid, of course. We'll speak of those details later, but we would all benefit. Because of you, our town would have a new business!"

Before Phebe could answer, there was a shuffling in the crowd, and Ella and Harold Browning edged to the front. Ella spoke first. "As you know, we have the new hotel here in town. Well, right now it's more a boarding house that serves meals to a sizeable portion of the fellows around here who shy away from doing their own cooking, but it has growing pains." A low ripple of appreciative laughter spread through the crowd. "We're newer to town than most of you folks, but that doesn't make any difference. We've been treated fine here and have every intention of staying." She turned to speak directly to Phebe. "If you're of a mind to do so, we have an extra room that we'd be most proud to let out to you, in exchange for helping around the place with cooking and such like when you aren't busy at the mercantile."

The blush had receded from Phebe's cheeks and she'd turned ghostly pale. She opened her mouth but no words came at first. She turned to Will and looked down at him with an intensely questioning expression. He searched her face. "Does this mean we get to stay here?"

"Yes, son, it does."

A light that had been absent from Will's features for many weeks burst forth, but, remembering his manly responsibilities, he said solemnly, "Sounds awful good to me, Ma." Then his dignity quite deserted him as he threw his hat into the air and let loose a joyful cheer.

The two remaining weeks before the scheduled auctioning off of Phebe's world passed swiftly as she did what she could to prepare for the sale. According to the contract Caleb had signed, the foreclosure included the land, house and outbuildings, and everything in them. Phebe and Will would literally be left with nothing except the clothes on their backs. She never spoke aloud of what this final, crushing blow did to her heart. The one thing she insisted on was that every article in the house that could be washed, dusted, scrubbed or polished, was. If these objects were going out of her life to new owners, they would go out sparkling clean.

Toward that end, her friends and neighbors, in town and out, again gathered to offer their elbow grease and their heart-deep support. On the last Saturday before the auction, Lillie, Brinna, Anne, and Libby, children in tow, gathered to put the finishing touches to the cleaning. Callie had come, too, with Amos, Carolina, and six-week-old Christopher. However, by a vote unanimous except for her lone dissent, instead of scrubbing walls and floors, she was elected to take charge of the children who had come with their mothers.

To Charity's dismay, Cora came with Libby. Cora seemed no happier than Charity about the situation. With subtle maneuvering, they managed to keep a sufficient enough distance apart that no one else noticed their mutual lack of regard as everyone set to washing down the walls and scrubbing the floors of the house. The day, which had started out chilly, turned warm and sunny, one of those golden gifts given in October before the winter snows blasted. The women agreed that the galloping wind would help dry everything inside well before evening.

The scrubbing job necessitated many trips back and forth to the creek for water, both to wash and rinse. On one of these treks, Libby noticed that with so much else going on the past weeks, Phebe's garden, stripped of its edibles, had not yet been cleared and "put to bed for the winter" as she expressed it. The women inspected the site and agreed that they'd tackle it the first thing after lunch. If Phebe wanted her possessions clean and sparkling before they went out of her care, her friends would clean and sparkle them for her, including the large, forlorn-looking plot before them.

After a well-deserved break, the women split into two groups. Brinna, Libby and Phebe stayed at the house to replace all the furnishings that had been moved outside to make the wall and floor scrubbing easier. Lillie, Anne, Cora, and Charity tackled the garden plot. In addition to the stalks and vines left behind, Phebe had temporarily pitched to the side the rocks she came across in her weeding, fully intending to later toss them by the creek bank. Completing this task, too, had been lost in the upheaval that her life had become.

Happy to spend time with Anne, no matter how short, Charity walked out with her to the fenced plot. She was secretly amazed that Caleb, always so occupied with his cattle and his fanciful schemes, had taken the time to build such a sturdy barrier around the garden. The tall posts had wire strung between them to keep out the mule deer and pronghorn that might be tempted by the feast inside. He had also placed a fine mesh wire, not unlike the window screens Charity had seen in Philadelphia, in the lower spaces to discourage rabbits and other such critters from joining the banquet. All in all, it was a strong, effective barricade that still let the sunlight in. *I bet Phebe and Will provided a lot more time and effort than Caleb supplied.* Charity immediately felt a guilty twinge for such an unkind observation about one who had so recently died. *He probably decided that if he wanted to eat, he'd better provide protection to the contributing source.* In spite of her remorse, her busy-as-a-bee brain insisted on having the last word as she quickly bent beside Anne to begin their task.

After the foliage residue had been gathered and added to the compost pile by the barn, they tackled the rocks lying haphazardly along the inside edge of the fence, deciding that transporting them in batches to the creek bank would be the quickest and easiest way. Since the wooden buckets they had earlier carried water in were now available, Lillie and Charity went to the house to fetch them.

Heavy as the rocks were, they couldn't fill the buckets all the way, but were still able to dispose of more each time than they would have if carrying them by hand. They made several trips, and Charity noticed that Cora managed to maintain her distance each time. That suited Charity just fine. On the final trek, however, all the stones had been tossed into the buckets and the whole group, with light hearts and merry chatter, started down the path to the creek.

Cora, who apparently had the lightest load, swished ahead of the others. Anne, Lillie, and Charity, strolling together, lugging their buckets, admitted they were too worn out to swish. As they came in sight of the creek bank, they were congratulating each other on the tremendous amount that had been accomplished that day. Even though they were now only a few feet from her, Cora, standing beside the pile of rocks they had dumped earlier, called to them that she would finish first because they were such slowpokes. She raised her bucket and started pouring the stones onto the pile. In a split second, her triumphant expression changed to sheer horror. She screamed. As she drew breath to scream again, Charity, who was closest to her, heard the buzzing rattle. A monstrous, icy hand squeezed her heart, freezing the flow of blood in her veins. In one eternal instant, she saw the slim, diamond-patterned figure launch itself at Mama. Mama was screaming. And screaming again ....

With another wild shriek, Cora smashed her empty wooden bucket down at the snake coiled a foot away, rattles whirring frantically, head up, tongue flicking as it precisely targeted its enemy. The weapon missed its mark, bouncing with a thunk against the rock on which the rattler was stretching up, reaching toward her. The snake, distracted for a split second by the object that had plunged between it and its intended victim, veered toward this new danger and thrust its fangs against the bucket's wooden side.

Even as it did so, Charity let out a banshee wail of her own. Scarcely aware that she was doing so, she grabbed a rock from her bucket and hurled it toward the rattler with all the precision she had once put into skipping stones across a creek. Her missile struck the snake's head. The force threw the rattler off balance, tipping it forward, its buttons continuing to buzz madly, filling Charity's ears with the menacing sound until it seemed to be whirring inside her. Propelled by a force she didn't know she possessed, she launched another rock at the snake, then another. As its head dropped down onto the rock, she shot forward, poised to dump her remaining rocks down on the still-twitching form. Before she could do so, the tail stopped vibrating and the rattles fell mercifully silent, leaving a vast hush on the autumn air.

She stared down at the snake, no longer menacing, no longer her mortal enemy. She started to tremble, but felt strong arms around her, holding her up as a voice murmured in her ear, "Charity, come away. There might be another one nearby." She allowed the arms and the voice to lead her to a spot away from the rocks and the motionless snake and the now-silent rattle buttons. "Charity, can you hear me?"

Recognition of sharp fear in the voice made her look up into Anne's worried face. "Yes. I can hear you." She shuddered. "I'm all right."

Anne looked hard into Charity's eyes. Reassured by what she saw, relief as sharp as her fear had been washed across her features and she gathered Charity into a fierce hug.

The other women, drawn to the spot by the wild screams, surrounded her, would have bundled her off to the house, but a shaky voice stopped them. "Charity."

She looked up. Cora was standing in front of her. All the icy resentment had been wiped from her features. Her eyes, so dark they were almost black, were enormous in her white face. "I—thank you," she said simply. "Thank you." Her expression crumpled. Libby took her daughter in her arms, holding her as tightly as Anne had held Charity.

Although Charity wished fiercely that it wouldn't, news of the afternoon's adventure spread rapidly through the community. She smiled as graciously as she could as she accepted the women's hugs and the men's gruff words of admiration that she'd "done good." But at night, when Phebe and Will slept, the scene replayed itself over and over against the backdrop of her heart. In those black hours of reliving those moments, she realized with shock that thinking about the snake no longer terrified her. When someone spoke of the event, she no longer quailed at the very mention of the word. She marveled that it could be so, but she was deeply grateful.

However, another result of the confrontation with the rattlesnake shook her to the foundations of her being. As the rattler's warning to Cora whirred menacingly, Charity was suddenly back in the old sheep pasture. She was four years old again, mouth open to scream but no sound escaping from her fear-closed throat, small body stiff with terror as she watched the snake lunge off the rock. Its rattle was thundering in her ears until there was no other sound in the world. And then she clearly saw her mother's face. During the fourteen years since her mother had died, her image had blurred, had become fainter and fainter until, in Charity's remembrance, there was only a wistful sensation of her presence. For a time after she and Pa had met Zane and Larissa Edwards, she even imagined that Mama had looked a lot like Mrs. Edwards. But Pa had told her that with her honey-gold hair and dark blue eyes, she was a mirror image of Mama. She had wondered how that could be, because when she stared hopefully in the mirror she saw only herself, never Mama smiling back at her. After a while, she had given up searching for her.

She told no one about how, in that flash of time, she had seen Mama, just as she had looked on that day. Her back was to Charity, and she was in the act of whirling to face the snake, the terror that must have come an instant later not yet marking her expression. Charity thanked God with all her heart for that mercy and for solving the puzzle. Long ago she had searched for her mother in the childish image that had looked back at her from the mirror. Now, when she gazed into those reflected depths, a young woman with honey-gold hair and dark blue eyes looked back at her, and smiled.

CHAPTER FORTY

With the auction scheduled to start at nine o'clock, Phebe, Will, and Charity were up early. Will was in the barn and Phebe and Charity were arranging the just-washed breakfast dishes when they heard the sound of a wagon and team approaching. The two women exchanged an anxious glance. It was not yet seven o'clock. Surely no one would be coming to the sale this early. Charity hurried to the door, then sighed with relief when she saw Ben assisting Anne down from the high wagon seat and Matt and Catty scrambling off over the sides. "It's the Claytons," she called back reassuringly to Phebe, as Ben reached up to swing Eve to the ground.

Phebe slumped with relief, then straightened her shoulders and joined Charity at the door, welcoming Anne and Ben, urging them to come in. "We don't have any coffee," she said apologetically. "We just washed the pot."

Anne laughed. "We thought that might be the case, so we brought some along." As proof, Ben hoisted the jug. "We just wanted to make sure you didn't need help getting everything ready." Anne looked about as she spoke. "It appears you're as set as can be."

"We're good in here. Will's out at the barn, checking everything there."

At her words, Ben motioned to Matt. "We'll just go on out and see if we c'n lend him a hand."

When the two had gone, Phebe brought glasses of milk for Catty and Eve. Setting the newly washed cups and saucers in front of Anne and Charity, she poured the still-steaming coffee. "It must have been boiling to beat all when you put it in the jug." Her attempt at a joke was feeble, but they smiled anyway.

When they finished, Charity rose to wash the cups again, and Anne put her hand on Phebe's arm. "You have everything done up here just beautifully. There's not another speck of work that you can do. There's no need for you to be here all day, watching the sale. Ben, Owen, and Cole will see to everything. Vincent and Ezra promised to keep an eye on the financial part. So we want you and Will to come home with us." Anne braced herself for Phebe's protest. "We won't take no for an answer."

Phebe started to speak, then pressed her lips firmly together. Her voice was only a little shaky as she said, "Thank you for understanding. Will and I accept your invitation."

In the wagon a little later, heads high, shoulders rigidly back, Phebe and Will stared ahead as their home receded in the distance.

The women managed to keep busy doing one thing and another during that long day. More to the point, they managed to keep Phebe busy and talking so that she had little time to dwell on what was taking place at the home that had been her security, and her son's, during all of her husband's schemes and dreams.

Late that afternoon, Ben rode in with Owen, Vincent, and Cole. The men came silently into the house. Phebe looked up at them, unable to speak. "It's done," Ben told her quietly. "Ezra's checkin' in with the bank to make sure it's all counted fair and proper."

She drew a deep breath and looked wildly around as if seeking a place she could escape to. There was no such place. She sank down onto a chair at the table. No one said anything, for there was nothing to say. Anne put her arm around Phebe's shoulders, the only comfort she could give.

"However, we do have somethin' f'r you." Ben spoke gruffly as he opened the door for Will and Matt to come in. They were lugging a wooden crate between them, which they hefted onto the table in front of her. Phebe stared at it blankly. It contained several cloth-wrapped objects.

"We couldn't get everythin', but we all pitched in for somethin'."

When she made no move to take anything out of the box, Anne reached over and pulled out the top bundle. She handed it to Phebe, who stirred as if waking from a dream—or a nightmare—and took it. Unwrapping it, she found her grandmother's sewing basket. Owen said gruffly, "That's from Callie and me. Callie knew how much it means to you."

Phebe stared at it and once more she tried to speak, but no words came. Anne handed her another piece from the box. Phebe unwrapped it to find her father's Bible. "That's from us," Anne said softly. "We couldn't let something so important go out of your life."

Phebe's eyes were swimming with tears, in spite of her efforts to hold them back. She unwrapped the other bundles. Her volumes of Shakespeare. "I know how much you enjoy reading them," Charity said quietly. Her china tea set from Ezra and Libby. The comb and brush set that had been her mother's from Brinna and Vince. Her grandmother's etched glass cake plate that had been passed down to her daughter, Phebe's mother. Link and Lillie had made certain that it would stay in Phebe's family.

The tears were running unchecked down Phebe's cheeks by the time she finished unwrapping everything. She had no words with which to thank them. The men shuffled their feet awkwardly as she buried her face against Anne's shoulder and cried.

Will had been standing back, fidgeting in embarrassment at his mother's emotional response. Now Ben said heartily, "I believe there's one more thing outside. Will, could you go check?"

The boy gave him a puzzled look, because he and Matt had been expressly charged with carrying the crate and its contents in to his mother. Obediently, however, he pulled open the door. Phebe, still sitting at the table, heard him give a wild whoop. Fearing he was under attack by wolves or bears at the least, she jumped up and flew out the door before anyone could stop her. Reaching the step, she halted in shock. Ben and Anne's oldest son, Jason, had come with the other men but had remained outside because he was sitting astride Will's horse, Wrangler.

Will was standing, open mouthed, staring at the pair. Then he walked slowly forward. Jason dismounted. "For me?" Will's question was scarcely a breath. Jason grinned and handed him the reins. The boy took them as if they might disappear when he touched them. He stepped to the horse and stroked his muzzle.

Ben said gruffly, "For you. A man can't be without his horse in this country."

Will, eyes shining, mounted and rode him around the yard as if getting to know him all over again. He drew the horse up in front of the little group standing by the steps. "Thank you." He could find no other words of manly appreciation.

"Why don't you take him over to the corral and unsaddle him?" Ben suggested.

Will did so, but as soon as he was out of sight of the others, he slid down and buried his tear-stained face in Wrangler's mane.

***

When Phebe moved to town, Charity went to stay with Ezra and Libby—and Cora. In spite of their truce, courtesy of the snake, Charity was still a little leery of Cora's motives, keeping in mind, as Pa liked to say, the advice about a leopard changing its spots. At any rate, she was too busy to spend precious time fretting over the color of Cora's intentions. At least until the afternoon she went into the store to buy chalk for school. She had neglected to purchase any until it was no longer possible to delay or she would be scratching the words on the board with her fingernails. She was in a hurry and her mind was on the history test she planned to give the older students the following day, so she didn't realize that neither Ezra nor Libby was in the room.

Only when she approached the counter did she become aware that Cora was standing behind it. The urgency of her errand notwithstanding, she would have put the chalk back and left as speedily as possible. Cora, however, as if reading her intentions, spoke quickly. "Charity, wait."

Despite her first instinct, Charity, keeping her expression as aloof as she could, waited stiffly for her to continue. Cora evidently saw the coolness in her eyes, for she took a deep breath. "I've been wanting to talk to you, but there hasn't been a chance until now." When Charity looked unconvinced at the flimsy excuse, Cora bit her lip. "I mean when no one else is around."

So no one else can hear your scorn and rudeness? Remembering her determination not to acknowledge Cora's distain, she didn't give voice to the thought that flashed through her mind.

As if for support, Cora gripped the edge of the counter with both hands. "I just wanted to tell you how sorry I am for being so nasty to you."

Charity blinked at this revelation but warily held her tongue.

"I know I've been awful to you." Shame tinged Cora's voice. "But, you see, I wanted the teaching position so very much. I was sure I would get it, and then they hired you. Someone they didn't even know, instead of me. I just couldn't believe it at first, and then when you came here, and you were so elegantly dressed, and so nice, and you were doing such a good job teaching, and everyone liked you so much—including Cork—" Her voice faltered before she hurried on. "I thought if I could convince the school board and everyone else that you weren't right for the job after all, they'd send you away and give me the position. And that Cork would pay attention to me then. So I said all those things about you. But it didn't work. Everyone still liked you, and Cork did, too. Then that day with the rattlesnake—" Her eyes grew wide. "You saved my life. Even after I was so awful to you. If you hadn't thrown those rocks, it would have—would have—" Her voice broke completely this time, and she gazed mutely at Charity, who had not moved during the disjointed confession.

So I was right about Cork. But I didn't know you were jealous about the teaching position, too. What can I possibly say? Cora was still staring at her, obviously waiting for her to respond. All she could manage was, "I understand, Cora. Truly I do." She did understand, more than Cora would ever realize. *Is this how Amity felt about me?*

"Can you ever forgive me?"

She saw the shine of tears in Cora's eyes, and heard the sincerity in her voice. She opened her mouth without knowing what she was going to say, and heard words falling out. Shock darted through her, but her voice kept going anyway, just as if it had a mind of its own. "Yes, Cora. I can forgive you. I never wanted there to be hostility between us. Now, knowing the reasons for it, I want those bad feelings even less."

Cora swallowed hard, unclenched one hand from the counter edge, and held it out to Charity. "Friends?"

Charity wasn't certain she wanted to go that far yet, but it was certainly better than Cora's hostility. She slowly put out her own hand.

"Can we settle for 'not enemies'?"

Cora stared at her in amazement. "It sounds good to me," she agreed, then suddenly started laughing. It was Charity's turn to stare at her in disbelief. "I've never had a 'not enemy' before," Cora choked. "I'm so pleased to meet my very first one." She shook Charity's hand as if they had just been introduced. As the absurdity of it struck her, Charity, too, started laughing.

***

By the middle of November, Clark's Valley had already been on the receiving end of several snowstorms that, in Charity's estimation, rated right along with some of the more memorable ones she'd experienced in Ohio, although none had kept her and the children from making it to school. But the folks who had been there for a few years and endured winter's blasts did not take these flurries, as they called them, lightly.

Because they knew that a storm could form quickly and become a whiteout almost instantaneously, one or another of the townsmen took to riding with Charity and the children to school. Once they were deposited safely there, the escort went about his business. And when it came time to go home, someone was there to accompany them. She noticed that the ranching families followed the same policy. She didn't fully understand their concern. She'd experienced blizzards before, and had never been caught out in a storm that would cause her to lose her way. After all, if people read the weather signs, wasn't there was plenty of warning before one struck? She wasn't, however, going to argue about it. This was one instance where the teacher obeyed the voices of higher authority. It wasn't long before she found abundant reason for their caution. Stubborn she might be, but she was glad she had listened.

Thanksgiving came late that year, falling on the last day of the month. Charity, finishing her time with the Clarks, had been dreading the holiday, the first one she'd spend without her family, even though she felt very much a part of the new community family she'd joined. Everyone participated in celebrating the day. Vince and Brinna had Doc Fergus come for dinner. The Monroes invited Sam McKnight, the blacksmith and farrier who had no family of his own. Phebe, at the boarding house, helped cook and serve the meal for all the other single men of the town who regularly ate there. Charity suspected that Phebe was secretly glad to be able to keep her hands so busy that she wouldn't have time to think about her first celebration without Caleb. She'd already had several eager proposals of marriage from the gentlemen who regularly graced the place with their presence. She had turned them all down.

Two days after Thanksgiving, Charity was to move out to the Claytons to stay with them for the month of December. The original plan had been for her to go to the Corleys, but Amos had come down with the mumps. Carolina and even baby Christopher had swiftly followed his lead. Charity had had the mumps before she and Pa moved from Michigan to Ohio. Doc Fergus warned her, however, that even though she did not run the risk of getting them again, it was possible for her to carry the infection to others. He advised her that being in constant close contact with the sick children by living with them would increase her risk of passing on the illness to others, particularly her students. Anne had urged her to stay with them instead, and Charity had gladly accepted.

Ben told her that he'd come into town on Saturday and transport her and her well-traveled trunk out to the ranch, but when she dismissed school on Friday afternoon, he was waiting by the front door with his wagon, on runners for the winter, and his shaggy-coated team. She saw that he already had her trunk in the back. Before she could ask, he said, "It's fixin' to storm up a good one tonight or tomorrow. Anne and me figured it'd be best if you come out to the ranch now, instead of waitin'."

Charity glanced at the azure sky with puzzlement. The day had actually been a mild one, and she certainly didn't see any storm clouds forming. She didn't ask him how he knew. Ben, she had learned, was keenly attuned to the weather, as were the other ranchers and townsmen. If he said a storm was coming, she'd take his word for it, especially if it meant she'd get to visit with Anne sooner than she had anticipated. Matt and Catty scrambled into the wagon bed. After Ben assured Griff that he'd see him safely home as well, the boy tied his horse to the back of the wagon and, grinning, quickly joined the other children. After waving the town children off under Link Monroe's watchful eye, Charity closed up the school and joined Ben on the wooden seat.

Anne greeted her happily as Ben and Matt continued on their way to take Griff home. There was no additional snow that night or the next morning. Ben, Jason, Luke, Nightowl, and Cork were out with the herd all that second day of December. As the morning wore on, Anne, checking her food supplies, stopped her work frequently to look out the kitchen window. She had Matt and Catty bring in extra water from the rain barrels stationed at the house corners. In the afternoon, she made sure the chickens were gathered securely in their house, with extra feed and water. She had Matt shut the other animals in the barn and give them generous portions of water and hay in addition to their usual rations. The sky was still clear, but there was a hush, as if nature were waiting for something.

In the late afternoon, the pounding of hooves mixed with the bawling of cattle drew them all to the door in time to see Ben driving his herd in the direction of the barn. The animals, sensing the coming storm, were balky and nervous, ready for any reason — or no reason — to bolt. Charity shot a bewildered look at Anne, whose expression reflected such relief that Charity stared, only then realizing the depth of the terrible apprehension the older woman had been concealing all day. Anne grabbed Matt's coat from the peg beside the door, thrust it at him, and said something that made him take off at a run for the corrals. He was there and swinging the gate wide when Ben turned the cattle toward the enclosure, and Charity finally understood what he was doing.

Anne watched Ben funnel the lead animals into the corral, the others dutifully following. She whirled back into the kitchen and Charity heard the stove lid clang as Anne lowered it. She hurried in to help make coffee and stir up the stew that had been simmering during the afternoon. By the time the men came into the house for the hot food and drink, the wind had begun to blow more forcefully than usual. Charity, glancing out the window as the noise increased, saw that the cattle were milling inside the corral and that Ben had snaked a rope from the gate to the porch post beside the back steps. That these usually unflappable people were taking such precautions was dire warning of what was coming.

The storm blew in early that evening. It was like nothing Charity had ever experienced. The wind swept the heavily falling snow before it so fiercely that at times it was literally impossible to see more than a foot ahead when she looked out the window. Even in the house they had to speak over the roar of the gale. The temperature plunged. Anne gathered the three children near the kitchen stove where it was warmer than at the other end of the room. She said nothing that would worry them, but each time a particularly loud blast rattled the door, she turned quickly toward it. Her men were out at the corral, protecting the herd in that wildness. Although they were in reality only yards away, it might as well have been miles for all that she could communicate with them and know whether they were safe. And there was nothing Charity could do or say to soothe her fear. Cork was out there, too.

Only by means of the rope Ben had strung were the men able to return to the house periodically for hot coffee and food and to get warm before going back out. The blizzard raged all that night and for two more days. When Charity saw that Anne was standing still, listening intently, she realized that the wind had slacked. Anne raised the window shutter to a world of glistening white and ran to the door as the men stumbled in. They found out later that the blizzard had blown the length of Wyoming Territory, stranding a train that had been unlucky enough to be caught out in it when drifts up to fifteen feet high blocked the tracks. Work trains were sent out from both directions to clear the way, but the blowing wind filled the cleared spaces almost as fast as they were shoveled out. It took several days before the work crews and the stranded passengers were brought to safety.

Ben hadn't been able to round up all his cattle, but by penning the ones in the corral and constantly prodding them to be up and moving rather than allowing them to lie down and freeze, the men were able to bring them through the storm. With the sky clear again, they set out to find the ones they had had to leave behind. They found some, but not all. Ben, his face strained, counted his losses. Charity finally understood the purpose of the enormous corral he had built and knew only too clearly that, but for his precautions, it would have been much, much worse.

***

Christmas brought gifts from her family. A knitted shawl the color of violets in the springtime from Rose. Admiring the finely executed stitches, she discovered the word "Kinsee" worked into the inside corner. She held it as if she were hugging the maker herself. Larissa sent *A Christmas Carol*, the book she had given Charity for Christmas years before and which they, as a family, had read each holiday since. Holding it tightly, Charity wondered how it could make them feel so far away and at the same time so very close. Merry sent a scribbled drawing which, Rose explained, was a picture of the snow man, snow lady, and snow sisters they had built. "After helping make one for each of us, she insisted that we do one of you, too." Ethan sent her a string of blue beads that, he wrote, had been her mother's, "and it's time they become yours." She pressed them to her cheek, overwhelmed by the realization that they were something her mother had actually touched.

Even Mac had included a gift. She opened it curiously and discovered a typically Mac offering. A school tablet not unlike the one she had used to write her farewell note to him so long ago. She strongly suspected it was the same one he had used to write his note when she had come here last summer. She didn't know whether to accept it as a joke or be indignant that he was poking fun at her. When she opened the cover to see if he had bothered to write an explanation, she abandoned both impulses. Pressed carefully inside was a dried oak leaf "from the tree beside the barn." The tears had been threatening with the unwrapping of each gift. Now they overflowed, such a mixture of loneliness and joy that she couldn't have said where one emotion ended and the other began.

CHAPTER FORTY-ONE

Although it seemed impossible that it should ever do so, the snows melted and spring burst over the prairie in a riot of green grass, pink and white prairie roses, and purple coneflowers. Charity could scarcely believe that she had been there almost a year. Looking back, she knew that she'd grown in many ways. Her cheeks turned pink when she thought of the young woman — scarcely more than a girl, she realized now — who had stepped off the train, looking for adventure. She had to admit, she had certainly found it.

***

While Charity had been in the midst of her transformation, changes had been coming Mac's direction also. Working alongside Doc Rawley each day, he knew the deep fulfillment of carrying on the work he was born to do. After their initial hesitation because he wasn't Doc and didn't have the seasoned look they were used to, the "new folks" in the community, who had not been around before his departure for medical school, accepted him. He was "Young Doc" to one and all, which tickled the older doctor no end.

Since his return home after leaving Amity in Philadelphia, he wrote to her each night, telling of his day and the events large and small of the community, "so that when you come back here, you'll be all caught up." On the evening that was to have been their marriage day, he returned to the farm and walked out to Mill Creek. He dropped down onto the rock that overhung the water, the place he had long ago dubbed his "sitting seat." It was here he used to come after a difficult day when Doc Rawley was teaching him medicine. The utter peace of the place, the water chuckling over the rocks, the breeze whispering through the oak and maple leaves, had soothed him when he had nowhere else to turn. For a long time that evening he sat on the rock and listened to the breeze whispering through the leaves and the water chuckling over the rocks.

Amity, too, wrote daily of her mother's friends who faithfully visited, since Matilda was still unable to go to them. A number of her own friends, whom Mac also knew, dropped by frequently and she reported to him the problems and pleasures, major and minor, that filled their lives. She tried to put a favorable light on her mother's condition, but as the weeks slid by, Mac, reading between the lines, realized that Matilda's situation had not measurably improved. He wrote to Dr. Terrill, who responded as one doctor to another how, in spite of her determined efforts, Matilda was not recovering as rapidly as they had hoped. There was improvement, however, he assured Mac, and they must not be discouraged that it was coming so slowly.

Mac, with a heavy heart, showed the letter to Doc Rawley who, after reading it, shook his head. He had never been one to mince words, and he did not do so now. "I've known Oliver a good many years. If he's worried, he has reason to be." Trained as Mac was to control his emotions, Doc saw the fear that flashed in his eyes and said sharply, "If he's still holding out hope, he has reason for that, too. Sure as green apples make bellyaches, we're just going to have to wait and see."

So Mac waited. And while he waited winter came, and another worry, faintly at first then more insistently, knocked at his heart. In early December, Amity gleefully informed him that she was now an honest to goodness aunt, and he'd better show her the respect such a high position deserved. Her sister Mercy had presented them with niece Matilda on Thanksgiving Day. Mother and baby were doing fine. Baby's father, grandparents, and aunt were ecstatic.

As in all her other letters, Amity wrote cheerfully this time of the people who came to see her, but she never spoke of going out to their homes, to the plays and other social events that he knew she so enjoyed. He feared that she was sacrificing her own pleasures to her mother's needs. His anxiety was confirmed in a letter from Dr. Terrill, who voiced his uneasiness over Amity's reluctance to leave the house. He didn't want to worry Mac, but he was concerned what it was doing to her health.

This revelation caused the anxiety that had gone before to seem like a mere trifle. Mac wrote to her urging her for her own well being to visit her friends, to go to parties, and other affairs that had been so much a part of her way of life. She wrote back that she was taking care of herself, that she was not ill in any way, and that attending social events was "simply no fun" without him. He would have gone to her then. He would have tossed aside his promise to Doc like wheat chaff in the wind, but he couldn't.

Winter, arriving, brought with it lower than usual icy temperatures. For the first time in his life, Doc was unable to tolerate the cold when riding out on house calls in his doctor's cutter. Even bundled under its deep hood that deflected the worst of the frigid air was not enough to keep him warm. He tried to brush it off, but the chill went deep into his bones, and Mac feared it would also attack his lungs. With Doc fussing a blue streak, Mac took over the outside calls, leaving him to tend those who came to the office. With so many other lives, including Doc's, now depending solely on him, he felt like a wire had been wrapped around his heart and was twisting tighter each day.

When a letter came from Jeff, admitting that he, too, was worried about Amity, Mac knew of only one way that she might be persuaded. He wrote back to Jeff, asking for his help, and received an affirmative answer by return mail. Because her well being depended on it, but feeling as if he were operating on his own heart without benefit of anesthetic, he wrote to Amity. He explained that he was deeply concerned about her health and expressed his wish that she allow Jeff to escort her to social functions. He did his best to make light of it, claiming that if she didn't follow doctor's orders, it would prove he was a very poor medical man and that the licensing board might just throw him out on his ear. He wrote to Oliver, explaining his high-handed approach, and mailed both letters before he lost his courage.

When he received Amity's response, it was so indignant that the paper almost scorched his fingers. He had to smile a little because he could picture her exasperation as she fired off the letter to him.

I am NOT in ill health, no matter what you have been told. I do NOT want to go out with Jeff or anyone else except you. But Father and Jeff are ganging up on me. And I don't want to get you in trouble with the medical board. Most of all, I don't want you worrying about me. So I will do as my doctor instructs. But that DOESN'T MEAN I'm going to enjoy myself!

The capitalization twice of *not* and then *doesn't mean* told him all he needed to know about how riled she was. But *my doctor* also told him all he needed to know about her love for him, and the tight wire around his heart eased a little.

***

Just as springtime had eventually arrived in Wyoming Territory, it came also to Fairvale. Feeling the warmth of the sun on his face, Mac knew that, finally, he could return to Philadelphia and Amity. He did so without delay.

Amity and Jeff met him at the train station. Mac drew her into his arms, held her close against his heart for a long time before he released her enough to look into her eyes, scarcely believing that he was really doing so. She smiled up at him, a little shakily, as if she couldn't really believe it either. He gently cupped her cheek with his hand. Her face held a new maturity, telling more clearly than words ever could how difficult the months of caring for her mother had been for her. One arm still holding her close to his side, he reached his other hand to Jeff, who had been standing discreetly back. Their hands met in a firm grasp that melted the months just past and renewed the bond of their friendship.

At the house, Dr. Terrill met them at the front door, as he had the summer before. Mac saw plainly that Oliver had aged severely in the months since their last meeting. His hair was snow white, and new lines had etched themselves around his eyes and mouth. His handshake, however, was as firm as ever, and his greeting as sincere.

In the front hallway, Amity squeezed Mac's arm. "Mother's waiting to see you, as soon as you get settled."

Mac wanted nothing more in the world than to be alone with Amity, but he could scarcely refuse to go to Mrs. Terrill when it was put to him by Amity herself. He expected to ascend the stairs to the bedroom, but Amity took his hand and led him down the hall. When he stepped through the doorway she indicated, he found a room bright with sunshine and festive with the greenery of lovingly-tended plants. Mrs. Terrill was in a chair by a window that overlooked a garden in which yellow daffodils and tulips of many hues were lifting their heads to the sun. She held out her hands to him and he went quickly to her, bent and kissed her cheek.

She studied him intently, then nodded to Amity who was standing close beside him. "It really is Mac, come back to us."

Amity slipped her hand into his. "Yes, Mother. It really is. I can hardly believe it, too."

When they went back out into the hallway, there was no one about. He took full advantage of the moment to draw her into his arms and kiss her as he had yearned to all the past months. At her ardent response, his arms tightened about her, holding her closer still. She drew an unsteady breath and buried her face against his shoulder. For the first time in many weeks, the tight wire around his heart fell away.

During the next few days, Mac was able to observe Mrs. Terrill and see for himself that she had made progress, but not as much as would have been expected by this time. He talked to Dr. Terrill who, almost as if unburdening himself, laid the facts before Mac. Oliver had evidently showed more optimism than he felt when he had kept Amity and Matilda apprised of her progress.

"She's reached the upper limit of her healing?" Mac forced the question past the tightness in his throat.

Oliver stared past Mac while he seemed to gather words. Then he looked him straight in the eye. "She may improve a fraction more, but, yes, she has reached the maximum point of her recovery."

***

Mac spent as much time as he could with Amity, when she wasn't, of necessity, with her mother or taking care of the innumerable details that cropped up in the running of a household. He was sitting out under his favorite maple tree late one afternoon while Amity dealt with a crisis in the kitchen. He was leaving the next day, and he had never wanted to do anything less in his life. Crisis apparently resolved, Amity found him there. He took her hand and pulled her down beside him, then slipped his arm around her, pulling her close. He was acutely aware of the strong possibility of being observed by any of the household or garden staff. At that moment, for himself he couldn't care less, but he would not jeopardize her respectability with those whom she supervised. "The days have gone by much too fast." He felt her nod her head against his shoulder in agreement.

He had promised Dr. Terrill he would not say anything about Matilda's prognosis. Oliver had said he would tell his wife and daughter when the last spark of hope was gone. Whether Mac agreed with his decision or not, Dr. Terrill was not only Matilda's husband and Amity's father; he was also the acting physician in the matter and had made his choice known. It was not Mac's place to override it. So he sat beside Amity, treasuring his last moments with her, refusing to look into the future, while the wire twisted around his heart again.

**

He arrived back in Fairvale, took up his medical duties, and tried to pretend that any of it mattered. Doc threw sharp glances at him but held his tongue because Mac performed his work as precisely as ever. On an afternoon two weeks after his return, he and Doc were in the office. Doc was rolling pills and Mac was recording the morning's round of calls. The door opened and Shawn Gallaway poked his head around the edge. "I was just at the post office for the afternoon mail. This came for you, Mac. Thought you might like to have it sooner than later." He grinned and held out an envelope. Mac took it and Shawn ducked back out the door.

His quick glance confirmed Amity's handwriting. Opening it, he sank into his chair and pulled out the closely written sheets. His smile of anticipation froze as he stared at the words she had written.

Dear Mac,

Father told me tonight that he believes Mother's health has improved as much as it is going to. That she will never be stronger and able to resume an active life as we had so hoped. This means that I must stay with her. I cannot come to Fairvale to be with you as we had dreamed and planned.

I also know that you cannot come to Philadelphia on a permanent basis. Just as I have my obligations here that cannot be set aside, you have yours in Fairvale that must be honored. I would not have you break the solemn promises you have made there, promises that have guided your life, in order to come here with me. You would be less than true to yourself if you did so, and I cannot bear the thought that I was the cause of it.

Because of this, I release you from any obligation our engagement has placed upon you.

This is the hardest letter I have ever had to write, but we cannot continue to dream of a future together when there is no future for us. I have treasured the time we have been together. You have given me so much joy.

Please do not write or try to contact me in any way.

Amity

"No!"

As Mac read his letter, Doc, frowning, had kept one eye on him while he continued with his pill-making. But when Mac uttered that single strangled word, Doc thrust aside the bottle he was capping and, fists on hips, planted himself beside Mac's chair. "What's going on? You might as well spit it out." Mac continued to stare at the letter in disbelief. "Mac," Doc barked.

Mac slowly turned his head. "She's broken our engagement," he said dully. "Her father told her that her mother will always be an invalid. Now Amity says she'll have to stay there permanently to take care of her, and she doesn't want me to contact her or even ever see her again."

Doc sank with a thump into his own chair. "Mac, I'm sorry," he said finally.

"I can't let her do this to us," Mac blurted. "I've got to go back to her. I've got to make her understand." He started to rise from his chair as if he were going to take off at that very moment.

Doc shot him a piercing glance. "Understand what?"

Mac stared at him. "That we can't let what we have end this way."

"End what way?"

"With her there taking care of her mother and me here, taking care of—"

"Taking care of what? Your obligations to the people here who've given you their trust, who are depending on you with their very lives? Is that how she put it?"

Mac nodded numbly.

"Seems to me you're not using the brains you were born with to give her the credit she deserves," Doc said flatly. "At least she sees the facts as they are, not as she wishes they could be. And she's being honest enough to tell you now, not waiting a hundred miles up the road and then saying, 'Oh, by the way, I can't marry you.'"

"But Doc—"

"Don't 'But Doc,' me. Suppose you break your promise to me? Or that I release you from it, if it comes to that. You've got as much integrity as any man I know. Only known one to have more, if it can be measured as such. Your Pa's word was good as gold. Never knew him to back out of anything once he'd spoken on it. I've been down enough roads to know that's a mighty rare commodity. You must have picked it up from him because as long as we've been together, you've shown the same grit."

Mac, hearing his words, stared at him as if he'd never seen him before.

"So if you've got all this high-falutin' integrity, where will you be if you toss aside what you've worked for all your life? Would you honestly be able to live with yourself? More important, what would that do to Amity, knowing you'd made that decision because of her?" Doc snapped his mouth shut and glared, full-force, at him.

Mac slowly sat back. The letter he had been clutching dropped to his lap, and he buried his face in his hands.

Doc rose from his chair, put his hand on Mac's shoulder and squeezed, hard. "Things are quiet here. If you want to take the rest of the day off, go ahead."

Mac nodded numbly and stood. As he reached for the doorknob, he said huskily, "Doc," and stopped as if unable to find any words, let alone appropriate ones.

Doc, who had followed him to the door, raised his hand as to stop him from saying words that were unnecessary, and shut the door after him. Then he walked slowly back to his chair and sank into it. Remembering the days of his own young love, and Marilla, and how the choice to be with her had been taken from him so many years ago, he stared straight ahead at nothing for a long time.

CHAPTER FORTY-TWO

Albany County, Wyoming Territory
May 1874

On a pleasantly warm afternoon the day before her twenty-first birthday, Charity was at the blackboard, writing questions for the next morning's geography test. Her wrist swooped across the surface, but she was not concentrating on tomorrow's examination. She was, rather, recalling the letter she had received yesterday from Pa. Among the snippets of farm and family life he had shared was the news that Hans was still working with Dr. Ingemar in Delaware County. When he'd first begun assisting there after Mac returned to Fairvale, Hans had made a point of coming home each weekend to see them. As time went on, his visits had become less frequent. Now, oddly enough, he was once more showing up at the farm with end-of-the-week regularity. Hans had offered no explanation for this renewed participation in the family's activities. "For some reason, however, Rose becomes considerably more animated whenever he appears on the doorstep, and they seem to have a lot to discuss between them when no one else is around. Ma and I are, of course, not drawing any conclusions from these events. We simply agree that you'll be interested in knowing about the friendship between the two."

I'm interested, all right! She could scarcely contain her glee. If there was a more perfect match than Rose and Hans, she couldn't name it. *How I wish I could be home to share in such momentous news.* It seemed like a lifetime since she had seen them. She suddenly realized that considering it as that span of time was not absurd, for she had grown in ways that she hadn't even dreamed when she had first come here "to expand her horizons." It was so hard to believe that her third year of teaching was drawing to a close and that she would soon be starting on her fourth.

She had left the outside door open to allow the fresh breeze into the room and didn't hear the footsteps behind her. "Excuse me, miss. I'm looking for the school ma'am. Would you know where I can find her?"

She jumped, causing the middle of her word to end in a jagged, chalky streak. There was no mistaking that voice. Ever since she left Fairvale she'd heard it in her dreams more nights than not. She whirled. Mac was standing in the doorway, watching her with a tentative smile. She drew a long breath and told her suddenly wildly flapping heart to calm down. She managed a friendly smile at him in return, as though his showing up in her classroom after not seeing him for three years was a commonplace occurrence. "The schoolteacher? Which one? We have such a large number of them in this district," she explained pompously.

"Why, I'm looking for Miss Michaels," he said solemnly. "I've heard that she's an excellent teacher. Can you tell me where her school is?"

"If you're looking for *that* Miss Michaels, it seems you've come to the right place after all."

He sighed with relief. "I'm sure glad. I can't tell you how many other schools I've stopped at this afternoon, looking for her."

Since she was still the only teacher in the district, their conversation was admittedly outlandish. He leaned against the door frame, the distance of the school room between them. She stood in front of the blackboard, absorbing the sight of him after so many months and acutely aware that he was studying her just as intently. Their eyes met.

"It's good to see you again, Charity. You don't look at all like that pesty little girl who used to follow me around, jabbering a blue streak."

"You mean the one you threatened to throw in the horse trough if she didn't quit asking so many dumb questions?"

"But I never actually dunked you and Rose," he pointed out virtuously. "I think I always knew that if I tried, the two of you would gang up on me and not just get me soaking wet but shove me down and hold me under."

"We considered it. We even had it all planned out, but you never did more than threaten us," she said with injured disappointment.

"I wasn't very smart sometimes, but I knew when to stay away from trouble, at least most of the time." His tone softened. "You look — amazing."

"Three years can bring a lot of changes," she admitted. He was dressed in his doctor's outfit of white shirt, black pants and coat, with his gold watch chain curving across his vest. She realized that he looked older than she had been picturing him. More mature, she decided. He had lost that take-on-the-world-and-win manner that had always before marked his approach to life. His hair was no longer flaming red, but a rich auburn. There was a gravity about his eyes that she had never seen before. She wondered fleetingly if it were the toll demanded of every doctor or whether Amity Terrill had put it there.

She had no time to dwell on it as her shock at seeing him wore off and the questions burst from her. "Is everyone all right at home? When did you get here? How did you get here? How long will you stay?" *Why did you come?* Fortunately, she clamped her teeth on her tongue before that inquiry followed all the others out of her mouth.

"Yes. This afternoon. On the train to Laramie, by rented horse to Clark's Valley, by horse and buggy here. For a few days, anyway, if that's agreeable to you."

It took her a second to realize he had answered her questions precisely in the order she had fired them at him. She almost stuck her tongue out at him, remembered her maturity in time, and was glad a moment later, for he was asking, "Will you walk with me, Charity? We have a lot of catching up to do."

She gestured to the board and realized she was still clutching the piece of chalk. She hastily stuck her hands behind her back. "I was just writing out a test for tomorrow."

He looked at the board and gave a low whistle. "Sure glad I don't have to answer those questions. Makes medical school seem like a breeze."

"My students do very well," she informed him with great dignity.

"I'm sure they do." The corners of his mouth twitched. "Do you use Miss Sullivan's tried and true methods?"

She wrinkled her nose at him. "Only in extreme cases, thank you."

He gestured around the room. "What do you need to do to close up? Since I interrupted you, I can do that while you finish the rest of the questions."

While he made sure the students had left their desks in good order and straightened up the books on their shelf, she finished writing out the test. When she put down the chalk, he glanced up from the volume he had been scanning. "*A Christmas Carol*. I remember your Pa reading it out loud to us. He was great at the ghostly voices parts." His eyes went to the blackboard. "Only five questions? Your students are lucky."

Deciding not to admit that she'd just shortened the test by half, she said airily, "The questions are quite comprehensive."

"I see." He nodded wisely as he read them. "Since you've finished writing your short, comprehensive test questions, shall we go?"

They put the shutters down and while she locked the door, he put her books and papers in the buggy next to his medical bag. "They'll be fine, there. Where shall we go?"

She led him over to the creek. "I like coming here. It reminds me of Mill Creek and home."

"I hear this is a good place for skipping stones," he said casually. He picked up a rock and shied it across the water. It bounced seven times.

She darted a suspicious look at him. Sure enough, he was grinning. "Someone told you," she said accusingly.

He tried to look innocent, but she glared him down. He raised his hands in surrender. "I confess. Rose told me. I think it was great, what you did."

First things first. "Rose told you? What did you do, dunk her in the horse trough?"

312

He managed to look completely guilty. "She did, and I didn't, I promise. I kind of wormed it out of her, though, so I'll take all the blame. You really beat the little monster at his own game all three times, skipping rocks, shooting marbles, and racing horses?"

She lifted her chin. "I did."

He shook his head, clearly impressed. "And did he behave himself after that?"

"He did." She spoke in firm defense of her pupil, ignoring the small voice that mentioned Luke's face-saving spitball antics afterwards. *All in all, he behaved himself pretty well. I think.*

To get his mind off her decidedly unscholarly methods, she gestured in a sweeping circle that took in the rippling creek, the schoolhouse and the wide-flung land stretching beyond them. "This great expanse puts me in mind of your Pa," she said softly. "The letters home he wrote that tried to portray the vast grasslands and the endless sky. I did get the sense of it from his descriptions, but I don't think the most profound words could ever adequately convey it. It's something you have to be in the midst of to really understand."

Silence stretched between them as his gaze swept then lingered over the immensity of their surroundings as the wind rushed past them. When he spoke, his voice held a note of wistfulness he couldn't conceal. "I thought about him a lot on the train out here. Somehow, being in the same place he was when he couldn't be home with us brings him so close I feel as though if I turned around, he'd be standing there." He gave a shaky laugh. "I can just hear him saying, 'By jingo, son, you've grown a mite since I saw you last.' And it would be like he'd never been away." He hesitated. "I told Ma I'd go visit his grave." He looked at her questioningly.

"Of course we can go," she said quietly. "I'm sure Ben would take us, no questions asked." Having assured him of her heartfelt support in his odyssey, sensing that he needed to change the subject, she led him over to the cottonwood tree near the creek. "The grass is still thick and green. In another month or so, it'll start drying up." She dropped down and patted the spot next to her for him to sit.

He eased down, leaned back on his elbows, and closed his eyes. "It's peaceful here."

She poked him. "Did you come all this way just to sleep?"

He abandoned his elbow-propped position to sit up beside her. "No," he said quietly. "I came to talk to you."

Her heart started flapping again, in spite of her stern orders for it to be still. She waited for him to go on.

"So much has happened in the three years since I've seen you," he said finally. "You're obviously doing very well here. Ma and Rose have shared your letters with me, and I appreciate the ones you sent me." She had continued to write to him, lightheartedly, just the way she always had. He had written back occasionally. He hesitated. "I gathered from those letters that you were seriously interested in a fellow named Cork." He looked over at her for confirmation.

"Yes," she said softly. "He's a very special man. I … think a great deal of him."

"Rose told me that he asked you to marry him, but you turned him down."

She felt her cheeks grow pink. *Thanks a lot, Rose*. On the other hand, Rose had also written her about Mac and Amity ending their engagement. "I care for him very much. But it just didn't feel all the way right, somehow. It's not something I can explain to you." She didn't dare look at him for fear he would see the explanation plainly on her face.

"I understand. Sometimes words just don't say what they're supposed to, no matter how hard we try." He pulled up a blade of grass, studied it intently, and began smoothing it between his fingers. "I ignored Amity's wishes," he confessed. "I wrote to her, of course, even after she told me not to. I sent telegrams that went unanswered. The letters came back unopened, marked 'return to sender' in her handwriting. I finally got a telegram from Dr. Terrill, telling me to stop trying to communicate with her because she was not going to change her mind and my insistence on contacting her was affecting her health. The knowledge that I was making her ill as well as miserable was too much. I just couldn't do that to her. It took me a long time to admit that she was right to do what she did, and even longer to realize that it wouldn't have worked out between her and me. Maybe for a little while, yes. But not for the long haul. We're from two different worlds and there was no way those two worlds were going to mesh happily ever after."

He suddenly shifted so that he was looking directly at her. She looked down at her hands to avoid his gaze. "Charity, however awkwardly this may come out, I want you to know. You've always been an important part of my life. I was just too blind and too busy being the perfect doctor to notice. I took it for granted that you'd always be around. But going out to the farm hasn't felt the same as it used to. I finally realized it's because you're not there joking and laughing and giving me holy blazes right back when I get high and mighty with you and Rose." He said slowly, "I want you to always be there."

She raised her head to look at him then. "I won't be a substitute for Amity," she said flatly.

"I don't want you to be a substitute for Amity," he said, just as determinedly. "She's herself. You are you. That's exactly as it should be." He studied the blade of grass still clutched between his fingers. "And before you ask, no, I'm not going to spend the rest of my life pining for her. Dr. Terrill's letters hint strongly that she and Jeff are nearing an understanding."

"Are you all right with that? He's your very good friend." She stared at him, waiting for his answer.

He looked directly back at her. "Yes. They're from the same world. There'll never be the differences between them that Amity and I would have had."

She held his gaze for a long moment. Seeing that he meant what he said, she released a quivery breath and bowed her head.

The silence lengthened between them until he said reluctantly, "It's getting late. The folks you're staying with will be worried about you. It's the Claytons this month, isn't it?"

"Yes. They will be wondering where I am if we don't go soon."

He rose and reached down to help her up. She raised her hands to his and he gripped them securely. Memory flashed and she was once again five years old, flailing around in that pond-sized mud puddle those older boys had shoved her into her first day of school in Fairvale. She was covered with muck and squalling to high heaven as she struggled to escape the wet, slimy depths. Suddenly a young boy with flame-red hair and deep blue eyes was squatting in front of her, palms out, offering to help her out of the puddle. She had given him her hands, and her heart, that day. It was true that he had willingly given her his hands when he pulled her out, but not his heart, then or any day after.

Now, so many years later, he drew her to her feet and they stood, hands clasped, each searching the other's face in wordless questioning. Releasing her hands, he circled his arms around her, drawing her close against the sure, steady beating of his heart. "Speck," he murmured. "My Speck. For now and always."

He had been calling her that ridiculous name since she was six years old. She had certainly never before thought of it as an endearment. But suddenly, it was exactly right, "For now and always," she whispered to his heart.

He slipped his hand gently under her chin, raising her face to his. His mouth found hers and she responded with an ardor that, for one eternal, blissful instant of time, sent the gurgling creek and the cottonwood tree they were standing under spinning crazily around them. The world slowly righted itself in her wonder of knowing that all the hopeless longings, all the unfulfilled dreams of so many years had come to this moment of sheer joy. His palms had touched hers, drawing her to her feet as he had done on that long gone day. As he did so, she had looked into the depths of his blue eyes and seen clearly that this time, as he was giving her his hands, he was giving her his heart, too.

About the Author

How does one piece together the life events that make up a biography? How to choose this event or that one when one incident flows into another so subtly that, suddenly, decades have been spanned. The adult we are looks back at the child we were, and we shake our heads in wonder at the swiftness of the journey.

I was born in Willows, California. My family moved to Southern California when I was eight. Grade school, high school, junior college. A weaving of memorizing Shakespeare in English class, playing clarinet in the high school marching band, and getting an "A" in gym class one semester—my sole physical education triumph. Marrying. Moving to Ohio and back to California. Moving to Washington State. Working nights in a nursing home for six years so that I could be home during the day with my children. Completing a secretarial degree and finding employment in an attorneys' office. Divorcing and forging a new life for my daughters and me. The opportunity to complete my college education "at home", instead of having to travel over two hundred miles, came when Western Washington University opened a branch campus at our local junior college. I graduated with my bachelor's degree in 1992. In the years since, I have studied sign language and learned to square dance. I served as secretary of our local square dance club for six years and was my club's editor of *Footnotes*, our state square dance magazine. I served as the Publicity Representative for our county unit of the American Cancer Society for twelve years. Each time I decided to quit and let someone else do the job, another person I cared about and loved was stricken with cancer, and I *couldn't* quit.

I had always enjoyed writing, but never dreamed that I could do it for real. When my younger daughter was three months old, I decided I wanted to do something for me that was inexpensive and could be done at home in my "spare" time. I began writing my first novel. Through the years, my quiet time became a source of much comfort in periods of stress and chaos, even when my characters were ornery and, refusing to do what I told them, went their own ways into situations I would never have willingly led them. I told them so, but they wouldn't listen.

My first novel, *The Longing of the Day*, was published in 2000, just a month before my younger daughter's twenty-fifth birthday. My "spare" time turned out to be a lot sparer than I had imagined! Since then, I have had three more novels published, *Day Star Rising, Days of Eternity*, and *Day Unto Day*. Each novel tells its own story, but the individuals' lives are bound, each to each, in ways they could never have foreseen.

ALL THINGS THAT MATTER PRESS

FOR MORE INFORMATION ON TITLES AVAILABLE FROM
ALL THINGS THAT MATTER PRESS, GO TO
http://allthingsthatmatterpress.com
or contact us at
allthingsthatmatterpress@gmail.com

www.ingramcontent.com/pod-product-compliance
Lightning Source LLC
Chambersburg PA
CBHW072100020726
47501CB00003B/661